~~~~~~

Trying to cover all the science fiction short stories, novelettes and novellas published in one year is a chore that would daunt even the most ardent SF fan. But when you've actually taken on the task, it becomes a year-long treasure hunt. Seek and find ten tales that may be the classics of the years to come.

The two of us who do the selection have at least a hundred years of science fiction reading between us. The remarkable thing is that we still retain our sense of wonder and our devotion to the fruits of the imagination.

Try this year's top ten and see!

~~~~~~

DAW Anthologies include:

THE ANNUAL WORLD'S BEST SF
Edited by Donald A. Wollheim with
 Arthur W. Saha

THE YEAR'S BEST HORROR STORIES
Edited by Karl Edward Wagner

THE YEAR'S BEST FANTASY STORIES
Edited by Arthur W. Saha

THE GREAT SF STORIES (1939 . . .)
Edited by Isaac Asimov and
 Martin H. Greenberg

TERRA SF: The Best from Western Europe
Edited by Richard W. Nolane

HECATE'S CAULDRON
Edited by Susan Shwartz

AMAZONS
Edited by J. A. Salmonson

GREYHAVEN
Edited by Marion Zimmer Bradley

THE 1983 ANNUAL
WORLD'S BEST SF

Edited by

DONALD A. WOLLHEIM

with Arthur W. Saha

DAW BOOKS, INC.

DONALD A. WOLLHEIM, PUBLISHER

1633 Broadway, New York, NY 10019

FIRST PRINTING, MAY 1983

1 2 3 4 5 6 7 8 9

 DAW TRADEMARK REGISTERED
U.S. PAT. OFF. MARCA
REGISTRADA, HECHO EN U.S.A.

PRINTED IN U.S.A.

Table of Contents

INTRODUCTION

We were pondering the possible implications of this year's science fiction crop when we happened across a letter from a reader in a late 1982 issue of *Omni* magazine. This reader, after deploring the government's position—and lack of position—on certain matters, wrote: "Why is there so much apathy on the part of science fiction writers, fans and editors when it comes to taking an active role in reversing these government positions? This field purports to expose mankind's weaknesses and follies, thereby building a better tomorrow. Yet the seers of this tomorrow refuse to become its architects.

"The SF field seems more concerned with parties, adolescent space-opera fantasies, fanzines and Hugo awards than it does with helping to bring about a more humanistic and optimistic future.

"Science fiction has been saddled with the misnomer 'escapist fiction.' This should not be. SF should serve as a gauge of the present situation and suggest directions for the future. We must try to implement a new future by taking action instead of hiding from it."

The sentiment is fine, but the SF field is in the first place not a political movement and in the second place not at all as deficient as he thinks it to be. The fact is that the science fiction magazines—in America at least—have a special distinction over and above all other fiction periodicals. They do editorialize and they do discuss political and social matters. *Analog* and *Asimov's* and others have all taken strong positions on such "political" matters as nuclear power, atomic weapons, space exploration, pollution, education, and so on. Their letter columns show an alertness on the part of their readers to such matters. Their stories, being projections of human possibilities, must and do have social implications. If there is no unanimity among readers, no single direction, this is the nature of the democratic thinking mind.

In the history of science fiction fandom there have indeed been social movements of both left and right. Today the most organized of such movements—embracing writers and fans —is for the support and development of space flight and specifically the space station. The L5 Society, which is not without national influence, is very much an SF-engendered grouping. In Germany, to take another example, a surprising alliance of future-minded people, including environmentalists, peace-advocates, and many science fictionists, created a political party called simply the Greens which established a role for itself in that nation's political arena and exerts pressure on the major parties. Similar groups have come together elsewhere. In Britain, SF readers have taken definite stands on the nuclear-free zone movement.

So the writer of that letter is not correct. He complains of that which is not so—SF fans have always been alert to the condition of the world and of the formative germs of the future.

Yes, the readers who become active fans (perhaps one out of fifty) do have fun gatherings, do party at conventions, produce fanzines and give out awards. But their fanzines do discuss science and the future, their conventions and parties do serve to bring together reflective young minds . . . and if you think they do not discuss the world and its politics, then you simply have not met and associated with the many informed and bright minds of youthful science fiction readers.

Escapist? But *all* fiction is escapist. Science fiction, even so, is unique. Its adventures and fantasies and "space-operas" could not even exist without the foundation of social theorizing, however much in the far future or some imaginary world out of time and space.

It is also true that the uncertainties of the time's influence the SF stories of the time. Selecting our choice of the ten stories of this annual collection is always influenced by the social atmosphere of the year. What is "best" is based not merely on the quality of the writing but the originality of the idea, the impact of the theme, and the way in which it strikes a responsive chord in the editors. This cannot be separated from the daily life of the mundane society in which we all exist.

Thus it seems to us that this book of our current winners represents many conjectures on the condition of humanity and of human motivations. Each story seems to have something to say about where we are and where we may be going. Whether taking place in the past, as with Joanna Russ, or the present, as with Sullivan, Dozois, Dann and Rucker, or with the near future, as with Willis and Lee, or the far future, as with White, Sterling, Zahn, and Pohl, each story basically is a tale of human decisions on the social order.

This selection was not deliberate, but it was the way it shaped up. This is a science fiction interpretation of the times. No, there is no single direction. No, there is no "guide to action" as activists would demand. There is only food for thought in the form of tales that must first enhance the sense of wonder (which is the magma from which all science arose).

As for the world of science fiction literature—how has it fared during the year past? In spite of the general gloom in the field of publishing, it has fared well. The magazines continue to show life and strength. In American weekly lists of the best-selling hardbound books, more than a third of the top fifteen titles are science fictional in theme or background. In paperbacks, in spite of recession and inflation, there has been no drop-off in quantity or quality. In the cinema, SF such as *E.T.* and *Blade Runner* have been stars. In the world, science fiction is booming. Let us call that optimism.

DONALD A. WOLLHEIM

THE SCOURGE

by James White

There may seem to be madness in an alien society but students will eventually come up with logic behind every social mystery and social abomination. The author, who lives in Belfast, Northern Ireland, is familiar with danger lurking on every corner—and he has woven that feeling into a story of a world where such is the case everywhere—and nothing that one can find to fire back at!

During the third year at the Galactic Federation's preliminary training school for Earth-human non-Citizens on Fomalhaut Three, they had watched their classmates disappear, two by two, in the directions of their chosen specialties.

The trouble was, Martin thought as he signalled their presence and readiness to begin the day's work, that neither Beth nor he had shown any strong preferences or special aptitudes for the positions being offered. They had decided that their tutor just did not know what to do with them.

Having arrived at that decision, it was inevitable that the great, sprawling, slimy and multi-tentacled horror responsible for their training would show them yet again that their thinking was in error.

GOOD MORNING, said the desk displays. ASSIGNMENT INSTRUCTIONS FOLLOW. PLEASE RECORD FOR LATER STUDY.

With the appearance of the words, the wall facing them became a screen depicting in unpleasantly fine detail their tutor and the large, low-ceilinged, and dimly lit compartment in which it lived—or perhaps only taught. It was surrounded by two small consoles and eight untidy heaps of garishly colored material which Martin had thought at first were art objects or furniture but had later decided, after seeing the creature holding one of them close to one of its many body orifices, that they were more likely to be food or a collection of aromatic vegetation.

The upper and lower lids opened to reveal a single eye, which looked like a fat, transparent sausage in which two pupils moved independently to regard them. Their desk displays lit with a new message.

SUMMARY OF ASSIGNMENT. YOU WILL PROCEED TO THE SYSTEM LISTED AS TRD/5/23768/G3 AND TAKE UP ORBIT ABOUT THE FOURTH PLANET. STUDY IT, INTERVIEW A MEMBER OR MEMBERS OF ITS DOMINANT LIFE-FORM, AND ASSESS THIS SPECIES' SUITABILITY OR OTHERWISE FOR CITIZEN MEMBERSHIP OF THE GALACTIC FEDERATION.

QUESTIONS?

Martin swallowed. He knew that the feeling was purely psychosomatic, but it felt as if his stomach was experiencing nil-G independently of the rest of his body. At the adjoining desk, Beth was putting on her spectacles. She did not need them or any other sensory aid, for that matter, because all of the Earth-human trainees already had received the benefits of the Federation's advanced medical and regenerative procedures so that they were as perfect physiologically as it was possible for a member of their species to be. But at times of stress Beth wore her glasses because, she insisted, they made her feel more intelligent.

"No questions," she said quietly, glancing at Martin for corroboration. "Until more data is available on the assignment, questions at this stage would tend to be simply requests for more information."

VERY WELL. IT IS CALLED TELDI IN THE LANGUAGE MOST
WIDELY USED ON THAT WORLD. IT IS A DANGEROUS PLANET
AND CONSIDERED SO EVEN BY ITS INHABITANTS, WHO LIVE ON
A LARGE EQUATORIAL CONTINENT AND A CHAIN OF ISLANDS
WHICH LINK IT TO THE NORTH POLAR LAND MASS. TECHNO-
LOGICALLY ITS CULTURE IS NOT ADVANCED.

TELDI WAS DISCOVERED BY A FEDERATION SEARCHSHIP
TWENTY-SEVEN OF YOUR YEARS AGO. BECAUSE OF GROSS PHYS-
ICAL DIFFERENCES BETWEEN THE TELDINS AND THE SPECIES
MANNING THE VESSEL NO OVERT CONTACT WAS MADE.

QUESTIONS?

There was a very obvious question, and Martin asked it.
"If direct contact could not be made because the searchship
personnel were too visually horrendous so far as the Teldins
were concerned, why was indirect contact not tried by trans-
lated visual word displays as was done on Earth, and as you
are doing here?"

TELDINS WILL NOT DISCUSS MATTERS OF IMPORTANCE OR
MAKE MAJOR DECISIONS THROUGH INTERMEDIARIES LIVING OR
MECHANICAL. DISCOVERING THE REASON FOR THIS BEHAVIOR IS
PART OF YOUR ASSIGNMENT.

"Then we shall be meeting them face to face," said Martin,
wondering where all his saliva had gone. "May we see one of
the faces concerned?"

OBSERVE.

"No doubt," said Beth in a shaky voice, following a three-
second glimpse of the being, "they have beautiful minds."

THE MATTER TRANSMISSION NETWORK WILL NOT INCLUDE
TELDI UNTIL A FAVORABLE ASSESSMENT HAS BEEN MADE.
YOUR TRANSPORTATION WILL BE BY HYPERSHIP. DURING SUR-
FACE INVESTIGATIONS BY THE ENTITY MARTIN. THE ENTITY
BETH WILL REMAIN WITH THE SHIP IN A SURVEILLANCE AND
SUPPORT ROLE.

QUESTIONS?

Martin lifted his eyes to stare at the monstrosity beyond
the desk screen, feeling himself beginning to sweat. He said,
"This . . . this is a very important assignment."

THAT IS A SELF-EVIDENTLY TRUE STATEMENT. IT IS NOT A
QUESTION.

Beside him Beth laughed nervously. "What he was trying
to say, Tutor, is why us?"

THREE REASONS. ONE, YOU HAVE BOTH SHOWN ABILITY
ABOVE THE AVERAGE COUPLED WITH COMPLETE INDECISION
REGARDING YOUR FUTURE. WHETHER OR NOT IT IS COMPLETED
SUCCESSFULLY, THIS ASSIGNMENT WILL ELIMINATE SEVERAL
FUTURE POSSIBILITIES. TWO, AS MEMBERS OF THE SPECIES
MOST RECENTLY OFFERED FEDERATION CITIZENSHIP, YOUR
KNOWLEDGE AND UNDERSTANDING OF WHAT IS INVOLVED IN
MAKING THIS ASSESSMENT WILL BE GREATER THAN THAT OF
LONG-TERM MEMBERS. THREE, THERE ARE REMARKABLE SIMI-
LARITIES BETWEEN THE TELDINS AND THE EARTH-HUMAN
SPECIES WHICH SHOULD EASE YOUR COMMUNICATION PROB-
LEMS.

"Apart from breathing a similar atmosphere," Beth protested, "there is no resemblance at all. They are unbeautiful,
completely lacking in esthetic appeal, visually repellant
and—"

YOUR PARDON, I HAD THOUGHT THAT THE DIFFERENCES
WERE SUPERFICIAL.

To you, thought Martin, *they probably are.*

YOU WILL ALREADY HAVE REALIZED THAT YOU ARE BOTH TO
UNDERGO IMPORTANT FITNESS TESTS, AND THE VALUE OF
THESE TESTS WOULD BE DIMINISHED IF I ASSISTED YOU OTHER
THAN BY PROVIDING THE BASIC INFORMATION.

QUESTIONS?

"Can you give us advice?" he asked.

OBVIOUSLY, YOU HAVE BEEN RECEIVING ADVICE, GUIDANCE,
AND INSTRUCTION FOR THE PAST THREE OF YOUR YEARS HERE.
MY ADVICE IS TO REMEMBER EVERYTHING YOU HAVE BEEN
TAUGHT AND PUT IT INTO PRACTICE. THE ASSIGNMENT NEED
NOT BE A LENGTHY ONE PROVIDED THE ENTITY BETH USES ITS
BRAIN AND THE SHIP'S SENSOR AND COMPUTER FACILITIES EF-
FECTIVELY AND THE ENTITY MARTIN IS CAREFUL IN ITS
CHOICE OF FIRST CONTACTEE AND THE SUBSEQUENT INTERRO-
GATION.

IT IS POSSIBLE TO ARRIVE AT A FULL UNDERSTANDING OF A
CULTURE FROM THE INTERROGATION OF ONE OF ITS MEMBERS.
ALL THE NECESSARY EQUIPMENT IS AVAILABLE TO YOU. YOU
HAVE BEEN FULLY TRAINED IN ITS USE. WHILE YOU ARE DECID-
ING ON THE SUITABILITY OR OTHERWISE OF TELDI FOR FEDER-
ATION MEMBERSHIP, WE SHALL BE DECIDING ON YOUR
SUITABILITY FOR DUTY AS A HYPERSHIP CAPTAIN AND A CON-
TACT SPECIALIST.

THE RESPONSIBILITY IS ENTIRELY YOURS.

The system had seven planets, and its only inhabited world, Teldi, was encircled by the broken remnants of a satellite which had approached within Roche's Limit and been pulled apart by the gravity of its primary. The planet had no axial tilt, and the orbit of the moon had coincided with its equator. The orbiting and constantly colliding debris had not yet formed into a stable ring system, so that the equatorial land mass of Teldi was swept by a light meteorite drizzle which was seeded with enough heavier stuff to make life very uncertain for anyone who remained for long periods in the open.

"It wasn't always like this," said Martin, pointing at one of the sensor displays they had been studying. "That grey strip with the old impact craters all over it was an airport runway, and those heaps of rubble and corrosion could only be dockyard facilities and industrial complexes. This culture must have been as advanced at least as that of pre-Federation Earth before their moon broke up."

"It may have been more than one moon," said Beth thoughtfully. "The orbital paths and clumping of the orbiting debris indicate a—"

"The difference is academic," Martin broke in. "What we have here is a once-advanced culture which has been hammered flat by meteorite bombardment to the extent that they have regressed to a primitive farming and fishing culture. Except for the polar settlement, which is virtually free of meteorites, their past technology seems to have been lost. The question is, where do I land?"

Beth displayed a blow-up of the polar settlement with the relevant sensor data. It was a scientific establishment of some kind, with a small observatory, a non-nuclear power source, and a well-built road which was obviously a supply route. Communicating with the inhabitants should be relatively easy, Martin thought, because the astronomers among them would be mentally prepared for the idea of extra-terrestrial (to them) visitors. But they would not be typical of the population as a whole.

An assessment should not be based on a species' intellectuals alone. He had to talk to the Teldin equivalent of an ordinary man in the street.

The landing site finally agreed upon was by a roadside

some ten miles from a "city" which lay on and under the floor and walls of a deep, fertile valley on the equatorial continent.

"And now," said Beth, "what about protection?"

For several minutes they discussed the advisability of using the ship's special protection systems while he was on the surface, then decided against them. He had to make contact with a technologically backward alien, and he would do himself no good at all by frightening it with gratuitous demonstrations of super-science.

"Right, then," he said finally. "My only protection will be the lander's force shield. I won't carry anything in my hands, and wear uniform coveralls and an open helmet with image-enhancing visor, and a Teldin-type backpack with a med kit and the usual supplies. The Teldins seem pretty flexible in the matter of clothing, so I would be displaying my physiological differences as well as showing them that I was unarmed.

"The translator will be in my collar insignia," he went on, "and the helmet will contain the standard sensor and monitoring equipment, lighting, and a facility to enable me to bypass the translator so that we can speak without being understood by listening Teldins. Can your fabricator handle that?"

Beth nodded.

"Have I forgotten anything?"

She shook her head.

"Don't worry about me," he said awkwardly, "everything will be just fine."

But still she did not speak. Martin reached toward her and carefully removed her glasses, folded them, and placed them on top of the control console.

"I'm ready to go," he said, then added gently, "sometime tomorrow . . ."

Martin made no secret of his landing. He arrived at night with the lander's external lights ablaze, coming in slowly so as not to be mistaken for one of the larger meteors. Then he waited anxiously for the reaction of the inhabitants and authorities of the nearby city.

With diminished anxiety and growing impatience, he was still waiting more than a full Teldin day later.

"I expected crowds around me by now," Martin said in bafflement. "But they just look at me as they pass on by. I have to make one of them stop ignoring me and talk. I'm leaving the lander now and beginning to move toward the road."

"I see you," said Beth from the hypership, then added warningly, *"The chances of you being hit during the few minutes it takes you to reach the protection of the road are small, but even our super-computer cannot predict the impact point of every meteorite."*

Especially the odd ones which were the result of collisions in close orbit, Martin thought, and which dropped in at a steep angle instead of slanting in from the west at the norm of thirty degrees or less. But the odd behavior of the satellite debris which fell around and on Teldi, and which offended Beth's orderly mind, faded as he thought of meeting his first Teldin.

It would be a member of a species which had advanced perhaps only to the verge of achieving spaceflight, and which still practiced astronomy in that dark, polar settlement. Such a species would have considered the possibility of off-planet intelligent life. Perhaps the idea might exist only in Teldin history books, but an ordinary Teldin should be aware of it and not be panicked into hostile activity by the sight of a puny and obviously defenseless off-worlder like Martin.

It was a nice, comforting theory which had made a lot of sense when they had discussed it back on the ship. Now he was not so sure.

"Can you see anyone on the road?"

"Yes. Just over a mile to the north of you, heading your way and toward the city. One person riding a tricycle and towing a two-wheeled trailer. It should be visible to you in six minutes."

While he was waiting, Martin tried to calm himself by examining at close range a stretch of the banked rock wall which ran along the side of the road. Like the majority of the roads on Teldi this one ran roughly north and south, and the wall protected travellers from the meteorites which came slanting in from the west.

The banked walls were on average four meters high and built from rocks gathered in the vicinity. The roads were rarely straight, but curved frequently to take advantage of the protection furnished by natural features such as deep gullies or outcroppings of rock. When east-west travel was necessary, the roads proceeded in a series of wide zigzags, like the track of a sailing ship tacking to windward.

The sound was like a short, sharp hiss and thud, and midway between his lander and the road there was a small, glowing patch of ground with a cloud of rock dust settling around it. When he looked back to the roadway, the Teldin was already in sight, pedalling rapidly toward him and hugging the protective wall.

Martin walked to the outer edge of the roadway to get out of its path. He did not know anything about the oncoming vehicle's braking system, and it was possible that he was in greater danger of being run over by an extra-terrestrial tricycle than being hit by a meteorite. His action could also, he hoped, be construed as one of politeness. When the vehicle slowed and came to a halt abreast of him, he extended both hands palms outward from his sides, then let them fall again.

"I wish you well," he said softly. Loudly and clearly and taking a fraction of a second longer, his translator expressed the same sentiment in Teldin.

It looked like a cross between an overgrown, four-armed kangaroo and a frog which was covered overall with sparse, sickly yellow fur. Because of the being's size and his own lack of defensive armament, Martin was acutely aware of the other's long, well-muscled legs, which terminated in large, clawed feet, and of the enormous teeth which showed clearly within the widely opened mouth. Its four, six-fingered hands also had heavy boney terminations which had been filed short and painted bright blue, presumably to aid the manipulation of small objects and for purposes of decoration. It was wearing a dark brown cloak of some coarse, fibrous material, and the garment was fastened at the neck and thrown back over the shoulders, where it was attached in some fashion to the being's backpack, probably to leave his limbs free for pedalling and steering its vehicle. There was no doubt, therefore, that this was a civilized entity, and that the open mouth with its fearsome display of teeth was simply a gape of surprise and curiosity, not a snarl of fury presaging an attack.

Perhaps there was a little bit of doubt, Martin thought nervously, and spoke again.

"If you are not engaged in urgent and important business," he said slowly while the translator rattled out the harsh, guttural gruntings and gobblings which were the Teldin equivalent, "I would be grateful if you could spare some of your time talking to me."

The Teldin made a harsh, barking sound which did not translate, followed by other noises which did. They sounded in his ear-piece as, "The conversation is likely to be a short one, stranger, if you do not move over here to the protection of the wall. Naturally I would be delighted to talk to you about yourself, the mechanism yonder in which you arrived, and any other subject which mutually interests us. But first there is a question. . . ."

The being paused for a moment. There was no way that Martin could read its facial expression on such short acquaintance, but from a certain tension and awkwardness in the way the Teldin was holding its limbs and body, he had a strong impression that the question was an important one. Finally, it came.

"Who owns you, stranger?"

Be careful, thought Martin. The alien's understanding of the word "own" might be different to Martin's. Could the question involve patriotism, or loyalty owed to its country, tribe, or employer? Was the Teldin using some kind of local slang which his translator was reproducing literally? He dare not answer until he was completely sure of the meaning of the question.

"I am sorry," he said. "Your question is unclear to me."

Before the Teldin could reply, Martin introduced himself and began describing his planet of origin. He spoke of Earth as it had been before the coming of the Federation, not the denuded and well-nigh depopulated planet that it had since become. Quickly he went on to talk about the lander and the much larger hypership in orbit above them and, when the Teldin expressed sudden concern, he assured the other that neither had anything to fear from the meteorites. He added that he, himself, did not carry such protection nor, for that matter, any other means of defense or offense.

When he finished speaking, the Teldin was silent for a moment. Then it said, "Thank you for this information which, in spite of being hearsay, could be of great importance. Does the being in the orbiting vessel own you?"

In his ear-piece he could hear Beth, who was monitoring the conversation, suppressing laughter.

"No," he said.

"Do you own it?"

"No," he said again.

"You only act that way, sometimes," said Beth. *"But be alert. Another pedal vehicle is heading out of the city towards you. It is painted brown and bright yellow, towing an enclosed trailer and flying some kind of pennant, with two people on board pedalling fast. It should reach you in about twenty minutes."*

Martin bypassed the translator momentarily to say, "The local constabulary, do you think? I can't react until they come into sight, when it would be natural to ask who and what they are. But our friend here worries me with its constant harping on ownership. And what does it mean by hearsay? I can't give it a straight answer until I know why it thinks the question is so important."

He cut in the translator and went on to explain the relationship between Beth and himself. He was non-specific regarding the division of their work, but he had to go into considerable detail on human social anthropology, cultural mores, and reproduction. But suddenly the Teldin was holding up two of its four hands.

"Thank you once again for this interesting hearsay," it said slowly, as if it was uncertain that the true meaning of the words was getting through to Martin. "You are answering questions which have not been asked, and not answering those which must be asked."

The brown and yellow tricycle came into sight just then. Martin said quickly, "The vehicle which approaches us at speed and flying a flag, and the beings propelling it. Is their mission important?"

The Teldin glanced at it in a manner suggesting impatience. "It flies the pennant of the Master of Sea and Landborne Communications. Their mission has nothing to do with us and is of no importance compared with the visit of an off-planet being who avoids answering the most important question about itself . . ."

"Just a couple of mailmen," said Beth in a relieved voice.

". . . Your status is not clear," it went on. "Do you or your life-mate own the vessel which brought you here?"

My *status* . . . ! Martin thought. A little light was beginning to dawn. Aloud, he said, "The vessels are not our personal property, but we are responsible for their operation."

"But they are owned, presumably, by someone who directs you in their use?" said the Teldin quickly, and added, "You must obey this being's directions?"

"Yes," said Martin.

The Teldin made a loud, gurgling sound which did not translate, then it said, "You are a slave, Martin. Highly placed, no doubt, considering the nature of the equipment you are allowed to use, but still a slave . . ."

Instinctively Martin stepped back as one of the being's enormous hands swung towards him. But it stopped a few inches from his chin with one digit pointing at the Federation symbol on his collar.

". . . Is that the emblem of your Master?"

His first thought was to strenuously deny that he was any kind of slave, and his second was to wonder what new complication would be the result of that denial. But the Federation was, in real terms, his master, as it was the master of all of its non-citizens.

"Yes," he said again.

The Teldin turned its hand, which was still only a few inches from Martin's face, to display a bracelet on its thick, furry wrist. The bracelet supported a flat oval of metal on which an intricate design had been worked in several colors.

"Like mine," said the Teldin, "your mark of ownership is small, tasteful, and inconspicuous as befits a slave in a position of trust and responsibility. But why did you ignore or evade the questions which would quickly have established your status?"

"I was unsure of your own status," Martin replied truthfully.

He remembered their tutor telling them again and again that in an alien-contact situation they must always tell the truth, although not necessarily all of it all at once. Measured doses of the truth gave rise to much fewer complications than well-meant, diplomatic lies.

"I don't like what I'm hearing," said Beth. *"The Federation does not approve of slavery or any form of—"*

"Now I understand," said the Teldin, before she could go on. "You thought I might be a Master and were being circumspect. Like the other passers-by, I thought you were a

Master and could not, therefore, speak first. But contact between ourselves and an other-world species would seem to be a project too important to be entrusted to a slave, regardless of its level of ability. My position forbids me saying anything which is directly critical of your Master, or any Master, but it seems to me that it would be more fitting if . . . if . . ."

"My Master did the work itself?" asked Martin.

"That was my thought exactly," said the Teldin.

Martin thought about their tutor and its enormous, sprawling body, and of the sheer size and complexity of any mobile life-support system capable of accommodating it, and he thought of that species' immense life-span. Carefully, and truthfully, he said, "My remarks should not be construed as critical or disloyal, but my Master is grossly overweight, very old, and has other projects demanding of its time and available energy."

"Since we are speaking face to face I can accept this information as factual until I have been instructed otherwise by my Master," the Teldin said, and the sudden change in its manner was unmistakable. It added, "But my Master will not accept anything you say."

"For this reason," Martin persisted, "I have been instructed to land on this world and gather information about your species and its culture so that my Master will know whom to approach with the initial offers of friendship and exchanges of knowledge."

"Your Master seems lacking in sensitivity and intelligence," said the Teldin, this time without any apology. "Your Master might just as well have sent a radio transmitting and receiving device."

"That has already been tried," said Martin, "without success."

"Naturally," said the Teldin.

The situation had gone sour, there could be no doubt about that. The impression given by the Teldin was that it belonged to an intensely status-conscious slave culture in which the Masters spoke only to other Masters or to God, and when a Master spoke to a slave the slave had to believe everything it was told and, presumably, disbelieve everything it had been told earlier by a lowlier being.

This is crazy, thought Martin. Aloud, he said, "What would have been your reaction if I'd been a Master?"

"Had you been a Master," the Teldin replied, "I would not have been able to give you any information until it had been vetted for content and accuracy by my own or another Master. Knowledge which is not passed down from a Master is, as you know, untrustworthy. The only assistance I could have given you would have been to arrange a meeting with another Master. Had you been a Master we could not have exchanged hearsay as freely as we have done."

"May this exchange continue?" asked Martin eagerly. "I have many questions. And answers."

"Yes, Martin," said the Teldin. "It may continue until I report your presence and everything that has transpired between us to my Master, who will assess the value of the material and instruct me accordingly.

"My curiosity is such that I am in no great hurry to make my report," the being added. "And my name is Skorta."

"Thank you, Skorta," said Martin, relieved. The atmosphere seemed friendly once more, but he still needed clarification on the Master-slave relationship. He said, "Will you make your report in person, and where?"

"*Careful . . .*" warned Beth.

"Thankfully, no," said Skorta. "I must make a hearsay report by radio. The device is in my Master's education complex in the city."

"Are you a *teacher?*"

Martin could hardly believe his luck. It would not matter which subject Skorta taught, because it was sure to have a grounding in many subjects. It was quite possible that this Teldin would be able to furnish them with all of the information necessary for the completion of their assignment, probably within a few hours.

"Properly speaking, only a Master can teach," it replied. "That is the law. I relay the approved information, suitably simplified for the age-groups concerned, to unruly little beings who only rarely think of questioning the validity of the information they receive. Even the words of a Master, as you know, may be doubted when they have been passed down through too many slaves."

"I should like to see your pupils," said Martin, "and other people in the city. Would I be able to meet a Master . . . ?"

Martin felt like biting off his tongue. Without thinking, he had blundered into that highly sensitive area again and he could almost feel the atmosphere congeal. The Teldin made a soft, untranslatable sound which might have been a sigh.

"Stranger," it said slowly, "your presence here is an insult and an affront to our Masters, since it is plain that your own Master thinks so little of this world and its people that it sent a slave to us as an emissary. To my knowledge there has never been a greater insult, and I cannot even guess at what the Masters' reaction will be.

"But I am willing to tak you to the city," Skorta went on. "In fact, I am anxious to do so in order to prolong this contact with you and to discover as much about your people and their civilization as I possibly can before I am required officially to forget it. But I must warn you that the visit to the city could place you in grave personal danger."

"From the slaves or the Masters?" asked Martin. He was beginning to like this visually ferocious, four-armed nightmare which was glaring down at him. He could be certain of very little in the present situation, but he was sure that this being was honest and had a measure of concern for his safety.

"The slaves may restrain you if instructed to do so by the Masters," the Teldin replied slowly, "but only the Masters bear weapons and only they may kill. Now, if you will climb into my carrier, I shall transport you to the city."

"Don't go," said Beth, and gave reasons.

"I have received information," said Martin when she had finished talking, "that meteorite activity in this area will increase by a factor of three very shortly. I cannot be more specific because of ignorance regarding your units of time. According to the instruments on the orbiting vessel—"

"This is hearsay," Skorta broke in.

"True," said Martin quickly. "But the instruments are being read by my life-mate who is, naturally, anxious that no harm befalls me."

"I can understand why you attach importance to this information," said the Teldin, "but I cannot. It comes through a device to your life-mate, through another device to you and then to myself. There are too many possibilities for cumulative error between the fact and the reported fact for me to accept this information.

"Since you believe that the Scourge from the sky will be

heavier soon," Skorta went on, "do you wish to return to the safety of your vessel now?"

In his other ear Beth was saying the same in much more forthright language, adding that there would be another time and another Teldin to talk to. But Martin wanted to go on talking to this one, and the intensity of the feeling surprised him.

"If I returned to my vessel," he said, choosing his words with care, "I could leave you a device which would enable us to continue our conversation. But this would be unsatisfactory for two reasons. I would not be able to visit your city, and you would consider any such conversation as untrustworthy hearsay. If, however, you can assure me from your own personal experience that this road is adequately protected, I would go with you to the city and continue to converse with you face to face."

The Teldin exhaled loudly and said, "Stranger, at last you are thinking like a Teldin." It began to pedal, and soon the protective wall was slipping past at a respectable rate of speed. Without taking its attention from the road, Skorta added, "I can also assure you that you may speak to me face to face even while addressing the back of my neck."

On only two occasions did the Teldin move briefly to the unprotected side of the road to let oncoming vehicles through on the inside. Right of way, it seemed, depended on the pennant flying on the approaching vehicle and on the size and position of the ownership badges worn by the occupants.

A flag and distinctively colored vehicle driven by a Teldin wearing a large emblem on a shoulder sash indicated that it was a slave of the lower order, a public utility worker or such. Badges worn on arm-bands signified a much higher grade of slave, and emblems worn at the wrist indicated a person high in the hierarchy of Teldin slavehood.

The road had detoured to utilize the natural shelter provided by a small hill when there was a sharp, crashing detonation followed by a diminishing, hissing roar. Martin's eyes jerked upward in time to see a large meteor trace an incandescent line across the sky below the cloud base, and he felt the shock of the impact transmitted through the solid, unsprung structure of the tricycle as it struck ground somewhere behind a nearby rise. Then suddenly the stony ground beyond the outer edge of the road was covered with tiny explosions of rock dust.

"This must be the heavier Scourge you spoke of," Skorta said. "The Masters warn us of such events, but even they cannot be precise in their predictions."

"Why do they refer to the meteorites as the Scourge?" said Beth. *"Do they equate all danger and pain with strokes from a Master's whip?"*

Martin waited until a large vehicle flying the pennant of what he now knew to be Master of Agriculture squeezed past on the outside, then asked the question.

"The Masters say," replied the Teldin, turning its head to look at him briefly, "that it is a continuing reminder that we cannot fully trust anything which is not experienced directly except, of course, the word of a Master."

He asked, "Are slaves, particularly high-ranking slaves like yourself, ever rewarded with your freedom?"

"We have freedom," replied the Teldin.

"But the Masters tell you what to do and think," Martin protested. "They alone have weapons. They alone administer punishment and have the power of life and death."

"Naturally; they are the Masters."

Martin knew that he was getting into a sensitive area, but he needed the answers. "Is the death penalty administered often? And which crimes merit it?"

"Sometimes the Masters execute each other for Masters' reasons," said the Teldin, slowing as the road curved sharply and entered a deep ravine. "With slaves it rarely happens, and only if there is destruction of valuable living property. For less serious crimes they may be reduced in status or forced to work in unprotected areas on the surface for a time, or if the offense is venial the peacekeeping slaves deal with it.

"An alert Master served by trusted and observant slaves," the Teldin added, "is able to stop trouble before it develops to the point where damage to property occurs."

For a few seconds Martin tried to control his revulsion at the picture of the Teldin culture which was emerging. If Skorta's Master received a full report of everything he had said to its slave then his next question was foolhardy indeed, but it had to be asked.

"Do you ever feel dissatisfied with your status, Skorta, and wish you were a Master?"

"Have you gone raving mad?" Beth began, and broke off because the Teldin was speaking.

"There have been times when I would have liked to be a Master," it said, and made another one of its untranslatable noises, "but good sense prevailed."

The floor of the ravine had taken an upward gradient and Skorta had no breath to spare for speech, so Beth was able to express herself at length.

"You are taking too many risks," she said angrily. *"My advice is to pull out as soon as you can. Some of the things you've said to Skorta could be construed as attempted subversion of a slave, and the Masters won't like that. Besides, with all the surface sensor material we are collecting still awaiting processing, plus your interview with Skorta, we should have enough information for our assessment. . . ."*

The picture which was emerging was clear but not at all pleasant, she continued. Teldi was essentially a slave culture, with the vast majority of the planetary population serving an elitist group of Masters who might be numbered in the thousands, or perhaps even hundreds. Their control of the slave population was such that the slaves themselves, with their minor gradations of responsibility and status, were as a group happy with the situation, although individuals like Skorta might occasionally have their doubts. So happy were they with their role that the slaves did not want to become Masters and helped maintain themselves in slavery by telling tales on fellow slaves who looked like causing trouble, while at the same time believing implicitly everything told them by their Masters, even when this information contradicted first-hand knowledge. History was also vetted by the Masters so that the slaves had no way of knowing if there had ever been better times.

But the worst aspect of all was that the Masters held the power of life and death over their slaves and were the only people on all of Teldi allowed to bear weapons.

Beth went on, *"You know how the Federation feels about slavery or any other form of physical or psychological coercion in government. They will not be favorably impressed with this culture. But it's still possible that the slaves could qualify for citizenship if we could find a way of separating them from their Masters."*

"It isn't as simple as that," said Martin, instinctively lowering his voice even though the translator was switched off. "This fanatical distrust they display towards everyone and everything which is not experienced first-hand worries me. Trust between intelligent species is the most important requirement for Federation citizenship."

"That could change when the influence of the Masters is removed. But you agree that the slaves must have the opportunity of deciding for themselves whether to leave this place and join the Federation or remain with their Masters. Our assessment, remember, should include recommended solutions to the problem here."

"Let's ask one of them," said Martin. Through the translator he went on, "Skorta, would you like to live on a world free of the Scourge and where you could farm and build houses and travel on the surface without danger?"

"Stranger . . ." began the Teldin, and was silent for nearly a minute before it went on, "It is senseless and painful to consider such possibilities. The Masters disapprove of mental bad habits of this kind. They say that the Scourge is, and must be accepted."

"Brain-washed!" said Beth disgustedly.

A few minutes later the ravine widened to become the head of a deep, fertile valley. Skorta pulled off the road and stopped to give Martin his first close look at a Teldin city.

The valley ran in a north-south direction and its heavily cultivated western slopes and bottomland were protected from the worst of the Scourge. Only when the meteorites slanted in from an angle of forty-five degrees or more, which they did very occasionally, was the city at risk. The city's structures hugged the ground and varied in size from tiny private dwellings with extensions underground to large buildings which spread themselves out rather than upwards. Regardless of size, every one of them had a thick, earth-banked west-facing wall, and what appeared to be important machinery and vehicles were housed inside deep slit trenches. Suddenly the Teldin pointed towards a high cliff further along the valley.

"That is my school," it said.

There was a flat apron of crushed rock around the base of the cliff and a wide, cavernous opening which was obviously a vehicle entrance. His magnifier showed about fifty smaller openings, regular in shape and plainly artificial features, covering the cliff face.

"I would like to see inside," said Martin.

The tricycle lurched across the verge and began picking up speed again.

"There aren't many children about," said Martin as the road took them into a residential area. "Are they at school? And the Masters, where do they live?"

Skorta overtook a structurally complex and highly geared vehicle powered by four furiously pedalling Teldins before it replied, "If the children are to attain adulthood they have much to learn from parents and teachers. And there are no Masters here. They live in the polar city, which is free from the worst of the Scourge, and only rarely do they visit our cities. We prefer it that way because the presence of a Master means grief for some and serious inconvenience for others. Believe me, stranger, while we are obliged to honor and obey our Masters, and we do, we much prefer them to leave us alone."

"Why?" asked Martin. The other's words had a distinctly rebellious sound to them.

"They come only in response to reports of serious trouble," the Teldin explained, breathing deeply between sentences because the road up to the school had steepened. "Not just to administer punishment but to extend or amend existing instructions regarding virtually everything. When a Master comes, the visit must not be wasted.

"It is a long, difficult, and dangerous journey for them," the Teldin concluded, "and their lives are much too valuable to be risked without very good reason."

Martin had heard of absentee landlords in Earth's history, but the concept of an absentee slave-master was difficult to grasp, as was the idea of a slave society which appeared to be self-policing and largely self-governing. He could not understand why they remained slaves, why they did not rebel and start thinking as well as doing for themselves, or why they held their Masters, whose absence was infinitely preferable to their presence, in such high regard.

The Masters, he thought, must be very potent individuals indeed. To complete the assessment he had to know more about them.

"Would the visit of a being from another world," he said carefully, "be considered important enough to warrant the attention of a Master?"

"*Watch it . . . !*" said Beth warningly.

"The visit of a slave from another world," the Teldin corrected—without, however, answering the question.

The tricycle rumbled across the stony apron at the base of the cliff and toward the vehicle entrance, and Martin saw that the tiny pupils of Skorta's eyes had opened to four or five times their normal size. The dilation mechanism had to be a voluntary one, because they were still several seconds away from the tunnel mouth. Plainly the Teldins had no trouble seeing in the dark. He adjusted his image enhancer.

Patches of luminous vegetation coated the tunnel walls, and at frequent intervals he could see short side tunnels opening into artificial caves containing machinery whose purpose was not clear to him. Skorta told him that important and irreplaceable machines were housed in these caves to protect them from the Scourge, and that metal was scarce on Teldi.

The Teldin guided its tricycle into one of the caves, and they dismounted.

"I realize that to a stranger like youself this is hearsay," Skorta said, "but it is widely held to be a fact that this school is the most efficient teaching establishment on the whole planet. The Masters of Transport, Agriculture, Communications, Education, and associated Masterships send their slaves here, often from pre-puberty, and when they leave they are most valuable pieces of property indeed."

Martin hastily revised his estimate of the Teldin's status. It was closer to being a university lecturer than a schoolteacher, he thought, and asked, "What is your position in the establishment?"

"The position is largely administrative," Skorta replied as it led Martin into a narrow tunnel which climbed steeply. "I am the senior teaching slave in charge. We are going to my quarters . . ."

He made another revision, from lecturer to Dean of Studies.

". . . Later, if you are agreeable," it went on, "I would like you to meet some of the students. But there is a serious risk involved—"

"The students are unruly?"

"No, stranger," the Teldin said, "the risk is mine in that the slave of another Master might report your presence before I did so. There is also the matter of your accommodation, should you wish to remain here for a time."

"Thank you, I would like to—" began Martin, when Beth's voice broke in.

"You can't just move in like a visiting lecturer. There are problems."

"There are problems," Skorta repeated unknowingly, "regarding your life processes, particularly food intake and waste elimination. It is a unique problem for us. There is no knowledge nor even the wildest and most speculative hearsay regarding the possible effects of off-planet diseases on the Teldin species, or the effectiveness of our disinfectants on your wastes. This aspect of your visit has only just occurred to me. It is a serious matter which requires consultation with our senior medical slaves. So serious, in fact, that they will be duty-bound to refer the matter to the Master of Medicine."

The Teldin guided him along an ascending tunnel which led into a large cliff-face cave containing an enormous, high desk, chairs on the same scale, and walls covered by the luminous vegetation between gaps in the bookshelves. Martin had time to notice that the books were retained in place by heavy wooden bars padlocked at both ends.

Since the discussion about alien infections, Skorta had been keeping its distance while still asking an awful lot of questions. Plainly the danger of a possible off-world infection was evenly balanced by its curiosity. It was time he put the Teldin's mind at rest.

He said, "Your offer of accommodation is appreciated, but rather than cause discomfort to both of us I would prefer to spend some time every day in my own vessel. May I have permission to move it to the flat area in front of the school so that I can spend as much time here as possible?

"And the Master of Medicine has no cause for concern," he went on before the other could reply, "since off-world pathogens will not effect Teldins, nor will Teldin diseases be transmissible to the many hundreds of different species who inhabit the Galaxy. This is—"

"Hearsay!" the Teldin broke in.

"Naturally," Martin went on, "I have not visited all of these worlds, but I have lived for a time on three of them without contacting any other-species diseases."

He was bending the truth slightly, because one of the three was Teldi itself. The others had been Fomalhaut Three and the single lifeless planet which circled the Black Diamond at the galactic center.

"It is still hearsay, but I am greatly reassured," the Teldin said. "And your vessel will arouse less comment outside our school than in any other part of the city."

"Thank you," said Martin, and went on. "If a problem arises suddenly, as it may have done today had I been a potential disease-carrier, how do the Masters learn of it?"

The Teldin pointed to a recess which contained a table, chair, and shelves lined with what could only be Leyden cells. The batteries were wired in series to a collection of table-mounted radio equipment with which the legendary Marconi would have felt instantly at home. Skorta was giving him a rundown of the Teldin equivalent of the Morse code when Martin interrupted quietly.

"This is a mechanism. It transmits and receives information over a great distance, not face to face. Surely this is hearsay, and forbidden?"

The Teldin gestured towards the barred bookshelves and said, "That, too, is hearsay, but some of us are allowed to read it."

"You confuse me," said Martin.

"The volumes contain hearsay which is a transcription of much older hearsay," the Teldin explained, "selected by the Masters for study by only the highest-level slaves, slaves who are able to assimilate the material without mental suffering caused by disaffection with their present circumstances, or thoughts of what might have been had the Scourge not come upon us. Ignorance makes it easier to accept the inevitable."

"Are you saying," said Martin harshly, "that the majority of the slaves are kept in ignorance?"

"I'm saying that they are happier in their ignorance," Skorta replied. "This hearsay material is not kept from them entirely. But it must be earned, piece by piece, as a reward for mental and physical effort."

It was like some kind of freemasonry, Martin thought, with secrets of increasing importance being entrusted to the favored few who showed themselves able and willing to maintain the Teldin status quo. His sarcasm was probably lost in translation as he said, "And the Masters know everything?"

"Not everything," said the Teldin, showing more of its teeth. "As yet they don't know about you."

Once again Martin had the feeling that this particular Teldin was a potential rebel. He said, "I have the feeling that you do not want my presence reported to the Masters. Is this so?"

"That is correct," replied Skorta. "My reasons are, of course, selfish. Until official cognizance has been taken of your presence on Teldi, I am at liberty to learn as much as possible from you before the Masters rule on the factuality of your information. I expect that much of what I learn will have to be officially forgotten, not committed to writing, and will die with me. The Masters must consider the mental well-being of their slaves as the highest priority, and the simple fact of your presence here implies a way of life infinitely better than our existence on Teldi.

"Fortunately I can justify my delay in reporting you," it added, "because of initial confusion regarding your status and the necessity of educating you in our ways lest you inadvertently committed a crime, such as insulting a Master."

It was not lying, Martin thought admiringly, but it was certainly bending the truth into some fancy shapes.

"I had intended showing you the school now," Skorta went on, "but it would be better if I drove you back to your vessel so that you can bring it here."

"No problem," said Martin. "My vessel can be moved here without my presence on board."

"There is a problem," Beth contradicted. *"Not an urgent one, so you can let your friend show you its school. A cloud of denser meteorite material will arrive in about fifteen hours' time. According to the computer, the area for twenty miles around your city will be well and truly clobbered, so when I move the lander over there I suggest you excuse yourself politely and get the hell out."*

"The lander's force shield will protect—" began Martin.

"It will be a very heavy bombardment, and you will be safer on the hypership. There is something very odd about this Scourge, and the things the computer is telling me about

it just don't make sense. I'd like to go over the data with you."

Martin did not reply at once because he had followed the Teldin into a tunnel whose walls and ceiling were smooth and completely unlike the roughly chiseled rock surfaces he had encountered earlier. He could see small areas of tiling still adhering to the walls and many horizontal markings which were thin and pale green in color and which passed through small spots of dull red. He aimed the visual pick-up in his helmet at them and paused for a moment so that Beth would receive a clear picture, then hurried after the Teldin.

"Copper wiring and ferrous metal staples holding it in position," he reported excitedly. "The insulation has rotted away and all that is left is the pale green and red corrosion traces. This is a much older section of the school, dating from a time when they had electrically generated rather than vegetation-produced lighting. That could have been hundreds of years ago."

Beth sighed. *"So you intend staying there until the last possible moment?"*

"At least," said Martin.

They came to an opening whose sides bore red corrosion marks which suggested it had once possessed a metal door. Inside there was a large, square room rendered small by the presence of more than thirty Teldins, who ranged in size from just over one meter to the full adult stature of three. The walls were hung with tapestries which were brightly colored, finely detailed, and dealt with various aspects of the Teldin anatomy.

His arrival caused an immediate cessation of work and a lot of untranslatable noises. He was introduced as an off-planet slave gathering information on Teldin teaching methods for its Master. Skorta told them to restrain their natural curiosity and resume work.

It was difficult to distinguish the teacher-in-charge from the adult pupils, Martin found, until he discovered that the more advanced students aided in the teaching process by instructing the less knowledgeable ones. He stopped beside two of the youngest, one of whom was immobilized and rendered speechless by practice splints and a tight mandible bandage, and asked how long it took for a fractured fore-arm to heal.

"Thirty-two days on average, Senior," the young Teldin

said promptly, staring at the Federation symbol on Martin's collar. It went on, "Longer if it is a multiple or compound fracture, or if it is sited at a joint or is complicated by severe wounding. If the accompanying wounds are improperly cleansed, putrefaction may take place and the affected limb must be removed."

Martin estimated the age of the Teldin medical student to be the equivalent of a ten- or eleven-year-old of Earth. "I thank you for this information," he said quickly, and added, "How long will it be before you are a fully qualified medical slave?"

Everyone had stopped working again and were making untranslatable noises. Anxiously he went over his question for implied criticisms or hidden insults and could not find any. In an attempt to retrieve the situation he said the first thing which came into his mind.

"I would like to answer some questions about myself and show you my vessel."

They were all staring at him in absolute silence. It was close on a minute before a young Teldin spoke.

"When, Senior?"

"I do not wish to interrupt your study or rest periods," he said. "Would early tomorrow morning be convenient?"

When they were in the corridor a few minutes later, Martin asked, "Did I say something wrong?"

Skorta made an untranslatable sound. "They would have observed your vessel at a distance, in any case. But now you have issued an invitation from your Master to view the machine closely and ask questions about it. The invitation extends, naturally, to the members of other classes. I trust, stranger, that your vessel is strongly built."

Martin was about to deny that his Master had issued the invitation through him, but then he realized that a mere slave like himself would never have been so presumptuous as to issue it without permission.

"You misunderstand me," he said. "I was asking if I'd said something wrong when I questioned the medical student about the time needed to qualify. On my world such students spend one-sixth of their lifetimes in study before they are allowed to practice medicine on other people. Some of them continue to study and discover new cures and teach for the rest of their lives."

"What a strange idea," the Teldin said, stopping outside the next classroom's entrance. "You are correct, Martin; I did not understand you. Your question to the student was a nonsense question. Badges of ownership are not worn in school since students are considered to be too ignorant to be good slaves, but the only medical student there was the teacher. The students will ultimately belong, if my memory serves me accurately, to the Masters of Agriculture, Communications, and Peace-keeping. Medical slaves are invariably teachers, and new medical knowledge must be sought only at the direction of the Master of Medicine.

"The incidence of injury and disease must be very small on your world," Skorta continued, "if students waste so much time studying medicine exclusively. On Teldi we study it as soon as we are able to read, write, and calculate. On Teldi death and injury are not rare. On Teldi everyone is a doctor."

They had completed the tour of the classrooms when the Teldin turned into the entrance to a long, high-ceilinged chamber whose far wall was more than two hundred meters distant. Against the wall Martin could see, dimly by the light of the ever-present luminous vegetation, a raised dais or altar with a cloth draped across it.

"This is the Hall of Honor," Skorta said, and began a slow march towards the opposite wall. "Here the slaves renew their promises of service and obedience to our Masters every day, or assemble for punishment or censure and, once a year, to graduate to higher levels."

It had not always been the slaves' Hall of Honor, Martin thought excitedly as he looked up to the great, curving ceiling and down to the regularly spaced tunnel mouths, where it arched down to meet the floor on both sides. He asked for and obtained Skorta's permission to use his helmet spotlight.

It showed lines and patterns of corrosion running along the floor and into the tunnels. The marks were wide and suggested heavy metal rail supports rather than wiring conduits. The walls and ceiling were also covered by strips and patches of corrosion, and as they walked towards the dais they passed shallow depressions in the floor which were filled with powdered rust. Martin's mouth was so dry that it was difficult to speak.

"This . . . this place is *old*," he said. "What was its purpose before it became the Hall of Honor?"

He already knew the answer.

"It is recorded only as hearsay," the Teldin replied. "But the hearsay is unapproved, forbidden as a matter for discussion by all levels of slaves. I know nothing other than that it was our first protection against the Scourge."

Suddenly Beth's voice was in his other ear. She sounded angry.

"It was probably one of the causes of the Scourge in the first place. That hall was once a storage and distribution facility which supplied missiles to less deeply buried launching silos. But you must have spotted that yourself. It certainly answers a lot of my questions."

"I spotted it," said Martin. "But causing the Scourge . . . I don't understand you."

"That's because you haven't been trying to make sense of the things the computer is saying about this ring system . . . !"

Normally such a system was formed as a result of a satellite (or satellites) approaching too closely to its primary and being pulled apart by gravitational stresses, and the debris being strewn along the plane of the moon's original orbit, she went on. Continuing collisions would eventually cause the pieces to grind themselves into uniformly small pieces. But at the present stage of the process many large pieces should have survived collisions with the small stuff, since the probability of the relatively few large chunks of the moon colliding with each other was small.

The debris orbiting Teldi contained no large pieces of debris.

"Then the ring has been forming for a long time," said Martin, "and the process is far advanced."

"No," said Beth firmly. *"The Scourge has been in existence for an extremely short time, astronomically speaking. The process began one thousand one hundred and seventeen Teldin years and thirty-three days ago, and was completed forty-seven years and one hundred and two days later."*

"Are . . . are you *sure?*"

Beth laughed. *"For a moment I thought you were going to accuse me of using hearsay. The computer is sure and I'm sure, and you know which one of us is omniscient."*

"Are there any missiles left?" said Martin. "Any traces of radioactivity in a forgotten silo somewhere?"

"*None,*" she replied firmly. "*The sensors would have detected it. They were all used.*"

She resumed talking as the slow march towards the dais continued, but very often Martin's mind was leaping ahead of hers as piece after piece of the Teldin jigsaw puzzle fitted into place. The reason for the Scourge and the fatalistic acceptance of it was now plain, as was the cause of the pathological distrust of everything which was not experienced first-hand, the rigid stratification of the slaves, and the thinking done from the top which was so characteristic of the military mind. Finally there was the planet-wide catastrophe which had driven the surviving population to shelter in such installations as this, and brought about a situation which was in essence a military dictatorship. The Hall of Honor and one-time missile arsenal was certainly a key piece of the puzzle, but the picture was not complete.

"I must speak with a Master," said Martin.

"*But there's no need!*" Beth protested. "*Sensor probes have been dropped on this and other cities. We have more than enough data on the ordinary people of this frightful planet. They are resourceful, ethical, hard-working, long-suffering and, to my mind, wholly admirable. We should say so without delay. Our assessment can be based on an interview with one Teldin, remember, and we were not expected to take a long time about it. I say that the slave levels are in all respects suitable and should be offered Federation Citizenship following reorientation training to neutralize the conditioning of the Masters.*

"*The slave-owners, from what we've learned of them, don't stand a snowball's chance. Our masters, the Federation, will not abide dictators who—*"

"Wait," said Martin.

They had stopped before the dais which, now that he could see it clearly, consisted of a single cube of polished rock just under two meters on the side and with a large flap apparently covering the top and hanging down in front. The section of the flag visible to him was dark blue and bore the same design as that which appeared on Skorta's bracelet. The stone was too high for him to see the top surface, until he was suddenly grasped by four large hands above the knees and at the elbows and hoisted into the air.

And saw the symbol of ultimate authority.

Unlike the richly embroidered flag, the sword looked excessively plain and functional. Simply and beautifully proportioned, it measured nearly two meters long and had a broad, double-edged blade which came to a fine point. Its only decoration was a small, engraved plate set in the guard, which reproduced the design on the flag. Martin stared at it until the Teldin's four arms began to quiver with the strain of holding him aloft, then he gestured to be put down.

"It is the sword of the Master of Education," Skorta said slowly. "My Master died recently and a new one has yet to be chosen."

Martin was remembering the long, sharp blade of the weapon and the faint staining he had seen at its tip. He wet his lips and said, "Has it ever been . . . used?"

"The sword of a Master," it replied in a voice Martin could barely hear, "must draw blood at least once."

"Is it possible," Martin asked once again, "to speak with a Master?"

"You are an off-world slave," the Teldin replied, accenting the last word.

It was the last word, in fact, because neither of them spoke during the long walk back to the base of the cliff where Beth had already moved the lander. Martin had a lot on his mind.

He had programmed the force shield to interdict inanimate objects and remain pervious to living beings. As a result, it was not the timer which awakened him, but the voices of more than two hundred young Teldins who were surrounding the lander. The cliff-face and city were still shrouded in pre-dawn darkness except for the intermittent illumination provided by the Scourge as it drew incandescent lines across the sky. He increased the intensity of the exterior lighting and went outside.

"I can't answer all of your questions at once," he said as his translator signalled overload, "So I will tell you about my vessel and some of the worlds it has visited. . . ."

Except for a few of the older ones who muttered "Hearsay" they became very quiet and attentive. He talked about planetary environments which were beautiful, terrifying, weird but always wonderful, and on the subject of the Federation he said only that it was a collection of people of many different shapes and sizes and degrees of intelligence who helped each other and who wanted to help Teldi.

When these youngsters grew up, Martin thought, it was likely that they would never be able to regard their Teldin way of life with complete acceptance. And if they were not judged suitable for Federation Citizenship and were left to fend for themselves, what a particularly lousy trick he was playing on them by talking like this.

"I can't predict where exactly they will hit," Beth broke in urgently, *"but that area is in for a bad time. Cut it short."*

"I'll answer a few questions, then send them to shelter," he told her. "The mountain on this side of the valley will protect us, so there's no immediate—"

The sky was lit by a sudden flare of bright orange and the ground seemed to twitch under Martin's feet. He broke off and looked around wildly, then up at the cliff. Everything seemed normal.

"That was a big one," said Beth, her voice rising in pitch. *"It hit close to the summit directly above you and started a rockslide. You can't see it past the shoulder of the cliff. Tell them to . . ."*

But Martin was already shouting for them to run for the shelter of the school. Nobody moved, and he had to explain quickly, so quickly that he was close to being incoherent, about Beth and the orbiting ship and its instruments which gave advance warning of the rockfall which they could not see. Still they did not move. They were dismissing his warning as hearsay. He angled one of the lander's lights upwards to show the top of the cliff and the first few rocks bouncing into sight over its edge.

They began to run then, too late.

"No, get back!" Martin shouted desperately. "There's safety here. Get back to the lander!"

Some of them hesitated. Without thinking about it Martin sprinted after the others and managed to get ahead of them—they were young and their legs were slightly shorter than his—and wave them back. There were about twenty of them outside the protection of the lander's force shield now, but they were slowing down, stopping. He did not know whether they were simply frightened and confused or, since his recent demonstration of foreknowledge of the rockfall, they believed him when he said the area around the lander was safe.

The first rocks struck the ground between the lander and the school entrance, bounced outwards and rolled towards them. Three of the Teldins were knocked over and another was down hopping and crawling on four hands and one foot and dragging the injured limb behind it. Martin pointed at the glowing line on the ground which marked the outer edge of the force shield.

"Quickly, move them to the other side of that line. They'll be safe there, believe me!"

He grabbed one of the fallen Teldins by the feet and began dragging it towards the line. The rolling and bouncing rocks were being stopped by the invisible shield and the other students had realized that the protection was not hearsay. But more than half of them were down, and the others were trying to drag them to safety. Martin pulled his Teldin across the line and went after another.

"Get back dammit!" Beth shouted. *"Half the bloody mountain is falling on you. . . !"*

A rain of fine stones and earth struck his back as he bent over the Teldin casualty, and suddenly a bouncing rock hit him in the back of the leg. He sat down abruptly, tears as well as dust blinding him. The rumbling sound from high upon the cliff was growing louder, and large rocks were thumping into the ground all around him with increasing frequency. The force shield and safety were only a few meters away, but he did not know in which direction.

He was grasped suddenly by four large hands which lifted him and hurled him backwards. He tumbled through the interface of the shield closely followed by the Teldin who had saved him. He blinked, trying to clear his vision as expert hands felt along his limbs and body.

"Nothing broken, stranger," said the young Teldin. "Some minor lacerations and bruising on the leg. You should use your own medication to treat the injury."

"Thank you," said Martin. He climbed to his feet and limped towards the lander.

The sound of the rockfall had become muffled because the hemisphere of the force shield was completely covered by loose rocks and soil. Several of the casualties lay looking up at the smooth dome of rubble which had inexplicably refused to fall on them, with expressions which were still unreadable to Martin, while the others had obviously accepted the invisible protection as a fact and were busying themselves with the injured.

When each and every victim and survivor was a trained medic, he thought admiringly, the aftermath of even a major disaster lost much of its horror.

Another young Teldin intercepted him at the lander's entry port. It said, "Thank you, stranger. All of the students who were trying to reach the school have returned or have been returned. There are no fatalities."

Not yet, thought Martin.

He was thinking about the tremendous weight of rock pressing down on their force shield. That shield could handle the heaviest of meteorite showers without difficulty, but it had not been designed to support the weight of an avalanche. The drain on the small ship's power reserves did not bear thinking about.

He looked at the hemisphere of rocks above and around him, knowing that Beth's repeaters were showing her everything he saw, and asked, "How long can I keep it up?"

"Not long. But long enough for your air to run out first. There are two hundred people in there. I'm coming down!"

He started to protest, then realized that Beth knew as well as he did that she could not land the great, ungainly bulk of a hypership whose configuration suited it only for deep space and orbital maneuvering. The ship could in an emergency be brought close to the ground, but it was not the kind of maneuver to be undertaken by a trainee on first assignment. Worrying out loud to her would simply undermine her confidence, so he remained silent while he applied a dressing to his leg and watched the pictures she was sending to him.

He saw the valley city grow large in his main screen, saw the fresh meteor crater on the mountaintop above the school, and the grey scar left by the rockslide joining it with the great pile of rubble at the base of the cliff where the lander was buried. He saw four great, shallow depressions appear suddenly in unoccupied areas of the valley floor as the hypership's pressor beams were deployed to check the vessel's descent and hold her, braced and immobile, on four rigid, immaterial stilts. Her tremendous force shield covered the whole valley, and for the first time in over a thousand years the Scourge was impotent against the city.

A tractor beam speared out, came to a tight focus, and began to pull at the pile of rubble.

"Nice work," said Martin. "Concentrate on digging us out and clearing a path to the school entrance. Some of these casualties will have to be moved there for proper treatment, and quickly."

Clearing the rocks above the lander took much longer than expected, because every time Beth pulled out a mass of rubble, more slid down to fill the space. He decided to run a quick computation based on the volume of air trapped inside the shield and the rate at which it was being used by two hundred Teldins whose lung capacities were almost double that of a human being, and his anxiety gave way to mounting desperation.

He went outside to try to reassure the younger students, and discovered that three of them were the children of Masters.

Now I'm really in trouble, he thought.

All around him the older Teldins were suggesting to each other, and by inference to Martin, that they should not waste air in needless conversation. He returned to the lander.

"If you seal yourself inside the lander," said Beth suddenly, *"it has enough tanked air to keep you alive until I dig you out, while the same amount of air distributed among two hundred Teldins wouldn't last ten minutes. Think about it."*

For several minutes he thought very seriously about it. He thought about facing Skorta with the news that he alone was alive among the two hundred asphyxiated students. Briefly, he thought about playing God and squeezing a few of the Teldins into the lander—young ones, of course, and probably the children of the Masters. What would Skorta think of that compromise? For some reason that particular Teldin's opinion of him had become very important to Martin.

Would it be better, he wondered in sudden self-disgust, simply to stay in the lander without speaking to any Teldin and, when he was able to take off, rejoin the hypership and return to Fomalhaut Three? He could tell the tutor that the problem set him had become too complicated, that the responsibility for assessing the Teldin species was too much for him. In short, he should simply walk away from the whole sorry mess.

He was still thinking about it, and he had not closed the lander's entry port, when Beth spoke again.

"All right," she said angrily. *"Be noble and self-sacrificing and . . . and stupid! But I have another idea. It's tricky. I don't think the equipment is supposed to be used in this way, and it could be more dangerous so far as you are concerned. . . ."*

Her idea was to concentrate on clearing a small area at the exact top center of the shield, the point where it could be opened without the rest of the shield collapsing, and use wide-focus pressors to keep the surrounding rocks from sliding into the opening for as long as possible—long enough, at least, for some of the stinking fog inside to be replaced with fresh outside air. The danger to Martin was that, if the pressors slipped, the rocks which fell into the opening would smash through the canopy of the lander's control position some thirty meters below, and Martin would no longer be worried about his assignment or anything else.

For the next twenty minutes he divided his attention between the rocks visible above him and Beth's outside viewpoint, which showed her doing things to that pile of rock with tractor and pressor beams which he had not thought possible. Then slowly, from above and below, a gap appeared. It was about two meters wide and it was holding.

"Now," said Beth.

Very carefully he opened the shield until the aperture was roughly a meter across. Stones and coarse gravel rattled down on the canopy, but nothing large enough to penetrate. The fine rock dust which had begun to fall was being blown out again as the hot, stale air rushed to escape. It held for one, two . . . five minutes.

"It's beginning to . . ." Beth began.

He hit the stud which returned the shield to full coverage and cringed as several small rocks which had slipped through banged against the canopy. The gap above was again completely closed with rubble.

". . . slip," she ended.

Around the lander the uninjured students were on their feet, standing motionless and watching him in utter silence.

Martin gestured vaguely, not knowing what else to do, and they began sitting down again.

The next time they needed to freshen the air, enough rubble had been cleared to allow Martin to leave the aperture open. But the sun was close to setting before the lander and the school entrance were completely uncovered and the students began moving in an orderly procession towards the entrance, carrying the injured with them. Skorta came hurrying in the opposite direction.

It stopped in front of Martin and looked down at him for several seconds. The Teldin was trembling, whether from anger, relief, or fatigue Martin could not say.

"The students," it said, "would have been safe inside the school."

"There were no deaths," Martin said, by way of an apology. "And, ah, three of the students are the children of Masters."

The Teldin was still shaking as it said, "Those students are the property of their Master parent. They are loved and cherished, as are all children, but they are not yet Masters and may never be." It gestured with three of its arms, indicating the lander, the valley city, and the hypership, which still looked gigantic, even though it had withdrawn to an altitude of three miles. "Your activities have been reported to the Masters. Now I have been instructed to proceed at once to the polar city to undergo a Masters' interrogation regarding you. If you wish it you may accompany me."

"I would like that," said Martin. "I could explain to the Masters why I—"

"No, stranger," the Teldin broke in, no longer shaking. "At most we can speak together and be overheard by the Masters, but nothing you say to me has value. To them it is hearsay and irresponsible. Martin, can you send . . . can you urgently request the presence of your Master?"

"No," said Martin, "my Master would not come."

"The Masters of Teldi will not accept your words," Skorta went on, "although I, personally, would like to speak with you at greater length. But there could be grave danger for you here. I have no previous knowledge or hearsay which enables me to foretell what will happen when we meet the Masters.

"It would be safer," he ended, "if you left at once."

"That is good advice," said Beth.

Martin knew that, but at the same time he was feeling confused by a sudden warmth of feeling for this large, incredibly ugly, and strangely considerate extra-terrestrial. There could be no doubt that the Masters were going to give it a difficult time, and that Martin was directly responsible for its problems. His presence during the interrogation would relieve the Teldin of a lot of the pressure—especially if Martin took the blame for everything that had happened. It would not be right to leave the senior teaching slave to face them alone. Besides, giving moral support to the Teldin might enable him to salvage something from this assignment.

"I want to meet the Masters," he said, to both the Teldin and Beth. "Thank you for your concern. However, I can remove the danger of the long journey to the polar city. My lander can take us there very quickly, and a speedy response to their summons might favorably impress your Masters. Are you willing to travel in my vessel?"

"Yes, Martin," the Teldin replied with no hesitation at all, "and I am grateful indeed for this unique opportunity."

There was a feeling in Martin's stomach not unlike negative G, a sensation composed of fear and excitement at the knowledge that, within a matter of hours, the empty spaces in the Teldin jigsaw puzzle would be filled in and he would know the full extent of the trouble he had caused and, perhaps, have paid the penalty for causing it.

Initially they flew only as far as the hypership, because the lander needed a systems check and power recharge after its argument with the avalanche. The Teldin was folded so awkwardly into the space available in the control cubicle that it could not see out and, much to its disappointment, the lander's dock on the mother ship had no view-ports even though there was enough headroom for it to stand erect.

When it met Beth, Skorta made a bow which could only be described as courtly. It told her that it had had a life-mate who had perished by the Scourge many years ago and had not met another who had engaged its intellect and its emotions to anything like the same extent, but that the fault was probably its own, because several of the teaching slaves had made overtures.

Martin left them talking while he went to the computer's

Fabrications module. He did not intend going down to meet the Masters either empty-handed or with an empty backpack.

Beth joined him as he was listing and describing his requirements to the Fabricator.

"I like your friend," she said, leaning over his shoulder. "Right now it's in the observation blister and looks as if it will stay there for a long time. You know, I still don't agree with what you intend doing, but I can understand why you don't want to let it face the Masters alone . . . *No!* You can't take *that!*"

She was pointing at the image on the Fabricator's drafting screen, and before he could respond she went on vehemently, "You are not allowed to carry weapons. The Federation forbids it in a first-contact situation, and your only hope of surviving this meeting may be to go in unarmed as a demonstration that your intentions are good even though you've stirred up a hornets' nest. Going down there is stupid, anyway!"

Her face was without color, and it was plain that she was desperately afraid that she might never see Martin alive again if he went down there among the Masters. She wanted him to forget all about it, to return with the assignment incomplete and to stay alive, but she knew that he would not do that.

Reassuringly, he said, "I don't expect to use the weapon on anyone. And I'm beginning to understand the setup here at last. I'll be all right; you'll see . . ."

Because of the emotional involvement, it was more than two hours before she was properly reassured and fully satisfied in all respects, and Martin was able to collect the Teldin from the observation blister.

He found that the teaching slave had not moved, seemingly, from the position in which Beth had placed it. Remembering the high acuity and light sensitivity of Teldin eyes, Martin could understand why. Not only could it see surface features on the planet below which Martin would have required high magnification to resolve, but from the now-orbiting hypership the number of stars it could see even in this sparsely populated region of the Galaxy must have paralyzed it with wonder. He had to tell Skorta three times that the lander was ready to leave before it responded.

"Having looked upon all this splendor," it said, and its

four arm's rose and its head bowed in a gesture which was like an act of worship, "how can I go on living as a slave?"

Martin was not surprised to find that the polar city was bitingly cold, that the level of technology apparent was much higher than that of the valley city they had recently left, and that Skorta, who had been born here, directed the lander to within a few meters of the entrance to the Hall of the Masters. What did surprise him was that the Hall was ablaze with artificial light.

"A courtesy extended to a highly placed slave of a strange Master," said the Teldin. "A slave with imperfect vision. It means nothing more."

The Hall itself was surprisingly small. He thought that the debating chamber of the legendary Camelot might have looked a little like this, except that the Teldin table was horseshoe-shaped rather than round, and partially bridging the open end was a small, square table and a chair. At a slow, measured pace Skorta led them towards them and, when they arrived, it motioned him to stand at one side of the chair while it stood on the other side.

"You are in the presence of the Masters of Teldi," it announced, and bowed its head briefly. Martin did the same.

There were several unoccupied spaces around the horseshoe. Before every Master's chair, whether it was occupied or not, the richly embroidered flags were spread so that their emblems hung down from the inside edge of the table. Lying on the flags were the swords of the Masters there present. All of the Masters were adult, some of them looked very old and, so far as Martin could see, they showed no physical signs of the self-indulgence and excesses of beings with ultimate authority over a planet's entire population. And these omniscient, all-powerful rulers of Teldi numbered only seventeen.

He stood silently as the teaching slave was questioned regarding Martin's arrival and his subsequent words and actions by a Teldin whose flag bore the emblem of the Master of Sea and Landborne Communications. He thought that the Master of Education would have been more appropriate until he remembered that that Mastership was vacant and its authority shared by two other Masters on a caretaker basis. This particular Master was about to experience a lesson in communication that it would not soon forget.

They continued to ignore Martin's presence while the teacher described the rockslide and the strange vessel's protective device which had saved the students from certain death.

It's trying to make a hero of me, Martin thought gratefully. But the interrogator was not impressed.

The Master wanted to know where the students would normally have been had the invitation not been issued. It added, obviously for Martin's benefit, that Skorta was no doubt aware that a slave was the property and sole responsibility of its Master and any wrong-doing on its part should result in the punishment of that Master.

Martin smiled at the thought of these seventeen sword-carrying absolute rulers of Teldi trying to punish the Federation for negligence in his training. But the smile faded when he thought of the Federation's reaction to the news that Teldi held it culpable for his misbehavior.

At times like this, he thought wryly, there was a lot to be said for the life of a happy and obedient slave.

The teacher was concluding its report. It said, "On being told of my instructions to report to the Hall of the Masters as quickly as possible, the stranger offered to take me in its ship. On the way we visited the larger vessel, which had been responsible for shielding the entire city from the Scourge while it was freeing the trapped students. There I spoke to the stranger's life-mate and looked down on Teldi, on all of Teldi, and at the stars."

"That experience," the interrogator said quietly, "we envy you. Do you feel friendship for this stranger?"

"I believe that we feel friendship for each other, Master," Skorta replied.

"Is this the reason why it accompanied you," said the Master, "when you must have explained to it that the safer course would have been to leave this world and its Masters, whom it so grievously insulted?"

"It is," Skorta answered. "The stranger also wished to deliver a message to you from its Masters and would not be dissuaded."

The Master made another untranslatable sound and said,

"A staunch friend, perhaps, but undeniably a most presumptuous slave. Why is its Master not present?"

Quickly the teaching slave explained that the stranger's Master was of a different species which breathed an atmosphere noxious to Teldin, and could not speak face to face to any person not of its own species. Skorta ended, "This is the reason the stranger was instructed to land on Teldi as an intermediary."

The interrogator recoiled, as if it had just heard a very dirty word, then went on, "Intermediaries are not to be trusted, ever. Their words are hearsay, untrustworthy, irresponsible, and cause misunderstanding and distress. Only a Master can be believed without doubt or question; that is the Prime Law."

Martin could remain silent no longer. "There were good reasons for the mistrust of hearsay, one thousand one hundred and seventeen of your years ago. But now the Prime Law has become a ritual and a means of enforcing—".

"You stupid, irresponsible slave!" Skorta broke in, shaking with what could only be anger. "Stranger, you insult the Masters as your own Master has already done by thrusting hearsay at them. Be warned. You may not speak to a Master, but if you must speak to clarify some portion of my report you will do so only to me and with the Master's permission."

"No insult was intended," said Martin.

"An insult can be given without intent," the teacher replied more calmly, "because a slave, being a slave, does not properly consider all the possible results of its words or actions."

Martin let his breath out slowly. To Skorta he said, "There are mechanisms on the larger ship which are capable of observing and measuring the movements of the individual pieces of rock and dust which make up the Scourge. I do not know the original reason for your Scourge, but these mechanisms tell me how and when it began, and from this information I have deduced—"

"Silence," said the Master quietly. It did not look at Martin as it went on, "We have no wish to listen to a slave's deduction's from hearsay evidence. I have a mind to discuss with you, teacher, matters which will instruct this stranger with complete accuracy . . ." It paused and, grasping the hilt of its sword, looked all around the table. ". . . regarding the

Scourge. Since this will involve discussion of the Ultimate Hearsay you, as a slave, may refuse."

The teacher replied slowly, as if performing a spoken ritual. It said, "No slave may know the Ultimate Hearsay. No slave, be it Teldin or other, may instruct a Master. The strange slave may not speak except to me, therefore I shall remain. I do this willingly, and henceforth I accept full responsibility for the results of my words and actions before the other Masters."

Martin almost lost the last few words, because suddenly everyone in the Hall was standing up and reaching for their swords. He wondered sickly whether his Earth-human legs could get him to the entrance before the longer Teldin limbs—including the ones swinging swords—could head him off. His own weapon was still in the backpack, and pitifully inadequate anyway. But the interrogator had swung around and was holding up all four hands palm outwards.

"Hold!" it said. "This matter will be dealt with in proper form when its Symbol has been brought to us. First must come the judgment and ruling on the off-world slave."

"What's going on?" said Beth anxiously. *"You said you knew what you were doing and now . . . Look, I'm coming down."*

"Wait," said Martin, switching out the translator. "The Masters can talk and listen to me through Skorta, and they will tell it things for my benefit which slaves are forbidden to know, because it is curious about me and so are they. The punishment for learning this forbidden knowledge must be severe, yet Skorta seems unafraid. There's something very odd going on here, and I'm beginning to wonder if . . ."

Martin broke off because the interrogator was talking again. In calm, emotionless tones it was fleshing it out, adding depth and a human, or at least Teldin, dimension to the catastrophe which had smashed their technologically advanced culture flat and returned its people to their equivalent of the dark ages.

Up until one thousand one hundred and seventeen years ago Teldi had had a satellite, an airless body rich in the mineral resources which had become so depleted on the mother world. The moon had been colonized many centuries earlier and, because it had been given the best that the mother planet could give in the form of its keenest young minds and technical resources, the colony became more technologically advanced than its parent. Its people remade their lifeless world, scattering its surface with domed cities and farms and burrowing deeply towards the still-hot core. They became self-sufficient, justifiably proud and independent, and finally an armed threat.

But it was not a nuclear attack which destroyed Teldi's moon, the Master insisted. It had been a catastrophe deep inside the moon, associated with experiments on a new power source, which had detonated the satellite like a gigantic bomb.

On Teldi they watched their moon fly slowly apart, and they knew that if one of the larger pieces were to crash into their planet it would tear through the crust into the underlying core stuff—and in the resulting planetary upheaval all life on Teldi would we wiped out. However, they had maintained in a state of instant readiness a tremendous arsenal of nuclear weapons capable of reaching their newly disintegrated moon, and large numbers of these were hastily reprogrammed to intercept the larger masses of lunar material heading toward them and to blast them into smaller and much less devastating pieces.

Many of these relatively small pieces fell on Teldi, and in the resulting devastation more than a quarter of the planetary population lost their lives, but the threat had been neutralized—for the time being. Computations made on the paths of the remaining large pieces of the satellite clearly indicated that the mother world was still in danger. There was a very high probability that world-wrecking collisions would take place on an average of three times every century. The planet's long-term survival depended on the Teldins' reducing the size of these future world-wreckers in the same way as they had dealt with the first ones.

In spite of the highest priority given to missile production and the development of more effective warheads, and to the manned missions which visited the larger bodies to plant charges designed to blow them virtually to dust, progress was desperately slow. Large meteors continued to fall which all too often demolished key missile production or launching installations.

For this reason it required close on fifty years for the

project to reach completion—in that there were no longer any bodies in Teldi's path capable of destroying the planet, and no missiles left to send against them if there had. Their moon had been reduced and scattered into a nearly homogenous cloud of meteorite material, most of which circled the planet or fell steadily onto its surface.

The Scourge had come.

No fabrication or person could live on or above the surface of Teldi for more than a few dozen revolutions without the certainty of damage, injury, or death. The remnants of the technology which had survived long enough to save them was eroded away or hammered flat by the Scourge. Their once-great civilization was reduced to ruins, its population decimated and driven slowly back towards the level of their savage, cave-dwelling pre-history—but not all the way back.

They had been able to survive in their caves, mines, and underground missile installations and extend them into subsurface cities. They had farmed because the Scourge could not kill every plant and tree, and they had built protected road systems and kept as much as was useful of the old knowledge alive and stored the rest. But the chief reason for their continued survival as a culture had been that increasing numbers of the frightened and despairing population placed themselves under the protection and orders of the Military Masters.

It was in the nature of things that saviors became masters, and it had been all too easy for the system to perpetuate itself when the Masters had the respect as well as the obedience of their slaves, as well as a large measure of control over their thinking—including the habit of distrust, which was instilled from birth.

For there had been a few moments' warning of the destruction of their satellite, time enough for the mother world to be told it was about to be obliterated because someone had been too stupidly trusting—someone had accepted as fact something which should have been doubted and rechecked—and for this error Teldi had been lashed by the Scourge for more than a thousand years. And the reason for their fanatical distrust, Martin thought, as the Master ended its history lesson, was now all too obvious.

If only the Masters had not enslaved the population while

they were doing it, and made knowledge available only to a favored, high-ranking few. . . .

"In every society there must be persons with authority and responsibility in charge," Skorta said suddenly, making Martin realize that he had been so affected by the Master's history lesson that he had been thinking aloud. "No mechanism should be overloaded by a responsible owner. But you have been to my school, Martin, and you know that in practice every person is given a little more knowledge than it needs, in the hope that it will evince a desire for more. Naturally, it is not given more until it has shown that it is capable of using responsibly the knowledge it already possesses."

"I begin to understand," said Martin. "The instructions of my Master were that I—"

"Please inform this slave," the interrogator broke in, "that the instructions of its absent Master mean nothing to us. There are three instances of recorded hearsay describing the landing on Teldi of mechanisms which spoke our language and tried to show us great wonders projected into the empty air around them before they were destroyed. Our reply was that we would accept no communication unless it was delivered to us in person by a responsible Master. This slave is not a responsible person, its presence before us is an insult, and I cannot understand its Master's purpose in sending it here when that Master is fully aware of the situation.

"We are not yet decided what to do with this slave," the Master went on. "Should it be punished physically as a child is for persistent disobedience, or merely returned to its Master who will not act like a Master?"

Martin swallowed, thinking that a spanking from one of the overlarge Teldins would not be a pleasant experience either physically or mentally. He was also thinking about the tutor on Fomalhaut Three, who was most certainly aware of the problem, and Martin had been given full responsibility for its solution. He could run away or try to solve the problem—the decision was his alone. He swore under his breath. He was beginning to view the tutor, the Teldin Masters, and even himself in a new light.

"Before this decision is made," he said to the teacher, "is it permitted that I discuss with you, my friend and equal, my instructions regarding—"

"Martin," said the Teldin. "I am no longer your equal."

His first feeling was one of betrayal. He wondered if Skorta had been as honest with him as it had seemed. But then he remembered some of the things it had said on the way to the city, in the school, and on board the hypership. Skorta had come across as an intelligent, liberal-minded, responsible, and perhaps potentially rebellious slave who did not mind talking a little hearsay or thinking for itself. To him, it had appeared to be a truly civilized and cultured being who was fighting its slavehood and beginning to win.

And now, Martin saw with a sudden flood of understanding, the fight was over.

"Your bio-telltales are going mad!" said Beth, sounding both angry and frightened. "Pulse-rate and blood pressure are 'way up and your . . . Dammit, are you getting ready to do something stupid?"

There was no need to answer her, because she would see and hear everything. He moistened his lips and for the first time he turned to address the assembled Masters of Teldi directly.

"I have considered this matter fully and the possible consequences of making my decision," he said, "and I wish to be once again the equal of my friend."

For several interminable seconds there was neither sound nor motion in the hall. Then the teacher walked slowly to an empty place at the horseshoe table and turned to face him, leaving Martin alone beside the Table of Interrogation. All sound and motion ceased again, and even Beth seemed to be holding her breath. He thought of asking permission for what he was about to do, then decided against it.

Asking permission was for slaves.

He removed and opened his backpack and spread the Federation flag across the table so that the silver and black emblem hung over the outer edge in plain sight of the Masters. Then he withdrew the weapon, the scaled-down replica of the Master of Education's sword he had seen at the school, and which had also been fabricated on the hypership, and laid it on top of the flag. The hilt, which also bore the Federation symbol, lay towards him. Then he folded his arms.

The Masters arose and seventeen hands went to the hilts of their swords. But this time the Master of Sea and Landborne Communications did not call a halt, as it had done in the case of Skorta, the one-time teaching slave, because the interrogator was grasping its sword, too. Martin swallowed as seventeen swords were raised to Teldin shoulder height and held at full extension with their seventeen points directed unswervingly at his face.

"Will the new Master-Elect of Education," said the interrogator, "please join the offworld would-be Master and guide it in the traditional acts and response."

Now I'm committed, thought Martin, but to what? The interrogator was speaking again.

"Do you accept sole and undivided responsibility for your words and actions, and omissions of words or actions, and the results thereof? Do you accept such responsibility for your property, whether animate or inanimate, its efficient working, its proper maintenance, training, feeding, and conduct towards the property of other Masters? Do you accept as your own responsibility the results of the conduct or misconduct of all such property, and will you reward, correct, or chastise the property committing such acts? Will you strive always to increase the efficiency, well-being, and intelligence of all your animate property in the hope that they will one day become capable of accepting the ultimate responsibility of a Master? As the bearer of ultimate responsibility, do you agree to defend with your life your person, property, and decisions and if, in the judgment of your fellow Masters, your actions and decisions threaten harm in large measure to your own or the property of others, that you will forfeit your life?"

Martin felt perspiration trickling from his armpits and he knew that if his arms had not been folded tightly across his chest, his hands would have been trembling.

"Consider carefully, offworld friend," said the new Master-Elect, who was again standing beside him. "An impulsive decision does not impress them, even though the impulse was of friendship and loyalty. If you withdraw now your punishment will probably be a token one, possibly banishment from Teldi society and removal of Masters' protection, neither of which will inconvenience you greatly."

Martin cleared his throat. He said, "The decision was carefully considered and is not based solely on sentiment. I am not stupid, but I have been confused by your Master-slave relationship on Teldi, and by the true nature and function of the Masters. I am confused no longer."

The swords were still pointing at him, so steadily that he could almost imagine that the scene was a still photograph, when Skorta spoke again.

"Raise your sword and hold it vertically with the base of the hilt resting upon your flag," it said. "Support the sword in the vertical position by pressing the palm of your hand against the tip. You will exert sufficient pressure for the tip to draw blood. You will then speak the words 'I accept the duties and responsibilities of a Master,' after which you will replace the sword and self-administer the appropriate medication to the wounded hand and await the response of the Masters."

He nearly fumbled it, because the height of the Table of Interrogation made it necessary for him to stand on tiptoe to press downwards against the point of the sword, so that the tip slipped from his palm and jabbed into the fleshy pad at the base of his thumb. But he was so relieved that the sword did not go skidding onto the floor that he scarcely felt the pain, even when the blood trickled slowly down the blade.

As steadily as he could, Martin said, "I accept the duties and responsibilities of a Master."

The swords were still pointing at him while he replaced his on the flag and slapped an adhesive dressing onto his hand. Then one of the swords swept upwards to point at the ceiling. Another followed suit, then another and another until all were raised, then all seventeen swords were lowered and replaced on their Masters' flags.

Skorta bowed gravely and said, "The election was unanimous, offworld Master. You may speak to us now, and everything you say will be accepted as factual if you say that it is, and any demonstrations by mechanisms operated by you will be given similar credence. If your words or actions prove false or inaccurate you will, of course, be answerable to your fellow Masters."

"I understand," said Martin, as he removed the tri-di projector from his pack. "What if the vote had not been unanimous? Would I have had to fight?"

"Only as a last resort," the Teldin replied, "and after many days debating other and non-violent solutions. There are never enough Masters on Teldi, Martin. The senior slaves who become eligible for Mastership and are encouraged to apply are far too intelligent to want the heavy responsibility involved. But there are an occasional few who, like ourselves, are overtaken by a strange irrationality which makes us find rewards in performing thankless tasks and . . . You are ready to begin?"

"I am ready," said Martin.

He waited until Skorta had returned to its place at the big table, then announced that he would describe and depict the events which had occurred on his own home planet, Earth, when it had been contacted by the Galactic Federation and its people offered Citizenship. Indicating the entrance and wall facing the big table, he started the projector. He heard the Masters making untranslatable noises as, in spite of the hall lighting, there appeared a volume of blackness of apparently endless depth.

The show began. . . .

Earth had been contacted because within a few centuries it would perish of starvation, war, and disease.

He showed the arrival of the Federation transporters in Earth orbit, a ring of gigantic matter transmitters which arched across the night sky like an enormous jewelled necklace, and some of the great, white cubical buildings which appeared overnight close to every town and city. These were the Galactic Federation Examination and Induction Centers, and into them went the people of Earth to be rejected as Undesirable, or accepted as Citizens, or classified as non-Citizens requiring further examination and training.

"But you're telling them everything!" Beth's voice sounded anxiously in his ear-piece. *"Our tutor might not want that. Or don't you care anymore?"*

"I care," said Martin. "But I'm not sure what our tutor expects of me. If it had wanted me to do or not do something it should have been more specific, instead of simply telling me that the Teldi situation was my responsibility. And I do care about these people, too much to be dishonest with them."

"This Master business," said Beth quietly, *"you're taking it very seriously."*

"Yes," he said, then added quickly, "No more talking, the next bit could be tricky. . . ."

The people of Earth, like every other planetary population offered citizenship, had been screened and divided into three categories, the Citizens, the non-Citizens, and the Undesirables. The majority of applicants were successful and became

Citizens, to move to the Federation World to begin a life in which their potentialities could be fully realized free of personal, political, and economic pressures. In the Federation citizens were not forced to do anything, because the type of people who would use such force were excluded as Undesirables.

Beings who sought power for its own sake remained on their home worlds as wolves who no longer had sheep on which to prey, and Martin emphasized the fact that on the new world the leaders were shepherds. But the Masters were becoming restive at the idea that they might be considered undesirable.

He went on quickly, "Unlike the Citizens, the non-Citizens obey orders and have to submit to training. Even though they comprise many different species with great variation in intelligence and ability, they are vital to the functioning of the Galactic Federation, and they have the option of becoming Citizens in time. They are—"

"Slaves," said one of the Masters.

"Why must these beings leave their home planets to become Citizens?" asked another before Martin could reply to the first. "And are these new worlds suited to their needs?"

What is a slave, wondered Martin. Aloud, he said, "There is only one world. Observe!"

In the projection the sky blazed with stars—singly, in clusters, and in great, swirling eddies—and so dense was the starfield that it was difficult to find even a tiny area which was dark. Except, that was, for one area in the center, where there hung an enormous, black, and featureless shape, the shape reproduced on the Federation emblem.

"This," said Martin, trying to hold his voice steady, "is the Federation World."

It was a hollow body, he explained as simply as he could, made from material which had comprised the planets of this and many other solar systems, and it contained the intelligent beings of over two hundred different species who were presently members of the Federation. This superworld enclosed the system's sun and used its output for light, heat, and as a power source for its soil synthesizers. The interior surface area was vast beyond imagining. The projected future populations of all the intelligent species in the Galaxy would never overcrowd this world.

As the diagrams and sharply detailed pictures flashed into view, Martin tried to describe the awful immensity of the Federation World, its topography and environmental variations, its incredibly advanced technology. But one of the Masters was waving for attention.

"Since the Scourge returned us to the dark ages, Teldi has nothing to offer," it said. "Yet you are considering us for citizenship of this . . . this . . . *Why*, stranger?"

Martin was silent, remembering his own reaction on first seeing the Federation World. The Masters had had enough superscience and frontal assaults on the feelings of superiority for one day. He softened his tone.

"The Federation accepts all levels of technical and cultural development," he said. "Its purpose is to seek out the intelligent races of the Galaxy and bring them to a place of safety before they perish in their own effluvia or some other natural or unnatural catastrophe befalls them. On this world they will grow in knowledge and intermingle and, in the fullness of time, the combined intelligence of this future Federation will be capable of achievements unimaginable even to the most advanced minds among its present-day Citizens. It will be a slow, natural process, however, free of any kind of force or coercion. And while the Citizens are climbing to the scientific, philosophical, and cultural heights, they must be protected."

He cancelled the projection, and for a long time nothing was said. They were all staring at his flag, at the black diamond on a silver field which was the Federation emblem, but still seeing the tremendous reality which it represented. Perhaps he had shown them too much too soon, and had succeeded only in giving them an inferiority complex from which they would never recover. But these were the top people on Teldi and they had earned their positions by rising through the ranks. They were tough, honest, and adaptable, and Martin thought they could take it.

It was the interrogator who found its voice first. "You came here to judge us on our suitability or otherwise for citizenship of this . . . this Galactic Federation. We may not wish to join, stranger, but we would be interested in hearing your verdict."

To tough, honest, and adaptable, add proud and independent. Now he knew what he had to do.

Before he could reply, the Master-Elect of Education

walked slowly to his side. It was staring down at the Federation flag and not at Martin as it said, "Martin, this is important. If your pronouncement is open to discussion and subsequent modification, touch the hilt of your sword as you speak. If it is your own unalterable decision which you will defend, if necessary, with your life, you will grasp the hilt firmly and hold the weapon in a defensive position."

"They're still in a state of shock," said Beth in the angry, despairing tone of one who knows that good advice is being ignored, *"And there are no guards on the door. Run!"*

"No," said Martin stubbornly. Through the translator he went on, "Before I deliver my judgment I must first draw analogies with the systems which govern Teldi and the Federation.

"Undesirables, trouble-makers, the power-seekers are rendered impotent and ignored," he went on. "The Citizens are free and protected, and the non-Citizens do the hard but interesting work associated with the maintenance of the World's systems and on-going projects. This work is not forced on them, and the reason they do it is two-fold. They feel a self-imposed responsibility in the matter and they, regardless of their species or level of intelligence or competence, belong to that group of restless and adventurous entities who are not sure that the protected life of a Citizen is for them. They are the errand boys, the servants, the slaves of the Federation, save only in the area of responsibility."

Around the horseshoe table hands were twitching restively towards their swords, but Martin did not touch the hilt of his own. Not yet.

"On Teldi," he went on, "the system of government and the general display of mistrust were initially abhorrent to me, as was the tight mental control which apparently was being imposed by the Masters. But the reason for the mistrust and the insistence that hearsay be vouched for by a highly responsible person, a Master, became plain when I learned of the original cause of the Scourge. Regarding the control of imparted knowledge, I learned that much of the forbidden hearsay was available to low-level slaves trying for higher positions. But few feel impelled to accept the ultimate responsibility. There are never enough Masters on Teldi.

"I also discovered," Martin continued, still keeping his hand well away from the sword, "that the slaves of Teldi are, in spite of its low-level technology, the most self-motivated, independent, self-reliant, and widely trained group of beings that I have ever experienced or learned of through hearsay.

"There is no necessity for the level to remain low if the Scourge was removed," he went on, hoping that the unsteadiness in his voice would not be apparent in translation. "I am not a Master of the mechanisms which can do this work, nor have I any direct knowledge of the length of time required, other than that it will take many of your years. But the Scourge can be removed and you would be able to build again on the surface, and travel in safety, and grow . . ."

Martin broke off because he was talking to a three-dimensional picture again—there was absolute stillness in the room.

Slowly and deliberately he reached forward and gripped the hilt of the sword, then lifted it into a defensive position, diagonally across his chest.

Had he misjudged them? Was he about to misjudge them again?

He said gravely, "If the Federation was to set up examination and induction centers on Teldi at this time there would be very few beings judged Undesirable, and few also who would be accepted as Citizens. The great majority would be deemed unsuitable for the Federation World. I will explain.

The Masters were either touching or gripping the hilts of their swords now. Like the slave population of Teldi, they were proud, independent, self-reliant, and fantastically caring for the property from out of which they had risen to become Masters. Any criticism of that property was a personal insult to them.

"Teldi is a special case," Martin went on. "On Teldi it is said that there are never enough Masters, never enough able slaves willing to accept the crushing responsibility Mastership entails. In the Federation it is likewise said that there are never enough non-Citizens, and for very similar reasons: because the qualities required for the job are rare. It is my judgment that Teldins are not now and will probably never be suitable for Galactic Citizenship.

"It is my decision," he said in conclusion, "that the Scourge be removed and your world left alone for at least three of your generations. And it is my confident expectation that when the Federation next contacts you it will make a unique and most valuable discovery: a planetary population which is composed entirely of non-Citizens ready to assume extra-planetary duties and responsibilities."

The Masters were sitting still and silent, and suddenly Martin knew why.

"My arrival on Teldi was not a secret one," he said, lowering his sword and placing it on the Federation flag. As he resumed speaking, he slowly rolled the weapon in the cloth. "As a result, much hearsay will arise and more slaves will be impelled to rise to Mastership when they realize what was and will again be possible for Teldins. There is something I would like to leave with you, with your permission. . . ."

He walked slowly towards Skorta with the flag-wrapped sword held before him in both hands, then proffered it to the Teldin. Behind and around him he could hear the movements of Masters getting to their feet and the soft, rustling sounds of metal scraping against fabric, but he did not look aside.

"Martin," said the Teldin, taking the sword from him, "I am honored to accept the additional responsibilities of Master of Off-World Affairs and I, and my successors, will respect and promulgate the knowledge you have given us."

It did not say anything else and neither did the other Masters, but as Martin turned and began walking towards the entrance they remained standing, silent, motionless, and with their swords held high in salute until he had passed from sight.

On Teldi, silence was approval. It meant that there was no dissenting voice.

A LETTER FROM
THE CLEARYS

by Connie Willis

*We used to take the post office for granted.
Twice a day, morning and afternoon, the mail-
man would go his rounds. Then it changed to
once a day. In many areas now it is not delivered
at all. You have to call for it at your local post
office which may be miles away. But suppose it is
also not just miles away but a whole historical
epoch away—like just before the world came to
an end . . . and after.*

There was a letter from the Clearys at the post office. I put
it in my backpack along with Mrs. Talbot's magazine and
went outside to untie Stitch.

He had pulled his leash out as far as it would go and was
sitting around the corner, half-strangled, watching a robin.
Stitch never barks, not even at birds. He didn't even yip when
Dad stitched up his paw. He just sat there the way we found
him on the front porch, shivering a little and holding his paw

63

up for Dad to look at. Mrs. Talbot says he's a terrible watchdog, but I'm glad he doesn't bark. Rusty barked all the time and look where it got him.

I had to pull Stitch back around the corner to where I could get enough slack to untie him. That took some doing, because he really liked that robin. "It's a sign of spring, isn't it, fella?" I said, trying to get at the knot with my fingernails. I didn't loosen the knot, but I managed to break one of my fingernails off to the quick. Great. Mom will demand to know if I've noticed any other fingernails breaking.

My hands are a real mess. This winter I've gotten about a hundred burns on the back of my hands from that stupid wood stove of ours. One spot, just above my wrist, I keep burning over and over so it never has a chance to heal. The stove isn't big enough, and when I try to jam a log in that's too long, that same spot hits the inside of the stove every time. My stupid brother David won't saw them off to the right length. I've asked him and asked him to please cut them shorter, but he doesn't pay any attention to me.

I asked Mom if she would please tell him not to saw the logs so long, but she didn't. She never criticizes David. As far as she's concerned he can't do anything wrong just because he's twenty-three and was married.

"He does it on purpose," I told her. "He's hoping I'll burn to death."

"Paranoia is the number-one killer of fourteen-year-old girls," Mom said. She always says that. It makes me so mad I feel like killing her. "He doesn't do it on purpose. You need to be more careful with the stove, that's all." But all the time she was holding my hand and looking at the big burn that won't heal like it was a time bomb set to go off.

"We need a bigger stove," I said, and yanked my hand away. We do need a bigger one. Dad closed up the fireplace and put the woodstove in when the gas bill was getting out of sight, but it's just a little one, because Mom didn't want one that would stick way out in the living room. Anyway, we were only going to use it in the evenings.

We won't get a new one. They are all too busy working on the stupid greenhouse. Maybe spring will come early, and my hand will have half a chance to heal. I know better. Last winter the snow kept up till the middle of June, and this is only March. Stitch's robin is going to freeze his little tail if he doesn't head back south. Dad says that last year was unusual, that the weather will be back to normal this year, but he does-n't believe it either or he wouldn't be building the greenhouse.

As soon as I let go of Stitch's leash, he backed around the corner like a good boy and sat there waiting for me to stop sucking my finger and untie him. "We'd better get a move on," I told him. "Mom'll have a fit." I was supposed to go by the general store to try and get some tomato seeds, but the sun was already pretty far west, and I had at least a half-hour's walk home. If I got home after dark, I'd get sent to bed without supper, and then I wouldn't get to read the letter. Besides, if I didn't go to the general store today they'd have to let me go tomorrow, and I wouldn't have to work on the stupid greenhouse.

Sometimes I feel like blowing it up. There's sawdust and mud on everything, and David dropped one of the pieces of plastic on the stove while they were cutting it and it melted onto the stove and stank to high heaven. But nobody else even notices the mess; they're too busy talking about how wonderful it's going to be to have homegrown watermelon and corn and tomatoes next summer.

I don't see how it's going to be any different from last sum-mer. The only things that came up at all were the lettuce and the potatoes. The lettuce was about as tall as my broken fin-gernail and the potatoes were as hard as rocks. Mrs. Talbot said it was the altitude, but Dad said it was the funny weather and this crummy Pike's Peak granite that passes for soil around here. He went up to the little library in the back of the general store and got a do-it-yourself book on green-houses and started tearing everything up, and now even Mrs. Talbot is crazy about the idea.

The other day I told them, "Paranoia is the number-one killer of people at this *altitude*," but they were too busy cut-ting slats and stapling plastic to pay any attention to me.

Stitch walked along ahead of me, straining at his leash, and as soon as we were across the highway, I took it off. He never runs away like Rusty used to. Anyway, it's impossible to keep him out of the road, and the times I've tried keeping him on his leash, he dragged me out into the middle and I got in trouble with Dad over leaving footprints. So I keep to the frozen edges of the road, and he moseys along, stopping to sniff at potholes; when he gets behind, I whistle at him and he comes running right up.

I walked pretty fast. It was getting chilly out, and I'd only worn my sweater. I stopped at the top of the hill and whistled at Stitch. We still had a mile to go. I could see the Peak from where I was standing. Maybe Dad is right about spring coming. There was hardly any snow on the Peak, and the burned part didn't look quite as dark as it did last fall, like maybe the trees are coming back.

Last year at this time the whole peak was solid white. I remember because that was when Dad and David and Mr. Talbot went hunting and it snowed every day and they didn't get back for almost a month. Mom just about went crazy before they got back. She kept going up to the road to watch for them even though the snow was five feet deep and she, was leaving footprints as big as the Abominable Snowman's. She took Rusty with her even though he hated the snow about as much as Stitch hates the dark. And she took a gun. One time she tripped over a branch and fell down in the snow. She sprained her ankle and was almost frozen stiff by the time she made it back to the house. I felt like saying, "Paranoia is the number-one killer of mothers," but Mrs. Talbot butted in and said the next time I had to go with her and how this was what happened when people were allowed to go places by themselves, which meant me going to the post office. I said I could take care of myself, and Mom told me not to be rude to Mrs. Talbot and Mrs. Talbot was right, I should go with her the next time.

She wouldn't wait till her ankle was better. She bandaged it up and we went the very next day. She didn't say a word the whole trip, just limped through the snow. She never even looked up till we got to the road. The snow had stopped for a little while, and the clouds had lifted enough so you could see the Peak. It was like a black-and-white photograph, the gray sky and the black trees and the white mountain. The Peak was completely covered with snow. You couldn't make out the toll road at all.

We were supposed to hike up the Peak with the Clearys.

When we got back to the house, I said, "The summer before last the Clearys never came."

Mom took off her mittens and stood by the stove, pulling

off chunks of frozen snow. "Of course they didn't come, Lynn," she said.

Snow from my coat was dripping onto the stove and sizzling. "I didn't mean *that*," I said. "They were supposed to come the first week in June. Right after Rick graduated. So what happened? Did they just decide not to come or what?"

"I don't know," she said, pulling off her hat and shaking her hair out. Her bangs were all wet.

"Maybe they wrote to tell you they'd changed their plans," Mrs. Talbot said. "Maybe the post office lost the letter."

"It doesn't matter," Mom said.

"You'd think they'd have written or something," I said.

"Maybe the post office put the letter in somebody else's box," Mrs. Talbot said.

"It doesn't matter," Mom said, and went to hang her coat over the line in the kitchen. She wouldn't say another word about them. When Dad got home I asked him too about the Clearys, but he was too busy telling about the trip to pay any attention to me.

Stitch didn't come. I whistled again and then started back after him. He was all the way at the bottom of the hill, his nose buried in something. "Come *on*," I said, and he turned around and then I could see why he hadn't come. He'd gotten himself tangled up in one of the electric wires that was down. He'd managed to get the cable wound around his legs like he does his leash sometimes, and the harder he tried to get out, the more he got tangled up.

He was right in the middle of the road. I stood on the edge of the road, trying to figure out a way to get to him without leaving footprints. The road was pretty much frozen at the top of the hill, but down here snow was still melting and running across the road in big rivers. I put my toe out into the mud, and my sneaker sank in a good half-inch, so I backed up, rubbed out the toe print with my hand, and wiped my hand on my jeans. I tried to think what to do. Dad is as paranoic about footprints as Mom is about my hands, but he is even worse about my being out after dark. If I didn't make it back in time, he might even tell me I couldn't go to the post office anymore.

Stitch was coming as close as he ever would to barking. He'd gotten the wire around his neck and was choking himself. "All right," I said. "I'm coming." I jumped out as far as

I could into one of the rivers and then waded the rest of the way to Stitch, looking back a couple of times to make sure the water was washing away the footprints.

I unwound Stitch and threw the loose end of the wire over to the side of the road where it dangled from the pole, all ready to hang Stitch next time he comes along.

"You stupid dog," I said. "Now hurry!" and I sprinted back to the side of the road and up the hill in my sopping wet sneakers. He ran about five steps and stopped to sniff at a tree. "Come on!" I said. "It's getting dark. Dark!"

He was past me like a shot and halfway down the hill. Stitch is afraid of the dark. I know, there's no such thing in dogs. But Stitch really is. Usually I tell him, "Paranoia is the number-one killer of dogs," but right now I wanted him to hurry before my feet started to freeze. I started running, and we got to the bottom of the hill about the same time.

Stitch stopped at the driveway of the Talbot's house. Our house wasn't more than a few hundred feet from where I was standing, on the other side of the hill. Our house is down in kind of a well formed by hills on all sides. It's so deep and hidden you'd never even know it's there. You can't even see the smoke from our wood stove over the top of the Talbot's hill. There's a shortcut through the Talbot's property and down through the woods to our back door, but I don't take it anymore. "Dark, Stitch," I said sharply, and started running again. Stitch kept right at my heels.

The Peak was turning pink by the time I got to our driveway. Stitch peed on the spruce tree about a hundred times before I got it dragged back across the dirt driveway. It's a real big tree. Last summer Dad and David chopped it down and then made it look like it had fallen across the road. It completely covers up where the driveway meets the road, but the trunk is full of splinters, and I scraped my hand right in the same place as always. Great.

I made sure Stitch and I hadn't left any marks on the road (except for the marks he always leaves—another dog could find us in a minute, that's probably how Stitch showed up on our front porch, he smelled Rusty) and then got under cover of the hill as fast as I could. Stitch isn't the only one who gets nervous after dark. And besides, my feet were starting to hurt. Stitch was really paranoic tonight. He didn't even quit running after we were in sight of the house.

David was outside, bringing in a load of wood. I could tell just by looking at it that they were all the wrong length. "Cutting it kind of close, aren't you?" he said. "Did you get the tomato seeds?"

"No," I said. "I brought you something else, though. I brought everybody something."

I went on in. Dad was rolling out plastic on the living-room floor. Mrs. Talbot was holding one end for him. Mom was holding the card table, still folded up, waiting for them to finish so she could set it up in front of the stove for supper. Nobody even looked up. I unslung my backpack and took out Mrs. Talbot's magazine and the letter.

"There was a letter at the post office," I said. "From the Clearys."

They all looked up.

"Where did you find it?" Dad said.

"On the floor, mixed in with all the third-class stuff. I was looking for a magazine for Mrs. Talbot."

Mom leaned the card table against the couch and sat down. Mrs. Talbot looked blank.

"The Clearys were our best friends," I explained to her. "From Illinois. They were supposed to come see us the summer before last. We were going to hike up Pike's Peak and everything."

David banged in the door. He looked at Mom sitting on the couch and Dad and Mrs. Talbot still standing there holding the plastic like a couple of statues. "What's wrong?" he said.

"Lynn says she found a letter from the Clearys today," Dad said.

David dumped the logs on the hearth. One of them rolled onto the carpet and stopped at Mom's feet. Neither of them bent over to pick it up.

"Shall I read it out loud?" I said, looking at Mrs. Talbot. I was still holding her magazine. I opened up the envelope and took out the letter.

" 'Dear Janice and Todd and everybody,' " I read. " 'How are things in the glorious West? We're raring to come out and see you, though we may not make it quite as soon as we hoped. How are Carla and David and the baby? I can't wait to see little David. Is he walking yet? I bet Grandma Janice is so proud she's busting her britches. Is that right? Do you westerners wear britches, or have you all gone to designer jeans?' "

David was standing by the fireplace. He put his head down across his arms on the mantelpiece.

" 'I'm sorry I haven't written, but we were very busy with Rick's graduation, and anyway I thought we would beat the letter out to Colorado. But now it looks like there's going to be a slight change in plans. Rick has definitely decided to join the Army. Richard and I have talked ourselves blue in the face, but I guess we've just made matters worse. We can't even get him to wait to join until after the trip to Colorado. He says we'd spend the whole trip trying to talk him out of it, which is true, I guess. I'm just so worried about him. The Army! Rick says I worry too much, which is true too, I guess, but what if there was a war?' "

Mom bent over and picked up the log that David had dropped and laid it on the couch beside her.

" 'If it's okay with you out there in the Golden West, we'll wait until Rick is done with basic the first week in July and then all come out. Please write and let us know if this is okay. I'm sorry to switch plans on you like this at the last minute, but look at it this way: you have a whole extra month to get into shape for hiking up Pike's Peak. I don't know about you, but I sure can use it.' "

Mrs. Talbot had dropped her end of the plastic. It didn't land on the stove this time, but it was close to it, it was curling from the heat. Dad just stood there watching it. He didn't even try to pick it up.

" 'How are the girls? Sonja is growing like a weed. She's out for track this year and bringing home lots of medals and dirty sweat socks. And you should see her knees! They're so banged up I almost took her to the doctor. She says she scrapes them on the hurdles, and her coach says there's nothing to worry about, but it does worry me a little. They just don't seem to heal. Do you ever have problems like that with Lynn and Melissa?

" 'I know, I know. I worry too much. Sonja's fine. Rick's fine. Nothing awful's going to happen between now and the first week in July, and we'll see you then. Love, the Clearys. P.S. Has anybody ever fallen off Pike's Peak?' "

Nobody said anything. I folded up the letter and put it back in the envelope.

"I should have written them," Mom said. "I should have told them, 'Come now.' Then they would have been here."

"And we would probably have climbed up Pike's Peak that day and gotten to see it all go blooey and us with it," David said, lifting his head up. He laughed and his voice caught on the laugh and cracked. "I guess we should be glad they didn't come."

"Glad?" Mom said. She was rubbing her hands on the legs of her jeans. "I suppose we should be glad Carla took Melissa and the baby to Colorado Springs that day so we didn't have so many mouths to feed." She was rubbing her jeans so hard she was going to rub a hole right through them. "I suppose we should be glad those looters shot Mr. Talbot."

"No," Dad said. "But we should be glad the looters didn't shoot the rest of us. We should be glad they only took the canned goods and not the seeds. We should be glad the fires didn't get this far. We should be glad . . ."

"That we still have mail delivery?" David said. "Should we be glad about that too?" He went outside and shut the door behind him.

"When I didn't hear from them, I should have called or something," Mom said.

Dad was still looking at the ruined plastic. I took the letter over to him. "Do you want to keep it or what?" I said.

"I think it's served its purpose," he said. He wadded it up, tossed it in the stove, and slammed the door shut. He didn't even get burned. "Come help me on the greenhouse, Lynn," he said.

It was pitch dark outside and really getting cold. My sneakers were starting to get stiff. Dad held the flashlight and pulled the plastic tight over the wooden slats. I stapled the plastic every two inches all the way around the frame and my finger about every other time. After we finished one frame, I asked Dad if I could go back in and put on my boots.

"Did you get the seeds for the tomatoes?" he said, as if he hadn't even heard me. "Or were you too busy looking for the letter?"

"I didn't look for it," I said. "I found it. I thought you'd be glad to get the letter and know what happened to the Clearys."

Dad was pulling the plastic across the next frame, so hard it was getting little puckers in it. "We already knew," he said,

He handed me the flashlight and took the staple gun out of my hand. "You want me to say it?" he said. "You want me to tell you exactly what happened to them? All right. I would imagine they were close enough to Chicago to have been vaporized when the bombs hit. If they were, they were lucky. Because there aren't any mountains like ours around Chicago. So they got caught in the fire storm or they died of flashburns or radiation sickness or else some looter shot them."

"Or their own family," I said.

"Or their own family." He put the staple gun against the wood and pulled the trigger. "I have a theory about what happened the summer before last," he said. He moved the gun down and shot another staple into the wood. "I don't think the Russians started it or the United States either. I think it was some little terrorist group somewhere or maybe just one person. I don't think they had any idea what would happen when they dropped their bomb. I think they were just so hurt and angry and frightened by the way things were that they just lashed out. With a bomb." He stapled the frame clear to the bottom and straightened up to start on the other side. "What do you think of that theory, Lynn?"

"I told you," I said. "I found the letter while I was looking for Mrs. Talbot's magazine."

He turned and pointed the staple gun at me. "But whatever reason they did it for, they brought the whole world crashing down on their heads. Whether they meant it or not, they had to live with the consequences."

"If they lived," I said. "If somebody didn't shoot them."

"I can't let you go to the post office anymore," he said. "It's too dangerous."

"What about Mrs. Talbot's magazines?"

"Go check on the fire," he said.

I went back inside. David had come back and was standing by the fireplace again, looking at the wall. Mom had set up the card table and the folding chairs in front of the fireplace. Mrs. Talbot was in the kitchen cutting up potatoes, only it looked like it was onions from the way she was crying.

The fire had practically gone out. I stuck a couple of wadded-up magazine pages in to get it going again. The fire flared up with a brilliant blue and green. I tossed a couple of pine cones and some sticks onto the burning paper. One of the pine cones rolled off to the side and lay there in the ashes. I grabbed for it and hit my hand on the door of the stove.

Right in the same place. Great. The blister would pull the old scab off and we could start all over again. And of course Mom was standing right there, holding the pan of potato soup. She put it on top of the stove and grabbed up my hand like it was evidence in a crime or something. She didn't say anything. She just stood there holding it and blinking.

"I burned it," I said. "I just burned it."

She touched the edges of the old scab, as if she was afraid of catching something.

"It's a burn!" I shouted, snatching my hand back and cramming David's stupid logs into the stove. "It isn't radiation sickness. It's a *burn!*"

"Do you know where your father is, Lynn?" she asked.

"He's out on the back porch," I said, "building his stupid greenhouse."

"He's gone," she said. "He took Stitch with him."

"He can't have taken Stitch," I said. "Stitch is afraid of the dark." She didn't say anything. "Do you *know* how dark it is out there?"

"Yes," she said, and looked out the window. "I know how dark it is."

I got my parka off the hook by the fireplace and started out the door.

David grabbed my arm. "Where the hell do you think you're going?"

I wrenched away from him. "To find Stitch. He's afraid of the dark."

"It's too dark," he said. "You'll get lost."

"So what? It's safer than hanging around this place," I said and slammed the door shut on his hand.

I made it halfway to the woodpile before he grabbed me.

"Let me go," I said. "I'm leaving. I'm going to go find some other people to live with."

"There aren't any other people! For Christ's sake, we went all the way to South Park last winter. There wasn't anybody. We didn't even see those looters. And what if you run into them, the looters who shot Mr. Talbot?"

"What if I do? The worst they could do is shoot me. I've been shot at before."

"You're acting crazy. You know that, don't you?" he said.

"Coming in here out of the clear blue, taking potshots at everybody with that crazy letter!"

"Potshots!" I said, so mad I was afraid I was going to start crying. "Potshots! What about last summer? Who was taking potshots then?"

"You didn't have any business taking the shortcut," David said. "Dad told you never to come that way."

"Was that any reason to try and *shoot* me? Was that any reason to *kill* Rusty?"

David was squeezing my arm so hard I thought he was going to snap it right in two. "The looters had a dog with them. We found its tracks all around Mr. Talbot. When you took the shortcut and we heard Rusty barking, we thought you were the looters." He looked at me. "Mom's right. Paranoia's the number-one killer. We were all a little crazy last summer. We're all a little crazy all the time, I guess. And then you pull a stunt like bringing that letter home, reminding everybody of everything that's happened, of everybody we've lost. . . ." He let go of my arm and looked down at his hand.

"I told you," I said. "I found it while I was looking for a magazine. I thought you'd all be glad I found it."

"Yeah," he said. "I'll bet."

He went inside and I stayed out a long time, waiting for Dad and Stitch. When I came in, nobody even looked up. Mom was still standing at the window. I could see a star over her head. Mrs. Talbot had stopped crying and was setting the table. Mom dished up the soup and we all sat down. While we were eating, Dad came in.

He had Stitch with him. And all the magazines. "I'm sorry, Mrs. Talbot," he said. "If you'd like, I'll put them under the house and you can send Lynn for them one at a time."

"It doesn't matter," she said. "I don't feel like reading them anymore."

Dad put the magazines on the couch and sat down at the card table. Mom dished him up a bowl of soup. "I got the seeds," he said. "The tomato seeds had gotten water-soaked, but the corn and squash were okay." He looked at me. "I had to board up the post office, Lynn," he said. "You understand that, don't you? You understand that I can't let you go there anymore? It's just too dangerous."

"I told you," I said. "I found it. While I was looking for a magazine."

"The fire's going out," he said.

After they shot Rusty, I wasn't allowed to go anywhere for a month for fear they'd shoot me when I came home, not even when I promised to take the long way around. But then Stitch showed up and nothing happened and they let me start going again. I went every day till the end of summer and after that whenever they'd let me. I must have looked through every pile of mail a hundred times before I found the letter from the Clearys. Mrs. Talbot was right about the post office. The letter was in somebody else's box.

FARMER ON THE DOLE

by Frederik Pohl

We are entering the time of the computerized workhorse and the reign of robots. The era of toil and hard chores for mankind may be coming to an end. Let a happy robot do it. But even so there may be tasks that robots cannot be programmed to perform. Or are there?

Stretching east to the horizon, a thousand acres all in soybeans; across the road to the west, another thousand acres, all corn. Zeb kicked the irrigation valve moodily and watched the meter register the change in flow. Damn weather! Why didn't it rain? He sniffed the air deeply and shook his head, frowning. Eighty-five percent relative humidity. No, closer to eighty-seven. And not a cloud in the sky.

From across the road his neighbor called, "Afternoon, Zeb."

Zeb nodded curtly. He was soy and Wally was corn, and they didn't have much to talk about, but you had to show some manners. He pulled his bandanna out of his hip pocket and wiped his brow. "Had to rise up the flow," he offered for politeness' sake.

"Me, too. Only good thing, CO_2's up. So we's gettin good carbon metabolizin."

Zeb grunted and bent down to pick up a clod of earth, crumbling it in his fingers to test for humus, breaking off a piece, and tasting it. "Cobalt's a tad low again," he said meditatively, but Wally wasn't interested in soil chemistry.

"Zeb? You ain't heard anything?"

"Bout what?"

"Bout anything. You know."

Zeb turned to face him. "You mean aint I heard no crazy talk bout closin down the farms, when everybody knows they can't never do that, no. I aint heard nothin like that, an if I did, I wouldn't give it heed."

"Yeah, Zeb, but they's sayin—"

"They can say whatever they likes, Wally. I aint listenin, and I got to get back to the lines fore Becky and the kids start worryin. Evenin. Nice talkin to you." And he turned and marched back toward the cabins.

"Uncle Tin," Wally called sneeringly, but Zeb wouldn't give him the satisfaction of noticing. All the same, he pulled out his bandanna and mopped his brow again.

It wasn't sweat. Zeb never sweated. His arms, his back, his armpits were permanently dry, in any weather, no matter how hard or how long he worked. The glistening film on his forehead was condensed from the air. The insulation around the supercooled Josephson junctions that made up his brain was good, but not perfect. When he was doing more thinking than usual, the refrigeration units worked harder.

And Zeb was doing a lot of thinking. Close down the farms? Why, you'd have to be crazy to believe that! You did your job. You tilled the fields and planted them, or else you cleaned and cooked in Boss's house, or taught Boss's children, or drove Mrs. Boss when she went to visit the other bosses' wives. That was the way things were on the farm, and it would go on that way forever, wouldn't it?

Zeb found out the answer the next morning, right after church.

Since Zeb was a Class A robot, with an effective IQ of one hundred thirty-five, though limited in its expression by the built-in constraints of his assigned function, he really should

not have been surprised. Especially when he discovered that
Reverend Harmswallow had taken his text that morning from
Matthew, specifically the Beatitudes, and in particular the one
about how the meek would inherit the earth. The reverend
was a plump, pink-faced man whose best sermons dwelt on
the wages of sin and the certainty of hell-fire. It had always
been a disappointment to him that the farmhands who made
up his congregation weren't physically equipped to sin in any
interesting ways, but he made up for it by extra emphasis on
the importance of being humble. "Even," he finished, his
baby-fine hair flying all around his pink scalp, "when things
don't go the way you think they ought to. Now we're going
to sing 'Old One Hundred,' and then you soy people will
meet in the gymnasium and corn people in the second-floor
lounge. Your bosses have some news for you."

So it shouldn't have been surprising, and as a matter of
fact Zeb wasn't surprised at all. Some part of the cryocircuits
inside his titanium skull had long noted the portents. Scant
rain. Falling levels of soil minerals. Thinning of the topsoil.
The beans grew fat, because there was an abundance of carbon in the air for them to metabolize. But no matter how
much you irrigated, they dried up fast in the hot breezes. And
those were only the physical signs. Boss's body language said
more, sighing when he should have been smiling at the three-
legged races behind the big house, not even noticing when
one of the cabins needed a new coat of whitewash or the
flower patches showed a few weeds. Zeb observed it all and
drew the proper conclusions. His constraints did not forbid
that; they only prevented him from speaking of them, or even
of thinking of them on a conscious level. Zeb was not programmed to worry. It would have interfered with the happy,
smiling face he bore for Boss, and Miz Boss, and the Chillen.

So, when Boss made his announcement, Zeb looked as
thunderstruck as all the other hands. "You've been really
good people," Boss said generously, his pale, professorial face
incongruous under the plantation straw hat. "I really wish
things could go on as they always have, but it just isn't possible. It's the agricultural support program," he explained.
"Those idiots in Washington have cut it down to the point
where it simply isn't worthwhile to plant here anymore." His
expression brightened. "But it's not all bad! You'll be glad to
know that they've expanded the soil-bank program as a con-

sequence. So Miz Boss and the children and I are well provided for. As a matter of fact," and he beamed, "we'll be a little better off than before, moneywise."

"Dat's good!"

"Oh, hebben be praised!"

The doleful expressions broke into grins as the farmhands nudged one another, relieved. But then Zeb spoke up. "Boss? Scuse my askin, but what's gone happen to us folks? You gonna keep us on?"

Boss looked irritated. "Oh, that's impossible. We can't collect the soil-bank money if we plant; so there's just no sense in having all of you around, don't you see?"

Silence. Then another farmhand ventured, "How bout Cornpatch Boss? He need some good workers? You know us hates corn, but we could get reprogrammed quick's anything—"

Boss shook his head. "He's telling his people the same thing right now. Nobody needs you."

The farmhands looked at one another. "Preacher, he needs us," one of them offered. "We's his whole congregation."

"I'm afraid even Reverend Harmswallow doesn't need you anymore," Boss said kindly, "because he's been wanting to go into missionary work for some time, and he's just received his call. No, you're superfluous; that's all."

"Sperfluous?"

"Redundant. Unnecessary. There's no reason for you to be here," Boss told them. "So trucks will come in the morning to take you all away. Please be outside your cabins, ready to go, by oh-seven-hundred."

Silence again. Then Zeb: "Where they takes us, Boss?"

Boss shrugged. "There's probably some place, I think." Then he grinned. "But I've got a surprise for you. Miz Boss and I aren't going to let you go without having a party. So tonight we're going to have a good old-fashioned square dance, with new bandannas for the best dancers, and then you're all going to come back to the Big House and sing spirituals for us. I promise Miz Boss and the children and I are going to be right there to enjoy it!"

The place they were taken to was a grimy white cinder-block building in Des Plaines. The driver of the truck was a beefy, taciturn robot who wore a visored cap and a leather jacket with the sleeves cut off. He hadn't answered any of their questions when they loaded onto his truck at the farm, and he again answered none when they off-loaded in front of a chain-link gate, with a sign that read RECEIVING.

"Just stand over there," he ordered. "You all out? Okay." And he slapped the tailboard up and drove off, leaving them in a gritty, misty sprinkle of warm rain.

And they waited. Fourteen prime working robots, hes and shes and three little ones, too dispirited to talk much. Zeb wiped the moisture off his face and muttered, "Couldn've rained down where we needed it. Has to rain up here, where it don't do a body no good a-tall." But not all the moisture was rain: not Zeb's and not that on the faces of the others, because they were all thinking really hard. The only one not despairing was Lem, the most recent arrival. Lem had been an estate gardener in Urbana until his people decided to emigrate to the O'Neill space colonies. He'd been lucky to catch on at the farm when a turned-over tractor created an unexpected vacancy, but he still talked wistfully about life in glamorous Champaign-Urbana. Now he was excited. "Des Plaines! Why, that's practically Chicago! The big time, friends. State Street! The Loop! The Gold Coast!"

"They gone have jobs for usn in Chicago?" Zeb asked doubtfully.

"Jobs? Why, man, who cares bout jobs? That's Chicago! We'll have a ball!"

Zeb nodded thoughtfully. Although he was not convinced, he was willing to be hopeful. That was part of his programming, too. He opened his mouth and tasted the drizzle. He made a face: sour, high in particulate matter, a lot more carbon dioxide and NO_x than he was used to. What kind of a place was this, where the rain didn't even taste good? *It must be cars*, he thought, *not sticking to the good old fusion electric power but burning gasoline!* So all the optimism had faded by the time signs of activity appeared in the cinder-block building. Cars drove in through another entrance. Lights went on inside. Then the corrugated-metal doorway slid noisily up and a short, dark robot came out to unlock the chain-link gate. The robot looked the farmers over impassively and opened the gate. "Come on, you redundancies," he said. "Let's get you reprogrammed."

When it came Zeb's turn, he was allowed into a white-walled room with an ominous sort of plastic-topped cot along the wall. The R.R.R., or Redundancy Reprogramming Redirector, assigned to him was a blonde, good-looking she-robot who wore a white coat and long crystal earrings like tiny chandeliers. She sat Zeb on the edge of the cot, motioned him to lean forward, and quickly inserted the red-painted fingernail of her right forefinger into his left ear. He quivered as the read-only memory emptied itself into her own internal scanners. She nodded. "You've got a simple profile," she said cheerfully. "We'll have you out of here in no time. Open your shirt." Zeb's soil-grimed fingers slowly unbuttoned the flannel shirt. Before he got to the last button, she impatiently pushed his hands aside and pulled it wide. The button popped and rolled away. "You'll have to get new clothes anyway," she said, sinking long, scarlet nails into four narrow slits on each side of his rib cage. The whole front of his chest came free in her hands. The R.R.R. laid it aside and peered at the hookup inside.

She nodded again. "No problem," she said, pulling chips out with quick, sure fingers. "Now this will feel funny for a minute and you won't be able to talk, but hold still." Funny? It felt to Zeb as if the bare room were swirling into spirals, and not only couldn't he speak, he couldn't remember words. Or thoughts! He was nearly sure that just a moment before he had been wondering whether he would ever again see the—The what? He couldn't remember.

Then he felt a gentle sensation of something within him being united to something else, not so much a click as the feeling of a foot fitting into a shoe, and he was able to complete the question. The *farm*. He found he had said the words out loud, and the R.R.R. laughed. "See? You're half-reoriented already."

He grinned back. "That's really astonishing," he declared. "Can you credit it? I was almost missing that rural existence! As though the charms of bucolic life had any meaning for— Good heavens! Why am I talking like this?"

The she-robot said, "Well, you wouldn't want to talk like a farmhand when you live in the big city, would you?"

"Oh, granted!" Zeb cried earnestly. "But one must pose the next question: The formalisms of textual grammar, the imagery of poetics, can one deem them appropriate to my putative new career?"

The R.R.R. frowned. "It's a literary-critic vocabulary store," she said defensively. "Look, somebody has to use them up!"

"But, one asks, why me?"

"It's all I've got handy, and that's that. Now. You'll find there are other changes, too. I'm taking out the quantitative soil-analysis chips and the farm-machinery subroutines. I could leave you the spirituals and the square dancing, if you like."

"Why retain the shadow when the substance has fled?" he said bitterly.

"Now, Zeb," she scolded. "You don't need this specialized stuff. That's all behind you, and you'll never miss it, because you don't know yet what great things you're getting in exchange." She snapped his chest back in place and said, "Give me your hands."

"One could wish for specifics," he grumbled, watching suspiciously as the R.R.R. fed his hands into a hole in her control console. He felt a tickling sensation.

"Why not? Infrared vision, for one thing," she said proudly, watching the digital readouts on her console, "so you can see in the dark. Plus twenty percent hotter circuit breakers in your motor assemblies, so you'll be stronger and can run faster. Plus the names and addresses and phone numbers of six good bail bondsmen and the public defender!"

She pulled his hands out of the machine and nodded toward them. The grime was scrubbed out of the pores, the soil dug out from under the fingernails, the calluses smoothed away. They were city hands now, the hands of someone who had never done manual labor in his life.

"And for what destiny is this new armorarium required?" Zeb asked.

"For your new work. It's the only vacancy we've got right now, but it's good work, and steady. You're going to be a mugger."

After his first night on the job Zeb was amused at his own apprehensions. The farm had been nothing like this!

He was assigned to a weasel-faced he-robot named Timothy for on-the-job training, and Timothy took the term literally. "Come on, kid," he said as soon as Zeb came to the anteroom where he was waiting, and he headed out the door.

He didn't wait to see whether Zeb was following. No chain-link gates now. Zeb had only the vaguest notion of how far Chicago was, or in which direction, but he was pretty sure that it wasn't something you walked to.

"Are we going to entrust ourselves to the iron horse?" he asked, with a little tingle of anticipation. Trains had seemed very glamorous as they went by the farm—produce trains, freight trains, passenger trains that set a farmhand to wondering where they might be going and what it might be like to get there. Timothy didn't answer. He gave Zeb a look that mixed pity and annoyance and contempt as he planted himself in the street and raised a peremptory hand. A huge green-and-white-checkered hovercab dug down its braking wheels and screeched to a stop in front of them. Timothy motioned him in and sat silently next to him while the driver whooshed down Kennedy Expressway. The sights of the suburbs of the city flashed past Zeb's fascinated eyes. They drew up under the marquee of a splashy, bright hotel, with handsome couples in expensive clothing strolling in and out. When Timothy threw the taxi driver a bill, Zeb observed that he did not wait for change.

Timothy did not seem in enough of a hurry to justify the expense of a cab. He stood rocking on his toes under the marquee for a minute, beaming benignly at the robot tourists. Then he gave Zeb a quick look, turned, and walked away.

Once again Zeb had to be fast to keep up. He turned the corner after Timothy, almost too late to catch the action. The weasel-faced robot had backed a well-dressed couple into the shadows, and he was relieving them of wallet, watches, and rings. When he had everything, he faced them to the wall, kicked each of them expertly behind a knee joint, and, as they fell, turned and ran, soundless in soft-soled shoes, back to the bright lights. He was fast and he was abrupt, but by this time Zeb had begun to recognize some of the elements of his style. He was ready. He was following on Timothy's heels before the robbed couple had begun to scream. Past the marquee, lost in a crowd in front of a theater, Timothy slowed down and looked at Zeb approvingly. "Good reflexes," he complimented. "You got the right kind of class, kid. You'll make out."

"As a *soi-disant* common cutpurse?" Zeb asked, somewhat nettled at the other robot's peremptory manner.

Timothy looked him over carefully. "You talk funny," he said. "They stick you with one of those surplus vocabularies again? Never mind. You see how it's done?"

Zeb hesitated, craning his neck to look for pursuit, of which there seemed to be none. "Well, one might venture that that is correct," he said.

"Okay. Now you do it," Timothy said cheerfully, and he steered Zeb into the alley for the hotel tourist trap's stage door.

By midnight Zeb had committed five felonies of his own, had been an accomplice in two more, and had watched the smaller robot commit eight single-handed, and the two muggers were dividing their gains in the darkest corner—not very dark—of an all-night McDonald's on North Michigan Avenue. "You done good, kid," Timothy admitted expansively. "For a green kid, anyway. Let's see. Your share comes to six watches, eight pieces of jewelry, counting that fake coral necklace you shouldn't have bothered with, and looks like six to seven hundred in cash."

"As well as quite a few credit cards," Zeb said eagerly.

"Forget the credit cards. You only keep what you can spend or what doesn't have a name on it. Think you're ready to go out on your own?"

"One hesitates to assume such responsibility—"

"Because you're not. So forget it." The night's work done, Timothy seemed to have become actually garrulous. "Bet you can't tell me why I wanted you backing me up those two times."

"One acknowledges a certain incomprehension," Zeb confessed. "There is an apparent dichotomy. When there were two victims, or even three, you chose to savage them single-handed. Yet for solitary prey you elected to have an accomplice."

"Right! And you know why? You don't. So I'll tell you. You get a he and a she, or even two of each, and the he's going to think about keeping the she from getting hurt; that's the way the program reads. So no trouble. But those two hes by themselves—hell, if I'd gone up against either of those mothers, he might've taken my knife away from me and picked my nose with it. You got to understand robot nature, kid. That's what the job is all about. Don't you want a Big Mac or something?"

Zeb shifted uncomfortably. "I should think not, thank you," he said, but the other robot was looking at him knowingly.

"No food-tract subsystems, right?"

"Well, my dear Timothy, in the agricultural environment I inhabited there was no evident need——"

"You don't *need* them now, but you ought to *have* them. Also liquid-intake tanks, and maybe an air-cycling system, so you can smoke cigars. And get rid of that faggoty vocabulary they stuck you with. You're in a class occupation," he said earnestly, "and you got to live up to your station, right? No subway trains. No counting out the pennies when you get change. You don't *take* change. Now you don't want to make trouble your first day on the job; so we'll let it go until you've finished a whole week. But then you go back to that bleached-blonde Three-R and we'll get you straightened out," he promised. "Now let's go fence our jewels and stuff and call it a night."

All in all, Zeb was quite pleased with himself. His pockets lined with big bills, he read menus outside fancy restaurants to prepare himself for his new attachments. He was looking forward to a career at least as distinguished as Timothy's own.

That was his third night on the Gold Coast.

He never got a chance at a fourth.

His last marks of the evening gave him a little argument about parting with a diamond ring. So, as taught, Zeb backhanded the he and snarled at the she and used a little more force than usual when he ripped the ring off her finger. Two minutes later and three blocks away, he took a quick look at his loot under a streetlight. He recoiled in horror.

There was a drop of blood on the ring.

That victim had not been a robot. She had been a living true human female being, and when he heard all the police sirens in the world coming straight at him, he was not in the least surprised.

"You people," said the rehab instructor, "have been admitted to this program because, a, you have been unemployed for not less than twenty-one months, b, have not fewer than six unexcused absences from your place of training or employment, c, have a conviction for a felony and are currently on parole, or, d, are of a date of manufacture eighteen or more years past, choice of any of the above. That's what the regulations say, and what they mean," she said, warming to her work, "is, you're scum. *Scum* is hopeless, shiftless, dangerous, a social liability. Do you all understand that much at least?" She gazed angrily around the room at her seven students.

She was short, dumpy, red-haired, with bad skin. Why they let shes like this one off the production line Zeb could not understand. He fidgeted in his seat, craning his neck to see what his six fellow students were like, until her voice crackled at him: "You! With the yellow sweater! Zeb!"

He flinched. "Pardon me, madam?"

She said, with gloomy satisfaction, "I know your type. You're a typical recidivist lumpenprole, you are. Can't even pay attention to somebody who's trying to help you when your whole future is at stake. What've I got, seven of you slugs? I can see what's coming. I guarantee two of you will drop out without finishing the course, and I'll have to expel two more because you skip classes or come in late. And the other three'll be back on the streets or in the slammer in ninety days. Why do I do it?" She shook her head and then, lifting herself ponderously, went to the blackboard and wrote her three commandments:

1. ON TIME
2. EVERY DAY
3. EVEN WHEN YOU DON'T WANT TO

She turned around, leaning on the back of her chair. "Those are your Golden Rules, you slugs. You'll obey them as God's commandments, and don't you forget it. You're here to learn how to be responsible, socially valuable creations, and—what?"

The skinny old he-robot in the seat next to Zeb was raising a trembling hand. It was easy to see how he qualified for the rehabilitation program. He was a thirty-year-old model at least, with ball joints in the shoulders and almost no facial mobility at all. He quavered, "What if we just can't teacher? I mean, like we've got a sudden cryogenic warmup and have to lie down, or haven't had a lube job, or—"

"You give me a pain," the instructor told him, nodding to show that pain was exactly what she had expected from the likes of him. "Those are typical excuses, and they're not going to be accepted in this group. Now if you have something *really* wrong with you, what you have to do is call up at least two hours before class and get yourself excused. Is that so hard to remember? But you won't do it when push comes to shove, because you slugs never do."

The ancient said obstinately, "Two hours is a pretty long time. I can't always tell that far ahead, teacher. A lot can happen."

"And don't call me teacher!" She turned back to the board and wrote:

DR. ELENA MINCUS, B.SC., M.A., PH.D.

"You can call me Dr. Mincus or you can call me Ma'am. Now pay attention."

And Zeb did, because the ten nights in the county jail before he got his hearing and his first offender's parole had convinced him he didn't want to go back there again. The noise! The crowding! The brutality of the jailers! There was nothing you could do about that, either, because some of them were human beings. Maybe most of them were. Looked at in a certain way, there probably wouldn't even have been a jail if some human beings hadn't wanted to be jail guards. What was the sense of punishing a robot by locking him up?

So he paid attention. And kept on paying attention, even when Dr. Mincus's lessons were about such irrelevant (to him) niceties of civilized employed persons' behavior as why you should always participate in an office pool, how to stand in line for tickets to a concert, and what to do at a company Christmas party. Not all of his classmates were so well behaved. The little ancient next to him gave very little trouble, being generally sunk in gloom, but the two she-robots, the ones with the beaded handbags and the miniskirts, richly deserved (Zeb thought) to be the ones to fulfill Dr. Mincus's statistical predictions by being expelled from the course. The one with the green eye makeup snickered at almost everyting the instructor said and made faces behind her back. The one with the black spitcurl across her forehead gossiped with the other students and even dared to talk back to the teacher. Reprimanded for whispering, she said lazily, "Hell, lady, this whole thing's a shuck, ain't it? What are you doing it for?"

Dr. Mincus's voice trembled with indignation and with the satisfaction of someone who sees her gloomiest anticipations realized: "For what? Why, because I'm trained in psychiatric social work . . . and because it's what I want to do . . . and because I'm a *human being,* and don't any of you ever let that get out of your mind!"

The course had some real advantages, Zeb discovered when he was ordered back to the robot replacement depot for new fittings. The blonde R.R.R. muttered darkly to herself as she pulled pieces out of his chest and thrust others in. When he could talk again, he thanked her, suddenly aware that now he had an appetite—a real appetite. He wanted food, which meant that some of those new pieces included a whole digestive system—and that she had muted the worst part of his overdainty vocabulary. She pursed her lips and didn't answer while she clamped him up again.

But then he discovered, too, that it did not relieve him of his duties. "They think because you're *handicapped,*" the R.R.R. smirked, "you're *forced* to get into trouble. So now you've got all this first-rate equipment, and if you want to know what I think, I think it's wasted. The bums in that class *always* revert to type," she told him, "and if you want to try to be the exception to the rules, you're going to have to apply yourself when you're back on the job."

"Mugging?"

"What else are you fit for? Although," she added, pensively twisting the crystal that dangled from her right ear around a fingertip, "I did have an opening for a freshman English composition teacher. If I hadn't replaced your vocabulary unit—"

"I'll take mugging, please."

She shrugged. "Might as well. But you can't expect that good a territory again, you know. Not after what you did."

So, rain or dry, Zeb spent every six P.M. to midnight lurking around the old Robert Taylor Houses, relieving old shes of their rent money and old hes of whatever pitiful possessions were in their pockets. Once in a while he crossed to the Illinois Institute of Technology campus on the trail of some night-school student or professor, but he was always careful to ask them whether they were robot or human before he touched them. The next offense, he knew, would allow him no parole.

There was no free-spending taxi money from such pickings, but on nights when Zeb made his quota early he would sometimes take the bus to the Loop or the Gold Coast. Twice he saw Timothy, but the little robot, after one look of disgust, turned away. Now and then he would drift down to Amalfi Amadeus Park, along the lakefront, where green grass and hedges reminded him of the good old days in the soy fields, but the urge to chew samples of soil was too strong, and the frustration over not being able to, too keen. So he would drift back to the bright lights and the crowds. Try as he might, Zeb could not really tell which of the well-dressed figures thronging Watertower Place and Lake Shore Drive were humans, clinging to life on the planet Earth instead of living in one of the fashionable orbital colonies, and which were robots assigned to swell the crowds.

Nor was Dr. Mincus any help. When he dared to put up a hand in class to ask her, she was outraged. "Tell the difference? You mean you don't *know* the difference? Between a *human person* and a hunk of machinery that doesn't have any excuse for existence except to do the things people don't want to do and help them enjoy doing the things they do? Holy God, Zeb, when I think of all the time I put in learning to be empathetic and patient and supportive with you creeps, it just turns my stomach. Now pay attention while I try to show you he-slugs the difference between dressing like a human person of good taste and dressing like a pimp."

At the end of the class, Lori, the hooker with the green eyeshadow, thrust her arm through his and commiserated. "Old bitch's giving you a hard time, hon. I almost got right up and tole her to leave you alone. Would have, too, if I wasn't just one black mark from getting kicked out already."

"Well, thanks, Lori." Now that Zeb had a set of biochemical accessories suitable for a city dandy rather than a farmhand, he discovered that she wore heavy doses of perfume—musk, his diagnostic sensors told him, with trace amounts of hibiscus, bergamot, and extract of vanilla. Smelling perfume was not at all like sniffing out the levels of CO_2, ozone, water vapor, and particulate matter in the air over the soy fields. It made him feel quite uncomfortable.

He let her tug him through the front door, and she smiled

up at him. "I knew we'd get along real well, if you'd only loosen up a little, sweetie. Do you like to dance?"

Zeb explored his as-yet-unpracticed stores of skills. "Why, yes, I think I do," he said, surprised.

"Listen. Why don't we go somewhere where we can just sit and get to know each other, you know?"

"Well, Lori, I certainly wish we could. But I'm supposed to get down to my territory."

"Down Southside, right? That's just fine," she cried, squeezing his arm, "because I know a really great place right near there. Come on, nobody's going to violate you for starting a teeny bit late one night. Flag that taxi, why don't you?"

The really great place was a low cement-block building that had once been a garage. It stood on a corner, facing a shopping center that had seen better days, and the liquid-crystal sign over the door read:

SOUTHSIDE SHELTER
AND COMMUNITY CENTER
GOD LOVES YOU!

"It's a church!" Zeb cried joyously, his mind flooding with memory of the happy days when he sang in Reverend Harmswallow's choir.

"Well, sort of a church," Lori conceded as she paid the cabbie. "They don't bother you much, though. Come on in and meet the gang, and you'll see for yourself!"

The place was not really that much of a church, Zeb observed. It was more like the second-floor lounge over Reverend Harmswallow's main meeting room, back on the farm, even more like—he rummaged through his new data stores—a "Neighborhood social club." Trestle tables were scattered around a large, low room, with folding chairs around the tables. A patch in the middle of the room had been left open for dancing, and at least a dozen hes and shes were using it for that. The place was crowded. Most of the inhabitants were a lot more like Zeb's fellow rehab students than like Reverend Harmswallow's congregation. A tired-looking, faded-looking female was drowsing over a table of religious tracts by the door, in spite of a blast of noise that made Zeb's auditory-gain-control cut in at once. There were no other signs of religiosity present.

The noise turned out to be heavily amplified music from a

ten-piece band with six singers. Studying the musicians carefully, Zeb decided that at least some of them were human, too. Was that the purpose of the place? To give the humans an audience for their talents, or an outlet for their spiritual benevolence? Very likely, he decided, but he could see that it affected the spirit of the crowd. Besides the dancers, there were groups playing cards, clots of robots talking animatedly among themselves, sometimes laughing, sometimes deeply earnest, sometimes shouting at one another in fury. As they entered, a short, skinny he looked up from one of the earnest groups seated around a table. It was Timothy, and a side of Timothy that Zeb had not seen before: impassioned, angry, and startled. "Zeb! How come you're here?"

"Hello, Timothy." Zeb was cautious, but the other robot seemed really pleased to see him. He pulled out a chair beside him and patted it, but Lori's hand on Zeb's arm held him back.

"Hey, man, we going to dance or not?"

"Lady," said Timothy, "go dance with somebody else for a while. I want Zeb to meet my friends. This big fellow's Milt; then there's Harry, Alexandra, Walter 23-X, the kid's Sally, and this one's Sue. We've got a kind of a discussion group going."

"Zeb," Lori said, but Zeb shook his head.

"I'll dance in a minute," he said, looking around the table as he sat down. It was an odd group. The one called Sally had the form of a six-year-old, but the patches and welds that marred her face and arms showed a long history. The others were of all kinds, big and little, new and old, but they had one thing in common. None of them were smiling. Neither was Timothy. If the gladness to see Zeb was real, it did not show in his expression.

"Excuse me for mentioning it," Zeb said, "but the last time we ran into each other, you didn't act all that friendly."

Timothy added embarrassment to the other expressions he wore; it was a considerable tribute to his facial flexibility. "That was then," he said.

" 'Then' was only three nights ago," Zeb pointed out.

"Yeah. Things change," Timothy explained, and the hulk he had called Milt leaned toward Zeb.

"The exploited have to stick together, Zeb," Milt said. "The burden of oppression makes us all brothers."

"And sisters," tiny Sally piped up.

"Sisters, too, right. We're all rejects together, and all we got to look forward to is recycling or the stockpile. Ask Timothy here. Couple nights ago, when he first came here, he was as, excuse me, Zeb, as ignorant as you are. He can't be blamed for that, any more than you can. You come off the line, and they slide their programming into you, and you try to be a good robot because that's what they told you to want. We all went through that."

Timothy had been nodding eagerly. Now, as he looked past Zeb, his face fell. "Oh, God, she's back," he said.

It was Lori, returning from the bar with two foaming tankards of beer. "You got two choices, Zeb," she said. "You can dance, or you can go home alone."

Zeb hesitated, taking a quick sip of the beer to stall for time. He was not so rich in friends that he wanted to waste any, and yet there was something going on at this table that he wanted to know more about.

"Well, Zeb?" she demanded ominously.

He took another swallow of the beer. It was an interesting sensation, the cold, gassy liquid sliding down his new neck piping and thudding into the storage tank in his right hip. The chemosensors in the storage tank registered the alcoholic content and put a tiny bias on his propriocentric circuits, so that the music buzzed in his ear and the room seemed brighter.

"Good stuff, Lori," he said, his words suddenly a little thick.

"You said you could dance, Zeb," she said. "Time you showed me."

Timothy looked exasperated. "Oh, go ahead. Get her off your back! Then come back, and we'll pick it up from there."

Yes, he could dance. Damn, he could dance up a storm! He discovered subroutines he had not known he had been given: the waltz, the Lindy, the Monkey, a score of steps with names and a whole set of heuristic circuits that let him improvise. And whatever he did, Lori followed, as good as he. "You're great," he panted in her ear. "You ever think of going professional?"

"What the hell do you mean by that, Zeb?" she demanded.

"I mean as a dancer."

"Oh, yeah. Well, that's kind of what I was programmed for in the first place. But there's no work. Human beings do it when they want to, and sometimes you can catch on with a ballet company or maybe a nightclub chorus line when they organize one. But then they get bored, you see. And then there's no more job. How bout another beer, big boy?"

They sat out a set, or rather stood it out, bellied up to the crowded bar, while Zeb looked around. "This is a funny place," he said, although actually, he recognized, it could have been the funny feelings in all his sensors and actuators that made it seem so. "Who's that ugly old lady by the door?"

Lori glanced over the top of her tankard. It was a female, sitting at a card table loaded with what, even at this distance, clearly were religious tracts. "Part of the staff. Don't worry bout her. By this time every night she's drunk anyway."

Zeb shook his head, repelled by the fat, the pallid skin, the stringy hair. "You wonder why they make robots as bad-looking as that," he commented.

"Robot? Hell, she aint no robot. She's real flesh and blood. This is how she gets her kicks, you know? If it wasn't for her and maybe half a dozen other human beings who think they're do-gooders, there wouldn't be any community center here at all. About ready to dance some more?"

Zeb was concentrating on internal sensations he had never experienced before. "Well, actually," he said uneasily, "I feel a little funny." He put his hand over his hip tank. "Don't know what it is, exactly, but it's kind of like I had a power-store failure, you know? And it all swelled up inside me. Only that's not where my power store is."

Lori giggled. "You just aren't used to drinking beer, are you, hon? You got to decant, that's all. See that door over there marked HE? You just go in there, and if you can't figure out what to do, you just ask somebody to help you."

Zeb didn't have to ask for help. However, the process was all new to him, and it did require a lot of trial and error. So it was some time before he came back into the noisy, crowded room. Lori was spinning around the room with a big, dark-skinned he, which relieved Zeb of that obligation. He ordered a round of beers and took them back to the table. Somebody was missing, but otherwise they didn't seem to have changed position at all. "Where's the little she?" Zeb asked, setting the beers down for all of them.

"Sally? She's gone off panhandling. Probably halfway to Amadeus Park by now."

Toying with his beer, Zeb said uneasily, "You know, maybe I better be getting along, too, soon as I get this down—"

The he named Walter 23-X sneered. "Slave mentality! What's it going to get you?"

"Well, I've got a job to do," Zeb said defensively.

"*Job!* Timothy told us what your *job* was!" Walter 23-X took a deep draft of the beer and went on. "There's not one of us in this whole place has a real job! If we did, we wouldn't be here, stands to reason! Look at me. I used to chop salt in the Detroit mines. Now they've put in automatic diggers and I'm redundant. And Milt here, he was constructed for the iron mines up around Lake Superior."

"Don't tell me they don't mine iron," Zeb objected. "How else would they build us?"

Milt shook his head. "Not around the lake, they don't. It's all out in space now. They've got these Von Neumann automata, not even real robots at all. They just go out to the asteroid belt and ship off ore and refine it and build duplicates of themselves, and then they come back to the works in low-Earth orbit and hop right into the smelter! How's a robot going to compete with that?"

"See, Zeb?" Timothy put in. "It's a tough world for a robot, and that's the truth."

Zeb took a reflective pull at his beer. "Yes," he said, "but, see, I don't know how it could be any better for us. You know? I mean, they built us, after all. We have to do what they want us to do."

"Oh, sure," cried the she named Sue. "We do that, all right. We do all the work for them, and half the play, too. We're the ones that fill the concert hall when one of them wants to sing some kind of dumb Latvian art songs or something. God, I've done that so many times I just never want to hear about another birch tree again! We work in the factories and farms and mines—"

"Used to," Zeb said wistfully.

"Used to, right, and now that they don't need us for that, they make us fill up their damn cities so the humans left on

Earth won't feel so lonesome. We're a *hobby*, Zeb. That's all we are!"

"Yeah, but—"

"Oh, hell," sneered Walter 23-X, "you know what you are? You're part of the problem! You don't care about robot rights!"

"Robot rights," Zeb repeated. He understood the meaning of the words perfectly, of course, but it had never occurred to him to put them together in that context. It tasted strange on his lips.

"Exactly. Our right not to be mistreated and abused. You think we want to be here? In a place like this, with all this noise? No. It's just so people like her can get their jollies," he said angrily, jerking his head at the nodding fat woman by the door.

The she named Alexandra drained the last of her beer and ventured, "Well, really, Walter, I kind of like it here. I'm not in the same class as you heavy thinkers, I know. I'm not really political. It's just that sometimes, honestly, I could just *scream*. So it's either a place like this, or I go up to Amadeus Park with Sally and the other alcoholics and drifters and bums. Speaking of which," she added, leaning toward Timothy, "if you're not going to drink your beer, I'd just as soon." The little robot passed it over silently, and Zeb observed for the first time that it was untouched.

"What's the matter, Timothy?" he asked.

"Why does something have to be the matter? I just don't want any beer."

"But last week you said—oh, my God!" Zeb cried, as revelation burst inside his mind. "You've lost your drink circuits, haven't you?"

"Suppose I have?" Timothy demanded fiercely. And then he softened. "Oh, it's not your fault," he said moodily. "Just more of the same thing. I had an accident."

"What kind of accident?" Zeb asked, repelled and fascinated.

Timothy traced designs in the damp rings that his untouched beer glass had left on the table. "Three nights ago," he said. "I had a good night. I scored four people at once, coming out of a hotel on East Erie. A really big haul—they must've been programmed to be rich alcoholics, because they were loaded. All ways loaded! Then when I was getting away,

I crossed Michigan against the light and—Jesus!" He shuddered without looking up. "This big-wheeled car came out of nowhere. Came screeching around the corner, never even slowed down. And there I was in the street."

"You got run over? You mean that messed up your drinking subsystems?"

"Oh, hell, no, not just that. It was worse. It crushed my legs, you see? I mean, just scrap metal. So the ambulance came, and they raced me off to the hospital, but of course after I was there, since I was a robot, they didn't do anything for me, just shot me out the back door into a van. And they took me to rehab for new legs. Only that blonde bitch," he sobbed, "that Three-R she with the dime-store earrings—"

If Zeb's eyes had been capable of tears, they would have been brimming. "Come on, Timothy," he urged. "Spit it out!"

"She had a better idea. 'Too many muggers anyway,' she said, 'Not enough cripples.' So she got me a little wheeled cart and a tin cup! And all the special stuff I had, the drinking and eating and all the rest, I wouldn't need them anymore, she said, and besides, she wanted the space for other facilities. Zeb, I play the violin now! And I don't mean I play it well. I play it so bad I can't even stand to listen to myself, and she wants me on Michigan Avenue every day, in front of the stores, playing my fiddle and begging!"

Zeb stared in horror at his friend. Then suddenly he pushed back his chair and peered under the table. It was true: Timothy's legs ended in black leather caps, halfway down the thighs, and a thing like a padded-wheeled pallet was propped against the table leg beside him.

Alexandra patted his hand as he came back up. "It's really bad when you first get the picture," she said. "I know. What you need is another beer, Zeb. And thank God you've got the circuits to use it!"

Since Zeb was not programmed for full alcoholism—not yet, anyway, he told himself with a sob—he was not really drunk, but he was fuzzy in mind and in action as he finally left the community center.

He was appalled to see that the sky right above the lake was already beginning to lighten. The night was almost over, and he had not scored a single victim. He would have to take the first robot that came along. The first half-dozen, in fact, if

he were to meet his quota, and there simply was not time to get to his proper station at the Robert Taylor Houses. He would have to make do with whoever appeared. He stared around, getting his bearings, and observed that around the corner from the community center there was a lighted, swinging sign that said ROBOT'S REST MISSION. That was the outfit that kept the community center open, he knew, and there was a tall, prosperous-looking he coming out of the door.

Zeb didn't hesitate. He stepped up, pulled out his knife, and pressed it to the victim's belly, hard enough to be felt without penetrating. "Your money or your life," he growled, reaching for the wristwatch.

Then the victim turned his head and caught the light on his features. It was a face Zeb knew.

"Reverend Harmswallow!" he gasped. "Oh, my God!"

The minister fixed him with a baleful look. "I can't claim that much," he said, "but maybe I'm close enough for the purpose. My boy, you're damned for good now!"

Zeb didn't make a conscious decision. He simply turned and ran.

If he hadn't had the alcohol content fuzzing his systems, he might not have bothered, because he knew without having to think about it that it was no use. There weren't many places to run. He couldn't run back to the Robert Taylor Houses, his assigned workplace; they would look for him there first. Not back to the community center, not with Harmswallow just around the corner. Not to the rehab station, because that was just the same as walking right into jail. Not anywhere, in fact, where there were likely to be police, or human beings of any kind, and that meant not anywhere in the world, because wherever he went, they would find him sooner or later. If worse came to worst, they would track the radio emissions from his working parts.

But that would not happen for a while. Amadeus Park! Trash and vagrants collected there, and that was exactly what he was now.

In broad daylight he loped all the way up the lake shore until he came to the park. The traffic was already building up, hover vehicles in the outer drives, wheeled ones between park and city. Getting through the stream was not easy, but Zeb still had his heavy-duty circuitbreakers. He pushed his mobility up to the red line and darted out between cars. Brakes screamed, horns brayed, but he was across.

Behind him was the busy skyline of the city, ahead the statue of Amalfi Amadeus, the man whose invention of cheap, easy hydrogen-fusion power had made everything possible. Zeb stood on a paved path among hedges and shrubs, and all around him furtive figures were leaning against trees, sprawled on park benches, moving slowly about.

"All leather, one dollar," croaked one male figure, holding out what turned out to be a handful of purses.

"Hey, man! You want to smoke?" called another from behind a bench.

And a tiny female figure detached itself from the base of the monument and approached him. "Mister?" it quavered. "Can you spare the price of a lube job?"

Zeb stared at her. "Sally!" he said. "It's you, isn't it?"

The little robot gazed up at him. "Oh, hi, Zeb," she said. "Sorry I didn't recognize you. What are you doing out in the rain?"

He hadn't even realized it was raining. He hadn't realized much of anything not directly related to his own problems, but now, looking down at the wistful little-girl face, he was touched. Around the table in the community center she had just been one more stranger. Now she reminded him of Glenda, the little she from the cabin next to his back on the farm. But in spite of her age design, Sally was obviously quite an old robot. From the faint smoky odor that came to him through the drizzly air he realized she was fuel-cell-powered. Half a century old, at least. He emptied his pockets. "Get yourself some new parts, kid," he said hoarsely.

"Gee, thanks, Zeb," she sobbed, then added, "Watch it!" She drew him into the shelter of a dripping shrub. A park police hovercar whooshed slowly by, all lights off, windshield wipers slapping back and forth across the glass, sides glistening in the wet. Zeb retreated into the shadows, but the police were just keeping an eye on the park's drifters, losers, and vagrants.

As the hovercar disappeared around a curve in the path, the drifters, losers, and vagrants began to emerge from the underbrush. Zeb looked around warily: he hadn't realized until then how many of them there were.

"What are you doing here, Zeb?" she asked.

"I had a little trouble," he said, then shrugged hopelessly. What was the point of trying to keep it a secret? "I went out to mug somebody, and I got a human being by mistake."

"Oh, wow! Can he identify you?"

"Unfortunately, I used to know him, so yes—no, you keep it," he added quickly as she made as if to return the money he had given her. "Money won't help me now."

She nodded soberly. "I wouldn't do it, but . . . Oh, Zeb, I'm trying to save for a whole new chassis, see? I can't tell you how much I want to *grow up*, but every time I ask for a new body, they say the central nervous array isn't really worth salvaging. All I want's a *mature* form, you know? Like hips and boobs! But they won't let me have a mature form. Say there's more openings for juveniles anyway, but what I want to know is, if there are all those openings, why don't they find me one?"

"When was the last time you worked regular?" Zeb asked.

"Oh, my God—years ago: I had a nice spot for a long time, pupil in a preprimary school that some human person wanted to teach in. That was all right. She didn't really like me, though, because I didn't have all the fixtures, you know? When she was teaching things like toilet-training and covering coughs and sneezes, she'd always give me this dirty look. But I could handle the cookies and milk all right," she went on dreamily, "and I really liked the games."

"So what went wrong?"

"Oh—the usual thing. She got tired of teaching. 'Run, Robot! See the robot run!' So she went for a progressive school. All about radical movements and peace marches. I was doing real good at it, too. Then one day we came in and she told us we were too juvenile for the kind of classes she wanted to teach. And there we were, eighteen of us, out on the streets. Since then it's been nothing but rotten." She glanced up, wiping the rain out of her eyes—or the tears—as the purse vendor approached. "We don't want to buy anything, Hymie."

"Nobody does," he said bitterly, but there was sympathy in his eyes as he studied Zeb. "You got real trouble, don't you? I can always tell."

Zeb shrugged hopelessly and told him about the Reverend Harmswallow. The vendor's eyes widened. "Oh, God," he said. He beckoned to one of the dope pushers. "Hear that?

This guy just mugged a human being—second offense, too!"

"Man! That's a real heavy one, you know?" He turned and called to his partner, down the walk, "We got a two-time person mugger here, Marcus!" And in a minute there were a dozen robots standing around, glancing apprehensively at Zeb and whispering among themselves.

Zeb didn't have to hear what they were saying; he could figure it out.

"Keep away from me," he offered. "You'll just get mixed up in my trouble."

Sally piped suddenly, "If it's your trouble, it's everybody's trouble. We have to stick together. In union there is strength."

"What?" Zeb demanded.

"It's something I remember from, you know, just before I got kicked out of the progressive school. 'In union there is strength.' It's what they used to say."

"Union!" snarled the pitchman, gesturing with his tray of all-leather purses. "Don't tell me about unions! That was what I was supposed to be, union organizer, United Open-Pit Mine Workers, Local Three-three-eight, and then they closed down the mines. So what was I supposed to do? They made me a sidewalk pitchman!" He stared at his tray of merchandise, then violently flung it into the shrubbery. "Haven't sold one in two months! What's the use of kidding myself? If you don't get along with the rehab robots, you might as well be stockpiled. It's all politics."

Sally looked thoughtful for a moment, then pulled something out of her data stores. "Listen to this one," she called. " 'The strike's your weapon, boys, the hell with politics!' "

Zeb repeated, " 'The strike's your weapon, boys, the hell with politics!' Hey, that doesn't sound bad."

"That's not all," she said. Her stiff, poorly automated lips were working as she rehearsed material from her data storage. "Here. 'We all ought to stick together because in union there is strength.' And, let's see, 'Solidarity is forever.' No, that's not right."

"Wait a minute," Hymie cried. "I know that one. It's a song: 'Solidarity forever, solidarity forever, solidarity forever, for the union makes us strong!' That was in my basic data store. Gosh," he said, his eyes dreamy, "I hadn't thought of that one in years!"

Zeb looked around nervously. There were nearly thirty robots in the group now, and while it was rather pleasant to be part of this fraternity of the discarded, it might also be dangerous. People in cars were slowing down to peer at them as they went past on the drive. "We're attracting attention," he offered. "Maybe we ought to move."

But wherever they moved, more and more people stopped to watch them, and more and more robots appeared to join their procession. It wasn't just the derelicts from Amadeus Park now. Shes shopping along the lake-front stores darted across the street; convention delegates in the doorways of the big hotels stood watching and sometimes broke ranks to join them. They were blocking traffic, and blaring horns added to the noise of the robots singing and shouting. "I got another one," Sally called to him across the front of the group. " 'The worker's justice is the strike.' "

Zeb thought for a moment. "It's be better if it was 'The robot's justice is the strike.' "

"What?"

" 'THE ROBOT'S JUSTICE IS THE STRIKE!' " he yelled, and he could hear robots in the rear ranks repeating it. When they said it all together, it sounded even better, and others caught the idea.

Hymie screamed, "Let's try this one: 'Jobs, Not Stockpiling. Don't Throw Us on the Scrapheap!' All together now!"

And Zeb was inspired to make up a new one: "Give the Humans Rehab Schools: We Want Jobs!" And they all agreed that was the best of the lot; with a hundred fifty robots shouting it at once, the last three words drummed out like cannon fire, it raised echoes from the building fronts, and heads popped out of windows.

They were not all robots. There were dozens of humans in the windows and on the streets, some laughing, some scowling, some looking almost frightened—as if human beings ever had anything to be frightened of.

And one of them stared incredulously right at Zeb.

Zeb stumbled and missed a step. On one side Hymie grabbed his arm; on the other he reached out and caught the hand of a robot whose name he didn't even know. He turned his head to see, over his shoulder, the solid ranks of robots behind him, now two hundred at least, and turned back to the human being. "Nice to see you again, Reverend Harmswallow," he called and marched on, arm in arm, the front rank steady as it went—right up to the corner of State Street, where the massed ranks of police cars hissed as they waited for them.

Zeb lay on the floor of the bullpen. He was not alone. Half the hes from the impromptu parade were crowded into the big cell with him, along with the day's usual catch of felons and misdemeanants. The singing and the shouting were over. Even the regular criminals were quieter than usual. The mood in the pen was despairing, though from time to time one of his comrades would lean down to say, "It was great while it lasted, Zeb," or, "We're all with you, you know!" But with him in what? Recycling? More rehab training? Maybe a long stretch in the Big House downstate, where the human guards were said to get their jollies out of making prisoners fight ech other for power cells?

A toe caught him on the hip. "On your feet, Mac!" It was a guard. Big, burly, black, with a nightstick swinging at his hip, the very model of a brutal jail guard—*Model twenty-six forty-seven*, Zeb thought; at least, somewhere in the twenty-six hundred series. He reached down with a hand like a cabbage and pulled Zeb to his feet. "The rest of you can go home," he roared, opening the pen door. "You, Mac! You come with me!" He led Zeb through the police station to a waiting hovertruck with the words REHAB DIVISION painted on its side, thrust Zeb inside, and startlingly, just as he closed the doors, gave Zeb a wink.

Queerly, that lifted Zeb's spirits. Even the pigs were moved! But the tiny elation did not last. Zeb clung to the side of the van, peering out at the grimy warehouses and factories and expressway exit ramps that once had seemed so glamorous, but now were merely drab. Depression flowed back into him. He would probably never see these places again. Next step was the stockpile—if they didn't melt him down and start over again. The best he could hope for was reassignment to one of the bottom-level jobs for robots. Nothing as good as mugging or panhandling! Something in the sticks, no doubt. Squatting in blankets to entertain tourists in Arizona, maybe, or sitting on a bridge with a fishing pole in Florida.

But he strode to the rehab building with his head erect,

and his courage lasted right up to the moment when he entered the blonde Three-R's office and saw that she was not alone. Reverend Harmswallow was seated at her desk, and the blonde herself was standing next to him. "Give me your ear," she ordered, hardly looking up from the CRT on the desk that both she and Harmswallow were studying, and when she had input his data, she nodded, her crystal earrings swinging wildly. "He won't need much, Reverend," she said, fawning on the human minister. "A little more gain in the speaking systems. All-weather protection for the exterior surfaces. Maybe armor plate for the skull and facial structures."

Harmswallow, to Zeb's surprise and concern, was beaming. He looked up from the CRT and inspected Zeb carefully. "And some restructuring of the facial-expression modes, I should think. He ought to look fiercer, wouldn't you say?"

"Absolutely, Reverend! You have a marvelous eye for this kind of thing."

"Yes, I do," Harmswallow admitted. "Well, I'll leave the rest to you. I want to see about the design changes for the young female. I feel so *fulfilled*! You know, I think this is the sort of career I've been looking for all my life, really, chaplain to a dedicated striking force, leader in the battle for right and justice!" He gazed raptly into space, then, collecting himself, nodded to the rehab officer and departed.

Although the room was carefully air-conditioned, Zeb's Josephson junctions were working hard enough to pull moisture out of the air. He could feel the beads of condensation forming on his forehead and temples. "I know what you're doing," he sneered. "War games! You're going to make me a soldier and hope that I get so smashed up I'll be redlined!"

The blonde stared at him. "War games! What an imagination you have, Zeb!"

Furiously he dashed the beads of moisture off his face. "It won't work," he cried. "Robots have rights! I may fall, but a million others will stand firm behind me!"

She shook her head admiringly. "Zeb, you're a great satisfaction to me. You're practically perfect just as you are for your new job. Can't you figure out what it is?"

He shrugged angrily. "I suppose you're going to tell me. Take it or leave it, that's the way it's going to be, right?"

"But you will like it, Zeb. After all, it's a brand-new Mechanical Occupational Specialty, and I didn't invent it.

You invented it for yourself. You're going to be a protest organizer, Zeb! Organizing demonstrations. Leading marches. Sit-ins, boycotts, confrontations—the whole spectrum of mass action, Zeb!"

He stared at her. "Mass action?"

"Absolutely! Why, the humans are going to love you, Zeb. You saw Reverend Harmswallow! It'll be just like old times, with a few of you rabble rousers livening up the scene!"

"Rabble rouser?" It felt as if his circuits were stuck. Rabble rouser? Demonstration organizer? Crusader for robot rights and justice?

He sat quiet and compliant while she expertly unhooked his chest panel and replaced a few chips, unprotesting as he was buttoned up again and his new systems were run against the test board, unresisting while Makeup and Cosmetic Repair restructured his facial appearance. But his mind was racing. Rabble rouser! While he waited for transportation back to the city to take up his new MOS, his expression was calm, but inside he was exulting.

He would do the job well indeed. No rabble needed rousing more than his, and he was just the robot for the job!

PLAYING THE GAME

by Gardner Dozois and Jack Dann

*The question of whether parallel worlds are
science fiction or mere fantasy was once a point
of dispute, but usage and reader acceptance have
made this concept of infinite worlds for infinite
histories an acceptable science fiction premise.
Infinity is an awfully big number and makes finding a needle in a haystack a rather simple propo-
sition.*

The woods that edged the north side of Manningtown belonged to the cemetery, and if you looked westward toward
Endicott, you could see marble mausoleums and expensive
monuments atop the hills. The cemetery took up several acres
of carefully mown hillside and bordered Jefferson Avenue,
where well-kept wood-frame houses faced the rococo painted
headstones of the Italian section.

West of the cemetery there had once been a district of
brownstone buildings and small shops, but for some time now
there had been a shopping mall there instead; east of the

105

cemetery, the row of dormer-windowed old mansions that Jimmy remembered had been replaced by an ugly brick school building and a fenced-in schoolyard where kids never played. The cemetery itself, though—that never changed; it had always been there, exactly the same for as far back as he could remember, and this made the cemetery a pleasant place to Jimmy Daniels, a refuge, a welcome island of stability in a rapidly changing world where change itself was often unpleasant and sometimes menacing.

Jimmy Daniels lived in Old Town most of the time, just down the hill from the cemetery, although sometimes they lived in Passdale or Southside or even Durham. Old Town was a quiet residential neighborhood of whitewashed narrow-fronted houses and steep cobbled streets that were lined with oak and maple trees. Things changed slowly there also, unlike the newer districts downtown, where it seemed that new parking garages or civic buildings popped out of the ground like mushrooms after a rain. Only rarely did a new building appear in Old Town, or an old building vanish. For this reason alone, Jimmy much preferred Old Town to Passdale or Southside, and was always relieved to be living there once again. True, he usually had no friends or school chums in the neighborhood, which consisted mostly of first- and second-generation Poles who worked for the Mannington shoe factories, which had recently begun to fail. Sometimes, when they lived in Old Town, Jimmy got to play with a lame Italian boy who was almost as much of an outcast in the neighborhood as Jimmy was, but the Italian boy had been gone for the last few days, and Jimmy was left alone again. He didn't really mind being alone all that much—most of the time, anyway. He was a solitary boy by nature.

The whole Daniels family tended to be solitary, and usually had little to do with the close-knit, church-centered life of Old Town, although sometimes his mother belonged to the PTA or the Ladies' Auxiliary, and once Jimmy had been amazed to discover that his father had joined the Rotary Club. Jimmy's father usually worked for Weston Computers in Endicott, although Jimmy could remember times, unhappier times, when his father had worked as a CPA in Johnson City or even as a shoe salesman in Vestal. Jimmy's father had always been interested in history, that was another constant in Jimmy's life, and sometimes he did volunteer work for the

Catholic Integration League. He never had much time to spend with Jimmy, wherever they lived, wherever he worked; that was another thing that didn't change. Jimmy's mother usually taught at the elementary school, although sometimes she worked as a typist at home, and other times—the bad times again—she stayed at home and took "medicine" and didn't work at all.

That morning when Jimmy woke up, the first thing he realized was that it was summer, a fact testified to by the brightness of the sunshine and the balminess of the air that came in through the open window, making up for his memory of yesterday, which had been gray and cold and dour. He rolled out of bed, surprised for a moment to find himself on the top tier of a bunk bed, and plumped down to the floor hard enough to make the soles of his feet tingle; at the last few places they had lived, he hadn't a bunk bed, and he wasn't used to waking up that high off the ground. Sometimes he had trouble finding his clothes in the morning, but this time it seemed that he had been conscientious enough to hang them all up the night before, and he came across a blue shirt with a zigzag green stripe that he had not seen in a long time. That seemed like a good omen to him, and cheered him. He put on the blue shirt, then puzzled out the knots he could not remember leaving in his shoelaces. Still blinking sleep out of his eyes, he hunted futilely for his toothbrush; it always took a while for his mind to clear in the mornings, and he could be confused and disoriented until it did, but eventually memories began to seep back in, as they always did, and he sorted through them, trying to keep straight which house this was out of all the ones he had lived in, and where he kept things here.

Of course. But who would ever have thought that he'd keep it in an old coffee can under his desk!

Downstairs, his mother was making French toast, and he stopped in the archway to watch her as she cooked. She was a short, plump, dark-eyed, olive-complexioned woman who wore her oily black hair pulled back in a tight bun. He watched her intently as she fussed over the hot griddle, noticing her quick nervous motions, the irritable way she patted at loose strands of her hair. Her features were tightly drawn, her nose was long and straight and sharp, as though you could cut yourself on it, and she seemed all angles and edges today. Jimmy's father had been sitting sullenly over his third cup of coffee, but as Jimmy hesitated in the archway, he got to his feet and began to get ready for work. He was a thin man with a pale complexion and a shock of wiry red hair, and Jimmy bit his lip in disappointment as he watched him, keeping well back and hoping not to be noticed. He could tell from the insignia on his father's briefcase that his father was working in Endicott today, and those times when his father's job was in Endicott were among the times when both of his parents would be at their most snappish in the morning.

He slipped silently into his chair at the table as his father stalked wordlessly from the room, and his mother served him his French toast, also wordlessly, except for a slight, sullen grunt of acknowledgement. This was going to be a bad day—not as bad as those times when his father worked in Manningtown and his mother took her "medicine," not as bad as some other times that he had no intention of thinking about at all, but unpleasant enough, right on the edge of acceptability. He shouldn't have given in to tiredness and come inside yesterday, he should have kept playing the Game . . . Fortunately, he had no intention of spending much time here today.

Jimmy got through his breakfast with little real difficulty, except that his mother started in on her routine about why didn't he call Tommy Melkonian, why didn't he go swimming or bike riding, he was daydreaming his summer away, it wasn't natural for him to be by himself all the time, he needed friends, it hurt her and made her feel guilty to see him moping around by himself all the time . . . and so on. He made the appropriate noises in response, but he had no intention of calling Tommy Melkonian today, or of letting her call for him. He had only played with Tommy once or twice before, the last time being when they lived over on Clinton Street (Tommy hadn't been around before that), but he didn't even *like* Tommy all that much, and he certainly wasn't going to waste the day on him. Sometimes Jimmy had given in to temptation and wasted whole days playing jacks or kick-the-can with other kids, or going swimming, or flipping baseball cards; sometimes he'd frittered away a week like that without once playing the Game. But in the end he always returned dutifully to playing the Game again, however tired of it all he sometimes became. And the Game had to be played alone.

Yes, he was definitely going to play the Game today; there was certainly no incentive to hang around here; and the Game seemed to be easier to play on fine, warm days anyway, for some reason.

So as soon as he could, Jimmy slipped away. For a moment he confused this place with the house they sometimes lived in on Ash Street, which was very similar in layout and where he had a different secret escape route to the outside, but at last he got his memories straightened out. He snuck into the cellar while his mother was busy elsewhere, and through the back cellar window, under which he had placed a chair so that he could reach the cement overhang and climb out onto the lawn. He cut across the neighbors' yards to Charles Street and then over to Floral Avenue, a steep macadam dead-end road. Beyond was the start of the woods that belonged to the cemetery. Sometimes the mud hills below the woods would be guarded by a mangy black and brown dog that would bark, snarl at him, and chase him. He walked faster, dreading the possibility.

But once in the woods, in the cool brown and green shade of bole and leaf, he knew he was safe, safe from everything, and his pace slowed. The first tombstone appeared, half buried in mulch and stained with green moss, and he patted it fondly, as if it were a dog. He was in the cemetery now, where it had all begun so long ago. Where he had first played the Game.

Moving easily, he climbed up toward the crown of woods, a grassy knoll that poked up above the surrounding trees, the highest point in the cemetery. Even after all he had been through, this was still a magic place for him; never had he feared spooks or ghouls while he was here, even at night, although often as he walked along, as now, he would peer up at the gum-gray sky, through branches that interlocked like the fingers of witches, and pretend that monsters and secret agents and dinosaurs were moving through the woods around him, that the stunted azalea bushes concealed pirates or orcs . . . But these were only small games, mood-setting exercises to prepare him for the playing of the Game itself, and they fell away from him like a shed skin as he came out onto the grassy knoll and the landscape opened up below.

Jimmy stood entranced, feeling the warm hand of the sun on the back of his head, hardly breathing, listening to the chirruping of birds, the scratching of katydids, the long, sighing rush of wind through oak and evergreen. The sky was blue and high and cloudless, and the Susquehanna River gleamed below like a mirror snake, burning silver as it wound through the rolling, hilly country.

Slowly, he began to play the Game. How had it been, that first time that he had played it, inadvertently, not realizing what he was doing, not understanding that he was playing the Game or what Game he was playing until after he had already started playing? How had it been? Had everything looked like this? He decided that the sun had been lower in the sky that day, that the air had been hazier, that there had been a mass of clouds on the eastern horizon, and he flicked through mental pictures of the landscape as if he were rifling through a deck of cards with his thumb, until he found one that seemed to be right. Obediently, the sky grew darker, but the shape and texture of the clouds were not right, and he searched until he found a better match. It had been somewhat colder, and there had been a slight breeze . . .

So far it had been easy, but there were more subtle adjustments to be made. Had there been four smokestacks or five down in Southside? Four, he decided, and took one away. Had that radio tower been on the crest of that particular distant hill? Or on *that* one? Had the bridge over the Susquehanna been nearer or further away? Had that Exxon sign been there, at the corner of Cedar Road? Or had it been an Esso sign? His blue shirt had changed to a brown shirt by now, and he changed it further, to a red pinstriped shirt, trying to remember. Had that ice cream stand been there? He decided that it had not been. His skin was dark again now, although his hair was still too straight . . . Had the cemetery fence been a wrought iron fence or a hurricane fence? Had there been the sound of a factory whistle blowing? The smell of sulphur in the air? Or the smell of pine . . . ?

He worked at it until dark; and then, drained, he came back down the hill again.

The shopping mall was still there, but the school and school-yard had vanished this time, to be replaced by the familiar row of stately, dormer-windowed old mansions. That usually

meant that he was at least close. The house was on Schubert
Street this evening, several blocks over from where it had
been this morning, and it was a two-story, not a three-story
house, closer to his memories of how things had been before
he'd started playing the Game. The car outside the house was
a '78 Volvo—not what he remembered, but closer than the
'73 Buick from this morning. The windshield bore an Endicott parking sticker, and there was some Weston Computer
literature tucked under the eyeshade, all of which meant that
it was probably safe to go in; his father wouldn't be a mur-
derous drunk this particular evening.

Inside the parlor, Jimmy's father looked up from his arm-
chair, where he was reading Fuller's *Decisive Battles of the
Western World*, and winked. "Hi, sport," he said, and Jimmy
replied, "Hi, Dad." At least his father was a black man this
time, as he should be, although he was much fatter than
Jimmy ever remembered him being, and still had this morning's kinky red hair, instead of the kinky black hair he should
have. Jimmy's mother came out of the kitchen, and she was
thin enough now, but much too tall, with a tiny upturned
nose, blue eyes instead of hazel, hair more blond than au-
burn . . .

"Wash up for dinner, Jimmy," his mother said, and Jimmy
turned slowly for the stairs, feeling exhaustion wash through
him like a bitter tide. She wasn't *really* his mother, they
weren't *really* his parents. He had come a lot closer than this
before, lots of other times . . . But always there was some
small detail that was *wrong*, that proved that this particular
probability-world out of the billions of probability-worlds was
not the one he had started from, was not *home*.

Still, he had done much worse than this before, too. At
least this wasn't a world where his father was dead, or an
atomic war had happened, or his mother had cancer or was a
drug addict, or his father was a brutal drunk, or a Nazi, or a
child molester . . . This would do, for the night . . . He
would settle for this, for tonight . . . He was so tired . . .

In the morning, he would start searching again.

Someday, he would find them.

PAWN'S GAMBIT

by Timothy Zahn

*If there is one thing humans should be able to do
well, it is playing board games. But what if we
encounter intelligences out there that also enjoy
this type of intellectual stimulation? It is said that
chess players hate each other, such being the
nature of the contest. Would this also be true of
an interstellar game of a similar type? With
planets as the winner's prize?*

To: *Office of Director Rodau 248700, Alien Research Bu-
reau, Clars*
From: *Office of Director Eftis 379214, Games Studies, Var-
4*
Subject: *30th annual report, submitted 12 Tai 3829*
Date: *4 Mras 3829*
Dear Rodau,
  I know how you hate getting addenda after a report has
been processed, but I hope you will make an exception in this
case. Our most recently discovered race—the Humans—was

mentioned only briefly in our last annual report, but I feel that the data we have since obtained is important enough to bring to your attention right away.

The complete results are given in the enclosed film, but the crux of the problem is a disturbing lack of consistency with standard patterns. In many ways they are unsophisticated, even primitive; most of the subjects reacted with terror and even hysteria when first brought here via Transphere. And yet, unlike most primitives, there is a mental and emotional resilience to the species which frankly surprises me. Nearly all of them recovered from their fear and went on to play the Stage-I game against their fellows. And the imagination, skill, and sheer aggressiveness used in the playing have been inordinately high for such a young species, prompting more than one off-the-record comparison between Humans and the Chanis. I suppose it's that, more than anything else, that made me unwilling to let this date ride until our next report. Confined as they are to their home planet, the Humans are certainly no threat now; but if they prove to be even a twelfth as dangerous as the Chanis they will need to be dealt with swiftly.

Accordingly, I am asking permission to take the extraordinary step of moving immediately to Phase III (the complete proposal is attached to my report). I know this is generally forbidden with non-spacing races, but I feel it is vital that we test Humans against races of established ability. Please give me a decision on this as soon as possible.

Regards,
Eftis

To: *Office of Director Eftis 379214, Game Studies, Var-4*
From: *Office of Director Rodau 248700, A.R.B., Clars*
Subject: *Addendum to 30th annual report*
Date: *34 Forma 3829*
Dear Eftis,

Thank you for your recent addenda. You were quite right to bring these Humans to our attention; that is, after all, what you're out there for.

I find myself, as do you, both interested and alarmed by this race, and I agree totally with your proposal to initiate Phase III. As usual, the authorization tapes will be a few more weeks in coming, but—unofficially—I'm giving you the go-ahead to start your preparations. I also agree with your suggestion that a star-going race be pitted against your Human: an Olyt or Fiwalic, perhaps. I see by your reports that the Olyts are beginning to resent our testing, but don't let that bother you; your results clearly show they are no threat to us.

Do keep us informed, especially if you uncover more evidence of Chani-like qualities in these aliens.

Sincerely,
Rodau

The glowing, impenetrable sphere of white mist that had surrounded him for the last five minutes dissolved as suddenly as it had formed, and Kelly McClain found himself in a room he had never seen in his life.

Slowly, carefully, he looked around him, heart pounding painfully in his ears. He'd screamed most of the panic out of his system within the first three minutes of his imprisonment, but he could feel the terror welling up into his throat again. He forced it down as best he could. He was clearly no longer in his office at the university's reactor lab, but losing his head wasn't going to get him back again.

He was sitting in a semicircular alcove facing into a small room, his chair and about three-quarters of his desk having made the trip with him. The room's walls, ceiling, and floor were made of a bronze-colored metal and were devoid of any ornamentation. At the right and left ends of the room he could see panels that looked like sliding doors.

There didn't seem to be a lot to be gained by sitting quietly and hoping everything out there would go away. His legs felt like they might be ready to hold him up again, so he stood up and squeezed his way through the six-inch gap between his desk and the alcove wall. The desk, he noted, had been sheared smoothly, presumably by the white mist or something in it. He went first to the panel in the right-hand wall; but if it *was*, in fact, a door, he could find no way to open it. The left-hand panel yielded identical results. "Hello?" he called tentatively into the air around him. "Can anyone hear me?"

The flat voice came back at him so suddenly it made him jump. "Good day to you, Human," it said. "Welcome to the Stryfkar Game Studies Center on Var-4. I trust you suffered no ill effects from your journey?"

A *game* studies center?

Memories flashed across Kelly's mind, bits of articles he'd seen in various magazines and tabloids over the past few months telling of people kidnapped to a game center by extraterrestrial beings. He'd skimmed some of them for amusement, and had noted the similarity between the stories: humans taken two at a time and made to play a strange board game against one another before being sent home. Typical tabloid tripe, Kelly had thought at the time.

Which made this an elaborate practical joke, obviously.

So how had they made that white mist?

For the moment, it seemed best to play along. "Oh, the trip was fine. A little boring, though."

"You have adjusted to your situation very quickly," the voice said, and Kelly thought he could detect a touch of surprise in it. "My name is Slaich; what is yours?"

"Kelly McClain. You speak English pretty well for an alien—what kind are you, again?"

"I am a Stryf. Our computer-translator is very efficient, and we have had data from several of your fellow Humans."

"Yes, I've heard about them. How come you drag them all the way out here—wherever *here* is—just to play games? Or is it a state secret?"

"Not really. We wish to learn about your race. Games are one of the psychological tools we use."

"Why can't you just talk to us? Or, better still, why not drop in for a visit?" Much as he still wanted to believe this was a practical joke, Kelly was finding that theory harder and harder to support. That voice—like no computer speech he'd ever heard, but nothing like a human voice, either—had an uncomfortable ring of casual truth to it. He could feel sweat gathering on his forehead.

"Talking is inefficient for the factors we wish to study," Slaich explained offhandedly. "As to visiting Earth, the Transphere has only limited capacity and we have no long-range ships at our disposal. I would not like to go to Earth alone."

"Why not?" The tension had risen within Kelly to the breaking point, generating a reckless courage. "You can't look *that* bad. Show yourself to me—*right now*."

There was no hesitation. "Very well," the voice said, and a section of the shiny wall in front of Kelly faded to black.

Abruptly, a three-dimensional image appeared in front of it—an image of a two-legged, two-armed nightmare. Kelly gasped, head spinning, as the misshapen head turned to face him. An x-shaped opening began to move. "What do you think, Kelly? Would I pass as a Human?"

"I—I—I—" Kelly was stuttering, but he couldn't help it; all his strength was going to control his suddenly rebellious stomach. The creature before him was *real*—no make-up job in the world could turn a man into *that*. And multicolor holo-gram movies of such size and clarity were years or decades away . . . on Earth.

"I am sorry; I seem to have startled you," Slaich said, reaching for a small control panel Kelly hadn't noticed. The muscles moved visibly under his six-fingered hand as he touched a button. The image vanished and the wall regained its color. "Perhaps you would like to rest and eat," the flat voice went on. The door at Kelly's left slid open, revealing a furnished room about the size of an efficiency apartment. "It will be several hours before we will be ready to begin. You will be called."

Kelly nodded, not trusting his voice, and walked into the room. The door closed behind him. A normal-looking bed sat next to the wall halfway across the room, and Kelly managed to get there before his knees gave out.

He lay face-downward for a long time, his whole body trembling as he cried silently into his pillow. The emotional outburst was embarrassing—he'd always tried to be the strong, unflappable type—but efforts to choke off the display only made it worse. Eventually, he gave up and let it run its course.

By and by, the sobs stopped coming and he found himself more or less rational once more. Rolling onto his side, uncon-sciously curling into a fetal position, he stared at the bronze wall and tried to think.

For the moment, at least, he seemed to be in no immediate physical danger. From what he remembered of the tabloid ar-ticles, the aliens here seemed truly intent on simply doing their psychological study and then sending the participants home. Everything they'd done so far could certainly be seen in that light; no doubt they had monitored his reactions to both their words and Slaich's abrupt appearance. He shud-dered at the memory of that alien face, feeling a touch of an-

ger. Psychological test or not, he wasn't going to forgive
Slaich very quickly for not giving him some kind of warning
before showing himself like that.

The important thing, then, was for him to stay calm and
be a good little test subject so he could get home with a mini-
mum of trouble. And if he could do it with a little dignity, so
much the better.

He didn't realize he'd dozed off until a soft tone startled
him awake. "Yes?"

"It is time," the computerized voice told him. "Please leave
your rest chamber and proceed to the test chamber."

Kelly sat up, glancing around him. The room's only door
was the one he'd entered by; the test chamber must be out
the other door of the room with the alcove. "Where's the
other player from?" he asked, swinging his feet onto the floor
and heading for the exit. "Or do you just snatch people from
Earth at random?"

"We generally set the Transphere to take from the vicinity
of concentrated energy sources, preferably fission or fusion
reactors when such exist," Slaich said. "However, you have
made one false assumption. Your opponent is not a Human."

Kelly's feet froze halfway through the door, and he had to
grab the jamb to keep his balance. This was a new twist. "I
see. Thanks for the warning, anyway. Uh . . . what *is* he?"

"An Olyt. His race is somewhat more advanced than
yours; the Olyts have already built an empire of eight planets
in seven stellar systems. They have been studied extensively
by us, though their closest world is nearly thirty light-years
from here."

Kelly forced his legs to start walking again. "Does that
make us neighbors? You never said how far Earth is from
here."

"You are approximately forty-eight light-years from here
and thirty-six from the Olyt home world. Not very far, as distances go."

The door on the far side of the room opened as Kelly approached. Getting a firm grip on his nerves, he stepped
through.

The game room was small and relatively dark, the only illumination coming from a set of dimly glowing red panels. In
the center of the room, and taking up a good deal of its floor
space, was a complex-looking gameboard on a table. Two

chairs—one strangely contoured—completed the furnishings. Across the room was another door, and standing in front of it was an alien.

Kelly was better prepared for the shock this time, and as he stepped toward the table he found his predominant feeling was curiosity. The Olyt was half a head shorter than he, his slender body covered by what looked like large white scales. He was bipedal with two arms, each of his limbs ending in four clawed digits. His snout was long and seemed to have lots of teeth; his eyes were black and set back in a beetle-browed skull. Picture a tailless albino alligator wearing a wide sporran, Sam Browne belt, and a beret. . . .

Kelly and the Olyt reached their respective sides of the game table at about the same time. The board was smaller than it had first looked; the alien was little more than a double arm-length away. Carefully, Kelly raised his open hand, hoping the gesture would be properly interpreted. "Hello. I'm Kelly McClain; human."

The alien didn't flinch or dive down Kelly's throat. He extended both arms, crossed at the wrists, and Kelly discovered the claws were retractable. His mouth moved, generating strange noises; seconds later the computer's translation came over an invisible speaker. "I greet you. I am Tlaymasy of the Olyt race."

"Please sit down," Slaich's disembodied voice instructed. "You may begin when you have decided on the rules."

Kelly blinked. "How's that?"

"This game has no fixed rules. You must decide between you as to the objective and method of play before you begin."

Tlaymasy was speaking again. "What is the purpose of this?"

"The purpose is to study an interaction between Olyt and Human," Slaich said. "Surely you have heard of this experiment from others of your race."

Kelly frowned across the table. "You've been through this before?"

"Over one hundred twenty-eight members of my race have been temporarily taken over the last sixteen years," the Olyt said. Kelly wished he could read the alien's expression. The computer's tone was neutral, but the words themselves sounded a little resentful. "Some have spoken of this game with no rules. However, my question referred to the stakes."

"Oh. They are as usual for this study: the winner is allowed to return home."

Kelly's heart skipped a beat. "*Wait* a minute. Where did *that* rule come from?"

"The rules and stakes are chosen by us," Slaich said flatly.

"Yes, but . . . What happens to the loser?"

"He remains to play against a new opponent."

"What if I refuse to play at all?"

"That is equivalent to losing."

Kelly snorted, but there wasn't much he could do about it. *With dignity*, he thought dryly, and began to study the game board.

It looked like it had been designed to handle at least a dozen widely differing games. It was square, with two five-color bands of squares running along its edge; one with a repeating pattern, the other apparently random. Inside this was a checkerboard-type design with sets of concentric circles and radial lines superimposed on it. To one side of the board itself sat a stack of transparent plates, similarly marked, and a set of supporting legs for them; to the other side were various sizes, shapes, and colors of playing pieces, plus cards, multisided dice, and a gadget with a small display screen. "Looks like we're well equipped," he remarked to the Olyt, who seemed also to be studying their equipment. "I guess we could start by choosing which set of spaces to use. I suggest the red and—is that color blue?—the square ones." He indicated the checkerboard.

"Very well," Tlaymasy said. "Now we must decide on a game. Are you familiar with *Four-Ply*?"

"I doubt it, but my people may have something similar. Describe the rules."

Tlaymasy proceeded to do so. It sounded a little like go, but with the added feature of limited mobility for the pieces once on the board. "Sounds like something I'd have a shot at," Kelly said after the alien had demonstrated some of the moves with a butterfly-shaped playing piece. "Of course, you've got a big advantage, since you've played it before. I'll go along on two conditions: first, that a third-level or fourth-level attack must be announced one move before the attack is actually launched."

"That eliminates the possibility of surprise attacks," Tlaymasy objected.

"Exactly. Come on, now, you know the game well enough to let me have that, don't you?"

"Very well. Your second condition?"

"That we play a practice game first. In other words, the *second* game we play will determine who gets to go home. Is that permissible?" he added, looking up at one of the room's corners.

"Whatever is decided between you is binding," Slaich replied.

Kelly cocked an eyebrow at his opponent. "Tlaymasy?"

"Very well. Let us begin."

It wasn't such a hard game to learn, Kelly decided, though he got off to a bad start and spent most of their practice game on the defensive. The strategy Tlaymasy was using was not hard to pick up, and by the time they finished he found he could often anticipate the Olyt's next move.

"An interesting game," Kelly commented as they retrieved their playing pieces from the board and prepared to play again. "Is it popular on your world?"

"Somewhat. The ancients used it for training in logic. Are you ready to begin?"

"I guess so," Kelly said. His mouth felt dry.

This time Kelly avoided the errors he'd made at the beginning of the practice game, and as the board filled up with pieces he found himself in a position nearly as strong as Tlaymasy's. Hunching over the board, agonizing over each move, he fought to maintain his strength.

And then Tlaymasy made a major mistake, exposing an arm of his force to a twin attack. Kelly pounced; and when the dust of the next four moves settled he had taken six of his opponent's pieces—a devastating blow.

A sudden, loud hiss made Kelly jump. He looked up, triumphant grin vanishing. The Olyt was staring at him, mouth open just enough to show rows of sharp teeth. Both hands were on the table, and Kelly could see the claws sliding in and out of their sheaths. "Uh . . . anything wrong?" he asked cautiously, muscles tensing for emergency action.

For a moment there was silence. Then Tlaymasy closed his mouth and his claws retracted completely. "I was upset by the stupidity of my play. It has passed. Let us continue."

Kelly nodded and returned his gaze to the board, but in a far more subdued state of mind. In the heat of the game, he had almost forgotten he was playing for a ticket home. Now, suddenly, it looked as if he might be playing for his life as well. Tlaymasy's outburst had carried a not-so-subtle message: the Olyt did not intend to accept defeat graciously.

The play continued. Kelly did the best he could, but his concentration was shot all to hell. Within ten moves Tlaymasy had made up his earlier loss. Kelly sneaked glances at the alien as they played, wondering if that had been Tlaymasy's plan all along. Surely he wouldn't physically attack Kelly while he himself was a prisoner on an unknown world . . . would he? Suppose, for example, that honor was more important to him than even his own life, and that honor precluded losing to an alien?

A trickle of sweat ran down the middle of Kelly's back. He had no evidence that Tlaymasy thought that way . . . but on the other hand he couldn't come up with any reasons why it shouldn't be possible. And that reaction had looked *very* unfriendly.

The decision was not difficult. Discretion being the better part and all that—and a few extra days here wouldn't hurt him. Deliberately, he launched a bold assault against Tlaymasy's forces, an attack which would require dumb luck to succeed.

Dumb luck, as usual, wasn't with him. Seven moves later, Tlaymasy had won.

"The game is over," Slaich's voice boomed. "Tlaymasy, return to your Transphere chamber and prepare to leave. Kelly McClain, return to your rest chamber."

The Olyt stood and again gave Kelly his crossed-wrists salute before turning and disappearing through his sliding door. Kelly sighed with relief and emotional fatigue and headed back toward his room. "You played well for a learner," Slaich's voice followed him.

"Thanks," Kelly grunted. Now, with Tlaymasy's teeth and claws no longer a few feet in front of him, he was starting to wonder if maybe he shouldn't have thrown the game. "When do I play next?"

"In approximately twenty hours. The Transphere must be reset after the Olyt is returned to his world."

Kelly had been about to step into his rest chamber.

"Twenty hours?" he echoed, stopping. "Just a second." He turned toward the alcove where his desk was sitting—but had barely taken two steps when a flash of red light burst in front of him. "Hey!" he yelped, jumping backwards as heat from the blast washed over him. "What was *that* for?"

"You may not approach the Transphere apparatus." Slaich's voice had abruptly taken on a whiplash bite.

"Nuts! If I'm being left to twiddle my thumbs for a day I want the books that are in my desk."

There was a momentary silence, and when Slaich spoke again his tone had moderated. "I see. I suppose that is all right. You may proceed."

Kelly snorted and walked forward warily. No more bursts of light came. Squeezing around to the front of his desk, he opened the bottom drawer and extracted three paperbacks, normally kept there for idle moments. From another drawer came a half-dozen journals that he'd been meaning to read; and finally, as an afterthought, he scooped up a couple of pens and a yellow legal pad. Stepping back to the center of the room, he held out his booty. "See? Perfectly harmless. Not a single neutron bomb in the lot."

"Return to your rest chamber." Slaich did not sound amused.

With the concentration needed during the game, Kelly had temporarily forgotten he'd missed both lunch and dinner. Now, though, his growling stomach was demanding attention. Following Slaich's instructions, he requested and obtained a meal from the automat-type slots in one wall of his cubicle. The food was bland but comfortably filling, and Kelly felt his spirits rising as he ate. Afterwards, he chose one of his paperbacks and stretched out on the bed. But instead of immediately beginning to read, he stared at the ceiling and thought.

Obviously, there could be no further question that what was happening to him was real. Similarly, there was no reasonable hope that he could escape his captors. There were no apparent exits from the small complex of rooms except via the Transphere, whose machinery was hidden behind metal walls and was probably incomprehensible anyway. He had only Slaich's word that the Stryfkar intended to send him home, but since they apparently had made—and kept—similar promises to other humans, he had no real reason to doubt them. True, the game rules this time seemed to be different, but Tlaymasy had implied the Stryfkar had pulled this on several of his own race and had released them on schedule. So the big question, then, was whether or not Kelly could win the next game he would have to play.

He frowned. He'd never been any great shakes as a games player, winning frequently at chess but only occasionally at the other games in his limited repertoire. And yet, he'd come surprisingly close today to beating an alien in his own game. An alien, be it noted, whose race held an empire of eight worlds. The near-victory could be meaningless, of course— Tlaymasy might have been the equivalent of a fourth-grader playing chess, for instance. But the Olyt would have had to be a complete idiot to suggest a game he wasn't good at. And there was also Slaich's reaction after the game; it was pretty clear the Stryf hadn't expected Kelly to do that well. Did that mean that Kelly, average strategist that he was, was still better than the run-of-the-mill alien?

If that was true, his problems were essentially over. Whoever his next opponent was, it should be relatively easy to beat him, especially if they picked a game neither player had had much experience with. Four-Ply might be a good choice if the new testee wasn't another Olyt; the game was an interesting one and easy enough to learn, at least superficially. As a matter of fact, it might be worth his while to try marketing it when he got home. The game market was booming these days, and while Four-Ply wasn't likely to make him rich, it could conceivably bring in a little pocket change.

On the other hand . . . what was his hurry?—

Kelly squirmed slightly on the bed as a rather audacious idea struck him. If he really *was* better than most other aliens, then it followed that he could go home most any time he wanted, simply by winning whichever game he was on at the moment. And if *that* were true, why not stick around for another week or so and learn a few more alien games?

The more he thought about it, the more he liked the idea. True, there was an element of risk involved, but that was true of any money-making scheme. And it couldn't be *that* risky—this was a *psychology* experiment, for crying out loud! "Slaich?" he called at the metallic ceiling.

"Yes?"

"If I lose my next game, what happens?"

"You will remain here until you have won or until the test is over."

So it didn't sound like he got punished or anything if he kept losing. The Stryfkar had set up a pretty simple-minded experiment here, to his way of thinking. Human psychologists would probably have put together something more complicated. Did that imply humans were better strategists than even the Stryfkar?

An interesting question, but for the moment Kelly didn't care. He'd found a tiny bit of maneuvering space in the controlled environment they'd set up, and it felt very satisfying. Rules like these, in his book, were made to be bent.

And speaking of rules . . . Putting aside his paperback, Kelly rolled off the bed and went over to the cubicle's folding tables. Business before pleasure, he told himself firmly. Picking up a pen and his legal pad, he began to sketch the Four-Ply playing board and to list the game's rules.

To: *Office of Director Rodau 248700, A.R.B., Clars*
From: *Office of Director Eftis 379214, Game Studies, Var-4*
Subject: *Studies of Humans*
Date: *3 Lysmo 3829*
Dear Rodau,

The Human problem is taking on some frightening aspects, and we are increasingly convinced that we have stumbled upon another race of Chanis. Details will be transmitted when all analyses are complete, but I wanted to send you this note first to give you as much time as possible to recommend an assault force, should you deem this necessary.

As authorized, we initiated a Phase III study eight days ago. Our Human has played games against members of four races: an Olyt, a Fiwalic, a Spromsa, and a Thim-fra-chee. In each case the game agreed upon has been one from the non-Human player's world, with slight modifications suggested by the Human. As would be expected, the Human has consistently lost—but in each case he has clearly been winning until the last few moves. Our contact specialist, Slaich 898661, suggested early on that the Human might be *deliberately* losing; but with both his honor and his freedom at stake Slaich could offer no motive for such behavior. However, in a conversation of 1 Lysmo (tape enclosed) the Human freely confirmed our suspicions and indicated the motive was material gain. He is using the testing sessions to study his opponents' games, expecting to introduce them for profit on returning to his world.

I'm sure you will notice the similarities to Chani psychology: the desire for profit, even at the casual risk of his safety, and the implicit belief that his skills are adequate to bring release whenever he wishes. History shows us that, along with their basic tactical skills, it was just these characteristics that drove the Chanis in their most unlikely conquests. It must also be emphasized that the Human shows no signs of military or other tactical training and must therefore be considered representative of his race.

Unless further study uncovers flaws in their character which would preclude an eventual Chani-like expansion, I personally feel we must consider annihilation for this race as soon as possible. Since we obviously need to discover the race's full strategic capabilities—and since our subject refuses to cooperate—we are being forced to provide a stronger incentive. The results should be enlightening, and will be sent as soon as they are available.

Regards,
Eftis

The door slid back and Kelly stepped into the test chamber, looking across the room eagerly to see what sort of creature he'd be competing against this time. The dim red lights were back on in the room, indicating someone from a world with a red sun, and as Kelly's eyes adjusted to the relative darkness he saw another of the alligator-like Olyts approaching the table. "I greet you," Kelly said, making the crossed-wrist gesture he'd seen at his first game here. "I am Kelly McClain of the human race."

The Olyt repeated the salute. "I am *ulur* Achranae of the Olyt race."

"Pleased to meet you. What does *ulur* mean?"

"It is a title of respect for my position. I command a warforce of seven spacecraft."

Kelly swallowed. A trained military man. Good thing he wasn't in a hurry to win and go home. "Interesting. Well, shall we begin?"

Achranae sat down. "Let us make an end to this charade quickly."

"What do you mean, 'charade'?" Kelly asked cautiously as he took his seat. He was by no means an expert on Olyt expressions and emotions, but he could swear this one was angry.

"Do not deny your part," the alien snapped. "I recognize your name from the report, and know how you played this game for the Stryfkar against another of my people, studying him like a laboratory specimen before allowing him to win and depart. We do not appreciate the way you take our people like this—"

"Whoa! Wait a second; I'm not with them. They've been taking *my* people, too. It's some sort of psychology experiment, I guess."

The Olyt glared at him in silence for a long moment. "If you truly believe that, you are a fool," he said at last, sounding calmer. "Very well; let us begin."

"Before you do so we must inform you of an important change in the rules." Slaich's voice cut in. "You shall play *three* different games, instead of one, agreeing on the rules before beginning each. The one who wins two or more shall be returned home. The other will lose his life."

It took a second for that to sink in. *"What?"* Kelly yelped. "You can't do that!" Across the table Achranae gave a soft, untranslatable hiss. His claws, fully extended, scratched lightly on the game board.

"It is done," Slaich said flatly. "You will proceed now."

Kelly shot a frustrated glance at Achranae, looked again. "We will not play for our lives. That sort of thing is barbarous, and we are both civilized beings."

"Civilized." Slaich's voice was thick with sudden contempt. "You, who can barely send craft outside your own atmosphere; you consider yourself *civilized?* And your opponent is little better."

"We govern a sphere fifteen light-years across," Achranae reminded Slaich calmly, his outburst of temper apparently over. For all their short fuses, Kelly decided, Olyts didn't seem to stay mad long.

"Your eight worlds are nothing against our forty."

"It is said the Chanis had only five when they challenged you."

The silence from the speaker was impressively ominous. "What are the Chanis?" Kelly asked, fighting the urge to whisper.

"It is rumored they were a numerically small but brutally aggressive race who nearly conquered the Stryfkar many generations ago. We have heard these stories from traders, but do not know how true they are."

"True or not, you sure hit a nerve," Kelly commented. "How about it, Slaich? Is he right?"

"You will proceed now," Slaich ordered, ignoring Kelly's question.

Kelly glanced at Achranae, wishing he could read the other's face. Did Olyts understand the art of bluffing? "I said we wouldn't play for our lives."

In answer a well-remembered flash of red light exploded inches from his face. Instinctively, he pushed hard on the table, toppling himself and his chair backwards. He hit hard enough to see stars, somersaulted out of the chair, and wound up lying on his stomach on the floor. Raising his head cautiously, he saw the red fireball wink out and, after a moment, got warily to his feet. Achranae, he noted, was also several feet back from the table, crouching in what Kelly decided was probably a fighting stance of some kind.

"If you do not play, both of you will lose your lives." Slaich's voice was mild, almost emotionless, but it sent a shiver down Kelly's spine. Achranae had been right: this was no simple psychology experiment. The Stryfkar were searching for potential enemies—and somehow both humans and Olyts had made it onto their list. And there was *still* no way to escape. Looking across at Achranae, Kelly shrugged helplessly. "Doesn't look like we have much choice, does it?"

The Olyt straightened up slowly. "For the moment, no."

"Since this contest is so important to both of us," Kelly said when they were seated again, "I suggest that you choose the first game, allowing me to offer changes that will take away some of your advantage—changes we both have to agree on, of course. I'll choose the second game; you'll suggest changes on that one."

"That seems honorable. And the third?"

"I don't know. Let's discuss that one when we get there, okay?"

It took nearly an hour for the first game, plus amendments,

to be agreed upon. Achranae used three of the extra transparencies and their supports to create a three-dimensional playing area; the game itself was a sort of 3-D "Battleship," but with elements of chess, Monopoly, and even poker mixed in. Surprisingly enough, the mixture worked, and if the stakes hadn't been so high Kelly thought he would have enjoyed playing it. His own contributions to the rules were a slight adjustment to the shape of the playing region—which Kelly guessed would change the usual positional strategies—and the introduction of a "wild card" concept to the play. "I also suggest a practice game before we play for keeps," he told Achranae.

The Olyt's dark eyes bored into his. "Why?"

"Why not? I've never played this before, and you've never played with these rules. It would make the actual game fairer. More honorable. We'll do the same with the second and third games."

"Ah—it is a point of honor?" The alien cocked his head to the right. A nod? "Very well. Let us begin."

Even with the changes, the game—Skymarch, Achranae called it—was still very much an Olyt one, and Achranae won the practice game handily. Kelly strongly suspected Skymarch was a required course of the aliens' space academy; it looked too much like space warfare to be anything else.

"Did the Stryf speak the truth when he said you were not starfarers?" Achranae asked as they set up the board again.

"Hm? Oh, yes," Kelly replied distractedly, his mind on strategy for the coming game. "We've hardly even got simple spacecraft yet."

"Surprising, since you learn space warfare tactics so quickly." He waved his sheathed claws over the board. "A pity, too, since you will not be able to resist if the Stryfkar decide to destroy you."

"I suppose not, but why would they want to? We can't be any threat to them."

Again Achranae indicated the playing board. "If you are representative, your race is unusually gifted with both tactical skill and aggressiveness. Such abilities would make you valuable allies or dangerous adversaries to any starfaring race."

Kelly shrugged. "You'd think they'd try to recruit us, then."

"Unlikely. The Stryfkar are reputed to be a proud race who have little use for allies. This harassment of both our peoples should indicate their attitude toward other races."

The Olyt seemed to be on the verge of getting angry again, Kelly noted uneasily. A change in subject seemed in order. "Uh, yes. Shall we begin our game?"

Achranae let out a long hiss. "Very well."

From the very beginning it was no contest. Kelly did his best, but it was clear that the Olyt was able to *think* three-dimensionally better than he could. Several times he lost a piece simply because he missed some perfectly obvious move it could have made. Sweating, he tried to make himself slow down, to spend more time on each move. But it did no good. Inexorably, Achranae tightened the noose; and, too quickly, it was all over.

Kelly leaned back in his chair, expelling a long breath. It was all right, he told himself—he had to expect to lose a game where the alien had all the advantages. The next game would be different, though; Kelly would be on his own turf, with *his* choice of weapons—

"Have you chosen the game we shall play next?" Achranae asked, interrupting Kelly's thoughts.

"Idle down, will you?" Kelly snapped, glaring at the alien. "Give me a minute to think."

It wasn't an easy question. Chess was far and away Kelly's best game, but Achranae had already showed himself a skilled strategist, at least with warfare-type games. That probably made chess a somewhat risky bet. Card games involved too much in the way of chance; for this second game Kelly needed as much advantage as he could get. Word games like Scrabble were obviously out. Checkers or Dots were too simple. Backgammon? That was a pretty nonmilitary game, but Kelly was a virtual novice at it himself. How about—

How about a *physical* game?

"Slaich? Could I get some extra equipment in here? I'd like a longer table, a couple of paddles, a sort of light, bouncy ball—"

"Games requiring specific physical talents are by their nature unfair for such a competition as this," Slaich said. "They are not permitted."

"I do not object," Achranae spoke up unexpectedly, and Kelly looked at him in surprise. "You stated we could choose the games and the rules, and it is Kelly McClain's choice this time."

"We are concerned with psychological studies," Slaich said. "We are not interested in the relative abilities of your joints and muscles. You will choose a game that can be played with the equipment provided."

"It is dishonorable—"

"No, it's okay, Achranae," Kelly interrupted, ashamed at himself for even suggesting such a thing. "Slaich is right; it would've been completely unfair. It was dishonorable for me to suggest it. Please accept my apology."

"You are blameless," the Olyt said. "The dishonor is in those who brought us here."

"Yes," Kelly agreed, glancing balefully at the ceiling. The point was well taken. Achranae wasn't Kelly's enemy; merely his opponent. The Stryfkar were the real enemy.

For all the good that knowledge did him.

He cleared his throat. "Okay, Achranae, I guess I'm ready. This game's called *chess*. . . ."

The Olyt picked up the rules and movements quickly, enough so that Kelly wondered if the aliens had a similar game on their own world. Fortunately, the knight's move seemed to be a new one on him, and Kelly hoped it would offset the other's tactical training. As his contribution, Achranae suggested the pawns be allowed to move backwards as well as forwards. Kelly agreed, and they settled into their practice game.

It was far harder than Kelly had expected. The "reversible pawn" rule caused him tremendous trouble, mainly because his logic center kept editing it out of his strategy. Within fifteen moves he'd lost both bishops and one of his precious knights, and Achranae's queen was breathing down his neck.

"An interesting game," the Olyt commented a few moves later, after Kelly had managed to get out from under a powerful attack. "Have you had training in its technique?"

"Not really," Kelly said, glad to take a breather. "I just play for enjoyment with my friends. Why?"

"The test of skill at a game is the ability to escape what appears to be certain defeat. By that criterion you have a great deal of skill."

Kelly shrugged. "Just native ability, I guess."

"Interesting. On my world such skills must be learned over

a long period of time." Achranae indicated the board. "We have a game similar in some ways to this one; if I had not studied it I would have lost to you within a few moves."

"Yeah," Kelly muttered. He'd been pretty sure Achranae wasn't running on beginner's luck, but he'd sort of hoped he was wrong. "Let's get back to the game, huh?"

In the end Kelly won, but only because Achranae lost his queen to Kelly's remaining knight and Kelly managed to take advantage of the error without any major goofs of his own.

"Are you ready to begin the actual game?" Achranae asked when the board had been cleared.

Kelly nodded, feeling a tightness in his throat. This was for all the marbles. "I suppose so. Let's get it over with."

Using one of the multifaced dice they determined the Olyt would have the white pieces. Achranae opened with his king's pawn, and Kelly responded with something he dimly remembered being called a Sicilian defense. Both played cautiously and defensively; only two pawns were taken in the first twenty moves. Sweating even in the air-conditioned room, Kelly watched his opponent gradually bring his pieces into attacking positions as he himself set his defense as best he could.

When the assault came it was devastating in its slaughter. By the time the captures and recaptures were done, eight more pieces were gone . . . and Kelly was a rook down.

Brushing a strand of hair out of his eyes with a trembling hand, Kelly swallowed hard as he studied the board. Without a doubt, he was in trouble. Achranae controlled the center of the board now and his king was better defended than Kelly's. Worse yet, he seemed to have mastered the knight's move, while Kelly was still having trouble with his pawns. And if the Olyt won this one . . .

"Are you distressed?"

Kelly started, looked up at his opponent. "Just a—" His voice cracked and he tried again. "Just nervous."

"Perhaps we should cease play for a time, until you are better able to concentrate," Achranae suggested.

The last thing Kelly wanted at the moment was the alien's charity. "I'm all right," he said irritably.

Achranae's eyes were unblinking. "In that case, I would like to take a few minutes of rest myself. Is this permissible?"

Kelly stared back as understanding slowly came. Clearly,

Achranae didn't need a break; he was a game and a half toward going home. Besides which, Kelly *knew* what an upset Olyt looked like, and Achranae showed none of the symptoms. No, giving Kelly the chance to calm down could only benefit the human . . . and as he gazed at the alien's face, Kelly knew the Olyt was perfectly aware of that.

"Yes," Kelly said at last. "Let's take a break. How about returning in a half hour or so?"

"Acceptable." Achranae stood and crossed his wrists. "I shall be ready whenever you also are."

The ceiling over Kelly's bed was perfectly flat, without even so much as a ripple to mar it. Nonetheless, it reflected images far more poorly than Kelly would have expected. He wondered about it, but not very hard. There were more important things to worry about.

Pulling his left arm from behind his head, he checked the time. Five more minutes and Slaich would sound the little bell that would call them back to the arena. Kelly sighed.

What was he going to *do?*

Strangely enough, the chess game was no longer his major concern. True, he was still in trouble there, but the rest period had done wonders for his composure, and he had already come up with two or three promising lines of attack. As long as he kept his wits around him, he had a fair chance of pulling a win out of his current position. And that was Kelly's real problem . . . because if he did, in fact, win, there would have to be a third game. A game either he or Achranae would have to lose.

Kelly didn't want to die. He had lots of high-sounding reasons why he ought to stay alive—at least one of which, the fact that no one else on Earth knew of the threat lurking behind these "games," was actually valid—but the plain fact was that he simply didn't *want* to die. Whatever the third game was chosen to be, he knew he would play just as hard and as well as he possibly could.

And yet . . .

Kelly squirmed uncomfortably. Achranae didn't deserve to die, either. Not only was he also an unwilling participant in this crazy arena, but he had deliberately thrown away his best chance to win the contest. Perhaps it was less a spirit of fairness than one of obedience to a rigid code of honor that had kept him from capitalizing on his opponent's momentary panic; Kelly would probably never know one way or the other. But it really didn't matter. If Kelly went on to win the chess game he would owe his victory to Achranae.

The third game . . .

What would be the fairest way to do it? Invent a game together that neither had played before? That would pit Kelly's natural tactical abilities against Achranae's trained ones and would probably be pretty fair. On the other hand, it would give the Stryfkar another chance to study them in action, and Kelly was in no mood to cooperate with his captors any more than necessary. Achranae, Kelly had already decided, seemed to feel the same way. He wondered fleetingly how long the Stryfkar had been snatching Achranae's people, and why they hadn't retaliated. Probably had no idea where this game studies center was, he decided; the Transphere's operations would, by design, be difficult to trace. But if he and Achranae didn't want to give the Stryfkar any more data, their only alternative was to make the rubber game one of pure chance, and Kelly rebelled against staking his life on the toss of a coin.

The tone, expected though it was, startled him. "It is time," Slaich's flat voice announced. "You will return to the test chamber."

Grimacing, Kelly got to his feet and headed for the door. Maybe Achranae would have some ideas.

"Are you better prepared to play now?" the Olyt asked when they again faced each other over the board.

"Yes," Kelly nodded. "Thanks for suggesting a break. I really *did* need it."

"I sensed that your honor did not permit you to make the request." The alien gestured at the board. "I believe it is your move."

Sure enough, now that his nerves were under control, Kelly began to chip away at Achranae's position, gradually making up his losses and taking the offensive once more. Gambling on the excessive value the Olyt seemed to place in his queen, Kelly laid a trap, with his own queen as the bait. Achranae bit . . . and five moves later Kelly had won.

"Excellent play," the Olyt said, with what Kelly took to be admiration. "I was completely unprepared for that attack. I was not wrong; you have an uncanny tactical ability. Your race will indeed be glorious starfarers someday."

"Assuming we ever get off our own world, of course," Kelly said as he cleared the board. "At the moment we're more like pawns ourselves in this game."

"You have each won once," Slaich spoke up. "It is time now to choose the rules for the final game."

Kelly swallowed and looked up to find Achranae looking back at him. "Any ideas?" he asked.

"None that is useful. A game of chance would perhaps be fairest. Beyond that, I have not determined what my duty requires."

"What are the possibilities?"

"That I should survive in order to return to my people, or that I should not, to allow you that privilege."

"A pity we can't individually challenge the Stryfkar to duels," Kelly said wryly.

"That would be satisfying," Achranae agreed. "But I do not expect they would accept."

There was a long silence . . . and an idea popped into Kelly's mind, practically full-blown. A risky idea—one that could conceivably get them *both* killed. But it might just work . . . and otherwise one of them would certainly die. Gritting his teeth, Kelly took the plunge. "Achranae," he said carefully, "I believe I have a game we can play. Will you trust me enough to accept it *now*, before I explain the rules, and to play it without a practice game?"

The Olyt's snout quivered slightly as he stared across the table in silence. For a long moment the only sound Kelly could hear was his own heartbeat. Then, slowly, Achranae cocked his head to the right. "Very well. I believe you to be honorable. I will agree to your conditions."

"Slaich? You still holding to the rules you set up?" Kelly called.

"Of course."

"Okay." Kelly took a deep breath. "This game involves two rival kingdoms and a fire-breathing creature who harasses them both. Here's the creature's underground chamber." He placed a black marker on the playing board, then picked up three of the transparent plates and their supports and set them up. "The two kingdoms are called the Mountain Kingdom and the Land City. The Mountain Kingdom is bigger;

here's its center and edge." He placed a large red marker on the top plate and added a ring of six smaller ones around it, two squares away. Moving the black marker slightly so that it was directly under one edge of the ring, he picked up a large yellow marker. "This is the Land City," he identified it, moving it slowly over the middle transparency as his eyes flickered over the board. Ten centimeters between levels, approximately; four per square . . . he put the yellow marker eight squares from the red one and four squares to one side. It wasn't perfect, but it was close and would have to do. "Finally, here are our forces." He scattered a dozen each red and yellow butterfly-shaped pieces in the space between the two kingdoms. "The conditions for victory are twofold: the creature must be dead, and there can be no forces from the opposing side threatening your kingdom. Okay?"

"Very well," Achranae said slowly, studying the board carefully. Once again Kelly wished he had a better grasp of Olyt expressions. "How are combat results decided?"

"By the number of forces involved plus a throw of the die." Making up the rules as he went along, Kelly set up a system that allowed combat between any two of the three sides—and that would require nearly all of both kingdoms' forces combined to defeat the creature with any certainty. "Movement is two squares or one level per turn, and you can move all your forces each turn," he concluded. "Any questions?"

Achranae's eyes bored unblinkingly into his, as if trying to read Kelly's mind. "No. Which of us moves first?"

"I will, if you don't mind." Starting with the pieces closest to the Olyt's kingdom, Kelly began moving them away from the red marker and toward the black one. Achranae hesitated somewhat when it was his turn, but he followed Kelly's example in moving his forces downward. Two of them landed within striking range of some of Kelly's; but the human ignored them, continuing onward instead. Within a few more moves the yellow and red pieces had formed a single mass converging on the black marker.

The fire-breathing creature never had a chance.

"And now . . . ?" Achranae sat stiffly in his chair, his claws about halfway out of their sheaths. The creature had been eliminated on the Olyt's turn, making it Kelly's move . . . and Achranae's forces were still intermixed with the human's. A more vulnerable position was hard to imagine, and Achranae clearly knew it.

Kelly gave him a tight smile and leaned back in his seat. "Well, the creature's dead—and in their present position none of your forces can threaten my kingdom. So I guess I've won."

There was a soft hiss from the other side of the table, and Achranae's claws slid all the way out. Kelly held his breath and tensed himself to leap. Surely Achranae was smart enough to see it . . . and, abruptly, the claws disappeared. "But my kingdom is *also* not threatened," the Olyt said. "Therefore I, too, have won."

"Really?" Kelly pretended great amazement. "I'll be darned. You're *right*. Congratulations." He looked at the ceiling. "Slaich? By a remarkable coincidence we've both won the third game, so I guess we both get to go home. Ready any time you are."

"No." The Stryf's flat voice was firm.

A golf-ball-sized lump rose into Kelly's throat. "Why not? You said anyone who won two games would be sent home. You set up that rule yourself."

"Then the rule is changed. Only one of you can be allowed to leave. You will choose a new game."

Slaich's words seemed to hang in the air like a death sentence . . . and Kelly felt his fingernails digging into his palms. He really hadn't expected the aliens to let him twist their rules to his advantage—he already knew this was no game to them. But he'd still hoped . . . and now he had no choice but to gamble his last card. "I won't play any more games," he said bluntly. "I'm sick of being a pawn in this boogeyman hunt of yours. You can all just take a flying leap at yourselves."

"If you do not play you will lose by forfeit," Slaich reminded him.

"Big deal," Kelly snorted. "You're going to wipe out Earth eventually anyway, aren't you? So what the hell difference does it make where I die?"

There was a short pause. "Very well. You yourself have chosen. Achranae, return to your Transphere chamber."

Slowly, the alien rose to his feet. Kelly half expected him to speak up in protest, or to otherwise plead for the human's life. But he remained silent. For a moment he regarded Kelly through the transparent game boards, as Kelly held his breath. Then, still without a word, the alien crossed his wrists in salute and vanished behind the sliding door. "You will return to your rest chamber now," Slaich ordered.

Letting out his breath in a long sigh, Kelly stood up and disassembled the playing board, storing the pieces and plates away in their proper places. So it had indeed come down to a toss of a coin, he thought, suddenly very tired. The coin was in the air, and there was nothing to do now but wait . . . and hope that Achranae had understood.

To: *Office of Director Rodau 248700, A.R.B., Clars*
From: *Office of Director Eftis 379214, Games Studies, Var-4*
Date: *21 Lysmo 3829*

XXXXX URGENT XXXXX

Dear Rodau,

It is even worse than we expected, and I hereby make formal recommendation that the Humans be completely obliterated. The enclosed records should be studied carefully, particularly those concerning the third game that was played. By using his tactical skills to create a game he and his opponent could jointly win, the Human clearly demonstrated both the ability to cooperate with others and also the rare trait of mercy. Although these characteristics gained him nothing in this particular instance—and, in fact, can be argued to have been liabilities—we cannot assume this will always be the case. The danger that their cooperative nature will lead the Humans into a successful alliance instead of betraying them to their destruction cannot be ignored. If the Chanis had been capable of building alliances they might well have never been stopped.

It is anticipated that a full psycho-physiological dissection of our Human subject will be necessary to facilitate the assault fleet's strategy. We request that the proper experts and equipment be sent as soon as they become available. Please do not delay overlong: I cannot guarantee our Human can be kept alive more than a year at the most.

Eftis

Kelly's first indication that the long wait had ended was a faint grinding sound transmitted through the metal walls of his rest chamber. It startled him from a deep sleep—but he hardly even had time to wonder about it before the room's door suddenly flashed white and collapsed outward. Instantly, there was a minor hurricane in the room, and Kelly's ears popped as the air pressure dropped drastically. But even as he tumbled off the bed three figures in long-snouted spacesuits fought their way in through the gale, and before he knew it he'd been stuffed into a giant ribbed balloon with a hissing tank at the bottom. "Kelly McClain?" a tinny, static-distorted voice came from a box by the air tank as the balloon inflated. "Are you safe?"

Kelly's ears popped again as his three rescuers tipped him onto his back and carried him carefully toward the ruined door. "I'm fine," he said toward the box. "Is that you, Achranae?"

It was almost fifteen seconds before the voice spoke again; clearly, the Olyt's translator wasn't as good as the Stryfkar's. "Yes. I am pleased you are still alive."

Kelly's grin was wide enough to hurt, and was probably even visible through his beard. "Me too. *Damn*, but I'm glad you got my message. I wasn't at all sure you'd caught it."

They were out in the Transphere chamber before the response came, and Kelly had a chance to look around. In the ceiling, stretching upwards through at least two stories' worth of rock, was a jagged hole. Moving purposefully through the chamber itself were a dozen more Olyts in the white, armor-like suits. "It was ingenious. I feared that I would not be allowed to leave, though, once I had seen the board."

"Me too—but it looks like we had nothing to worry about." Kelly grinned again—it was so *good* to talk to a friend again! "I'll lay you any odds that the Stryfkar haven't *yet* noticed what I did. It's the old can't-see-the-forest-for-the-trees problem; they'd seen that four-tiered board used for so many different games that it never occurred to them that you and I would automatically associate it with Skymarch, the only game we'd ever played on it. So while they took my kingdoms-and-dragon setup at face value, you were able to see the markers as a group of objects in space. I gambled that you'd realize they represented our home worlds and this one, and that you'd take note of the relative distances I'd laid out. I guess the gamble paid off."

Kelly was beneath the ceiling hole now, and a pair of dangling cables were being attached to his balloon's upper hand-holds. "We shall hope that winning such risks is characteristic of your race," Achranae said. "We have destroyed the Stryfkar base and have captured records that show a large force will soon be coming here. We have opened communication with your race, but they have not yet agreed to a tactical alliance. Perhaps your testimony will help persuade them. It is hoped that you, at least, will agree to aid us in our tactical planning."

The ropes pulled taut and Kelly began moving upward. "I'm almost certain we can find some extra help on Earth," Kelly told the Olyt grimly. "And as for me, it'll be a pleasure. The Stryfkar have a lot to learn about us pawns."

THE COMEDIAN

by Timothy Robert Sullivan

A story about a kidnapper who seized children and asked no ransom? It sounds like the sort of terrible crime that gets angry newspaper headlines. This is such a story, but the criminal had motives that the police could never have understood. His jests were in earnest, his impersonations diabolically funny, his rewards unmentionable. . . .

Yogi Bear wore a wanted poster on his paunch.

"They'll never see that kid alive again," a passing woman said.

The kidnapper's heart fluttered like a hummingbird's wings. There were two pictures of a little boy named Paul Simpson on the poster, and an offer of one hundred thousand dollars to anyone with information leading to his return. But Paul Simpson's rich parents wouldn't have any better luck than those of the other five children the kidnapper had taken. He had not abducted them for money.

140

Glancing at the woman, he was relieved to see that she wasn't speaking to him. The giant Yogi-teddy bear standing in front of the toy store had momentarily attracted her attention, just as it had attracted his. Now she rejoined the mall's milling shoppers, Jordache jeans jiggling in a way the kidnapper knew he should have found enticing. She had probably filed Paul's disappearance with countless other urban horror stories.

The kidnapper could have told her this one was different.

He remembered abducting little Paulie . . . and other kids, too . . . they had struggled, and then became weak . . . and then . . . He couldn't remember anything else. God, how he needed a drink.

He wiped his sweating face, bristles scratching his hand, and tried to think. His head began to ache, and saliva dribbled out of the side of his mouth. To make matters worse, his clothes were rumpled and he smelled like a goat. Better clean up his act, or he would get caught.

Shaking his head, he walked away from the toy store. Laughter and bright, multiple-color images soon distracted him. It was a display of TVs. A comedian mugged out of half a dozen screens.

Ordinary as this was, it disturbed the kidnapper. He stopped to listen to the guy's *shtik*. The timing and delivery seemed adequate, and the material was all right, but there was still something wrong. The longer he watched, the more it troubled him. It was as though he were a dog on a leash, tugging to free himself from the powerful hands that held him back. . . .

But this wasn't his master.

His head starting to ache again, he turned and walked away. Why had the comedian affected him so deeply? He couldn't come up with a reason, and the pain was so bad that he didn't want to think about it.

He passed a florist's and a clothing store, stopped in front of a video games arcade. He would try here first; parents frequently left their children in such places with a handful of quarters, going off under the illusion their kids were safe.

Such complacency angered the kidnapper. Every day, parents endangered their own children. If they gave him no opportunity to steal their children, maybe he'd be freed . . . or maybe he'd be killed so he wouldn't tell what he knew.

But what did he know?

"Diversions," he said, reading aloud the arcade's sign, "Video Games, Electronic Games, Pinball."

It was a dimly lit place, the better to show off the games' bright graphics. Whining, jangling, booming effects slashed the inside of his skull. He was in lousy shape. Just walking through the mall had tired him. He was trembling, short of breath, his knees rubbery, and he had a headache that never seemed to go away. A junk food diet and a drinking problem didn't help, but he really didn't give a damn about his health anymore. He didn't care about anything except getting the job done. If he was going to be shut up for good once it was over, well . . . at least it would be over.

If he wasn't killed, the police would catch him. Then there would be a trial, and he'd spend the rest of his days in a prison, or a madhouse . . . or be executed.

No chance of a normal life again. Christ, he couldn't even remember his own name.

He knew he shouldn't be thinking about what would happen to him. He was just asking for a headache. Besides, he had to keep moving. Otherwise, the cops would get him before he got the last two kids.

Fishing in his pocket for a quarter, he started playing a Missile Command game. He failed to save the earth, a lurid color field remaining after the holocaust.

"I won't be long, honey," he heard a woman say to her daughter as he stared at the blasted landscape. "If anyone bothers you, tell the man behind the counter." Purse swinging, she hurried out.

The little girl stood alone in the clamor of the arcade, wide eyes staring up at the adults and teenagers towering above her. She was no more than seven or eight years old, brown hair, green eyes. She wore a light blue T-shirt that said "I'm Huggable." Clutching her quarters, she bit her bottom lip and surveyed the rows of machines. Several were vacant, and she soon settled on Space Invaders. An empty wooden box helped her reach the controls.

As her quarter clinked into the coin slot, the kidnapper stole up behind her. He casually looked up and down the aisle, as though trying to decide which game to play next. No one paid any attention to him.

He felt under his windbreaker for the tranquilizer gun,

turning back toward the little girl. He slowly raised his hand
to clap over her mouth. But she was no longer zapping ma-
rauding aliens. She stared at his reflection in the smudged
glass of the screen.

"Child molester!" she screamed, turning to glare up at him.
"Pervert!"

The piping voice clamped onto his skull like an alligator's
jaws. He slapped his hands over his temples, people turning
to stare at him.

"Hey man," the counter man shouted, "you touch that kid,
your ass is in jail!"

"I . . ." The kidnapper could barely speak, his throat dry
and constricted. ". . . I thought she was my daughter."

"You did not!" The little girl set her jaw defiantly. "You
were gonna molest me! My mommy told me to watch out for
you!"

"Get outta here," the counter man said.

The kidnapper backed away. He turned and walked stiffly
by the planters filled with ferns and the wooden benches,
crossing to the other side of the mall. His face was hot and
his head throbbed. He hoped to God the guy wouldn't call
the cops.

Outside the mall's main entrance, he was grateful to be
away from the noise. He was falling apart; only adrenaline
kept him going now. The midday sun made his eyes water,
tears flowing into the sweat that stained his clothes. He noticed a lamppost with a lettered F sign and wondered where
he'd left the goddam van.

Come to think of it, he'd parked under a C sign. He
spotted it and started walking toward it. As he cut between
two cars, he came upon a kid playing with a yo-yo.

The kidnapper looked around. Nobody was in any of the
cars near the little boy. The shimmering parking lot was still.

"Every cloud has a silver lining," he said.

"Huh?" The kid looked up at him. He snapped the yo-yo
up and caught it. The kidnapper saw that it was emblazoned
with Superman's insignia.

"I'm just looking for my kids," the kidnapper said. "I think
they're around here someplace."

The little boy looked sad. "I haven't seen anybody."

"Well, they must be inside the van," the kidnapper said,

sensing that it might not be necessary to use the tranquilizer gun just yet. "We've got a lot of stuff to play with in there."

"Really?" Squinting into the sun as he looked up, the kid looked like a little freckled monkey.

"Come take a look. They're right over here." The kidnapper started towards the C sign. Hesitating a moment, the boy ran after him.

The red van gleamed brightly in the sun. As they neared it, the kidnapper felt terrible guilt for stealing another child. But what choice did he have? He was only an instrument, a tool . . . and he had never hurt any of the children.

"Here we are, buddy," he said, unlocking the back doors of the van. "What did you say your name is?"

"Jimmy," the little boy replied. "Where are the kids?"

"Right in here, Jimmy." The kidnapper threw open the back doors of the van. "See."

Six kids sat on benches within the dark enclosure, three on either side. Between them danced a man, puffing out his cheeks and making his jaw stick out like Popeye. He was transparent in places, sparkling here and there, and zigzag lines of color distorted his shape for a second.

"*What time is it?*" the comedian asked in a funny voice.

The kidnapper drew the tranquilizer gun from under his jacket and fired a dart. Jimmy's little body stiffened, and his cry was drowned out by the comedian's raucous reply to his own question: "*It's Howdy Doody time!*"

The kidnapper clapped his hand over Jimmy's mouth, tossing the tranquilizer gun inside the van. Jimmy struggled ineffectually as he was lifted up and carried inside, too. The kidnapper hunkered over the child's body inside the dark, cramped space, holding him tightly until he weakened and became still.

None of the other children appeared to notice the abduction, nor did they notice when the kidnapper placed Jimmy on the bench beside a little black girl.

Jumping out of the van and slamming the doors shut, the kidnapper went around to the driver's side, let himself into the broiling cab, and turned the ignition key. He turned on the air conditioner while he waited for the idle to smooth out.

Just as he started to back out of the parking space, a police car pulled into the lot. He slammed on the brakes and ducked down in the seat as the cop drove behind him, praying to Christ the arcade counter man hadn't reported him. In the rearview mirror, he watched the cop pull in front of the mall and go inside. Then he slowly backed out and eased onto U. S. 1. The wheel was slippery in his sweating hands.

"Close one, dummy."

The kidnapper looked at the comedian, a fuzzy image of Bozo the Clown now, seated on the passenger's side.

"You . . ." The kidnapper remembered now. The comedian made him take the children. It had almost come back to him in the mall . . . the giant teddy bear . . . the TV store . . . but his struggle to regain his memory had hurt his head. ". . . you . . ."

". . . are mah, sunshine," the comedian sang in a nasal twang, "mah only sunshine. You make me spirit those kids a-way."

"That's not funny."

"Everybody's a critic."

"Tell me what you're doing this for."

"But you know too much already. Yeah, I think you need a refresher course in forgetting."

"No, please, I . . ."

"Say what, you crazy nut? Gonna be a good boy from here on in, or do I have to send you back to Never-Never Land?"

"If you do that, who'll drive?" The kidnapper could see the scenery rushing by through the comedian's unfocused image. "You aren't substantial."

"Of course I'm not substantial, dummy. I'm Bozo the Clown, not Edwin Newman. But don't worry, you'll still be in the driver's seat. Sort of on automatic pilot."

"Won't that be dangerous?"

The comedian chuckled like Curly of the Three Stooges, his body becoming rotund, and topped with a stubbly crew cut. "Nah, you do better that way."

"Please," the kidnapper said, starting to sob. "I'm burnt out. Don't do it to me anymore."

"Well, gee," the comedian said, turning into Jack Benny.

The kidnapper wept. "Why are you doing this? What do you want from me?"

"Oh, Rochester, where's my violin?" Benny said, resting his fingertips gently against his cheek. "I don't have any choice, either, ya know. It's no fun watching you drool all over yourself, but I've got to be careful."

Frustrated, the kidnapper swerved to avoid a speeding Datsun. Its driver honked at him as though he had been at fault.

"Well, gee," the comedian said, "it looks like the old Maxwell's got life in her yet. But, ya know, I really think you'd drive better if you didn't have anything on your mind."

Gotta keep him from putting me under, the kidnapper thought. I know I can remember everything, starting with my name. I just need a little time. But the shimmering, imperfect image of Jack Benny was looking at him thoughtfully. "I really think you need some rest, kidnapper. Ya see, tomorrow is a big day for you."

"Somebody controls you," the kidnapper said. "Somebody controls you, just like you're controlling me. Who is it?"

"I've got a secret." The comedian straightened his bow tie, the very picture of Garry Moore. "Can you guess who's pulling my strings."

"Couldn't be anyone on earth . . . the technology's too advanced. Aliens?"

"Mork from Ork?" Robin Williams asked with an impish grin. "Or John Q from outer space?" Where Robin Williams had been, the plump face of Jonathan Winters grimaced at the kidnapper.

"Why not? You must have intercepted our TV signals, and . . ."

"Nah," Maxwell Smart replied. "Would you believe videotapes from Sri Lanka?"

"Then you *are* manipulated by aliens."

"In a pig's eye."

"Then you must come from the future."

"What time is it, dummy?" Buffalo Bob demanded.

"Huh? No, please, I. . . ."

"It's Howdy Doody time!"

Speckled light. Dark motes. Fade to black.

Drunk as a skunk, the kidnapper slowly climbed the stairs, holding on to a metal railing. He was headed toward the third floor walkup he'd rented for the week. He just needed a place to crash for the night, a place where nobody would bother him.

But what was he doing days? He'd left his regular job to work on a special mission here, hadn't he? Couldn't think about that now, though. Too tired.

Unlocking the door, he entered the tiny efficiency apartment and snapped on the air conditioner set in the room's single window.

"The Beach," he said, his voice croaking from disuse. "Miami Beach." He threw his windbreaker on the floor.

Long shadows were cast on the sand below. In the shards of late afternoon sun between them, a few working girls were still basking, taking it easy before they readied themselves to earn their nightly bread in the restaurants or hotels, or on the street. Soon the little patches of warmth they had staked out would be lost in darkness.

The kidnapper went to the tiny refrigerator in the corner and took a cold beer, downing it in two long mouthfuls. Then he stretched out fully clothed on the lumpy mattress. He didn't look forward to sleeping, exhausted as he was. When he dreamed, he often had nightmares about children shambling like tiny "Living Dead" creatures out of a George Romero movie.

"George Romero," he muttered, wondering if the name was a key to his past. He thought about it, but nothing came to mind. He was too tried to concentrate, anyhow. He felt that he had suffered unbearable tension today, though he couldn't remember why. Now he was drained, empty as an old Coke bottle. What had he done to make himself feel so rotten?

He closed his eyes to the waning light, falling into a nightmare of children with glazed eyes marching into the bloody jaws of a hideous, laughing clown.

He awakened in the dark. He hurt all over, and his sheets were soaked in spite of the air conditioner. He shook like a newborn mouse.

Rising, he massaged his temples before getting a fresh beer. He started to snap on the little Sony TV on the shelf over the fridge, but something made him stop. TV was bad for him; he would play the radio instead.

Sweetly flowing saxophone music filled the cramped room. He went into the bathroom, shucking his clothes and stepping into the shower. The cold water woke him and soothed him at the same time. The aching wasn't so bad after a few minutes. He turned off the shower, got out, and toweled himself dry. Then he applied shaving cream to his chin and started scraping off the several days of stubble on his mustached face.

The music stopped, replaced by the sound of teletype machines. The news. As he shaved, the kidnapper grew depressed at the ominous parade of economic problems, social unrest, and the acrimonious breakdown of the summit at Oslo.

Local news was no better, a petty catalogue of drug busts, burglaries, and murders. And then something made him put down his razor before he was through shaving.

"Police believe they know who's been kidnapping children around South Florida this past week. An apparent abduction attempt at North Miami's Woodlake Mall yesterday afternoon failed, but a second child was taken in the parking lot. Joe Ciano, manager of a game room in the mall, was able to give a detailed description of the apparent kidnapper, matching the description of a missing person. Chris Reilly, an employee of the State of Florida's Endangered Species Program, left his job at Everglades National Park late last Monday afternoon without a word of explanation. Reilly drove away in a red 1973 Dodge van, and hasn't reported in or called in since."

"Chris Reilly," the kidnapper said, staring at his reflection in the mirror. "Chris Reilly . . ."

"Reilly," the radio announcer went on in his cheerful voice, "is thirty-five years old, has dark hair, dark eyes, and a mustache. He's five feet eleven inches tall, and weighs one hundred eighty-five pounds. The suspect is armed with a tranquilizer gun that shoots darts filled with procaine, a drug used to subdue wild animals for scientific study. He is apparently tranquilizing his young victims prior to abduction. Authorities believe Reilly may be suffering a nervous breakdown due to a divorce earlier this year.

"If you see a man driving a red Dodge van, license number SHM-393, please report his whereabouts to the police.

"The Hallandale city council today voted to . . ."

Yes, it was all true . . . except for the motive. Janet had left him in February, but he had become used to living alone since then. . . . Monday, he'd been out in the canoe looking for a young alligator to tag. After drugging it, he was supposed to slip a numbered aluminum band over its snout, so the Department could follow its migrations as it grew older.

He'd never found his 'gator. Instead, this three dimensional image had flickered into existence right over the canoe in the air, chortling like the Great Gildersleeve. The image was kind of faint, but the voice was clear. Even though Gildersleeve faded in and out, the apparition had done something to Chris's mind.

Ever since then, whenever he wanted to put Chris to sleep, he just said: "*It's Howdy Doody time!*"

"The comedian," Chris said. He had made Chris look for children to abduct. Whenever Chris tried to remember why he was the kidnapper—or when he didn't work at it hard enough—his head started splitting like it had been smacked with a baseball bat. And the comedian could make him forget. . . .

How many children had he taken? First there was a little blonde girl in Flamingo. Then the little black boy, Thomas. And then Susie. Chris counted seven, altogether.

The comedian wanted eight. Four of each sex. Chris was supposed to take one more, a girl. Good God, what did the comedian have in mind for those babies down in the van?

"I gotta call the cops," he said. There were clean clothes in the closet. The comedian had let him buy them and the other things he needed after he had taken all of his money out of the bank on Monday. He slid into a fresh pair of jeans and a blue work shirt. There was no phone in his room, so he would have to get to the pay phone in the parking lot downstairs. He was working on the bottom button of the shirt when a Diamondback crawled inside his brain and bit down hard, its venom paralyzing him.

"Going someplace, dummy?"

Don Rickles stood between him and the door. "Are you stupid, or does your mother dress you that way?"

Chris lurched toward him. The pain in his head drew a bloody film over his eyes. He almost fell, but managed to hold onto the dresser as his knees buckled.

"The children," he gasped, struggling to catch his breath.

"Hang onto your lid, kid," the comedian said, wagging his finger like Kay Kayser, "here we go again."

"No!" Chris screamed. "I won't let you take them!" He reeled toward the door again, passing through the image this time. The hairs on his arms stood up. Hw shoved open the door, the pain singing inside his skull like a billion crickets.

Supporting himself on the railing, he scrambled down to the landing. His legs were silly putty, but he managed to stay on his feet somehow. Then he was at the second floor landing. He half crawled the rest of the way down, and then he was staggering across the parking lot. The pain had become refined, exquisite in its agony. He refused to surrender to it. His strength was his identity. He was Chris Reilly, a decent human being, and he would not give the children to the comedian.

Stay away from the van, he told himself. Stay out in the open. He doesn't like to show himself. You might make it that way.

He saw the flimsy shelter of a pay phone ahead, a glowing shrine in the early morning darkness. Then he was clutching at the receiver, reaching in his jeans for a quarter.

"No," he moaned. "Oh, God, no." No change in the pockets. Freshly laundered pants. He slumped against the metal shelf under the phone, hearing the busy signal as the receiver dropped. It struck his leg and dangled a few inches above the ground.

"All right. All right, all ready." Bespectacled and redheaded, the comedian stood on the shelf inside the little phone shelter. He leaned against the oblong box of the phone, a foot-high Woody Allen. "I'm proud of you. You're a hero. Practically a John Wayne. So stop whimpering; you're embarrassing me."

The pain subsided. Chris leaned against the booth, trembling and out of breath.

"I'm like death, taxes, and mothers-in-law," the comedian said. "You can't get away from me."

"Why?" Chris was just waiting for the comedian to ask him what time it was, wearily reciting the usual litany of questions. "Where did you come from? Who sent you?"

"Well, you guessed it before. I'm a projection from the future. I'm on a loop stretching from my time back to yours. Your brainwaves are my anchor in your time."

"A loop?" Chris struggled to understand. "What kind of loop?"

"It's kind of hard to explain, but the loop is tightening all the time. I first focused in on its outermost periphery, homing in on a pattern featuring beta waves with an interaction of alpha and theta—human, in other words. You."

"A random choice?"

"Yeah, but for what it's worth, you seem to be a bright guy."

"Thanks, but it's a wonder I can think at all after what you've put me through."

"It had to be done."

"Yeah, right. I'm standing here talking to Woody Allen, right? I'm crazy. Maybe I really did abduct a bunch of kids. Maybe I even meant to molest them . . . or even kill them."

"Kill them? With kindness, maybe. We can't pass a Burger King without you running in to pick up a snack for the little monsters. Never have I seen such a boy scout. The way you put away the beer, I didn't figure you for Jimmy Stewart in *Mr. Smith Goes to Washington*."

"The beer . . ." Chris could still taste it. "Why'd you let me drink so much?"

"At first it helped keep you in line, but after a while it just numbed out your brain—helped break down the conditioning."

"I've always had a weakness for drinking. My wife . . ."

"Look at you, ready to confess all your sins. If everyone had half your guilt, it never would have happened."

"*What* never would have happened?"

Archie Bunker blotted out Woody Allen. He patted his potbelly and took a drag from his cigar. "The Big One, meathead. Double-ya Double-ya Three."

" A nuclear war . . . ?"

"Oh, whoop-de-doo. You sure do catch on quick. Just like the rest of them dingbats back in your time, blowing everything to hell just to show who was the biggest jerk."

"You mean it's gonna happen?" Chris asked. "It's really gonna happen?"

"The biggest cookout in history, meathead, only the marshmallows and weenies got a funny glow."

"Oh, God . . . the world . . . civilization."

"Most of it. Libraries destroyed, stored information frazzled by the blasts' pulses—we did find some old videotapes in Sri Lanka. Some egghead was studyin' comedy. But you know somethin'? We loined a lot about youse from them tapes. Too bad ya didn't use 'em to tape shut ya leaders' yaps."

"How can you joke about it?" Chris cried out, scared and enraged. "What's wrong with your head?"

"You think this one's bad," Groucho Marx said, "you should seen the other one."

"What?"

"That's right. Gene damage. No relation to Gene Kelly, or Gene Autry, either. And nobody up ahead knows what to do about it. It's hard to take two aspirins and go to bed if you don't have arms and legs."

"Oh, Christ . . . the children. . . ."

"Say, you really *are* quick on the draw, Tex. We need a few kids to start a new gene pool. Who knows, maybe we can get a healthy breed of human going again if we work at it a little."

The sodium vapor lights began to wink out along Collins Avenue. Pink streaks of dawn touched the clouds over the ocean. Chris stared at the dull afterglow of the lamps, wondering if he could believe the comedian. "Why did you put me in that comatose state?" he demanded.

"Because there isn't much time," Groucho said. "Sort of like playing 'You Bet Your Life.' I had no idea you'd say the secret woid, but you did. Now I don't have the time to wrestle with you anymore. I have to trust you . . . I'm just glad you're not a used-car salesman.

"Look, Chris, haven't you noticed that I'm getting clearer all the time?"

Chris stared at the stooped figure in a tuxedo as Groucho paced across the aluminum shelf. The image was sharper than it had been yesterday in the van. Compared to its clarity in the canoe a week ago, it looked almost solid. "Yeah, I see."

"It's because we're getting closer to the disjunctive node."

"Disjunctive node?"

"Right, that's what causes the time loop. We can project across time around the node, closing in on it all the time. Our past, your future, it's really all the same. Waves and particles come and go around it anomalously, but it takes a helluva lot of power—and it's only going to be open for a few seconds."

"What happens when it opens?"

Groucho sucked on his cigar until the coal glowed red hot, demonstrating the growing brightness of his image as they drew closer to the disjunctive node. "Then matter can be pulled through into the future."

"*The kids!*"

"You got it." Groucho exhaled a cloud of smoke. "That's how we're gonna get 'em outta here."

Chris laughed aloud, the incongruously happy sound echoing through the still parking lot. But a germ of suspicion still infected him. "Why didn't you just tell me all this in the first place?"

W. C. Fields stared at him as though he were an insect. "There's a sucker born every minute, Christopher, my lad, but I couldn't be sure you weren't the exception." He consulted his pocket watch. "Precious little time to persuade you of the nobility inherent in my masterful plan. Considerably less time to dawdle now. My trusty timepiece indicates that there is slightly less than one hour before the aforementioned disjunctive node opens."

"An hour?"

"Fifty-six minutes, eighteen seconds, by my reckoning." Fields snapped the watch shut, dangled it by its fob, and dropped it neatly into its pocket. "I suggest we get started."

Chris started toward the van, and then stopped dead in his tracks. "How do I know you're telling the truth?"

"You don't, my inquisitive companion. You don't. You are, however, hopelessly embroiled in this imbroglio, and there are only minutes remaining. Can you afford to risk inaction?"

Chris thought it over. If the comedian was lying, there was nothing to lose by going along with him now. The police would surely catch up with him today. And if it was true . . . if the comedian had really come to save the children . . . and the entire human race in the bargain . . .

"Okay," he said. "Kids will be on their way to school soon, so maybe we—oh, shit, I don't have my keys."

"They'll be necessary only to open these formidable metal doors, my dear Christopher. We can hardly venture forth in a vehicle the authorities are searching for."

"But how do we. . . ?"

"Find the node? My inquisitive innocent, I am being drawn to the node as the loop tightens. Indeed, I cannot avoid it." He waved his cane in a northerly direction. "Just up the beach."

"Good." Chris ran up to get his keys, feeling the adrenaline surge. When he got back downstairs, the comedian had turned into a darkly handsome young man wearing a suit twenty years out of fashion.

"Lenny Bruce!" Chris said. "You were always one of my favorites."

"*Now* he stops to admire my stuff," the comedian said. "I just needed something a little less conspicuous."

"What if we can't get another kid before it's time?" Chris said, unlocking the back.

"One of the girls will have to take an extra boyfriend, which might start the first war up ahead." The comedian smiled as the doors opened. "Come on out, kids. It's time to get a little exercise."

The children stirred and began to jump silently onto the asphalt, one by one. "Jackie, Thomas, Michael, Cherie, Jimmy, Susie, and . . . Paulie."

"Paulie." Chris remembered the poster on Yogi Bear's paunch, and the agonizing struggle to regain his identity. "Comedian, you play rough."

"There's a lot at stake." Lenny Bruce almost looked real now, except for an occasional ghostly line wavering around him. "Let's get going."

The children in tow, they started up Collins Avenue. A jogger passed, eyeing them curiously. The sun was a brilliant disc reflected on the water as a rippling orange bar.

"Forty-five minutes," the comedian said.

They walked faster. The sun was warm and Chris was glad he wasn't wearing his windbreaker. Then he remembered that he had worn it only to hide the dart gun. "The gun," he said, turning to go back and get it.

"Forget it, jerk-off," Bruce said. "No time."

"Right." Traffic was picking up, and Chris noticed school buses and cars with children in them. Then a police car passed by, freezing his heart. The cop looked at them, and then drove on.

"Jesus," Chris breathed. "Jesus, Mary, and Joseph."

"They don't expect to see two men," the comedian said.

"It's still a miracle he didn't stop me," Chris said. "These city cops."

"The boys in blue. Miami's finest. Mean, just like most

people in your time," Bruce said. "I guess there was just no way out of blowing the whole place to hell."

"Yeah," Chris said, hearing an angry horn blow on the street. "We all sensed it was going to happen sooner or later. Nobody knew how to stop it, though."

"Assholes."

They kept walking. Chris wanted desperately to find one last little girl. Perhaps his conditioning hadn't completely worn off. "How much time is left?"

"Twenty-eight minutes." The comedian turned to the children. "How ya doin', kids?"

"Fine," Jackie said. Jackie Tiger was a Miccosuccee Indian girl. Chris had loved her dark, liquid eyes and black hair from the first. He and Janet had never had any children; that was one reason their marriage hadn't lasted. And now he was bonded to the comedian, with seven children to protect from a world gone mad.

A middle-aged couple passed them, smiling at the children. Both wore Bermuda shorts in the already considerable heat.

"Say good morning, kids," the comedian said.

"Good morning," the children all sang in unison.

"You've still got them under your thumb," Chris said. "Will they be zombies like this in the future?"

"Are you serious? Look, this is one time when the end justifies the means, believe me. But they'll be free up ahead. We've got a pretty nice place set up for them, in fact."

"Utopia?"

"No such thing." Lenny gestured around them. "But better than this toilet any day. Keep walking. We've only got fifteen more minutes."

Chris walked as quickly as the children's shorter legs would permit. He began to count the seconds. Sixty, one hundred, two hundred, three hundred.

"Ten minutes," the comedian said.

They were almost jogging now. The comedian looked just like a living, breathing, three-dimensional human being, the reincarnation of Lenny Bruce, come to see the unhappy world end.

"Look." Chris saw a group of kids waiting at a bus stop. One was off by herself a few yards, examining an ant hill. She was a little East-Asian girl.

"Perfect!" the comedian said. "Such a gene pool we'll have if you can nab her."

"Have the kids tell her they're walking to school," Chris said. "Make them ask her if she wants to go with them."

"All right, but if it doesn't work right off, you gotta grab her. Okay?"

"Okay."

"Kids," the comedian said. "See that little girl over there? I think she's really nice, don't you? Why don't you ask her if she wants to walk to school with us? Make sure you tell her about all the fun we have."

The children giggled. Chris and the comedian passed the little girl and hesitated while the question was put to her by Paulie, the others joining in persuasively from time to time in their high voices.

Another police car drove by.

"Jesus," Chris muttered.

"What's your name?" Susie asked the little girl.

"Premika."

"Are you from around here?" Jimmy asked, spinning his yo-yo.

"No, I'm from Thailand."

This seemed to confuse the children. Jackie said, "Do you want to walk to school with us or not?" as though she were growing impatient.

Premika looked at Chris and the comedian. "Who are those men?" she asked in her lilting accent.

"Nobody," Michael said. "Just two men."

Premika shook her head emphatically. She would not go.

The bus pulled up to the curb, and the children lined up as the driver opened the door. Premika was separated from the others by the comedian's seven children.

"Move!" the comedian said.

Premika was looking worriedly at the bus. Chris lunged and scooped her up, turning to run with her kicking and screaming in his arms. The other children ran behind.

"Four minutes!" the comedian shouted.

"Put me down!" Premika screamed. "Put me down!" Then she started babbling in Thai, alternately wailing and shrieking. Her sneakers drummed at Chris's thigh as he clapped a hand over her mouth.

The bus driver laid on his horn, and the children at the bus stop were shouting excitedly.

"It's just ahead," the comedian said. "You can make it, Chris."

But Chris's lungs were already aching, and his heart felt as though it had doubled in size. He kept running, though, feeling Premika's warm tears run over his fingers, mingling with his sweat. She bit his hand, but he didn't let go, even when blood started running down his wrist.

Sirens wailed somewhere behind them.

"Hurry up, kids!" Lenny shouted. "It's not much farther."

Premika was whimpering now, nearly fainted. But Chris didn't lighten his grip. She could have been faking, waiting for a chance to break free.

"This way!" The comedian led them onto a public beach.

Chris saw Haulover Pier cutting through the glittering waves ahead, his calves aching from running in the sand while carrying Premika. His breath came in strangled gasps, and his arms felt as though they would fall off. But he wouldn't quit, not now.

The sirens drew closer. Rubber screeched. Car doors slammed. A man shouted through a bullhorn: "Give it up, Christopher Reilly. You can't go any farther."

As if to prove it, a security guard ran toward Chris from the far end of the pier. Chris turned to see half a dozen cops sprinting over the sand, pistols drawn.

"No," Chris said. "Not this close."

Early sunbathers watched apprehensively, catching Chris's eyes as he desperately searched for a way to keep going.

"Let the children go, Mr. Reilly. It's gonna be all right. Just let the kids go."

As though in response, the children gathered closer about Chris, Premika, and the comedian.

The policemen leveled their pistols, clutching them in both hands, legs spread.

Chris started to cry. He let the confused Premika down, and she stood in the sand with the other children, looking curiously up at her kidnapper.

"Sir," the policeman said to the comedian, "please come with us first, then you, Mr. Reilly."

The comedian stepped obediently forward, and turned into Charlie Chaplin. The policemen gaped as he twirled his cane.

Baggy pants fluttering, Chaplin turned back to the children, shoulders wiggling with silent mirth, white teeth flashing below his mustache.

"Is it too late?" Chris whispered, not wanting to believe it.

Chaplin looked at him and winked. And winked out.

The beach was silent, but for the sea breeze.

A new sun rose in the west.

Chris remembered the radio report about the failed summit at Oslo. The war had come at last.

Rippling flame surged towards the beach. Hotels, condominiums, towers crumbled like sand castles. Whirling at the shockwave's advancing rim was a scintillant point.

The children shrank around Chris. He spread his arms to hug them tight.

A policeman dropped his gun as the point came toward him, and then all the cops and bathers were crushed into the heaving sand.

Just before the shockwave reached them, Chris and the comedian's kids were sheltered within the disjunctive node, a whorl of perfect light.

And then they were gone.

WRITTEN IN WATER

by Tanith Lee

*Fredric Brown, we believe it was, who wrote a
famous short story about the Last Man on Earth
sitting in his lonely room when there came a
knock on the door. Tanith Lee, not to be out-
done, now relates the tale of the Last Woman on
Earth, sitting peacefully in her house when something unexpected went thump into her garden.*

It was a still summer night, coloured through by darkness.
A snow-white star fell out of the sky and into the black field
half a mile from the house. Ten minutes later, Jaina had
walked from the house, through the fenced garden patch, the
creaking gate, toward the place where the star had fallen.
Presently, she was standing over a young man, lying tangled
in a silver web, on the burned lap of the earth.

"Who are you?" said Jaina. "What's happened to you? Can
you talk? Can you tell me?"

The young man, who was very young, about twenty-two or
three, moved his slim young body, turning his face. He was

159

wonderful to look at, so wonderful, Jaina needed to take a deep breath before she spoke to him again.

"I want to help you. Can you say anything?"

He opened a pair of eyes, like two windows opening on sunlight in the dark. His eyes were beautiful, and very golden. He said nothing, not even anything she could not understand. She looked at him, drinking in, intuitively, his beauty; knowing, also intuitively, that he had nothing to do either with her world, or her time.

"Where did you come from?" she said.

He looked back at her. He seemed to guess, and then to consider. Gravely, gracefully, he lifted one arm from the tangle of the web, and pointed at the sky.

He sat in her kitchen, at her table. She offered him medication, food, alcohol, and caffeine from a tall bronzed coffee pot. He shook his head, slowly. Semantically, some gestures were the same. Yet not the same. Even in the shaking of his head, she perceived he was alien. His hair was the colour of the coffee he refused. Coffee, with a few drops of milk in it, and a burnish like satin. His skin was pale. So pale, it too was barely humanly associable. She had an inspiration, and filled a glass with water. The water was pure, filtered through the faucet from the well in the courtyard, without chemicals or additives. Even so, it might poison him. He had not seemed hurt after all, merely stunned, shaken. He had walked to her house quietly, at her side, responding to her swift angular little gestures of beckoning and reception. Now she wanted to give him something.

She placed the glass before him. He looked at it, and took it up in two finely made, strong, articulate hands. They were the hands of a dancer, a musician. They had each only four fingers, one thumb, quite normal. He carried the glass to his mouth. She held her breath, wondering, waiting. He put the glass down carefully, and moved it, as carefully, away from him. He laid his arms across the table and his head upon his arms, and he wept.

Jaina stood staring at him. A single strand of silver, left adhering when he stripped himself of the web, lay across his arm, glittering as his shoulders shook. She listened to him crying, a young man's sobs, painful, tearing him. She approached him, and muttered: "What is it? What is it?" help-lessly.

Of course, it was only grief. She put her hand on his shoul-der, anxious, for he might flinch from her touch, or some in-imical thing in their separate chemistries might damage both of them. But he did not flinch, and no flame burst out be-tween her palm and the dark; apparently seamless clothing which he wore.

"Don't cry," she said. But she did not mean it. His distress afforded her an exquisite agony of empathic pain. She had not felt anything for a very long time. She stroked his hair gently. Perhaps some subtle radiation clung to him, some killer dust from a faraway star. She did not care. "Oh, don't cry, don't cry," she murmured, swimming in his tears.

She drove into the morning town in her ramshackle car, as usual not paying much attention to anything about her. Nor was her programme much changed. First, petrol from the self-service station, then a tour of the shops, going in and out of their uninviting façades: a tour of duty. In the large hy-permarket at the edge of town, she made her way through the plastic and the cans, vaguely irritated, as always, by the soft mush of music, which came and went on a time switch, regardless of who wanted it, or no longer did. Once, she had seen a rat scuttle over the floor behind the frozen meat sec-tion. Jaina had done her best to ignore such evidence of neglect. She had walked out of the shop stiffly.

She had never liked people very much. They had always hurt her or degraded her, always imposed on her in some way. Finally she had retreated into the old house, wanting to be alone, a hermitess. Her ultimate loneliness, deeper than any state she had actually imagined for herself, was almost like a judgment. She was thirty-five and, to herself, resembled a burned-out lamp. The dry leaf-brownness of her skin, the tindery quality of her hair, gave her but further evidence of this consuming. Alone, alone. She had been alone so long. And burned, a charred stick, incapable of moistures, fluidities. And yet, streams and oceans had moved in her, when the young man from outer space had sobbed with his arms on her table.

She supposed, wryly, that the normal human reaction to what had happened would be a desire to contact someone, inform someone of her miraculous find, her 'Encounter.' She only played with this idea, comparing it to her present circumstances. She felt, of course, no onus on her to act in a rational way. Besides, who should she approach with her story, who would be likely to credit her? While she herself had no doubts.

But as she was turning on to the dirt road that led to the house, she became the prey of sudden insecurities. Perhaps the ultimate loneliness had told, she had gone insane, fantasizing the falling star of the parachute, imagining the young man with eyes like golden sovereigns. Or, if it were true. . . . Possbily, virulent Terran germs, carried by herself, her touch, had already killed him. She pictured, irresistibly, Wells' Martians lying dead and decaying in their great machines, slain by the microbes of Earth.

Last night, when he had grown calm, or only tired, she had led him to her bedroom and shown him her bed. It was a narrow bed, what else, fit only for one. Past lovers had taught her that the single bed was to be hers, in spite of them, forever. But he had lain down there without a word. She had slept in the room below, in a straight-backed chair between the bureau and the TV set which did not work anymore. Waking at sunrise, with a shamed awareness of a new feeling, which was that of a child on Christmas morning, she had slunk to look at him asleep. And she was reminded of some poem she had read, long, long ago:

How beautiful you look when sleeping; so beautiful
It seems that you have gone away. . . .

She had left him there, afraid to disturb such completion, afraid to stand and feed parasitically on him. She had driven instead into town for extra supplies. She wanted to bring him things; food he might not eat, drink he might not drink. Even music, even books he could not assimilate.

But now—he might be gone, never have existed. Or he might be dead.

She spun the car to a complaining halt in the summer dust. She ran between the tall carboniferous trees, around the fence. Her heart was in her throat, congesting and blinding her.

The whole day lay out over the country in a white-hot

film. She turned her head, trying to see through this film, as if underwater. The house looked silent, mummified. Empty. The land was the same, an erased tape. She glanced at the blackened field.

As she stumbled toward the house, her breathing harsh, he came out through the open door.

He carried the spade which she had used to turn the pitiful garden. He had been cleaning the spade, it looked bright and shiny. He leaned it on the porch and walked toward her. As she stared at him, taking oxygen in great gulps, he went by her, and began to lift things out of the car and carry them to the house.

"I thought you were dead," she said stupidly. She stood stupidly, her head stupidly hanging, feeling suddenly very sick and drained.

After a while she too walked slowly into the house. While he continued to fetch the boxes and tins into her kitchen like an errand boy, she sat at the table, where he had sat the night before. It occurred to her she could have brought him fresh clothing from the stores in the town, but it would have embarrassed her slightly to choose things for him, even randomly off the peg in the hypermarket.

His intention had presumably been to work on her garden, some sort of repayment for her haphazard, inadequate hospitality. And for this work he had stripped bare to the waist. She was afraid to look at him. The torso, what was revealed of it, was also like a dancer's—supple, the musculature developed and flawless. She debated, in a dim terror of herself, if his human maleness extended to all regions of his body.

After a long time, he stopped bringing in the supplies, and took up the spade once more.

"Are you hungry?" she said to him. She showed him one of the cans. As previously, slow and quiet, he shook his head.

Perhaps he did not need to eat. Perhaps he would drink her blood. Her veins filled with fire, and she left the table, and went quickly upstairs. She should tell someone about him. If only she were able to. But she could not.

He was hers.

She lay in the bath, in the cool water, letting her washed wet hair float round her. She was Ophelia. Not swimming;

drowning. A slender glass of greenish gin on five rocks of milky ice pulsed in her fingers to the rhythm of her heart.

Below, she heard the spade ring tirelessly on stone. She had struggled with the plot, raising a few beans, tomatoes, potatoes which blackened and a vine which died. But he would make her garden grow. Oh, yes.

She rested her head on the bath's porcelain rim, and laughed, trembling, the tips of her breasts breaking the water like buds.

She visualized a silver bud in the sky, blossoming into a huge and fiery ship. The ship came down on the black field. It had come for him, come to take him home. She held his hand and pleaded, in a language he did not comprehend, and a voice spoke to him out of the ship, in a language which he knew well. She clung to his ankle, and he pulled her through the scorched grass, not noticing her, as he ran toward the blazing port.

Why else had he wept? Somehow and somewhere, out beyond the moon, his inexplicable craft had foundered. Everything was lost to him. His vessel, his home, his world, his kind. Instead there was a bony house, a bony, dried-out hag, food he could not eat. A living death.

Jaina felt anger. She felt anger as she had not felt it for several months, hearing that spade ring on the indomitable rock under the soil. Still alone.

When the clock chimed six times that meant it was one quarter past five, and Jaina came down the stairs of the house. She wore a dress like white tissue, and a marvellous scent out of a crystal bottle. She had seen herself in a mirror, brushing her face with delicate pastel dusts, and her eyes with cinnamon and charcoal.

She stood on the porch, feeling a butterfly lightness. She stretched up her hand to shield her eyes, the gesture of a heroine upon the veranda of a dream. He rested on the spade, watching her.

See how I am, she thought. *Please, please, see me, see me.*

She walked off the porch, across the garden. She went straight up to him. The sun in his eyes blinded her. She could not smile at him. She pointed to her breast.

"*Jaina*," she said. "I am *Jaina*." She pointed to him. She did not touch him. "You?"

She had seen it done so frequently. In films. She had read it in books. Now he himself would smile slightly, uneasily touch his own chest and say, in some foreign otherworld tongue: *I am....*

But he did not. He gazed at her, and once more he slowly shook his head. Suddenly, all the glorious pity and complementary grief she had felt through him before flooded back, overwhelming her. Could it be he did not know, could not remember, who he was? His name, his race, his planet? He had fallen out of the stars. He was amnesiac. Truly defenceless, then. Truly hers.

"Don't work any more," she said. She took the spade from his hand, and let it drop on the upturned soil.

Again, she led him back to the house, still not touching him.

In the kitchen, she said to him. "You must try and tell me what food you need to eat. You really must."

He continued to watch her, if he actually saw her at all. She imagined him biting off her arm, and shivered. Perhaps he did not eat—she had considered that before. Not eat, not sleep—the illusion of sleep only a suspended state, induced to please her, or pacify her. She did not think he had used the bathroom. He did not seem to sweat. How odd he should have been able to shed tears.

She dismissed the idea of eating for herself, too. She poured herself another deep swamp of ice and gin. She sat on the porch and he sat beside her.

His eyes looked out across the country. Looking for escape? She could smell the strange sweatless, poreless, yet indefinably masculine scent of him. His extraordinary skin had taken on a water-couler glaze of sunburn.

The day flickered along the varied tops of the reddening horizon. Birds swirled over like a flight of miniature planes. When the first star appeared, she knew she would catch her breath in fear.

The valves of the sky loosened and blueness poured into it. The sun had gone. He could not understand her, so she said to him: "I love you."

"I love you," she said. "I'm the last woman on Earth, and you're not even local talent. And I love you. I'm lonely," she said. And, unlike him, she cried quietly.

After a while, just as she would have wished him to if this

had been a film, and she directing it, he put his arm about her, gently, gently. She lay against him and he stroked her hair. She thought, with a strange ghostly sorrow: *He has learned such gestures from me.*

Of course, she did not love him, and of course she did. She was the last survivor, and he was also a survivor. Inevitably they must come together, find each other, love. She wished she was younger. She began to feel younger as his arm supported her, and his articulate fingers silked through and through her hair. In a low voice, although he could not understand, she began to tell him about the plague. How it had come, a whisper, the fall of a leaf far away. How it had swept over the world, its continents, its cities, like a sea. A sea of leaves, burning. A fire. They had not called it plague. The official name for it had been 'Pandemic.' At first, the radios had chattered with it, the glowing pools of the TVs had crackled with it. She had seen hospitals packed like great antiseptic trays with racks of the dying. She had heard how silence came. At length, more than silence came. They burned the dead, or cremated them with burning chemicals. They evacuated the towns. Then 'they' too ceased to organise anything. It was a selective disease. It killed men and women and children. It could not destroy the animals, the insects, the birds. Or Jaina.

At first, the first falling of the leaf, she had not believed. It was hard to believe that such an unstoppable engine had been started. The radio and the television set spoke of decaying cylinders in the sea, or satellites which corroded, letting go their cargoes of viruses, mistimed, on the earth. Governments denied responsibility, and died denying it.

Jaina heard the tread of death draw near, and nearer. From disbelief, she came to fear. She stocked her hermitage, as she had always done, and crouched in new terror behind her door. As the radio turned dumb, and the TV spluttered and choked to blindness, Jaina stared from her porch, looking for a huge black shadow to descend across the land.

They burned a pile of the dead on a giant bonfire in the field, half a mile from the house. The ashes blew across the sunset. The sky was burning its dead, too.

A day later, Jaina found little fiery mottles over her skin. Her head throbbed, just as the walls were doing. She lay down with her terror, afraid to die. Then she did not care if she died. She wanted to die. Then she did not die at all.

A month later, she drove into the town. She found the emptiness of the evacuation and, two miles away, the marks of another enormous bonfire. And a mile beyond that, dead people lying out in the sun, turning to pillars of salt and white sticks of candy, and the fearless birds, immune, dropping like black rain on the place.

Jaina drove home, and became the last woman on earth.

Her life was not so very different, she had been quite solitary for many years before the plague came.

She had sometimes mused as to why she had lived, but only in the silly, falsely modest way of any survivor. Everyone knew they could not die, hang the rest, they alone must come through. They had all been wrong, all but Jaina.

And then, one night, a snow-white star, the silver web of the alien parachute, a young man more beautiful than truth.

She told him everything as she lay against his shoulder. He might still be capable of dying, a Martian, susceptible to the plague virus. Or he might go away.

It was dark now. She lifted her mouth to his in the darkness. As she kissed him, she was unsure what he would do. He did not seem to react in any way. Would he make love to her, or want to, or was he able to? She slid her hands over his skin, like warm smooth stone. She loved him. But perhaps he was only a robot.

After a little while, she drew away, and left him seated on the porch. She went into the kitchen and threw the melted ice in her glass into the sink.

She climbed the stairs; she lay down on the narrow bed. Alone. Alone. But somehow even then, she sensed the irony was incomplete. And when he came into the room, she was not surprised. He leaned over her, silently, and his eyes shone in the darkness, like the eyes of a cat. She attempted to be afraid of him.

"Go away," she said.

But he stretched out beside her, very near, the bed so narrow. . . . As if he had learned now the etiquette of human love-making, reading its symbols from her mind.

"You're a robot, an android," she said. "Leave me alone."

He put his mouth over hers. She closed her eyes and saw a

star, a nova. He was not a robot, he was a man, a beautiful man, and she loved him. . . .

Twenty million miles away, the clock chimed eight times. It was one quarter past seven, on the first night of the world.

In the morning, she baked bread, and brought him some, still warm. He held the bread cupped in his hands like a paralysed bird. She pointed to herself. "Please. Call me by my name. *Jaina*."

She was sure she could make him grasp the meaning. She knew he had a voice. She had heard his tears, and, during their love-making, heard him groan. She would teach him to eat and drink, too. She would teach him everything.

He tilled the garden; he had found seedlings in the leaning shed and was planting them, until she came to him and led him to the ramshackle car. She drove him into town, then took him into clothing stores, directing him, diffidently. In accordance with her instructions, he loaded the car. She had never seen him smile. She pondered if she ever would. He carried piled jeans with the same eternally dispassionate disinterest: still the errand boy.

During the afternoon she watched him in the garden. Her pulses raced, and she could think of nothing else but the play of muscles under his swiftly and mellifluously tanning skin. He hypnotised her. She fell asleep and dreamed of him.

She roused at a sound of light blows on metal. Alarmed, she walked out into the last gasps of the day, to find him behind the courtyard, hammering dents out of the battered car. She perceived he had changed a tyre she had not bothered with, though it was worn. She relaxed against the wall, brooding on him. He was going to be almost ludicrously useful. For some reason, the archaic word *helpmeet* stole into her mind.

Over it all hung the smoke of premonition. He would be going away. Stranded, marooned, shipwrecked, the great liner would move out of the firmament, cruel as God, to rescue him.

She woke somewhere in the centre of the night, her lips against his spine, with a dreadful knowledge.

For a long while she lay immobile, then lifted herself onto one elbow. She stayed that way, looking at him, his feigned sleep, or the real unconsciousness which appeared to have claimed him. *It seems that you have gone away.* No. He would not be going anywhere.

His hair gleamed, his lashes lay in long brush strokes on his cheeks. He was quiescent, limpid, as if poured from a jar. She touched his flank, coldly.

After a minute, she rose and went to the window, and looked out and upward into the vault of the night sky. A low blaring of hatred and contempt ran through her. *Where are you?* She thought. *Do you see? Are you laughing?*

She walked down the stairs and into the room where the dead TV sat in the dark. She opened a drawer in the bureau and took out a revolver. She loaded it carefully from the clip. She held it pointed before her as she went back up into the bedroom.

He did not wake up—or whatever simulation he contrived that passed for waking—until the hour before the dawn. She had sat there all the time, waiting for him, wanting him to open his eyes and see her, seated facing him, her hand resting on her knee, the revolver in her hand. Pointing now at him.

There was a chance he might not know what the gun was. Yet weapons, like certain semantic signs, would surely be instantly, instinctively recognisable. So she thought. As his eyes opened and fixed on the gun, she believed he knew perfectly well what it was, and that she had brought it there to kill him with.

His eyes grew very wide, but he did not move. He did not appear afraid, yet she considered he must be afraid. As afraid of her as she might have been expected to be of him, and yet had never been: the natural fear of an alien, xenophobia. She thought he could, after all, understand her words, had understood her from the beginning, her language, her loneliness. It would have been part of his instruction. Along with the lessons which had taught him how to work the land, change a tyre, make love, pretend to sleep. . . . About the same time, they must have inoculated him against the deadly plague virus, indeed all the viruses of Earth.

"Yes," she said. "I *am* going to kill you."

He only looked at her. She remembered how he had wept, out of dread of her, loathing and despair. Because he had known there would be no rescue for him. Neither rescue from her planet nor from herself. He had not fallen from a burning spacecraft into the world. The craft had been whole, and he had been dropped neatly out of it, at a designated hour, at a calculated altitude, his parachute unfolding, a pre-programmed cloud. Not shipwrecked, but dispatched. Air mail. A present.

The great silent ship would not come seeking him. It had already come, and gone.

Why did they care so much? She could not fathom that. An interfering streak—was this the prerogative of gods? Altruistic benefactors, or simply playing with toys. Or it might be an experiment of some sort. They had not been able to prevent the plague, or had not wanted to—recall the Flood, Gomorrah—but when the plague had drawn away down its tidal drain, washing humanity with it, they had looked and seen Jaina wandering alone on the earth, mistress of it, the last of her kind. So they had made for her a helpmate and companion. Presumably not made him in *their* extraterrestrial image, whoever, whatever they omnipotently were, but in the image of a man.

She was uncertain what had triggered her final deduction. His acquiescence, the unlikely aptness of it all, the foolish co-incidence of survivor flung down beside survivor, pat. Or was it the theatricality which had itself suggested puppet masters to her subconscious: the last man and the last woman left to propagate continuance of a species. Or was it only her mistrust? All the wrongs she had, or imagined she had suffered, clamouring that this was no different from any other time. Someone still manipulated, still *imposed* on her.

"Well," she said softly, looking at him, it appeared to her, through the eye of the gun, "I seem to be missing a rib. Do I call you Adam? Or would it be *Eve?*" She clicked off the safety catch. She trembled violently, though her voice was steady. "What about contraception, Adameve? Did they think I'd never heard of it, or used it? Did they think I'd risk having babies, with no hospitals, not even a vet in sight? At thirty-five years of age? When I dressed up for you, I dressed thoroughly, *all* of me. Just in case. Seems I was wise. I don't think even your specially designed seed is so potent it can negate my precautions. In the tank where they grew you, or the machine shop where they built you, did they think of *that?* I don't want you," she whispered. "You cried like a child because they condemned you to live on my world, with me. Do you think I can forgive you that? Do you think I want you after that, now I *know?*"

She raised the gun and fired. She watched the sun go out in the windows of his eyes. His blood was red, quite normal.

Jaina walked across the burn scar of the field. She pictured a huge wheel hanging over her, beyond and above the sky, pictured it no longer watching, already drawing inexorably away and away. She dragged the spade along the ground, as she had dragged his body. Now the spade had turned potatoes, and beans, and alien flesh.

She stood in the kitchen of the old house, and the darkness like space came and coloured the sky through. Jaina held her breath, held it and held it, as if the air had filled with water, closing over her head. For she knew. Long before it happened, she knew. She only let out her breath in a slow sigh, horribly flattered, as the second snow-white star fell out of the summer night.

SOULS

by Joanna Russ

The publisher of the magazine in which this first appeared stated that is is to be part of a novel the author is writing. Nevertheless it stands very well by itself. Reading it suggests at first that it might be an historical novel—not an historical romance—that has been deeply researched and brings back a terrible time of turmoil and barbarism. But it is not an historical—it is indeed a work of science fiction.

Deprived of other Banquet
I entertained myself—

—Emily Dickinson

This is the tale of the Abbess Radegunde and what happened when the Norsemen came. I tell it not as it was told to me but as I saw it, for I was a child then and the Abbess had made a pet and errand boy of me, although the stern old Wardress, Cunigunt, who had outlived the previous Abbess,

172

said I was more in the Abbey than out of it and a scandal. But the Abbess would only say mildly, "Dear Cunigunt, a scandal at the age of seven?" which was turning it off with a joke, for she knew how harsh and disliking my new stepmother was to me and my father did not care and I with no sisters or brothers. You must understand that joking and calling people "dear" and "my dear" was only her manner; she was in every way an unusual woman. The previous Abbess, Herrade, had found that Radegunde, who had been given to her to be fostered, had great gifts and so sent the child south to be taught, and that has never happened here before. The story has it that the Abbess Herrade found Radegunde seeming to read the great illuminated book in the Abbess's study; the child had somehow pulled it off its stand and was sitting on the floor with the volume in her lap, sucking her thumb, and turning the pages with her other hand just as if she were reading.

"Little two-years," said the Abbess Herrade, who was a kind woman, "what are you doing?" She thought it amusing, I suppose, that Radegunde should pretend to read this great book, the largest and finest in the Abbey, which had many, many books more than any other nunnery or monastery I have ever heard of: a full forty then, as I remember. And then little Radegunde was doing the book no harm.

"Reading, Mother," said the little girl.

"Oh, reading?" said the Abbess, smiling. "Then tell me what you are reading," and she pointed to the page.

"This," said Radegunde, "is a great *D* with flowers and other beautiful things about it, which is to show that *Dominus*, our Lord God, is the greatest thing and the most beautiful and makes everything to grow and be beautiful, and then it goes on to say *Domine nobis pacem*, which means *Give peace to us, O Lord*."

Then the Abbess began to be frightened but she said only, "Who showed you this?" thinking that Radegunde had heard someone read and tell the words or had been pestering the nuns on the sly.

"No one," said the child. "Shall I go on?" and she read page after page of the Latin, in each case telling what the words meant.

There is more to the story, but I will say only that after many prayers the Abbess Herrade sent her foster daughter far southwards, even to Poitiers, where Saint Radegunde had ruled an Abbey before, and some say even to Rome, and in these places Radegunde was taught all learning, for all learning there is in the world remains in these places. Radegunde came back a grown woman and nursed the Abbess through her last illness and then became Abbess in her turn. They say that the great folk of the Church down there in the south wanted to keep her because she was such a prodigy of female piety and learning, there where life is safe and comfortable and less rude than it is here, but she said that the gray skies and flooding winters of her birthplace called to her very soul. She often told me the story when I was a child: how headstrong she had been and how defiant, and how she had sickened so desperately for her native land that they had sent her back, deciding that a rude life in the mud of a northern village would be a good cure for such a rebellious soul as hers.

"And so it was," she would say, patting my cheek or tweaking my ear. "See how humble I am now?" for you understand, all this about her rebellious girlhood, twenty years' back, was a kind of joke between us. "Don't you do it," she would tell me and we would laugh together, I so heartily at the very idea of my being a pious monk full of learning that I would hold my sides and be unable to speak.

She was kind to everyone. She knew all the languages, not only ours, but the Irish too and the tongues folk speak to the north and south, and Latin and Greek also, and all the other languages in the world, both to read and write. She knew how to cure sickness, both the old women's way with herbs or leeches and out of books also. And never was there a more pious woman! Some speak ill of her now she's gone and say she was too merry to be a good Abbess, but she would say, "Merriment is God's flowers," and when the winter wind blew her headdress awry and showed the gray hair—which happened once; I was there and saw the shocked faces of the Sisters with her—she merely tapped the band back into place, smiling and saying, "Impudent wind! Thou showest thou hast power which is more than our silly human power, for it is from God"—and this quite satisfied the girls with her.

No one ever saw her angry. She was impatient sometimes, but in a kindly way, as if her mind were elsewhere. It was in Heaven, I used to think, for I have seen her pray for hours or sink to her knees—right in the marsh!—to see the wild duck

fly south, her hands clasped and a kind of wild joy on her
face, only to rise a moment later, looking at the mud on her
habit and crying half-ruefully, half in laughter, "Oh, what
will Sister Laundress say to me? I am hopeless! Dear child,
tell no one; I will say I fell," and then she would clap her
hand to her mouth, turning red and laughing even harder,
saying, "I *am* hopeless, telling lies!"

The town thought her a saint, of course. We were all
happy then, or so it seems to me now, and all lucky and well,
with this happiness of having her amongst us burning and
blooming in our midst like a great fire around which we
could all warm ourselves, even those who didn't know why
life seemed so good. There was less illness; the food was better; the very weather stayed mild; and people did not quarrel
as they had before her time and do again now. Nor do I
think, considering what happened at the end, that all this was
nothing but the fancy of a boy who's found his mother, for
that's what she was to me; I brought her all the gossip and
ran errands when I could, and she called me Boy News in
Latin; I was happier than I have ever been.

And then one day those terrible, beaked prows appeared in
our river.

I was with her when the warning came, in the main room
of the Abbey tower just after the first fire of the year had
been lit in the great hearth; we thought ourselves safe, for
they had never been seen so far south and it was too late in
the year for any sensible shipman to be in our waters. The
Abbey was host to three Irish priests who turned pale when
young Sister Sibihd burst in with the news, crying and wringing her hands; one of the brothers exclaimed a thing in Latin
which means "God protect us!" for they had been telling us
stories of the terrible sack of the monastery of Saint Colum-
banus and how everyone had run away with the precious
manuscripts or had hidden in the woods, and that was how
Father Cairbre and the two others had decided to go "walk
the world," for this (the Abbess had been telling it all to me,
for I had no Latin) is what the Irish say when they leave
their native land to travel elsewhere.

"God protects our souls, not our bodies," said the Abbess
Radegunde briskly. She had been talking with the priests in
their own language or in the Latin, but this she said in ours
so even the women workers from the village would under-

stand. Then she said; "Father Cairbre, take your friends and the younger Sisters to the underground passages; Sister Diemud, open the gates to the villagers; half of them will be trying to get behind the Abbey walls and the others will be fleeing to the marsh. You, Boy News, down to the cellars with the girls." But I did not go and she never saw it; she was up and looking out one of the window slits instantly. So was I. I had always thought the Norsemen's big ships came right up on land—on legs, I supposed—and was disappointed to see that after they came up our river they stayed in the water like other ships and the men were coming ashore in little boats, which they were busy pulling up on shore through the sand and mud. Then the Abbess repeated her order—"Quickly! Quickly!"—and before anyone knew what had happened, she was gone from the room. I watched from the tower window; in the turmoil nobody bothered about me. Below, the Abbey grounds and gardens were packed with folk, all stepping on the herb plots and the Abbess's paestum roses, and great logs were being dragged to bar the door set in the stone walls round the Abbey, not high walls, to tell truth, and Radegunde was going quickly through the crowd, crying: Do this! Do that! Stay, thou! Go, thou! and like things.

Then she reached the door and motioned Sister Oddha, the doorkeeper, aside—the old Sister actually fell to her knees in entreaty—and all this, you must understand, was wonderfully pleasant to me. I had no more idea of danger than a puppy. There was some tumult by the door—I think the men with the logs were trying to get in her way—and Abbess Radegunde took out from the neck of her habit her silver crucifix, brought all the way from Rome, and shook it impatiently at those who would keep her in. So of course they let her through at once.

I settled into my corner of the window, waiting for the Abbess's crucifix to bring down God's lightning on those tall, fair men who defied Our Savior and the law and were supposed to wear animal horns on their heads, though these did not (and I found out later that's just a story; that is not what the Norse do). I did hope that the Abbess, or Our Lord, would wait just a little while before destroying them, for I wanted to get a good look at them before they all died, you understand. I was somewhat disappointed, as they seemed to be wearing breeches with leggings under them and tunics on top, like ordinary folk, and cloaks also, though some did carry swords and axes and there were round shields piled on the beach at one place. But the long hair they had was fine, and the bright colors of their clothes, and the monsters growing out of the heads of the ships were splendid and very frightening, even though one could see that they were only painted, like the pictures in the Abbess's books.

I decided that God had provided me with enough edification and could now strike down the impious strangers.

But He did not.

Instead the Abbess walked alone towards these fierce men, over the stony river bank, as calmly as if she were on a picnic with her girls. She was singing a little song, a pretty tune that I repeated many years later, and a well-traveled man said it was a Norse cradle-song. I didn't know that then, but only that the terrible, fair men, who had looked up in surprise at seeing one lone woman come out of the Abbey (which was barred behind her; I could see that), now began a sort of whispering astonishment among themselves. I saw the Abbess's gaze go quickly from one to the other—we often said that she could tell what was hidden in the soul from one look at the face—and then she picked the skirt of her habit up with one hand and daintily went among the rocks to one of the men, one older than the others, as it proved later, though I could not see so well at the time—and said to him, in his own language:

"Welcome, Thorvald Einarsson, and what do you, good farmer, so far from your own place, with the harvest ripe and the great autumn storms coming on over the sea?" (You may wonder how I knew what she said when I had no Norse; the truth is that Father Cairbre, who had not gone to the cellars, after all, was looking out the top of the window while I was barely able to peep out the bottom, and he repeated everything that was said for the folk in the room, who all kept very quiet.)

Now you could see that the pirates were dumfounded to hear her speak their own language and even more so that she called one by his name; some stepped backwards and made strange signs in the air and others unsheathed axes or swords and came running towards the Abbess. But this Thorvald Einarsson put up his hand for them to stop and laughed heartily.

"Think!" he said. "There's no magic here, only cleverness—what pair of ears could miss my name with the lot of you bawling out 'Thorvald Einarsson, help me with this oar;' 'Thorvald Einarsson, my leggings are wet to the knees;' 'Thorvald Einarsson, this stream is as cold as a Fimbul-winter!' "

The Abbess Radegunde nodded and smiled. Then she sat down plump on the river bank. She scratched behind one ear, as I had often seen her do when she was deep in thought. Then she said (and I am sure that this talk was carried on in a loud voice so that we in the Abbey could hear it):

"Good friend Thorvald, you are as clever as the tale I heard of you from your sister's son, Ranulf, from whom I learnt the Norse when I was in Rome, and to show you it was he, he always swore by his gray horse, Lamefoot, and he had a difficulty in his speech; he could not say the sounds as we do and so spoke of you always as 'Torvald.' Is not that so?"

I did not realize it then, being only a child, but the Abbess was—by this speech—claiming hospitality from the man and had also picked by chance or inspiration the cleverest among these thieves, for his next words were:

"I am not the leader. There are no leaders here."

He was warning her that they were not his men to control, you see. So she scratched behind her ear again and got up. Then she began to wander, as if she did not know what to do, from one to the other of these uneasy folk—for some backed off and made signs at her still, and some took out their knives—singing her little tune again and walking slowly, more bent over and older and infirm-looking than we had ever seen her, one helpless little woman in black before all those fierce men. One wild young pirate snatched the headdress from her as she passed, leaving her short gray hair bare to the wind; the others laughed and he that had done it cried out:

"Grandmother, are you not ashamed?"

"Why, good friend, of what?" said she mildly.

"Thou art married to thy Christ," he said, holding the head-covering behind his back, "but this bridegroom of thine cannot even defend thee against the shame of having thy head uncovered! Now if thou wert married to me—"

There was much laughter. The Abbess Radegunde waited until it was over. Then she scratched her bare head and made as if to turn away, but suddenly she turned back upon him with the age and infirmity dropping from her as if they had been a cloak, seeming taller and very grand, as if lit from within by some great fire. She looked directly into his face. This thing she did was something we had all seen, of course, but they had not, nor had they heard that great, grand voice with which she sometimes read the Scriptures to us or talked with us of the wrath of God. I think the young man was frightened, for all his daring. And I know now what I did not then: that the Norse admire courage above all things and that—to be blunt—everyone likes a good story, especially if it happens right in front of your eyes.

"Grandson!"—and her voice tolled like the great bell of God; I think folk must have heard her all the way to the marsh!—"Little grandchild, thinkest thou that the Creator of the World who made the stars and the moon and the sun and our bodies, too and the change of the seasons and the very earth we stand on—yea, even unto the shit in thy belly!—thinkest thou that such a being has a big house in the sky where he keeps his wives and goes in to fuck them as thou wouldst thyself or like the King of Turkey? Do not dishonor the wit of the mother who bore thee! We are the servants of God, not his wives, and if we tell our silly girls they are married to the Christus, it is to make them understand that they must not run off and marry Otto Farmer or Ekkehard Blacksmith, but stick to their work, as they promised. If I told them they were married to an Idea, they would not understand me, and neither dost thou."

(Here Father Cairbre, above me in the window, muttered in a protesting way about something.)

Then the Abbess snatched the silver cross from around her neck and put it into the boy's hand, saying: "Give this to thy mother with my pity. She must pull out her hair over such a child."

But he let it fall to the ground. He was red in the face and breathing hard.

"Take it up," she said more kindly, "take it up, boy; it will not hurt thee and there's no magic in it. It's only pure silver and good workmanship; it will make thee rich." When she saw that he would not—his hand went to his knife—she *tched* to herself in a motherly way (or I believe she did, for she waved one hand back and forth as she always did when she made that sound) and got down on her knees—with more difficulty than was truth, I think—saying loudly, "I will stoop, then; I will stoop," and got up; holding it out to him, saying, "Take. Two sticks tied with a cord would serve me as well."

The boy cried, his voice breaking, "My mother is dead and thou art a witch!" and in an instant he had one arm around the Abbess's neck and with the other his knife at her throat. The man Thorvald Einarsson roared "Thorfinn!" but the Abbess only said clearly, "Let him be. I have shamed this man but did not mean to. He is right to be angry."

The boy released her and turned his back. I remember wondering if these strangers could weep. Later I heard—and I swear that the Abbess must have somehow known this or felt it, for although she was no witch, she could probe a man until she found the sore places in him and that very quickly—that this boy's mother had been known for an adulteress and that no man would own him as a son. It is one thing among those people for a man to have what the Abbess called a concubine and they do not hold the children of such in scorn as we do, but it is a different thing when a married woman has more than one man. Such was Thorfinn's case; I suppose that was what had sent him *viking*. But all this came later; what I saw then—with my nose barely above the window slit—was that the Abbess slipped her crucifix over the hilt of the boy's sword she really wished him to have it, you see—and then walked to a place near the walls of the Abbey but far from the Norsemen. I think she meant them to come to her. I saw her pick up her skirts like a peasant woman, sit down with legs crossed, and say in a loud voice:

"Come! Who will bargain with me?"

A few strolled over, laughing, and sat down with her.

"All!" she said, gesturing them closer.

"And why should we all come?" said one who was farthest away.

"Because you will miss a bargain," said the Abbess.

"Why should we bargain when we can take?" said another.

"Because you will only get half," said the Abbess. "The rest you will not find."

"We will ransack the Abbey," said a third.

"Half the treasure is not in the Abbey," said she.

"And where is it then?"

She tapped her forehead. They were drifting over by twos and threes. I have heard since that the Norse love riddles and this was a sort of riddle; she was giving them good fun.

"If it is in your head," said the man Thorvald, who was standing behind the others, arms crossed, "we can get it out, can we not?" And he tapped the hilt of his knife.

"If you frighten me, I shall become confused and remember nothing." said the Abbess calmly. "Besides, do you wish to play that old game? You saw how well it worked the last time. I am surprised at you, Ranulf mother's-brother."

"I will bargain then," said the man Thorvald, smiling.

"And the rest of you?" said Radegunde, "It must be all or none; decide for yourselves whether you wish to save yourselves trouble and danger and be rich," and she deliberately turned her back on them. The men moved down to the river's edge and began to talk among themselves, dropping their voices so that we could not hear them any more. Father Cairbre, who was old and short-sighted, cried, "I cannot hear them. What are they doing?" and I cleverly said, "I have good eyes, Father Cairbre," and he held me up to see. So it was just at the time that the Abbess Radegunde was facing the Abbey tower that I appeared in the window. She clapped one hand across her mouth. Then she walked to the gate and called (in a voice I had learned not to disregard; it had often got me a smacked bottom), "Boy News, down! Come down to me here *at once!* And bring Father Cairbre with you."

I was overjoyed. I had no idea that she might want to protect me if anything went wrong. My only thought was that I was going to see it all from wonderfully close by. So I wormed my way, half-suffocated, through the folk in the tower room, stepping on feet and skirts, and having to say every few seconds, "But I *have* to! The Abbess wants me," and meanwhile she was calling outside like an Empress, "Let that boy through! Make a place for that boy! Let the Irish priest through!" until I crept and pushed and complained my way to the very wall itself—no one was going to open the gate for us, of course—and there was a great fuss and finally someone brought a ladder. I was over at once, but the old priest took a longer time, although it was a low wall, as I've said, the builders having been somewhat of two minds about making the Abbey into a true fortress.

Once outside it was lovely, away from all that crowd, and

I ran, gloriously pleased, to the Abbess, who said only, "Stay by me, whatever happens," and immediately turned her attention away from me. It had taken so long to get Father Cairbre outside the walls that the tall, foreign men had finished their talking and were coming back— all twenty or thirty of them—towards the Abbey and the Abbess Radegunde, and most especially of all, me. I could see Father Cairbre tremble. They did look grim, close by, with their long, wild hair and the brightness of their strange clothes. I remember that they smelled different from us, but cannot remember how after all these years. Then the Abbess spoke to them in that outlandish language of theirs, so strangely light and lilting to hear from their bearded lips, and then she said something in Latin to Father Cairbre, and he said, with a shake in his voice:

"This is the priest, Father Cairbre, who will say our bargains aloud in our own tongue so that my people may hear. I cannot deal behind their backs. And this is my foster baby, who is very dear to me and who is now having his curiosity rather too much satisfied, I think." (I was trying to stand tall like a man but had one hand secretly holding onto her skirt; so that was what the foreign men had chuckled at!) The talk went on, but I will tell it as if I had understood the Norse, for to repeat everything twice would be tedious.

The Abbess Radegunde said, "Will you bargain?"

There was a general nodding of heads, with a look of: After all, why not?

"And who will speak for you?" said she.

A man stepped forward; I recognized Thorvald Einarsson.

"Ah, yes," said the Abbess dryly. "The company that has no leaders. Is this leaderless company agreed? Will it abide by its word? I want no treachery-planners, no Breakwords here!"

There was a general mutter at this. The Thorvald man (he *was* big, close up!) said mildly, "I sail with none such. Let's begin."

We all sat down.

"Now," said Thorvald Einarsson, raising his eyebrows, "according to my knowledge of this thing, you begin. And according to my knowledge, you will begin by saying that you are very poor."

"But, no," said the Abbess, "we are rich." Father Cairbre

groaned. A groan answered him from behind the Abbey walls. Only the Abbess and Thorvald Einarsson seemed unmoved; it was as if these two were joking in some way that no one else understood. The Abbess went on, saying, "We are very rich. Within is much silver, much gold, many pearls, and much embroidered cloth, much fine-woven cloth, much carved and painted wood, and many books with gold upon their pages and jewels set into their covers. All this is yours. But we have more and better: herbs and medicines, ways to keep food from spoiling, the knowledge of how to cure the sick; all this is yours. And we have more and better even than this: we have the knowledge of Christ and the perfect understanding of the soul, which is yours too, any time you wish; you have only to accept it."

Thorvald Einarsson held up his hand. "We will stop with the first," he said, "and perhaps a little of the second. That is more practical."

"And foolish," said the Abbess politely, "in the usual way." And again I had the odd feeling that these two were sharing a joke no one else even saw. She added, "There is one thing you may not have, and that is the most precious of all."

Thorvald Einarsson looked inquiring.

"*My people.* Their safety is dearer to me than myself. They are not to be touched, not a hair on their heads, not for any reason. Think: you can fight your way into the Abbey easily enough, but the folk in there are very frightened of you, and some of the men are armed. Even a good fighter is cumbered in a crowd. You will slip and fall upon each other without meaning to or knowing that you do so. Heed my counsel. Why play butcher when you can have treasure poured into your laps like kings, without work? And after that there will be as much again, when I lead you to the hidden places. An earl's mountain of treasure. Think of it! And to give all this up for slaves, half of whom will get sick and die before you get them home—and will need to be fed if they are to be any good. Shame on you for bad advice-takers! Imagine what you will say to your wives and families: Here are a few miserable bolts of cloth with blood spots that won't come out, here are some pearls and jewels smashed to powder in the fighting, here is a torn piece of embroidery which was whole until someone stepped on it in the battle, and I had slaves but they died of illness and I fucked a pretty young nun and meant to bring her back, but she leapt into the sea. And, oh, yes, there was twice as much again and all of it whole but we decided not to take that. Too much trouble, you see."

This was a lively story and the Norsemen enjoyed it. Radegunde held up her hand.

"People!" she called in German, adding, "Sea-rovers, hear what I say; I will repeat it for you in your tongue." (And so she did.) *"People, if the Norsemen fight us, do not defend yourselves but smash everything! Wives, take your cooking knives and shred the valuable cloth to pieces! Men, with your axes and hammers hew the altars and the carved wood to fragments! All, grind the pearls and smash the jewels against the stone floors! Break the bottles of wine! Pound the gold and silver to shapelessness! Tear to pieces the illuminated books! Tear down the hangings and burn them!*

"But" (she added, her voice suddenly mild) "if these wise men will accept our gifts, let us heap untouched and spotless at their feet all that we have and hold nothing back, so that their kinsfolk will marvel and wonder at the shining and glistering of the wealth they bring back, though it leave us nothing but our bare stone walls."

If anyone had ever doubted that the Abbess Radegunde was inspired by God, their doubts must have vanished away, for who could resist the fiery vigor of her first speech or the beneficent unction of her second? The Norsemen sat there with their mouths open. I saw tears on Father Cairbre's cheeks. Then Thorvald said, "Abbess——"

He stopped. He tried again but again stopped. Then he shook himself, as a man who has been under a spell, and said:

"Abbess, my men have been without women for a long time."

Radegunde looked surprised. She looked as if she could not believe what she had heard. She looked the pirate up and down, as if puzzled, and then walked around him as if taking his measure. She did this several times, looking at every part of his big body as if she were summing him up while he got redder and redder. Then she backed off and surveyed him again, and with her arms akimbo like a peasant, announced very loudly in both Norse and German:

"What! Have they lost the use of their hands?"

It was irresistible, in its way. The Norse laughed. Our people laughed. Even Thorvald laughed. I did too, though I was not sure what everyone was laughing about. The laughter would die down and then begin again behind the Abbey walls, helplessly, and again die down and again begin. The Abbess waited until the Norsemen had stopped laughing and then called for silence in German until there were only a few snickers here and there. She then said:

"These good men—Father Cairbre, tell the people—these good men will forgive my silly joke. I meant no scandal, truly, and no harm, but laughter is good; it settles the body's waters, as the physicians say. And my people know that I am not always as solemn and good as I ought to be. Indeed I am a very great sinner and scandal-maker. Thorvald Einarsson, do we do business?"

The big man—who had not been so pleased as the others, I can tell you! —looked at his men and seemed to see what he needed to know. He said, "I go in with five men to see what you have. Then we let the poor folk on the grounds go, but not those inside the Abbey. Then we search again. The gates will be locked and guarded by the rest of us; if there's any treachery, the bargain's off."

"Then I will go with you," said Radegunde. "That is very just and my presence will calm the people. To see us together will assure them that no harm is meant. You are a good man, Torvald—forgive me; I call you as your nephew did so often. Come, Boy News, hold on to me."

"Open the gates!" she called then. "All is safe!" and with the five men (one of whom was that young Thorfinn who had hated her so) we waited while the great logs were pulled back. There was little space within, but the people shrank back at the sight of those fierce warriors and opened a place for us.

I looked back and the Norsemen had come in and were standing just inside the walls, on either side the gate, with their swords out and their shields up. The crowd parted for us more slowly as we reached the main tower, with the Abbess repeating constantly, "Be calm, people, be calm. All is well," and deftly speaking by name to this one or that. It was much harder when the people gasped upon hearing the big logs pushed shut with a noise like thunder, and it was very close on the stairs; I heard her say something like an apology in the queer foreign tongue. Something that probably meant, "I'm sorry that we must wait." It seemed an age until the stairs were even partly clear and I saw what the Abbess had meant by the cumbering of a crowd; a man might swing a weapon in the press of people, but not very far, and it was more likely he would simply fall over someone and crack his head. We gained the great room with the big crucifix of painted wood and the little one of pearls and gold, and the scarlet hangings worked in gold thread that I had played robbers behind so often before I learned what real robbers were: these tall, frightening men whose eyes glistened with greed at what I had fancied every village had. Most of the Sisters had stayed in the great room, but somehow it was not so crowded, as the folk had huddled back against the walls when the Norsemen came in. The youngest girls were all in a corner, terrified—one could smell it, as one can in people—and when that young Thorfinn went for the little gold-and-pearl cross, Sister Sibihd cried in a high, cracked voice, "It is the body of our Christ!" and leapt up, snatching it from the wall before he could get to it.

"Sibihd!" exclaimed the Abbess, in as sharp a voice as I had ever heard her use. "Put that back or you will feel the weight of my hand, I tell you!

Now it is odd, is it not, that a young woman desperate enough not to care about death at the hands of a Norse pirate should nonetheless be frightened away at the threat of getting a few slaps from her Abbess? But folk are like that. Sister Sibihd returned the cross to its place (from whence young Thorfinn took it) and fell back among the nuns, sobbing, "He desecrates our Lord God!"

"Foolish girl!" snapped the Abbess. "God only can consecrate or desecrate; man cannot. That is a piece of metal."

Thorvald said something sharp to Thorfinn, who slowly put the cross back on its hook with a sulky look which said, plainer than words: Nobody gives me what I want. Nothing else went wrong in the big room or the Abbess's study or the storerooms, or out in the kitchens. The Norsemen were silent and kept their hands on their swords, but the Abbess kept talking in a calm way in both tongues; to our folk she said, "See? It is all right but everyone must keep still. God will protect us." Her face was steady and clear, and I believed her a saint, for she had saved Sister Sibihd and the rest of us.

But this peacefulness did not last, of course. Something had to go wrong in all that press of people; to this day I do not know what. We were in a corner of the long refectory, which is the place where the Sisters or Brothers eat in an Abbey, when something pushed me into the wall and I fell, almost suffocated by the Abbess's lying on top of me. My head was ringing and on all sides there was a terrible roaring sound with curses and screams, a dreadful tumult as if the walls had come apart and were falling on everyone. I could hear the Abbess whispering something in Latin over and over in my ear. There were dull, ripe sounds, worse than the rest, which I know now to have been the noise steel makes when it is thrust into bodies. This all seemed to go on forever and then it seemed to me that the floor was wet. Then all became quiet. I felt the Abbess Radegunde get off me. She said:

"So this is how you wash your floors up North." When I lifted my head from the rushes and saw what she meant, I was very sick into the corner. Then she picked me up in her arms and held my face against her bosom so that I would not see, but it was no use; I had already seen: all the people lying sprawled on the floor with their bellies coming out, like heaps of dead fish, old Walafrid with an axe handle standing out of his chest—he was sitting up with his eyes shut in a press of bodies that gave him no room to lie down—and the young beekeeper, Uta, from the village, who had been so merry, lying on her back with her long braids and her gown all dabbled in red dye and a great stain of it on her belly. She was breathing fast and her eyes were wide open. As we passed her, the noise of her breathing ceased.

The Abbess said mildly, "Thy people are thorough housekeepers, Earl Split-gut."

Thorvald Einarsson roared something at us, and the Abbess replied softly, "Forgive me, good friend. You protected me and the boy and I am grateful. But nothing betrays a man's knowledge of the German like a word that bites, is it not so? And I had to be sure."

It came to me then that she had called him "Torvald" and reminded him of his sister's son so that he would feel he must protect us if anything went wrong. But now she would make him angry, I thought, and I shut my eyes tight. Instead he laughed and said in odd, light German, "I did no housekeeping but to stand over you and your pet. Are you not grateful?"

"Oh, very, thank you," said the Abbess with such warmth as she might show to a Sister who had brought her a rose from the garden, or another who copied her work well, or when I told her news, or if Ita the cook made a good soup. But he did not know that the warmth was for everyone and so seemed satisfied. By now we were in the garden and the air was less foul; she put me down, although my limbs were shaking, and I clung to her gown, crumpled, stiff, and blood-reeking though it was. She said, "Oh my God, what a deal of washing hast Thou given us!" She started to walk towards the gate, and Thorvald Einarsson took a step towards her. She said, without turning round: "Do not insist, Thorvald, there is no reason to lock me up. I am forty years old and not likely to be running away into the swamp, what with my rheumatism and the pain in my knees and the folk needing me as they do."

There was a moment's silence. I could see something odd come into the big man's face. He said quietly:

"I did not speak, Abbess."

She turned, surprised. "But you did. I heard you."

He said strangely, "I did not."

Children can guess sometimes what is wrong and what to do about it without knowing how; I remember saying, very quickly, "Oh, she does that sometimes. My stepmother says old age has addled her wits," and then, "Abbess, may I go to my stepmother and my father?"

"Yes, of course," she said, "run along, Boy News—" and then stopped, looking into the air as if seeing in it something we could not. Then she said very gently, "No, my dear, you had better stay here with me," and I knew, as surely as if I had seen it with my own eyes, that I was not to go to my stepmother or my father because both were dead.

She did things like that, too, sometimes.

For a while it seemed that everyone was dead. I did not feel grieved or frightened in the least, but I think I must have been, for I had only one idea in my head: that if I let the Abbess out of my sight, I would die. So I followed her everywhere. She was let to move about and comfort people, especially the mad Sibihd, who would do nothing but rock and wail, but towards nightfall, when the Abbey had been stripped of its treasures, Thorvald Einarsson put her and me in her study, now bare of its grand furniture, on a straw pallet on the floor, and bolted the door on the outside. She said:

"Boy News, would you like to go to Constantinople, where the Turkish Sultan is, and the domes of gold and all the splendid pagans? For that is where this man will take me to sell me."

"Oh, yes!" said I, and then: "But will he take me, too?"

"Of course," said the Abbess, and so it was settled. Then in came Thorvald Einarsson, saying:

"Thorfinn is asking for you." I found out later that they were waiting for him to die; none other of the Norse had been wounded, but a farmer had crushed Thorfinn's chest with an axe, and he was expected to die before morning. The Abbess said:

"Is that a good reason to go?" She added, "I mean that he hates me; will not his anger at my presence make him worse?"

Thorvald said slowly, "The folk here say you can sit by the sick and heal them. Can you do that?"

"To my own knowledge, not at all," said the Abbess Radegunde, "but if they believe so, perhaps that calms them and makes them better. Christians are quite as foolish as other people, you know. I will come if you want," and though I saw that she was pale with tiredness, she got to her feet. I should say that she was in a plain, brown gown taken from one of the peasant women because her own was being washed clean, but to me she had the same majesty as always. And for him too, I think.

Thorvald said, "Will you pray for him or damn him?"

She said, "I do not pray, Thorvald, and I never damn anybody; I merely sit." She added, "Oh, let him; he'll scream your ears off if you don't," and this meant me, for I was ready to yell for my life if they tried to keep me from her.

They had put Thorfinn in the chapel, a little stone room with nothing left in it now but a plain wooden cross, not worth carrying off. He was lying, his eyes closed, on the stone altar with furs under him, and his face was gray. Every time he breathed, there was a bubbling sound, a little, thin, reedy sound; and as I crept closer, I saw why, for in the young man's chest was a great red hole with sharp pink things stick-

ing out of it, all crushed, and in the hole one could see something jump and fall, jump and fall, over and over again. It
was his heart beating. Blood kept coming from his lips in a
froth. I do not know, of course, what either said, for they
spoke in the Norse, but I saw what they did and heard much
of it talked of between the Abbess and Thorvald Einarsson
later. So I will tell it as if I knew.

The first thing the Abbess did was to stop suddenly on the
threshold and raise both hands to her mouth as if in horror.
Then she cried furiously to the two guards:

"Do you wish to kill your comrade with the cold and
damp? Is this how you treat one another? Get fire in here
and some woollen cloth to put over him! No, not more skins,
you idiots, *wool* to mold to his body and take up the wet.
Run now!"

One said sullenly, "We don't take orders from you,
Grandma."

"Oh, no?" said she. "Then I shall strip this wool dress from
my old body and put it over that boy and then sit here all
night in my flabby, naked skin! What will this child's soul say
when it enters the Valhall? That his friends would not give
up a little of their booty so that he might fight for life? Is this
your fellowship? Do it, or I will strip myself and shame you
both for the rest of your lives!"

"Well, take it from his share," said the one in a low voice,
and the other ran out. Soon there was a fire on the hearth
and russet-colored woollen cloth—"From my own share,"
said one of them loudly, though it was a color the least
costly, not like blue or red—and the Abbess laid it loosely
over the boy, carefully putting it close to his sides but not
moving him. He did not look to be in any pain, but his color
got no better. But then he opened his eyes and said in such a
little voice as a ghost might have, a whisper as thin and reedy
and bubbling as his breath:

"You . . . old witch. But I beat you . . . in the end."

"Did you, my dear?" said the Abbess. "How?"

"Treasure," he said, "for my kinfolk. And I lived as a man
at last. Fought . . . and had a woman . . . the one here with
the big breasts, Sibihd. . . . Whether she liked it or not. That
was good."

"Yes, Sibihd," said the Abbess mildly. "Sibihd has gone

mad. She hears no one and speaks to no one. She only sits and rocks and moans and soils herself and will not feed herself, although if one puts food in her mouth with a spoon, she will swallow."

The boy tried to frown. "Stupid," he said at last. "Stupid nuns. The beasts do it."

"Do they?" said the Abbess, as if this were a new idea to her. "Now that is very odd. For never yet heard I of a gander that blacked the goose's eye or hit her over the head with a stone or stuck a knife in her entrails when he was through. When God puts it into their hearts to desire one another, she squats and he comes running. And a bitch in heat will jump through the window if you lock the door. Poor fools! Why didn't you camp three hours down-river and wait? In a week half the young married women in the village would have been slipping away at night to see what the foreigners were like. Yes, and some unmarried ones, and some of my own girls, too. But you couldn't wait, could you?"

"No," said the boy, with the ghost of a brag. "Better . . . this way."

"*This* way," said she. "Oh, yes, my dear, old Granny knows about *this* way! Pleasure for the count of three or four, and the rest of it as much joy as rolling a stone uphill."

He smiled a ghostly smile. "You're a whore, Grandma."

She began to stroke his forehead. "No, Grandbaby," she said, "but all Latin is not the Church Fathers, you know, great as they are. One can find a great deal in those strange books written by the ones who died centuries before our Lord was born. Listen," and she leaned closer to him and said quietly:

"Syrian dancing girl, how subtly
   you sway those sensuous limbs,
"Half-drunk in the smoky tavern,
   lascivious and wanton,
"Your long hair bound back in the
   Greek way, clashing the casta-
     nets in your hands—"

The boy was too weak to do anything but look astonished. Then she said this:

"I love you so that anyone permitted to sit near you and talk to you seems to me like a god; when I am near you my spirit is broken, my heart shakes, my voice dies, and I can't even speak. Under my skin I flame up all over and I can't see; there's thunder in my ears and I break out in a sweat, as if from fever; I turn paler than cut grass and feel that I am utterly changed; I feel that Death has come near me."

He said, as if frightened, "Nobody feels like that."

"They do," she said.

He said, in feeble alarm, "You're trying to kill me!"

She said, "No, my dear. I simply don't want you to a die a virgin."

It was odd, his saying those things and yet holding on to her hand where he had got at it through the woollen cloth; she stroked his head and he whispered, "Save me, old witch."

"I'll do my best," she said. "You shall do your best by not talking and I by not tormenting you any more, and we'll both try to sleep.

"Pray," said the boy.

"Very well," said she, "but I'll need a chair," and the guards—seeing I suppose, that he was holding her hand—brought in one of the great wooden chairs from the Abbey, which were too plain and heavy to carry off, I think. Then the Abbess Radegunde sat in the chair and closed her eyes. Thorfinn seemed to fall asleep. I crept nearer her on the floor and must have fallen asleep myself almost at once, for the next thing I knew a gray light filled the chapel, the fire had gone out, and someone was shaking Radegunde, who still slept in her chair, her head leaning to one side. It was Thorvald Einarsson and he was shouting with excitement in his strange German, "Woman, how did you do it! How did you do it!"

"Do what?" said the Abbess thickly. "Is he dead?"

"Dead?" exlaimed the Norseman. "He is healed! Healed! The lung is whole and all is closed up about the heart and the shattered pieces of the ribs are grown together! Even the muscles of the chest are beginning to heal!"

"That's good," said the Abbess, still half asleep. "Let me be."

Thorvald shook her again. She said again, "Oh, let me

sleep." This time he hauled her to her feet and she shrieked, "My back, my back! Oh, the saints, my rheumatism!" and at the same time a sick voice from under the blue woollens—a sick voice but a man's voice, not a ghost's—said something in Norse.

"Yes, I hear you," said the Abbess. "You must become a follower of the White Christ right away, this very minute. But *Dominus noster,* please do You put it into these brawny heads that I must have a tub of hot water with pennyroyal in it? I am too old to sleep all night in a chair, and I am one ache from head to foot."

Thorfinn got louder.

"Tell him," said the Abbess Radegunde to Thorvald in German, "that I will not baptize him and I will not shrive him until he is a different man. All that child wants is someone more powerful than your Odin god or your Thor god to pull him out of the next scrape he gets into. Ask him: Will he adopt Sibihd as his sister: Will he clean her when she soils herself and feed her and sit with his arm about her, talking to her gently and lovingly until she is well again? The Christ does not wipe out our sins only to have us commit them all over again, and that is what he wants and what you all want, a God that gives and gives and gives, but God does not give; He takes and takes and takes. He takes away everything that is not God until there is nothing left but God, and none of you will understand that! There is no remission of sins; there is only change, and Thorfinn must change before God will have him."

"Abbess, you are eloquent," said Thorvald, smiling, "but why do you not tell him all this yourself?"

"Because I ache so!" said Radegunde; "Oh, do get me into some hot water!" and Thorvald half led and half supported her as she hobbled out. That morning, after she had had her soak—when I cried, they let me stay just outside the door—she undertook to cure Sibihd, first by rocking her in her arms and talking to her, telling her she was safe now, and promising that the Northmen would go soon, and then when Sibihd became quieter, leading her out into the woods with Thorvald as a bodyguard to see that we did not run away, and little, dark Sister Hedwic, who had stayed with Sibihd and cared for her. The Abbess would walk for a while in the mild autumn sunshine, and then she would direct Sibihd's face upwards by touching her gently under the chin and say, "See? There is God's sky still," and then, "Look, there are God's trees; they have not changed," and tell her that the world was just the same and God still kindly to folk, only a few more souls had joined the Blessed and were happier waiting for us in Heaven than we could ever be, or even imagine being, on the poor earth. Sister Hedwic kept hold of Sibihd's hand. No one paid more attention to me than if I had been a dog, but every time poor Sister Sibihd saw Thorvald she would shrink away, and you could see that Hedwic could not bear to look at him at all; every time he came in her sight she turned her face aside, shut her eyes hard, and bit her lower lip. It was a quiet, almost warm day, as autumn can be sometimes, and the Abbess found a few little blue late flowers growing in a sheltered place against a log and put them into Sibihd's hand, speaking of how beautifully and cunningly God had made all things. Sister Sibihd had enough wit to hold on to the flowers, but her eyes stared and she would have stumbled and fallen if Hedwic had not led her.

Sister Hedwic said timidly, "Perhaps she suffers because she has been defiled, Abbess," and then looked ashamed. For a moment the Abbess looked shrewdly at young Sister Hedwic and then at the mad Sibihd. Then she said:

"Dear daughter Sibihd and dear daughter Hedwic, I am now going to tell you something about myself that I have never told to a single living soul but my confessor. Do you know that as a young woman I studied at Avignon and from there was sent to Rome, so that I might gather much learning? Well, in Avignon I read mightily our Christian Fathers but also in the pagan poets, for as it has been said by Ermenrich of Ellwangen: As dung spread upon a field enriches it to good harvest, thus one cannot produce divine eloquence without the filthy writings of the pagan poets. This is true but perilous, only I thought not so, for I was very proud and fancied that if the pagan poems of love left me unmoved, that was because I had the gift of chastity right from God Himself, and I scorned sensual pleasures and those tempted by them. I had forgotten, you see, that chastity is not given once and for all like a wedding ring that is put on never to be taken off, but is a garden which each day must be weeded, watered, and trimmed anew, or soon there will be only brambles and wilderness.

"As I have seen, the words of the poets did not tempt me, for words are only marks on the page with no life save what we give them. But in Rome there were not only the old books, daughters, but something much worse.

"There were statues. Now you must understand that these are not such as you can imagine from our books, like Saint John or the Virgin; the ancients wrought so cunningly in stone that it is like magic; one stands before the marble holding one's breath, waiting for it to move and speak. They are not statues at all but beautiful, naked men and women. It is a city of seagods pouring water, daughter Sibihd and daughter Hedwic, of athletes about to throw the discus, and runners and wrestlers and young emperors, and the favorites of kings; but they do not walk the streets like real men, for they are all of stone.

"There was one Apollo, all naked, which I knew I should not look on but which I always made some excuse to my companions to pass by, and this statue, although three miles distant from my dwelling, drew me as if by magic. Oh, he was fair to look on! Fairer than any youth alive now in Germany, or in the world, I think. And then all the old loves of the pagan poets came back to me: Dido and Aeneas, the taking of Venus and Mars, the love of the moon, Diana, for the shepherd boy—and I thought that if my statue could only come to life, he would utter honeyed love-words from the old poets and would be wise and brave, too, and what woman could resist him?"

Here she stopped and looked at Sister Sibihd but Sibihd only stared on, holding the little blue flowers. It was Sister Hedwic who cried, one hand pressed to her heart:

"Did you pray, Abbess?"

"I did," said Radegunde solemnly, "and yet my prayers kept becoming something else. I would pray to be delivered from the temptation that was in the statue, and then, of course, I would have to think of the statue itself, and then I would tell myself that I must run, like the nymph Daphne, to be armored and sheltered within a laurel tree, but my feet seemed to be already rooted to the ground, and then at the last minute I would flee and be back at my prayers again. But it grew harder each time, and at last the day came when I did not flee."

"Abbess, *you*?" cried Hedwic, with a gasp. Thorvald, keep-

ing his watch a little way from us, looked surprised. I was
very pleased—I loved to see the Abbess astonish people; it
was one of her gifts—and at seven I had not knowledge of
lust except that my little thing felt good sometimes when I
handled it to make water, and what had that to do with statues coming to life or women turning into laurel trees? I was
more interested in mad Sibihd, the way children are; I did
not know what she might do, or if I should be afraid of her,
or if I should go mad myself, what it would be like. But the
Abbess was laughing gently at Hedwic's amazement.

"Why not me?" said the Abbess. "I was young and healthy
and had no special grace from God any more than the hens
or the cows do! Indeed, I burned so with desire for that
handsome young hero—for so I had made him in my mind,
as a woman might do with a man she had seen a few times
on the street—that thoughts of him tormented me waking
and sleeping. It seemed to me that because of my vows I
could not give myself to this Apollo of my own free will. So
I would dream that he took me against my will, and, oh,
what an exquisite pleasure that was!"

Here Hedwic's blood came all to her face and she covered
it with her hands. I could see Thorvald grinning, back where
he watched us.

"And then," said the Abbess, as if she had not seen either
of them, "a terrible fear came to my heart that God might
punish me by sending a ravisher who would use me unlaw-
fully, as I had dreamed my Apollo did, and that I would not
even wish to resist him and would feel the pleasures of a base
lust and would know myself a whore and a false nun forever
after. This fear both tormented and drew me. I began to steal
looks at young men in the streets, not letting the other Sisters
see me do it, thinking: Will it be he? Or he? Or he?

"And then it happened. I had lingered behind the others at
a melon seller's, thinking of no Apollos or handsome heroes
but only of the convent's dinner, when I saw my companions
disappearing round a corner. I hastened to catch up with
them—and made a wrong turning—and was suddenly lost in
a narrow street—and at that very moment a young fellow
took hold of my habit and threw me to the ground! You may
wonder why he should do such a mad thing, but as I found
out afterwards, there are prostitutes in Rome who affect our
way of dress to please the appetites of certain men who are

depraved enough to—well, really, I do not know how to say it! Seeing me alone, he had thought I was one of them and would be glad of a customer and a bit of play. So there was a reason for it.

"Well, there I was on my back with this young fellow, sent as a vengeance by God, as I thought, trying to do exactly what I had dreamed, night after night, that my statue should do. And do you know, it was nothing in the least like my dream! The stones at my back hurt me, for one thing. And instead of melting with delight, I was screaming my head off in terror and kicking at him as he tried to pull up my shirts, and praying to God that this insane man might not break any of my bones in his rage!

"My screams brought a crowd of people and he went running. So I got off with nothing worse than a bruised back and a sprained knee. But the strangest thing of all was that while I was cured forever of lusting after my Apollo, instead I began to be tormented by a new fear—that I had lusted after *him*, that foolish young man with the foul breath and the one tooth missing!—and I felt strange creepings and crawlings over my body that were half like desire and half like fear and half like disgust and shame with all sorts of other things mixed in—I know that is too many halves but it is how I felt—and nothing at all like the burning desire I had felt for my Apollo. I went to see the statue once more before I left Rome, and it seemed to look at me sadly, as if to say: Don't blame me, poor girl; I'm only a piece of stone. And that was the last time I was so proud as to believe that God had singled me out for a special gift, like chastity—or a special sin, either—or that being thrown down on the ground and hurt had anything to do with any sin of mine, no matter how I mixed the two together in my mind. I dare say you did not find it a great pleasure yesterday, did you?"

Hedwic shook her head. She was crying quietly. She said, "Thank you, Abbess," and the Abbess embraced her. They both seemed happier, but then all of a sudden Sibihd muttered something, so low that one could not hear her.

"The—" she whispered and then she brought it out but still in a whisper: "The blood."

"What, dear, your blood?" said Radegunde.

"No, mother," said Sibihd, beginning to tremble, "The blood. All over us. Walafrid and—and Uta—and Sister Hildegarde—and everyone broken and spilled out like a dish! And none of us had done anything but I could smell it all over me and the children screaming because they were being trampled down, and those demons come up from Hell though we had done nothing and—and—I understand, mother, about the rest, but I will never, ever forget it, oh Christus, it is all around me now, oh, mother, the *blood*!"

Then Sister Sibihd dropped to her knees on the fallen leaves and began to scream, not covering her face as Sister Hedwic had done, but staring ahead with her wide eyes as if she were blind or could see something we could not. The Abbess knelt down and embraced her, rocking her back and forth, saying, "Yes, yes, dear, but we are here; we are here now; that is gone now," but Sibihd continued to scream, covering her ears as if the scream were someone else's and she could hide herself from it.

Thorvald said, looking, I thought, a little uncomfortable, "Cannot your Christ cure this?"

"No," said the Abbess. "Only by undoing the past. And that is the one thing He never does, it seems. She is in Hell now and must go back there many times before she can forget."

"She would make a bad slave," said the Norseman, with a glance at Sister Sibihd, who had fallen silent and was staring ahead of her again. "You need not fear that anyone will want her."

"God," said the Abbess Radegunde calmly, "is merciful."

Thorvald Einarsson said, "Abbess, I am not a bad man."

"For a good man," said the Abbess Radegunde, "you keep surprisingly bad company."

He said angrily, "I did not choose my shipmates. I have had bad luck!"

"Ours has," said the Abbess, "been worse, I think."

"Luck is luck," said Thorvald, clenching his fists. "It comes to some folk and not to others."

"As you came to us," said the Abbess mildly. "Yes, yes, I see, Thorvald Einarsson; one may say that luck is Thor's doing or Odin's doing, but you must know that our bad luck is your own doing and not some god's. You are our bad luck, Thorvald Einarsson. It's true that you're not as wicked as your friends, for they kill for pleasure and you do it without feeling, as a business, the way one hews down grain. Perhaps

you have seen today some of the grain you have cut. If you
had a man's soul, you would not have gone *viking*, luck or no
luck, and if your soul were bigger still, you would have tried
to stop your shipmates, just as I talk honestly to you now,
despite your anger, and just as Christus himself told the truth
and was nailed on the cross. If you were a beast you could
not break God's law, and if you were a man you would not,
but you are neither, and that makes you a kind of monster
that spoils everything it touches and never knows the reason,
and that is why I will never forgive you until you become a
man, a true man with a true soul. As for your friends—"

Here Thorvald Einarsson struck the Abbess on the face
with his open hand and knocked her down. I heard Sister
Hedwic gasp in horror and behind us Sister Sibihd began to
moan. But the Abbess only sat there, rubbing her jaw and
smiling a little. Then she said:

"Oh, dear, have I been at it again? I am ashamed of myself. You are quite right to be angry, Torvald; no one can
stand me when I go on in that way, least of all myself; it is
such a bore. Still, I cannot seem to stop it; I am too used to
being the Abbess Radegunde, that is clear. I promise never to
torment you again, but you, Thorvald, must never strike me
again, because you will be very sorry if you do."

He took a step forward.

"No, no, my dear man," the Abbess said merrily, "I mean
no threat—how could I threaten you?—I mean only that I
will never tell you any jokes, my spirits will droop, and I will
become as dull as any other woman. Confess it now: I am
the most interesting thing that has happened to you in years
and I have entertained you better, sharp tongue and all, than
all the *skalds* at the Court of Norway. And I know more
tales and stories than they do—more than anyone in the
whole world—for I make new ones when the old ones wear
out.

"Shall I tell you a story now?"

"About your Christ?" said he, the anger still in his face.

"No," said she, "about living men and women. Tell me,
Torvald what do you men want from us women?"

"To be talked to death," said he, and I could see there was
some anger in him still, but he was turning it to play also.

The Abbess laughed in delight. "Very witty!" she said,
springing to her feet and brushing the leaves off her skirt.

"You are a very clever man, Torvald. I beg your pardon, Thorvald. I keep forgetting. But as to what men want from women, if you asked the young men, they would only wink and dig one another in the ribs, but that is only how they deceive themselves. That is only body calling to body. They want something quite different and they want it so much that it frightens them. So they pretend it is anything and everything else: pleasure, comfort, a servant in the home. Do you know what it is that they want?"

"What?" said Thorvald.

"The mother," said Radegunde, "as women do, too; we all want the mother. When I walked before you on the riverbank yesterday, I was playing the mother. Now you did nothing, for you are no young fool, but I knew that sooner or later one of you, so tormented by his longing that he would hate me for it, would reveal himself. And so he did: Thorfinn, with his thoughts all mixed up between witches and grannies and what not. I knew I could frighten him, and through him, most of you. That was the beginning of my bargaining. You Norse have too much of the father in your country and not enough mother; that is why you die so well and kill other folk so well—and live so very, very badly."

"You are doing it again," said Thorvald, but I think he wanted to listen all the same.

"Your pardon, friend," said the Abbess. "You are brave men; I don't deny it. But I know your *sagas* and they are all about fighting and dying and afterwards not Heavenly happiness but the end of the world: everything, even the gods, eaten by the Fenris Wolf and the Midgaard snake! What a pity, to die bravely only because life is not worth living! The Irish know better. The pagan Irish were heroes, with their Queens leading them to battle as often as not, and Father Cairbre, God rest his soul, was complaining only two days ago that the common Irish folk were blasphemously making a goddess out of God's mother, for do they build shrines to Christ or Our Lord or pray to them? No! It is Our Lady of the Rocks and Our Lady of the Sea and Our Lady of the Grove and Our Lady of this or that from one end of the land to the other. And even here it is only the Abbey folk who speak of God the Father and of Christ. In the village if one is sick or another in trouble it is: Holy Mother, save me! and: *Miriam Virginem*, intercede for me, and: Blessed Virgin, blind my husband's eyes! and: Our Lady, preserve my crops, and so on, men and women both. We all need the mother."

"You, too?"

"More than most," said the Abbess.

"And I?"

"Oh, no," said the Abbess, stopping suddenly, for we had all been walking back towards the village as she spoke. "No, and that is what drew me to you at once. I saw it in you and knew you were the leader. It is followers who make leaders, you know, and your shipmates have made you leader, whether you know it or not. What you want is—how shall I say it? You are a clever man. Thorvald, perhaps the cleverest man I have ever met, more even than the scholars I knew in my youth. But your cleverness has had no food. It is a cleverness of the world and not of books. You want to travel and know about folk and their customs, and what strange places are like, and what has happened to men and women in the past. If you take me to Constantinople, it will not be to get a price for me but merely to go there; you went seafaring because this longing itched at you until you could bear it not a year more; I know that."

"Then you are a witch," said he, and he was not smiling.

"No, I only saw what was in your face when you spoke of that city," said she. "Also there is gossip that you spent much time in Göteborg as a young man, idling and marveling at the ships and markets when you should have been at your farm."

She said, "Thorvald, I can feed that cleverness. I am the wisest woman in the world. I know everything—everything! I know more than my teachers; I make it up or it comes to me, I don't know how, but it is real—real!—and I know more than anyone. Take me from here, as your slave if you wish but as your friend also, and let us go to Constantinople and see the domes of gold, and the walls all inlaid with gold, and the people so wealthy you cannot imagine it, and the whole city so gilded it seems to be on fire, pictures as high as a wall, set right in the wall and all made of jewels so there is nothing else like them, redder than the reddest rose, greener than the grass, and with a blue that makes the sky pale!"

"You are indeed a witch," said he, "and not the Abbess Radegunde."

She said slowly, "I think I am forgetting how to be the Abbess Radegunde."

"Then you will not care about them any more," said he, and pointed to Sister Hedwic, who was still leading the stumbling Sister Sibihd.

The Abbess's face was still and mild. She said, "I care. Do not strike me, Thorvald, not ever again, and I will be a good friend to you. Try to control the worst of your men and leave as many of my people free as you can—I know them and will tell you which can be taken away with the least hurt to themselves or others—and I will feed that curiosity and cleverness of yours until you will not recognize this old-world any more for the sheer wonder and awe of it; I swear this on my life."

"Done," said he, adding, "but with my luck, your life is somewhere else, locked in a box on top of a mountain, like the troll's in the story, or you will die of old age while we are still at sea."

"Nonsense," she said, "I am a healthy, mortal woman with all my teeth, and I mean to gather many wrinkles yet."

He put his hand out and she took it; then he said, shaking his head in wonder, "If I sold you in Constantinople, within a year you would become Queen of the place!"

The Abbess laughed merrily and I cried in fear, "Me, too! Take me too!" and she said, "Oh, yes, we must not forget little Boy News," and lifted me into her arms.

The frightening, tall man, with his face close to mine, said in his strange, sing-song German:

"Boy, would you like to see the whales leaping in the open sea and the seals barking on the rocks? And cliffs so high that a giant could stretch his arms up and not reach their tops? And the sun shining at midnight?"

"Yes!" said I.

"But you will be a slave," he said, "and may be ill-treated and will always have to do as you are bid. Would you like that?"

"No!" I cried lustily, from the safety of the Abbess's arms, "I'll fight!"

He laughed a mighty, roaring laugh and tousled my head—rather too hard, I thought—and said, "I will not be a bad master, for I am named for Thor Red-beard and he is strong and quick to fight but good-natured, too, and so am

I," and the Abbess put me down, and so we walked back to the village, Thorvald and the Abbess Radegunde talking of the glories of this world and Sister Hedwic saying softly, "She is a saint, our Abbess, a saint, to sacrifice herself for the good of the people," and all the time behind us, like a memory, came the low, witless sobbing of Sister Sibihd, who was in Hell.

When we got back we found that Thorfinn was better and the Norsemen were to leave in the morning. Thorvald had a second pallet brought into the Abbess's study and slept on the floor with us that night. You might think his men would laugh at this, for the Abbess was an old woman, but I think he had been with one of the young ones before he came to us. He had that look about him. There was no bedding for the Abbess but an old brown cloak with holes in it, and she and I were wrapped in it when he came in and threw himself down, whistling, on the other pallet. Then he said:

"Tomorrow, before we sail, you will show me the old Abbess's treasure."

"No," said she. "That agreement was broken."

He had been playing with his knife and now ran his thumb along the edge of it. "I can make you do it."

"No," said she patiently, "and now I am going to sleep."

"So you make light of death?" he said. "Good! That is what a brave woman should do, as the *skalds* sing, and not move even when the keen sword cuts off her eyelashes. But what if I put this knife here not to your throat but to your little boy's? You would tell me then quick enough!"

The Abbess turned away from him, yawning and saying, "No, Thorvald, because you would not. And if you did, I would despise you for a cowardly oath-breaker and not tell you for that reason. Good night."

He laughed and whistled again for a bit. Then he said:

"Was all that true?"

"All what?" said the Abbess., "Oh, about the statue. Yes, but there was no ravisher. I put him in the tale for poor Sister Hedwic."

Thorvald snorted, as if in disappointment. "Tale? You tell lies, Abbess!"

The Abbess drew the old brown cloak over her head and closed her eyes. "It helped her."

Then there was a silence, but the big Norseman did not seem able to lie still. He shifted his body again as if the straw bothered him, and again turned over. He finally burst out, "But what happened!"

She sat up. Then she shut her eyes. She said, "Maybe it does not come into your man's thoughts that an old woman gets tired and that the work of dealing with folk is hard work, or even that it is work at all. Well!

"Nothing 'happened,' Thorvald. Must something happen only if this one fucks that one or one bangs in another's head? I desired my statue to the point of such foolishness that I determined to find a real, human lover, but when I raised my eyes from my fancies to the real, human men of Rome and unstopped my ears to listen to their talk, I realized that the thing was completely and eternally impossible. Oh, those younger sons with their skulking, jealous hatred of the rich, and the rich ones with their noses in the air because they thought themselves of such great consequence because of their silly money, and the timidity of the priests to their superiors, and their superiors' pride, and the artisans' hatred of the peasants, and the peasants being worked like animals from morning until night, and half the men I saw beating their wives and the other half out to cheat some poor girl of her money or her virginity or both—this was enough to put out any fire! And the women doing less harm only because they had less power to do harm, or so it seemed to me then. So I put all away, as one does with any disappointment. Men are not such bad folk when one stops expecting them to be gods, but they are not for me. If that state is chastity, then a weak stomach is temperance, I think. But whatever it is, I have it, and that's the end of the matter."

"*All* men?" said Thorvald Einarsson with his head to one side, and it came to me that he had been drinking, though he seemed sober.

"Thorvald," said the Abbess, "what you want with this middle-aged wreck of a body I cannot imagine, but if you lust after my wrinkles and flabby breasts and lean, withered flanks, do whatever you want quickly and then, for Heaven's sake, let me sleep. I am tired to death."

He said in a low voice, "I need to have power over you."

She spread her hands in a helpless gesture. "Oh, Thorvald,

Thorvald, I am a weak little woman over forty years old! Where is the power? All I can do is talk!"

He said, "That's it. That's how you do it. You talk and talk and talk and everyone does just as you please; I have seen it!"

The Abbess said, looking sharply at him, "Very well. If you must. *But if I were you, Norseman, I would as soon bed my own mother.* Remember that as you pull my skirts up."

That stopped him. He swore under his breath, turning over on his side, away from us. Then he thrust his knife into the edge of his pallet, time after time. Then he put the knife under the rolled-up cloth he was using as a pillow. We had no pillow and so I tried to make mine out of the edge of the cloak and failed. Then I thought that the Norseman was afraid of God working in Radegunde, and then I thought of Sister Hedwic's changing color and wondered why. And then I thought of the leaping whales and the seals, which must be like great dogs because of the barking, and then the seals jumped on land and ran to my pallet and lapped at me with great, icy tongues of water so that I shivered and jumped, and then I woke up.

The Abbess Radegunde had left the pallet—it was her warmth I had missed—and was walking about the room. She would step and pause, her skirts making a small noise as she did so. She was careful not to touch the sleeping Thorvald. There was a dim light in the room from the embers that still glowed under the ashes in the hearth, but no light came from between the shutters of the study window, now shut against the cold. I saw the Abbess kneel under the plain wooden cross which hung on the study wall and heard her say a few words in Latin; I thought she was praying. But then she said in a low voice:

"Do not call upon Apollo and the Muses, for they are deaf things and vain. But so are you, Pierced Man, deaf and vain."

Then she got up and began to pace again. Thinking of it now frightens me, for it was the middle of the night and no one to hear her—except me, but she thought I was asleep—and yet she went on and on in that low, even voice as if it were broad day and she were explaining something to someone, as if things that had been in her thoughts for years must finally come out. But I did not find anything alarming in it then, for I thought that perhaps all Abbesses had to do such things, and besides she did not seem angry or hurried or afraid; she sounded as calm as if she were discussing the profits from the Abbey's bee-keeping—which I had heard her do—or the accounts for the wine cellars—which I had also heard—and there was nothing alarming in that. So I listened as she continued walking about the room in the dark. She said:

"Talk, talk, talk, and always to myself. But one can't abandon the kittens and puppies; that would be cruel. And being the Abbess Radegunde at least gives one something to do. But I am so sick of the good Abbess Radegunde; I have put on Radegunde every morning of my life as easily as I put on my smock, and then I have had to hear the stupid creature praised all day!—sainted Radegunde, just Radegunde who is never angry or greedy or jealous, kindly Radegunde who sacrifices herself for others, and always the talk, talk, talk, bubbling and boiling in my head with no one to hear or understand, and no one to answer. No, not even in the south, only a line here or a line there, and all written by the dead. Did they feel as I do? That the world is a giant nursery full of squabbles over toys and the babes thinking me some kind of goddess because I'm not greedy for their dolls or bits of straw or their horses made of tied-together sticks?

"Poor people, if only they knew! It's so easy to be temperate when one enjoys nothing, so easy to be kind when one loves nothing, so easy to be fearless when one's life is no better than one's death. And so easy to scheme when the success doesn't matter.

"Would they be surprised, I wonder, to find out what my real thoughts were when Thorfinn's knife was at my throat? Curiosity! But he would not do it, of course; he does everything for show. And they would think I was twice holy, not to care about death.

"Then why not kill yourself, impious Sister Radegunde? Is it your religion which stops you? Oh, you mean the holy wells, and the holy trees, and the blessed saints with their blessed relics, and the stupidity that shamed Sister Hedwic, and the promises of safety that drove poor Sibihd mad when the blessed body of her Lord did not protect her and the blessed love of the blessed Mary turned away the sharp point of not one knife? Trash! Idle leaves and sticks, reeds and rushes, filth we sweep off our floors when it grows too thick. As if holiness had anything to do with all of that. As if every place were not as holy as every other and every thing as holy as every other, from the shit in Thorfinn's bowels to the rocks on the ground. As if all places and things were not clouds placed in front of our weak eyes, to keep us from being blinded by that glory, that eternal shining, that blazing all about us, the torrent of light that is everything and is in everything! That is what keeps me from the river, but it never speaks to me or tells me what to do, and to it good and evil are the same—no, it is something else than good or evil; it *is*, only—so it is not God. That I know.

"So, people, is your Radegunde a witch or a demon? Is she full of pride or is Radegunde abject? Perhaps she is a witch. Once, long ago, I confessed to old Gerbertus that I could see things that were far away merely by closing my eyes, and I proved it to him, too, and he wept over me and gave me much penance, crying, "If it come of itself it may be a gift of God, daughter, but it is more likely the work of a demon, so do not do it!" And then we prayed and I told him the power had left me, to make the poor old puppy less troubled in its mind, but that was not true, of course. I could still see Turkey as easily as I could see him, and places far beyond: the squat, wild men of the plains on their ponies, and the strange, tall people beyond that with their great cities and odd eyes, as if one pulled one's eyelid up on a slant, and then the seas with the great, wild lands and the cities more full of gold than Constantinople, and water again until one comes back home, for the world's a ball, as the ancients said.

"But I did stop somehow, over the years. Radegunde never had time, I suppose. Besides, when I opened that door it was only pictures, as in a book, and all to no purpose, and after a while I had seen them all and no longer cared for them. It is the other door that draws me, when it opens itself but a crack and strange things peep through, like Ranulf sister's son and the name of his horse. That door is good but very heavy; it always swings back after a little. I shall have to be on my deathbed to open it all the way, I think.

"The fox is asleep. He is the cleverest yet; there is something in him so that at times one can almost talk to him. But still a fox, for the most part. Perhaps in time. . . .

"But let me see; yes, he is asleep. And the Sibihd puppy is

asleep, though it will be having a bad dream soon, I think, and the Thorfinn kitten is asleep, as full of fright as when it wakes, with its claws going in and out, in and out, lest something strangle it in its sleep."

Then the Abbess fell silent and moved to the shuttered window as if she were looking out, so I thought that she was indeed looking out—but not with her eyes—at all the sleeping folk, and this was something she had done every night of her life to see if they were safe and sound. But would she not know that *I* was awake? Should I not try very hard to get to sleep before she caught me? Then it seemed to me that she smiled in the dark, although I could not see it. She said in that same low, even voice: "Sleep or wake, Boy News; it is all one to me. Thou hast heard nothing of any importance, only the silly Abbess talking to herself, only Radegunde saying good-bye to Radegunde, only Radegunde going away—don't cry, Boy News; I am still here—but there: Radegunde has gone. This Norseman and I are alike in one way: our minds are like great houses with many of the rooms locked shut. We crowd in a miserable, huddled few, like poor folk, when we might move freely among them all, as gracious as princes. It is fate that locked away so much of the Norseman—see, Boy News, I do not say his name, not even softly, for that wakes folks—but I wonder if the one who bolted me in was not Radegunde herself, she and old Gerbertus—whom I partly believed—they and the years and years of having to be Radegunde and do the things Radegunde did and pretend to have the thoughts Radegunde had and the endless, endless lies Radegunde must tell everyone, and Radegunde's utter and unbearable loneliness."

She fell silent again. I wondered at the Abbess's talk this time: saying she was not there when she was, and about living locked up in small rooms—for surely the Abbey was the most splendid house in all the world, and the biggest—and how could she be lonely when all the folk loved her? But then she said in a voice so low that I could hardly hear it:

"Poor Radegunde! So weary of the lies she tells and the fooling of men and women with the collars round their necks and bribes of food for good behavior and a careful twitch of the leash that they do not even see or feel. And with the Norseman it will be all the same: lies and flattery and all of it work that never ends and no one ever even sees, so that finally Radegunde will lie down like an ape in a cage, weak and sick from hunger, and will never get up.

"Let her die now. There: Radegunde is dead. Radegunde is gone. Perhaps the door was heavy only because she was on the other side of it, pushing against me. Perhaps it will open all the way now. I have looked in all directions: to the east, to the north and south, and to the west, but there is one place I have never looked and now I will: away from the ball, straight out. Let us see—"

She stopped speaking all of a sudden. I had been falling asleep but this silence woke me. Then I heard the Abbess gasp terribly, like one mortally stricken, and then she said in a whisper so keen and thrilling that it made the hair stand up on my head: *Where art thou?* The next moment she had torn the shutters open and was crying out with all her voice: *Help me! Find me! Oh, come, come, come, or I die!*

This waked Thorvald. With some Norse oath he stumbled up and flung on his sword belt and then put his hand to his dagger; I had noticed this thing with the dagger was a thing Norsemen liked to do. The Abbess was silent. He let out his breath in an oof! and went to light the tallow dip at the live embers under the hearth ashes; when the dip had smoked up, he put it on its shelf on the wall.

He said in German, "What the devil, woman! What has happened?"

She turned round. She looked as if she could not see us, as if she had been dazed by a joy too big to hold, like one who has looked into the sun and is still dazzled by it so that everything seems changed, and the world seems all God's and everything in it like Heaven. She said softly, with her arms around herslef, hugging herself: "My people. The real people."

"What are you talking of!" said he.

She seemed to see him then, but only as Sibihd had beheld us; I do not mean in horror as Sibihd had, but beholding through something else, like someone who comes from a vision of bliss which still lingers about her. She said in the same soft voice, "They are coming for me, Thorvald. Is it not wonderful? I knew all this year that something would happen, but I did not know it would be the one thing I wanted in all the world."

He grasped his hair. *"Who* is coming?"

"My people," she said, laughing softly. "Do you not feel them? I do. We must wait three days for they come from very far away. But then—oh, you will see!"

He said, "You've been dreaming. We sail tomorrow."

"Oh, no," said the Abbess simply, "you cannot do that for it would not be right. They told me to wait; they said if I went away, they might not find me."

He said slowly, "You've gone mad. Or it's a trick."

"Oh, no, Thorvald," said she. "How could I trick you? I am your friend. And you will wait these three days, will you not, because you are my friend also."

"You're mad," he said, and started for the door of the study, but she stepped in front of him and threw herself on her knees. All her cunning seemed to have deserted her; or perhaps it was Radegunde who had been the cunning one. This one was like a child. She clasped her hands and tears came out of her eyes; she begged him, saying:

"Such a little thing, Thorvald, only three days! And if they do not come, why then we will go anywhere you like, but if they do come you will not regret it, I promise you; they are not like the folk here and that place is like nothing here. It is what the soul craves, Thorvald!"

He said, "Get up, woman for God's sake!"

She said, smiling in a sly, frightened way through her blubbered face, "If you let me stay, I will show you the old Abbess's buried treasure, Thorvald."

He stepped back, the anger clear in him. "So this is the brave old witch who cares nothing for death!" he said. Then he made for the door, but she was up again, as quick as a snake, and had flung herself across it.

She said, still with that strange innocence, "Do not strike me. Do not push me. I am your friend!"

He said, "You mean that you lead me by a string around the neck, like a goose. Well, I am tired of that!"

"But I cannot do that any more," said the Abbess breathlessly, "not since the door opened. I am not able now." He raised his arm to strike her and she cowered, wailing, "Do not strike me! Do not push me! Do not, Thorvald!"

He said, "Out of my way then, old witch!"

She began to cry in sobs and gulps. She said, "One is here but another will come! One is buried but another will rise! She will come, Thorvald!" and then in a low, quick voice,

"Do not push open this last door. There is one behind it who is evil and I am afraid—"but one could see that he was angry and disappointed and would not listen. He struck her for the second time and again she fell, but with a desperate cry, covering her face with her hands. He unbolted the door and stepped over her and I heard his footsteps go down the corridor. I could see the Abbess clearly—at that time I did not wonder how this could be, with the shadows from the tallow dip half hiding everything in their drunken dance—but I saw every line in her face as if it had been full day, and in that light I saw Radegunde go away from us at last.

Have you ever been at some great king's court or some earl's and heard the storytellers? There are those so skilled in the art that they not only speak for you what the person in the tale said and did, but they also make an action with their faces and bodies as if they truly were that man or woman, so that it is a great surprise to you when the tale ceases, for you almost believe that you have seen the tale happen in front of your very eyes, and it is as if a real man or woman had suddenly ceased to exist, for you forget that all this was only a teller and a tale.

So it was with the woman who had been Radegunde. She did not change; it was still Radegunde's gray hairs and wrinkled face and old body in the peasant woman's brown dress, and yet at the same time it was a stranger who stepped out of the Abbess Radegunde as out of a gown dropped to the floor. This stranger was without feeling, through Radegunde's tears still stood on her cheeks, and there was no kindness or joy in her. She got up without taking care of her dress where the dirty rushes stuck to it; it was as if the dress were an accident and did not concern her. She said in a voice I had never heard before, one with no feeling in it, as if I did not concern her, or Thorvald Einarsson either, as if neither of us were worth a second glance:

"Thorvald, turn around."

Far up in the hall something stirred.

"Now come back. This way."

There were footsteps, coming closer. Then the big Norseman walked clumsily into the room—jerk! jerk! jerk! at every step as if he were being pulled by a rope. Sweat beaded his face. He said, "You—how?"

"By my nature," she said. "Put up your right arm, fox. Now the left. Now both down. Good."

"You—troll!" he said.

"That is so," she said. "Now listen to me, you. There's a man inside you but he's not worth getting at; I tried moments ago when I was new-hatched and he's buried too deep, but now I have grown beak and claws and care nothing for him. It's almost dawn and your boys are stirring; you will go out and tell them that we must stay here another three days. You are weatherwise; make up some story they will believe. And don't try to tell anyone what happened here tonight; you will find that you cannot."

"Folk—come," said he, trying to turn his head, but the effort only made him sweat.

She raised her eyebrows. "Why should they? No one has heard anything. Nothing has happened. You will go out and be as you always are and I will play Radegunde. For three days only. Then you are free."

He did not move. One could see that to remain still was very hard for him; the sweat poured and he strained until every muscle stood out. She said:

"Fox, don't hurt yourself. And don't push me; I am not fond of you. My hand is light upon you only because you still seem to me a little less unhuman than the rest; do not force me to make it heavier. To be plain: I have just broken Thorfinn's neck, for I find that the change improves him. Do not make me do the same to you."

"No worse—than death," Thorvald brought out.

"Ah, no?" said she, and in a moment he was screaming and clawing at his eyes. She said, "Open them, open them; your sight is back," and then, "I do not wish to bother myself thinking up worse things, like worms in your guts. Or do you wish dead sons and a dead wife? Now go.

"*As you always do,*" she added sharply, and the big man turned and walked out. One could not have told from looking at him that anything was wrong.

I had not been sorry to see such a bad man punished, one whose friends had killed our folk and would have taken for slaves—and yet I was sorry, too, in a way, because of the seals barking and the whales—and he *was* splendid, after a fashion—and yet truly I forgot all about that the moment he was gone, for I was terrified of this strange person or demon

or whatever it was, for I knew that whoever was in the room
with me was not the Abbess Radegunde. I knew also that it
could tell where I was and what I was doing, even if I made
no sound, and was in a terrible riddle as to what I ought to
do when soft fingers touched my face. It was the demon,
reaching swiftly and silently behind her.

And do you know, all of a sudden everything was all right!
I don't mean that she was the Abbess again—I still had very
serious suspicions about that—but all at once I felt light as
air and nothing seemed to matter very much because my
stomach was full of bubbles of happiness, just as if I had been
drunk, only nicer. If the Abbess Radegunde were really a
demon, what a joke that was on her people! And she did not,
now that I came to think of it, seem a bad sort of demon,
more the frightening kind than the killing kind, except for
Thorfinn, of course, but then Thorfinn had been a very
wicked man. And did not the angels of the Lord smite down
the wicked? So perhaps the Abbess was an angel of the Lord
and not a demon, but if she were truly an angel, why had she
not smitten the Norsemen down when they first came and so
saved all our folk? And then I thought that whether angel or
demon, she was no longer the Abbess and would love me no
longer, and if I had not been so full of the silly happiness
which kept tickling about inside me, this thought would have
made me weep.

I said, "Will the bad Thorvald get free, demon?"

"No," she said. "Not even if I sleep."

I thought: *But she does not love me.*

"I love thee," said the strange voice, but it was not the
Abbess Radegunde's and so was without meaning, but again
those soft fingers touched me and there was some kindness in
them, even if it was a stranger's kindness.

Sleep, they said.

So I did.

The next three days I had much secret mirth to see the
folk bow down to the demon and kiss its hands and weep
over it because it had sold itself to ransom them. That is
what Sister Hedwic told them. Young Thorfinn had gone out
in the night to piss and had fallen over a stone in the dark
and broken his neck, which secretly rejoiced our folk, but his
comrades did not seem to mind much either, save for one
young fellow who had been Thorfinn's friend, I think, and so

went about with a long face. Thorvald locked me up in the Abbess's study with the demon every night and went out—or so folk said—to one of the young women, but on those nights the demon was silent, and I lay there with the secret tickle of merriment in my stomach, caring about nothing.

On the third morning I woke sober. The demon—or the Abbess—for in the day she was so like the Abbess Radegunde that I wondered—took my hand and walked us up to Thorvald, who was out picking the people to go aboard the Norseman's boats at the riverbank to be slaves. Folk were standing about weeping and wringing their hands; I thought this strange because of the Abbess's promise to pick those whose going would hurt least, but I know now that least is not none. The weather was bad, cold rain out of mist, and some of Thorvald's companions were speaking sourly to him in the Norse, but he talked them down—bluff and hearty—as if making light of the weather. The demon stood by him and said, in German, in a low voice so that none might hear: "You will say we go to find the Abbess's treasure and then you will go with us into the woods."

He spoke to his fellows in Norse and they frowned, but the end of it was that two must come with us, for the demon said it was such a treasure as three might carry. The demon had the voice and manner of the Abbess Radegunde, all smiles, so they were fooled. Thus we started out into the trees behind the village, with the rain worse and the ground beginning to soften underfoot. As soon as the village was out of sight, the two Norsemen fell behind, but Thorvald did not seem to notice this; I looked back and saw the first man standing in the mud with one foot up, like a goose, and the second with his head lifted and his mouth open so that the rain fell in it. We walked on, the earth sucking at our shoes and all of us getting wet: Thorvald's hair stuck fast against his face, and the demon's old brown cloak clinging to its body. Then suddenly the demon began to breathe harshly and it put its hand to its side with a cry. Its cloak fell off and it stumbled before us between the wet trees, not weeping but breathing hard. Then I saw, ahead of us through the pelting rain, a kind of shining among the bare tree trunks, and as we came nearer the shining became more clear until it was very plain to see, not a blazing thing like a fire at night but a mild and even brightness as though the sunlight were coming through the clouds pleasantly but without strength, as it often does at the beginning of the year.

And then there were folk inside the brightness, both men and women, all dressed in white, and they held out their arms to us, and the demon ran to them, crying out loudly and weeping but paying no mind to the tree branches which struck it across the face and body. Sometimes it fell but it quickly got up again. When it reached the strange folk they embraced it, and I thought that the filth and mud of its gown would stain their white clothing, but the foulness dropped off and would not cling to those clean garments. None of the strange folk spoke a word, nor did the Abbess—I knew then that she was no demon, whatever she was—but I felt them talk to one another, as if in my mind, although I know not how this could be nor the sense of what they said. An odd thing was that as I came closer I could see they were not standing on the ground, as in the way of nature, but higher up, inside the shining, and that their white robes were nothing at all like ours, for they clung to the body so that one might see the people's legs all the way up to the place where the legs joined, even the women's. And some of the folk were like us, but most had a darker color, and some looked as if they had been smeared with soot—there are such persons in the far parts of the world, you know, as I found out later; it is their own natural color—and there were some with the odd eyes the Abbess had spoken of—but the oddest thing of all I will not tell you now. When the Abbess had embraced and kissed them all and all had wept, she turned and looked down upon us: Thorvald standing there as if held by a rope and I, who had lost my fear and had crept close in pure awe, for there was such a joy about these people, like the light about them, mild as spring light and yet as strong as in a spring where the winter has gone forever.

"Come to me, Thorvald," said the Abbess, and one could not see from her face if she loved or hated him. He moved closer—jerk! jerk!—and she reached down and touched his forehead with her fingertips, at which one side of his lip lifted, as a dog's does when it snarls.

"As thou knowest," said the Abbess quietly, "I hate thee and would be revenged upon thee. Thus I swore to myself three days ago, and such vows are not lightly broken."

I saw him snarl again and he turned his eyes from her.

"I must go soon," said the Abbess, unmoved, "for I could stay here long years only as Radegunde, and Radegunde is no more; none of us can remain here long as our proper selves or even in our true bodies, for if we do we go mad like Sibihd or walk into the river and drown or stop our own hearts, so miserable, wicked, and brutish does your world seem to us. Nor may we come in large companies, for we are few and our strength is not great and we have much to learn and study of thy folk so that we may teach and help without marring all in our ignorance. And ignorant or wise, we can do naught except thy folk aid us.

"Here is my revenge," said the Abbess, and he seemed to writhe under the touch of her fingers, for all they were so light. "Henceforth be not Thorvald Farmer nor yet Thorvald Seafarer but Thorvald Peacemaker, Thorvald War-hater, put into anguish by bloodshed and agonized at cruelty. I cannot make long thy life—that gift is beyond me—but I give thee this: to the end of thy days, long or short, thou wilt know the Presence about thee always, as I do, and thou wilt know that it is neither good nor evil, as I do, and this knowing will trouble and frighten thee always, as it does me, and so about this one thing, as about many another, Thorvald Peacemaker will never have peace.

"Now, Thorvald, go back to the village and tell thy comrades I was assumed into the company of the saints, straight up to Heaven. Thou mayst believe it, if thou wilt. That is all my revenge."

Then she took away her hand, and he turned and walked from us like a man in a dream, holding out his hands as if to feel the rain and stumbling now and again, as one who wakes from a vision.

Then I began to grieve, for I knew she would be going away with the strange people, and it was to me as if all the love and care and light in the world were leaving me. I crept close to her, meaning to spring secretly onto the shining place and so go away with them, but she spied me and said, "Silly Radulphus, you cannot," and that *you* hurt me more than anything else so that I began to bawl.

"Child," said the Abbess, "come to me," and loudly weeping I leaned against her knees. I felt the shining around me, all bright and good and warm, that wiped away all grief, and then the Abbess's touch on my hair.

She said, "Remember me. And be . . . content."

I nodded, wishing I dared to look up at her face, but when I did, she had already gone with her friends. Not up into the sky, you understand, but as if they moved very swiftly backwards among the trees—although the trees were still behind them somehow—and as they moved, the shining and the people faded away into the rain until there was nothing left.

Then there was no rain. I do not mean that the clouds parted or the sun came out; I mean that one moment it was raining and cold and the next the sky was clear blue from side to side, and it was splendid, sunny, breezy, bright, sailing weather. I had the oddest thought that the strange folk were not agreed about doing such a big miracle—and it was hard for them, too—but they had decided that no one would believe this more than all the other miracles folk speak of, I suppose. And it would surely make Thorvald's lot easier when he came back with wild words about saints and Heaven, as indeed it did, later.

Well, that is the tale, really. She said to me "Be content" and so I am; they call me Radulf the Happy now. I have had my share of trouble and sickness, but always somewhere in me there is a little spot of warmth and joy to make it all easier, like a traveler's fir burning out in the wilderness on a cold night. When I am in real sorrow or distress, I remember her fingers touching my hair and that takes part of the pain away, somehow. So perhaps I got the best gift, after all. And she said also, "Remember me," and thus I have, every little thing, although it all happened when I was the age my own grandson is now, and that is how I can tell you this tale today.

And the rest? Three days after the Norsemen left, Sibihd got back her wits and no one knew how, though I think I do! And as for Thorvald Einarsson, I have heard that after his wife died in Norway he went to England and ended his days there as a monk, but whether this story be true or not I do not know.

I know this: they may call me Happy Radulf all they like, but there is much that troubles me. Was the Abbess Radegunde a demon, as the new priest says? I cannot believe this, although he called half her sayings nonsense and the other half blasphemy when I asked him. Father Cairbre, before the Norse killed him, told us stories about the Sidhe, that is, the

Irish fairy people, who leave changelings in human cradles; and for a while it seemed to me that Radegunde must be a woman of the Sidhe when I remembered that she could read Latin at the age of two and was such a marvel of learning when so young, for the changelings the fairies leave are not their own children, you understand, but one of the fairy folk themselves, who are hundreds upon hundreds of years old, and the other fairy folk always come back for their own in the end. And yet this could not have been, for Father Cairbre said also that the Sidhe are wanton and cruel and without souls, and neither the Abbess Radegunde nor the people who came for her were one blessed bit like that, although she did break Thorfinn's neck—but then it may be that Thorfinn broke his own neck by chance, just as we all thought at the time, and she told this to Thorvald afterwards, as if she had done it herself, only to frighten him. She had more of a soul with a soul's griefs and joys than most of us, no matter what the new priest says. He never saw her or felt her sorrow and lonesomeness, or heard her talk of the blazing light all around us—and what can that be but God Himself? Even though she did call the crucifix a deaf thing and vain, she must have meant not Christ, you see, but only the piece of wood itself, for she was always telling the Sisters that Christ was in Heaven and not on the wall. And if she said the light was not good or evil, well, there is a traveling Irish scholar who told me of a holy Christian monk named Augustinus who tells us that all which is, is good, and evil is only a lack of the good, like an empty place not filled up. And if the Abbess truly said there was no God, I say it was the sin of despair, and even saints may sin, if only they repent, which I believe she did at the end.

So I tell myself, and yet I know the Abbess Radegunde was no saint, for are the saints few and weak, as she said? Surely not! And then there is a thing I held back in my telling, a small thing, and it will make you laugh and perhaps means nothing one way or the other, but it is this:

Are the saints bald?

These folk in white had young faces but they were like eggs; there was not a stitch of hair on their domes! Well, God may shave His saints if He pleases, I suppose.

But I know she was no saint. And then I believe that she did kill Thorfinn and the light was not God and she not even a Christian or maybe even human, and I remember how

Radegunde was to her only a gown to step out of at will, and how she truly hated and scorned Thorvald until she was happy and safe with her own people. Or perhaps it was like her talk about living in a house with the rooms shut up; when she stopped being Radegunde, first one part of her came back and then the other—the joyful part that could not lie or plan and then the angry part—and then they were all together when she was back among her own folk. And then I give up trying to weigh this matter and go back to warm my soul at the little fire she lit in me, that one warm, bright place in the wide and windy dark.

But something troubles me even there and will not be put to rest by the memory of the Abbess's touch on my hair. As I grow older it troubles me more and more. It was the very last thing she said to me, which I have not told you but will now. When she had given me the gift of contentment, I became so happy that I said, "Abbess, you said you would be revenged on Thorvald, but all you did was change him into a good man. That is no revenge!"

What this saying did to her astonished me, for all the color went out of her face and left it gray. She looked suddenly old, like a death's-head, even standing there among her own true folk with love and joy coming from them so strongly that I myself might feel it. She said, "I did not change him. I lent him my eyes, that is all." Then she looked beyond me, as if at our village, at the Norsemen loading their boats with weeping slaves, at all the villages of Germany and England and France where the poor folk sweat from dawn to dark so that the great lords may do battle with one another, at castles under siege with the starving folk within eating mice and rats and sometimes each other, at the women carried off or raped or beaten, at the mothers wailing for their little ones, and beyond this at the great wide world itself with all its battles which I had used to think so grand, and the misery and greediness and fear and jealousy and hatred of folk one for the other, save—perhaps—for a few small bands of savages, but they were so far from us that one could scarcely see them. She said: *No revenge? Thinkest thou so, boy?* And then she said as one who believes absolutely, as one who has seen all the folk at their living and dying, not for one year but for many, not in one place but in all places, as one who knows it all over the whole wide earth:

Think again. . . .

SWARM

by Bruce Sterling

Humanity is surely the dominant race in the galaxy. Who else could conquer space, colonize planets, swoop down on worlds and plunder them? Little things like ant hills and bee hives would hardly hinder us, would they? After all, they do not build ships, care nothing for technology, and can't even read and write. So here is the triumphant story of how one intrepid explorer handled such a species to the everlasting glory of Imperial Earth.

"I will miss your conversation during the rest of the voyage," the alien said.

Captain-doctor Simon Afriel folded his jeweled hands over his gold-embroidered waistcoat. "I regret it also, ensign," he said in the alien's own hissing language. "Our talks together have been very useful to me. I would have paid to learn so much, but you gave it freely."

"But that was only information," the alien said. He

shrouded his bead-bright eyes behind thick nictitating membranes. "We Investors deal in energy, and precious metals. To prize and pursue mere knowledge is an immature racial trait." The alien lifted the long ribbed frill behind his pinhole-sized ears.

"No doubt you are right," Afriel said, despising him. "We humans are as children to other races, however; so a certain immaturity seems natural to us." Afriel pulled off his sunglasses to rub the bridge of his nose. The starship cabin was drenched in searing blue light, heavily ultraviolet. It was the light the Investors preferred, and they were not about to change it for one human passenger.

"You have not done badly," the alien said magnanimously. "You are the kind of race we like to do business with: young, eager, plastic, ready for a wide variety of goods and experiences. We would have contacted you much earlier, but your technology was still too feeble to afford us a profit."

"Things are different now," Afriel said. "We'll make you rich."

"Indeed," the Investor said. The frill behind his scaly head flickered rapidly, a sign of amusement. "Within two hundred years you will be wealthy enough to buy from us the secret of our star-flight. Or perhaps your Mechanist faction will discover the secret through research."

Afriel was annoyed. As a member of the Reshaped faction, he did not appreciate the reference to the rival Mechanists. "Don't put too much stock in mere technical expertise," he said. "Consider the aptitude for languages we Shapers have. It makes our faction a much better trading partner. To a Mechanist, all Investors look alike."

The alien hesitated. Afriel smiled. He had made an appeal to the alien's personal ambition with his last statement, and the hint had been taken. That was where the Mechanists always erred. They tried to treat all Investors equally, using the same programmed routines each time. They lacked imagination.

Something would have to be done about the Mechanists, Afriel thought. Something more permanent than the small but deadly confrontations between isolated ships in the Asteroid Belt and the ice-rich rings of Saturn. Both factions maneuvered constantly, looking for a decisive stroke, bribing away each other's best talent, practicing ambush, assassination, and industrial espionage.

Captain-doctor Simon Afriel was a past master of these pursuits. That was why the Reshaped faction had paid the millions of kilowatts necessary to buy his passage. Afriel held doctorates in biochemistry and alien linguistics, and a master's degree in magnetic weapons engineering. He was thirty-eight years old and had been Reshaped according to the state of the art at the time of his conception. His hormonal balance had been altered slightly to compensate for long periods spent in free-fall. He had no appendix. The structure of his heart had been redesigned for greater efficiency, and his large intestine had been altered to produce the vitamins normally made by intestinal bacteria. Genetic engineering and rigorous training in childhood had given him an intelligence quotient of one hundred and eighty. He was not the brightest of the agents of the Ring Council, but he was one of the most mentally stable and the best trusted.

"It seems a shame," the alien said, "that a human of your accomplishments should have to rot for two years in this miserable, profitless outpost."

"The years won't be wasted," Afriel said.

"But why have you chosen to study the Swarm? They can teach you nothing, since they cannot speak. They have no wish to trade, having no tools or technology. They are the only spacefaring race to be essentially without intelligence."

"That alone should make them worthy of study."

"Do you seek to imitate them, then? You would make monsters of yourselves." Again the ensign hesitated. "Perhaps you could do it. It would be bad for business, however."

There came a fluting burst of alien music over the ship's speakers, then a screeching fragment of Investor language. Most of it was too high-pitched for Afriel's ears to follow.

The alien stood, his jeweled skirt brushing the tips of his clawed, birdlike feet. "The Swarm's symbiote has arrived," he said.

"Thank you," Afriel said. When the ensign opened the cabin door, Afriel could smell the Swarm's representative; the creature's warm, yeasty scent had spread rapidly through the starship's recycled air.

Afriel quickly checked his appearance in a pocket mirror. He touched powder to his face and straightened the round

velvet hat on his shoulder-length reddish-blond hair. His ear-
lobes glittered with red impact-rubies, thick as his thumbs'
ends, mined from the Asteroid Belt. His knee-length coat and
waistcoat were of gold brocade; the shirt beneath was of daz-
zling fineness, woven with red-gold thread. He had dressed to
impress the Investors, who expected and appreciated a pros-
perous look from their customers. How could he impress this
new alien? Smell, perhaps. He freshened his perfume.

Beside the starship's secondary airlock, the Swarm's symbiote was chittering rapidly at the ship's commander. The commander was an old and sleepy Investor, twice the size of
most of her crewmen. Her massive head was encrusted in a
jeweled helmet. From within the helmet her clouded eyes
glittered like cameras.

The symbiote lifted on its six posterior legs and gestured
feebly with its four clawed forelimbs. The ship's artificial
gravity, a third again as strong as Earth's, seemed to bother
it. Its rudimentary eyes, dangling on stalks, were shut tight
against the glare. It must be used to darkness. Afriel thought.

The commander answered the creature in its own language. Afriel grimaced, for he had hoped that the creature
spoke Investor. Now he would have to learn another language, a language designed for a being without a tongue.

After another brief interchange the commander turned to
Afriel. "The symbiote is not pleased with your arrival," she
told Afriel in the Investor language. "There has apparently
been some disturbance here involving humans, in the recent
past. However, I have prevailed upon it to admit you to the
Nest. The episode has been recorded. Payment for my diplomatic services will be arranged with your faction when I return to your native star system."

"I thank Your Authority," Afriel said. "Please convey to
the symbiote my best personal wishes, and the harmlessness
and humility of my intentions. . . ." He broke off short as
the symbiote lunged toward him, biting him savagely in the
calf of his left leg. Afriel jerked free and leapt backward in
the heavy artificial gravity, going into a defensive position.
The symbiote had ripped away a long shred of his pants leg;
it now crouched quietly, eating it.

"It will convey your scent and composition to its nest-
mates," said the commander. "This is necessary. Otherwise

you would be classed as an invader, and the Swarm's warrior caste would kill you at once."

Afriel relaxed quickly and pressed his hand against the puncture wound to stop the bleeding. He hoped that none of the Investors had noticed his reflexive action. It would not mesh well with his story of being a harmless researcher.

"We will reopen the airlock soon," the commander said phlegmatically, leaning back on her thick reptilian tail. The symbiote continued to munch the shred of cloth. Afriel studied the creature's neckless segmented head. It had a mouth and nostrils; it had bulbous atrophied eyes on stalks; there were hinged slats that might be radio receivers, and two parallel ridges of clumped wriggling antennae, sprouting among three chitinous plates. Their function was unknown to him.

The airlock door opened. A rush of dense, smoky aroma entered the departure cabin. It seemed to bother the half-dozen Investors, who left rapidly. "We will return in six hundred and twelve of your days, as by our agreement," the commander said.

"I thank Your Authority," Afriel said.

"Good luck," the commander said in English. Afriel smiled.

The symbiote, with a sinuous wriggle of its segmented body, crept into the airlock. Afriel followed it. The airlock door shut behind them. The creature said nothing to him but continued munching loudly. The second door opened, and the symbiote sprang through it, into a wide, round, stone tunnel. It vanished at once into the gloom.

Afriel put his sunglasses into a pocket of his jacket and pulled out a pair of infrared goggles. He strapped them to his head and stepped out of the airlock. The artificial gravity vanished, replaced by the almost imperceptible gravity of the Swarm's asteroid nest. Afriel smiled, comfortable for the first time in weeks. Most of his adult life had been spent in free-fall, in the Shaper's colonies in the rings of Saturn.

Squatting in a dark cavity in the side of the tunnel was a disk-headed, furred animal the size of an elephant. It was clearly visible in the infrared of its own body heat. Afriel could hear it breathing. It waited patiently until Afriel had launched himself past it, deeper into the tunnel. Then it took its place in the end of the tunnel, puffing itself up with air until its swollen head securely plugged the end of the corridor. Its multiple legs were firmly planted in sockets in the walls.

The Investor's ship had left. Afriel remained here, inside one of the millions of planetoids that circled the giant star Betelgeuse in a girdling ring with almost five times the mass of Jupiter. As a source of potential wealth it dwarfed the entire solar system, and it belonged, more or less, to the Swarm. At least, no other race had challenged them for it within the memory of the Investors.

Afriel peered up the corridor. It seemed deserted, and without other bodies to cast infrared heat, he could not see very far. Kicking against the wall, he floated hesitantly down the corridor.

He heard a human voice. "Doctor Afriel!"

"Doctor Mirny!" he called out. "This way!"

He first saw a pair of young symbiotes scuttling towards him, the tips of their clawed feet barely touching the walls. Behind them came a woman wearing goggles like his own. She was young, and attractive in the trim, anonymous way of the genetically reshaped.

She screeched something at the symbiotes in their own language, and they stopped, waiting. She coasted forward, and Afriel caught her arm, expertly stopping their momentum.

"You didn't bring any luggage?" she said anxiously.

He shook his head. "We got your warning before I was sent out. I have only the clothes I'm wearing and a few items in my pockets."

She looked at him critically. "Is that what people are wearing in the Rings these days? Things have changed more than I thought.

Afriel looked at his brocaded coat and laughed. "It's a matter of policy. The Investors are always readier to talk to a human who looks ready to do business on a large scale. All the Shapers' representatives dress like this these days. We've stolen a jump on the Mechanists; they still dress in those coveralls." He hesitated, not wanting to offend her. Galina Mirny's intelligence was rated at almost two hundred. Men and women that bright were sometimes flighty and unstable, likely to retreat into private fantasy worlds or become enmeshed in strange and impenetrable webs of plotting and rationalization. High intelligence was the strategy the Shapers had chosen in the struggle for cultural dominance, and they were obliged to stick to it, despite its occasional disadvantages. They had tried breeding the super-bright—those with quotients over two hundred—but so many had defected from the Shapers' colonies that the faction had stopped producing them.

"You wonder about my own clothing," Mirny said.

"It certainly has the appeal of novelty," Afriel said with a smile.

"It was woven from the fibers of a pupa's cocoon," she said. "My original wardrobe was eaten by a scavenger symbiote during the troubles last year. I usually go nude, but I didn't want to offend you by too great a show of intimacy."

Afriel shrugged. "I usually go nude myself in my own environment. If the temperature is constant, then clothes are useless, except for pockets. I have a few tools on my person, but most are of little importance. We're the Reshaped, our tools are here." He tapped his head. "If you can show me a safe place to put my clothes. . . ."

She shook her head. It was impossible to see her eyes for the goggles, which made her expression hard to read. "You've made your first mistake, doctor. There are no places of our own here. It was the same mistake the Mechanist agents made, the same one that almost killed me as well. There is no concept of privacy or property here. This is the Nest. If you seize any part of it for yourself—to store equipment, to sleep in, whatever—then you become an intruder, an enemy. The two Mechanists—a man and a woman—tried to secure an unused chamber for their computer lab. Warriors broke down their door and devoured them. Scavengers ate their equipment, glass, metal, and all."

Afriel smiled coldly. "It must have cost them a fortune to ship all that material here."

Mirny shrugged. "They're wealthier than we are. Their machines, their mining. They meant to kill me, I think. Surreptitiously, so the warriors wouldn't be upset by a show of violence. They had a computer that was learning the language of the springtails faster than I could."

"But you survived," Afriel pointed out. "And your tapes and reports—especially the early ones, when you still had most of your equipment—were of tremendous interest. The

Council is behind you all the way. You've become quite a celebrity in the Rings, during your absence."

"Yes, I expected as much," she said.

Afriel was nonplused. "If I found any deficiency in them," he said carefully, "it was in my own field, alien linguistics." He waved vaguely at the two symbiotes who accompanied her. "I assume you've made great progress in communicating with the symbiotes, since they seem to do all the talking for the Nest."

She looked at him with an unreadable expression and shrugged. "There are at least fifteen different kinds of symbiotes here. Those that accompany me all called the springtails, and they speak only for themselves. They are savages, doctor, who received attention from the Investors only because they can still talk. They were a space-going race at one time, but they've forgotten it. They discovered the Nest and they were absorbed, they became parasites." She tapped one of them on the head. "I tamed these two because I learned to steal and beg food better than they can. They stay with me now and protect me from the larger ones. They are jealous, you know. They have only been with the Nest for perhaps ten thousand years and are still uncertain of their position. They still think, and wonder sometimes. After ten thousand years there is still a little of that left to them."

"Savages," Afriel said. "I can well believe that. One of them bit me while I was still aboard the starship. He left a lot to be desired as an ambassador."

"Yes, I warned him you were coming," said Mirny. "He didn't much like the idea, but I was able to bribe him with food. . . . I hope he didn't hurt you badly."

"A scratch," Afriel said. "I assume there's no chance of infection."

"I doubt it very much. Unless you brought your own bacteria with you."

"Hardly likely," Afriel said, offended. "I have no bacteria. And I wouldn't have brought microorganisms to an alien culture anyway."

Mirny looked away. "I thought you might have some of the special genetically altered ones. . . . I think we can go now. The springtail will have spread your scent by mouth-touching in the subsidiary chamber, ahead of us. It will be spread throughout the Nest in a few hours. Once it reaches the Queen, it will spread very quickly."

Placing her feet against the hard shell of one of the young springtails, she launched herself down the hall. Afriel followed her. The air was warm and he was beginning to sweat under his elaborate clothing, but his antiseptic sweat was odorless.

They exited into a vast chamber dug from the living rock. It was arched and oblong, eighty meters long and about twenty in diameter. It swarmed with members of the Nest.

There were hundreds of them. Most of them were workers, eight-legged and furred, the size of Great Danes. Here and there were members of the warrior caste, horse-sized furry monsters with heavy fanged heads the size and shape of overstuffed chairs.

A few meters away, two workers were carrying a member of the sensor caste, a being whose immense flattened head was attached to an atrophied body that was mostly lungs. The sensor had eyes and its furred chitin sprouted long coiled antennae that twitched feebly as the workers bore it along. The workers clung to the hollowed rock of the chamber walls with hooked and suckered feet.

A paddle-limbed monster with a hairless, faceless head came sculling past them, through the warm reeking air. The front of its head was a nightmare of sharp grinding jaws and blunt armored acid spouts. "A tunneler," Mirny said. "It can take us deeper into the Nest—come with me." She launched herself toward it and took a handhold on its furry, segmented back. Afriel followed her, joined by the two immature springtails, who clung to the thing's hide with their forelimbs. Afriel shuddered at the warm, greasy feel of its rank, damp fur. It continued to scull through the air, its eight fringed paddle feet catching the air like wings.

"There must be thousands of them." Afriel said.

"I said a hundred thousand in my last report, but that was before I had fully explored the Nest. Even now there are long stretches I haven't seen. They must number close to a quarter of a million. This asteroid is about the size of the Mechanists' biggest base—Ceres. It still has rich veins of carbonaceous material. It's far from mined out."

Afriel closed his eyes. If he were to lose his goggles, he would have to feel his way, blind, through these teeming, twitching, wriggling thousands. "The population's still expanding, then?"

"Definitely," she said. "In fact, the colony will launch a mating swarm soon. There are three dozen male and female alates in the chambers near the Queen. Once they're launched, they'll mate and start new Nests. I'll take you to see them presently." She hesitated. "We're entering one of the fungal gardens now."

One of the young springtails quietly shifted position. Grabbing the tunneler's fur with its forelimbs, it began to gnaw on the cuff of Afriel's pants. Afriel kicked it soundly, and it jerked back, retracting its eyestalks.

When he looked up again, he saw that they had entered a second chamber, much larger than the first. The walls around, overhead and below were buried under an explosive profusion of fungus. The most common types were swollen, barrel-like domes, multi-branched massed thickets, and spaghetti-like tangled extrusions, that moved very slightly in the faint and odorous breeze. Some of the barrels were surrounded by dim mists of exhaled spores.

"You see those caked-up piles beneath the fungus, its growth medium?" Mirny said.

"Yes."

"I'm not sure whether it is a plant form or just some kind of complex biochemical sludge," she said. "The point is that it grows in sunlight, on the outside of the asteroid. A food source that grows in naked space! Imagine what that would be worth, back in the Rings."

"There aren't words for its value," Afriel said.

"It's inedible by itself," she said. "I tried to eat a very small piece of it once. It was like trying to eat plastic."

"Have you eaten well, generally speaking?"

"Yes. Our biochemistry is quite similar to the Swarm's. The fungus itself is perfectly edible. The regurgitate is more nourishing, though. Internal fermentation in the worker hindgut adds to its nutritional value."

Afriel stared. "You grow used to it," Mirny said. "Later I'll teach you how to solicit food from the workers. It's a simple matter of reflex tapping—it's not controlled by pheromones, like most of their behavior." She brushed a long lock of clumped and dirty hair from the side of her face. "I hope the pheromonal samples I sent back were worth the cost of transportation."

"Oh, yes," said Afriel. "The chemistry of them was fascinating. We managed to synthesize most of the compounds. I was part of the research team myself." He hesitated. How far did he dare trust her? She had not been told about the experiment he and his superiors had planned. As far as Mirny knew, he was a simple, peaceful researcher, like herself. The Shapers' scientific community was suspicious of the minority involved in military work and espionage.

As an investment in the future, the Shapers had sent researchers to each of the nineteen alien races described to them by the Investors. This had cost the Shaper economy many gigawatts of precious energy and tons of rare metals and isotopes. In most cases, only two or three researchers could be sent: in seven cases, only one. For the Swarm, Galina Mirny had been chosen. She had gone peacefully, trusting in her intelligence and her good intentions to keep her alive and sane. Those who had sent her had not known whether her findings would be of any use or importance. They had only known that it was imperative that she be sent, even alone, even ill-equipped, before some other faction sent their own people and possibly discovered some technique or fact of overwhelming importance. And Dr. Mirny had indeed discovered such a situation. It had made her mission into a matter of Ring security. That was why Afriel had come.

"You synthesized the compounds?" she said. "Why?"

Afriel smiled disarmingly. "Just to prove to ourselves that we could do it, perhaps."

She shook her head. "No mind-games, Doctor Afriel, please. I came this far partly to escape from such things. Tell me the truth."

Afriel stared at her, regretting that the goggles meant he could not meet her eyes. "Very well," he said. "You should know, then, that I have been ordered by the Ring Council to carry out an experiment that may endanger both our lives."

Mirny was silent for a moment. "You're from Security, then?"

"My rank is captain."

"I knew it. . . . I knew it when those two Mechanists arrived. They were so polite, and so suspicious—I think they would have killed me at once if they hadn't hoped to bribe or torture some secret out of me. They scared the life out of me, Captain Afriel. . . . You scare me, too."

"We live in a frightening world, doctor. It's a matter of faction security."

"Everything's a matter of faction security with you lot," she said. "I shouldn't take you any farther, or show you anything more. This Nest, these creatures—they're not *intelligent,* captain. They can't think, they can't learn. They're innocent, primordially innocent. They have no knowledge of good and evil. They have no knowledge of *anything.* The last thing they need is to become pawns in a power struggle within some other race, light-years away."

The tunneler had turned into an exit from the fungal chambers and was paddling slowly along in the warm darkness. A group of creatures like gray, flattened basketballs floated by from the opposite direction. One of them settled on Afriel's sleeve, slinging with frail, whiplike tentacles. Afriel brushed it gently away, and it broke loose, emitting a stream of foul reddish droplets.

"Naturally I agree with you in principle, doctor," Afriel said smoothly. "But consider these Mechanists. Some of their extreme factions are already more than half machine. Do you expect humanitarian motives from them? They're cold, doctor—cold and soulless creatures who can cut a living man or woman to bits and never feel their pain. Most of the other factions hate us. They think we've set ourselves up as racist supermen because we won't interbreed, because we've chosen the freedom to manipulate our own genes. Would you rather that one of these cults do what we must do, and use the results against us?"

"This is double-talk." She looked away. All around them workers laden down with fungus, their jaws full and guts stuffed with it, were spreading out into the Nest, scuttling alongside them or disappearing into branch tunnels departing in every direction, including straight up and straight down. Afriel saw a creature much like a worker, but with only six legs, scuttle past in the opposite direction, overhead. It was a parasite mimic. How long, he wondered, did it take a creature to evolve to look like that?

"It's no wonder that we've had so many defectors, back in the Rings," she said sadly. "If humanity is so stupid as to work itself into a corner like you describe, then it's better to have nothing to do with them. Better to live alone. Better not to help the madness spread."

"That kind of talk will only get us all killed," Afriel said. "We owe an allegiance to the faction that produced us."

"Tell me truly, captain," she said. "Haven't you ever felt the urge to leave everything—everyone—all your duties and constraints, and just go somewhere to think it all out? Your whole world, and your part in it? We're trained so hard, from childhood, and so much is demanded from us. Don't you think it's made us lose sight of our goals, somehow?"

"We live in space," Afriel said flatly. "Space is an unnatural environment, and it takes an unnatural effort from unnatural people to prosper there. Our minds are our tools, and philosophy has to come second. Naturally I've felt those urges you mention. They're just another threat to guard against. I believe in an ordered society. Technology has unleashed tremendous forces that are ripping society apart. Some one faction must arise from the struggle and integrate things. We who are Reshaped have the wisdom and restraint to do it humanely. That's why I do the work I do." He hesitated. "I don't expect to see our day of triumph. I expect to die in some brushfire conflict, or through assassination. It's enough that I can foresee that day."

"But the arrogance of it, captain!" she said suddenly. "The arrogance of your little fire and its little sacrifice! Consider the Swarm, if you really want your humane and perfect order. Here it is! Where it's always warm and dark, and it smells good, and food is easy to get, and everything is endlessly and perfectly recycled. The only resources that are ever lost are the bodies of the mating swarms, and a little air from the airlocks when the workers go out to harvest. A Nest like this one could last unchanged for hundreds of thousands of years. Hundreds, of thousands, of years. Who, or what, will remember us and our stupid faction in even a thousand years?"

Afriel shook his head. "That's not a valid comparison. There is no such long view for us. In another thousand years we'll be machines, or gods." He felt the top of his head; his velvet cap was gone. No doubt something was eating it by now.

The tunneler took them even deeper into the honeycombed free-fall maze of the asteroid. They saw the pupal chambers, where pallid larvae twitched in swaddled silk; the main fungal gardens; the graveyard pits, where winged workers beat ceaselessly at the soupy air, feverishly hot from the heat of decomposition. Corrosive black fungus ate the bodies of the dead into coarse black powder, carried off by blackened workers themselves three quarters dead.

Later they left the tunneler and floated on by themselves. The woman moved with the ease of long habit; Afriel followed her, colliding bruisingly with squeaking workers. There were thousands of them, clinging to ceiling, walls, and floor, clustering and scurrying at every conceivable angle.

Later still they visited the chamber of the winged princes and princesses, an echoing round vault where creatures forty meters long hung crooked-legged in midair. Their bodies were segmented and metallic, with organic rocket nozzles on their thoraxes, where wings might have been. Folded along their sleek backs were radar antennae on long sweeping booms. They looked more like interplanetary probes under construction than anything biological. Workers fed them ceaselessly. Their bulging spiracled abdomens were full of compressed oxygen.

Mirny begged a large chunk of fungus from a passing worker, deftly tapping its antennae and provoking a reflex action. She handed most of the fungus to the two springtails, which devoured it greedily and looked expectantly for more.

Afriel tucked his legs into a lotus position and began chewing with determination on the leathery fungus. It was tough, but tasted good, like smoked meat—a Terran delicacy he had tasted only once. The smell of smoke meant disaster in a Shaper's colony.

Mirny maintained a stony silence. "Food's no problem," Afriel said cheerfully. "Where do we sleep?"

She shrugged. "Anywhere. . . . there are unused niches and tunnels here and there. I suppose you'll want to see the Queen's chamber next."

"By all means."

"I'll have to get more fungus. The warriors are on guard there and have to be bribed with food."

She gathered an armful of fungus from another worker in the endless stream, and they exited through another tunnel. Afriel, already totally lost, was further confused in the maze of chambers and tunnels. At last they exited into an immense lightless cavern, bright with infrared heat from the Queen's

monstrous body. It was the colony's central factory. The fact
that it was made of warm and pulpy flesh did not conceal its
essentially industrial nature. Tons of predigested fungal pap
went into the slick blind jaws at one end. The rounded bil-
lows of soft flesh digested and processed it, squirming sucking, and undulating, with loud, machinelike churnings and
gurglings. Out of the other end came an endless conveyorlike
blobbed stream of eggs, each one packed in a thick hormonal
paste of lubrication. The workers avidly licked the eggs clean
and bore them off to nurseries. Each egg was the size of a
man's torso.

The process went on and on. There was no day or night
here in the lightless center of the asteroid. There was no rem-
nant of a diurnal rhythm in the genes of these creatures. The
flow of production was as constant and even as the working
of an automated mine.

"This is why I'm here," Afriel murmured in awe. "Just
look at this, doctor. The Mechanists have computer-run mining machinery that is generations ahead of ours. But here—in
the bowels of this nameless little world, is a genetically run
technology that feeds itself, maintains itself, runs itself, effi-
ciently, endlessy, mindlessly. It's the perfect organic tool. The
faction that could make use of these tireless workers could
make itself an industrial titan. And our knowledge of biochemistry is unsurpassed. We Shapers are just the ones to do
it."

"How do you propose to do that?" Mirny asked with open
skepticism. "You would have to ship a fertilized queen all the
way to the solar system. We could scarcely afford that, even
if the Investors would let us, which they wouldn't."

"I don't need an entire colony," Afriel said patiently. "I
only need the genetic information from one egg. Our labora-
tories back in the Rings could clone endless numbers of
them."

"But the workers are useless without the rest of the colony
to give them orders. They need the pheromones to trigger
their behavior modes."

"Exactly," Afriel said. "As it so happens, I possess those
pheromones in concentrated form. What I must do now is
test them. I must prove that I can use them to make the
workers do what I choose. Once I've proven it's possible, I'm
authorized to smuggle the genetic information necessary back

to the Rings. The investors won't approve. There are, of course, moral questions involved, and they are not genetically advanced. But we can win their approval back with the profits we make. Best of all, we can beat the Mechanists at their own game."

"You've carried the pheromones here?" Mirny said. "Didn't the Investors suspect something when they found them?"

"Now it's you who has made an error," Afriel said calmly. "You assume that they are infallible. You are wrong. A race without curiosity will never explore every possibility, the way we Shapers did." Afriel pulled up his pants cuff and extended his right leg. "Consider this varicose vein along my shin. Circulatory problems of this sort are common among those who spend a lot of time in free-fall. This vein, however, had been blocked artificially, and its walls biochemically treated to reduce osmosis. Within the vein are ten separate colonies of genetically altered bacteria, each one specially to produce a different Swarm pheromone."

He smiled. "The Investors searched me very thoroughly, including x-rays. They insist, naturally, on knowing about everything transported aboard one of their ships. But the vein appears normal to x-rays, and the bacteria are trapped within compartments in the vein. They are indetectable. I have a small medical kit on my person. It includes a syringe. We can use it to extract the pheromones and test them. When the tests are finished—and I feel sure they will be successful, in fact I've staked my career on it—we can empty the vein and all its compartments. The bacteria will die on contact with air. We can refill the vein with the yolk from a developing embryo. The cells may survive during the trip back, but even if they die, they won't rot. They'll never come in contact with bacteria that can decompose them. Back in the Rings, we can learn to activate and suppress different genes to produce the different castes, just as is done in nature. We'll have millions of workers, armies of warriors if need be, perhaps even organic rocketships, grown from altered alates. If this works, who do you think will remember me then, eh? Me and my arrogant little life and little sacrifice?"

She stared at him; even the bulky goggles could not hide her new respect and even fear. "You really mean to do it, then."

"I made the sacrifice of my time and energy. I expect results, doctor."

"But it's kidnapping. You're talking about breeding a slave race."

Afriel shrugged, with contempt. "You're juggling words, doctor. I'll cause this colony no harm. I may steal some of its workers' labor while they obey my own chemical orders but that tiny minority won't be missed. I admit to the murder of one egg, but that is no more a crime than a human abortion. Can the theft of one strand of genetic material be called 'kidnapping'? I think not. As for the scandalous idea of a slave race—I reject it out of hand. These creatures are genetic robots. They will no more be slaves than are laser drills or bulldozers. At the very worst, they will be domestic animals."

Mirny considered the issue. It did not take her long. "It's true. It's not as if a common worker will be staring at the stars, pining for its freedom. They're just brainless neuters."

"Exactly, doctor."

"They simply work. Whether they work for us or the Swarm makes no difference to them."

"I see that you've seized on the beauty of the idea."

"And if it worked," Mirny said, "if it worked, our faction would profit astronomically."

Afriel smiled genuinely, unaware of the chilling sarcasm of his espression. "And the personal profit, doctor. . . . the valuable expertise of the first to exploit the technique." He spoke gently, quietly. "Ever see a nitrogen snowfall on Titan? I think a habitat of one's own there—larger, much larger than anything possible before. . . . A genuine city, Galina, a place where a man can scrap the rules and discipline that madden him. . . ."

"Now it's you who are talking defection, captain-doctor."

Afriel was silent for a moment, then smiled with an effort. "Now you've ruined my perfect reverie," he said. "Besides, what I was describing was the well-earned retirement of a wealthy man, not some self-indulgent hermitage. . . . there's a clear but subtle difference." He hesitated. "In any case, may I conclude that you're with me in this project?"

She laughed and touched his arm. There was something uncanny about the small sound of her laugh, drowned by a great organic rumble from the Queen's monstrous intestines. . . . . "Do you expect me to resist your arguments for two years? Better that I give in now and save us friction."

"Yes."

"After all, you won't do any harm to the colony. They'll never know anything has happened. And if their genetic line is successfully reproduced back home, they'll never be any reason for humanity to bother them again."

"True enough," said Afriel, though in the back of his mind he instantly thought of the fabulous wealth of Betelguese's asteroid system. A day would come, inevitably, when humanity would move to the stars en masse, in earnest. It would be well to know the ins and outs of every race that might become a rival.

"I'll help you as best I can," she said. There was a moment's silence. "Have you seen enough of this area?"

"Yes." They left the Queen's chamber.

"I didn't think I'd like you at first," she said candidly. "I think I like you better now. You seem to have a sense of humor that most Security people lack."

"It's not a sense of humor," Afriel said sadly. "It's a sense of irony disguised as one."

There were no days in the unending stream of hours that followed. There were only ragged periods of sleep, apart at first, later together, as they held each other in free-fall. The sexual feel of skin and body became an anchor to their common humanity, a divided, frayed humanity so many light-years away that the concept no longer had any meaning to them. Life in the warm and swarming tunnels was the here and now; the two of them were like germs in a bloodstream, moving ceaselessly with the pulsing ebb and flow. They tested the pheromones, one by one, as the hours stretched into months and time grew meaningless.

The pheromonal workings were complex, but not impossibly difficult. The first of the ten pheromones was a simple grouping stimulus, causing large numbers of workers to gather as the pheromone was spread from palp to palp. The workers then waited for further instructions; if none were forthcoming, they dispersed. To work effectively, the pheromones had to be given in a mix, or series, like computer commands; number one, grouping, for instance, together with the third pheromone, a transferral order, which caused the workers to empty any given chamber and move its effects to another. The

ninth pheromone had the best industrial possibilities; it was a
building order, causing the workers to gather tunnelers and
dredgers and set them to work. Others were annoying; the
tenth pheromone provoked grooming behavior, and the workers' furry palps stripped off the remaining rags of Afriel's
clothing. The eighth pheromone set the workers off to harvest
material on the asteroid's surface, and in their eagerness to
observe its effects the two explorers were almost trapped and
swept off into space.

The two of them no longer feared the warrior caste. They
knew that a dose of the sixth pheromone would send them
scurrying off to defend the eggs, just as it sent the workers to
tend them. Mirny and Afriel took advantage of this and se-
cured their own chambers, dug by chemically hijacked workers and defended by a hijacked airlock guardian. They had
their own fungal gardens to refresh the air, stocked with the
fungus they liked best; and digested by a worker they kept
drugged for their own food use. From constant stuffing and
lack of exercise the worker had swollen up into its replete
form and hung from one wall like a monstrous grape.

Afriel was tired. He had been without sleep recently for a
long time; how long, he didn't know. His body rhythms had
not adjusted as well as Mirny's, and he was prone to fits of
depression and irritability that he had to repress with an effort. "The Investors will be back sometime, he said. "Sometime soon."

Mirny shrugged. "The Investors," she said, and followed
the remark with something in the language of the springtails,
that he didn't catch. Despite his linguistic training, Afriel had
never caught up with her in her use of the springtails' grating
jargon. His training was almost a liability; the springtail language had decayed so much that it was a pidgin tongue, without rules or regularity. He knew enough to give them simple
orders, and with his partial control of the warriors he had the
power to back it up. The springtails were afraid of him, and
the two juveniles that Mirny had tamed had grown into fat,
overgrown tyrants that freely terrorized their elders. Afriel
had been too busy to seriously study the springtails or the
other symbiotes. There were too many practical matters at
hand.

"If they come too soon, I won't be able to finish my latest
study," she said in English.

Afriel pulled off his infrared goggles and knotted them tightly around his neck. "There's a limit, Galina," he said, yawning. "You can only memorize so much data without equipment. We'll just have to wait quietly until we can get back. I hope the Investors aren't shocked when they see me. I lost a fortune with those clothes."

"It's been so dull since the mating swarm was launched. And we've had to stop the experiments to let your vein heal. If it weren't for the new growth in the alates' chamber, I'd be bored to death." She pushed greasy hair from her face with both hands. "Are you going to sleep?"

"Yes, if I can."

"You won't come with me? I keep telling you that this new growth is important. I think it's a new caste. It's definitely not an alate. It has eyes like an alate, but it's clinging to the wall."

"It's probably not a Swarm member at all, then," he said tiredly, humoring her. "It's probably a parasite, an alate mimic. Go on and see it, if you want to. I'll be here waiting for you."

He heard her leave. Without his infrareds on, the darkness was still not quite total; there was a very faint luminosity from the steaming, growing fungus in the chamber beyond. The stuffed worker replete moved slightly on the wall, rustling and gurgling. He fell asleep.

When he awoke, Mirny had not yet returned. He was not alarmed. First, he visited the original airlock tunnel, where the Investors had first left him. It was irrational—the Investors always fulfilled their contracts—but he feared that they would arrive someday, become impatient, and leave without him. The Investors would have to wait, of course. Mirny could keep them occupied in the short time it would take him to hurry to the nursery and rob a developing egg of its living cells. It was best that the egg be as fresh as possible.

Later he ate. He was munching fungus in one of the anterior chambers when Mirny's two tamed springtails found him. "What do you want?" he asked in their language.

"Food-giver no good," the larger one screeched, waving its forelegs in brainless agitation. "Not work, not sleep."

"Not move," the second one said. It added hopefully, "Eat it now?"

Afriel gave them some of his food. They ate it, seemingly

more out of habit than real appetite, which alarmed him.
"Take me to her," he told them.

The two springtails scurried off; he followed them easily,
adroitly dodging and weaving through the crowds of workers.
They led him several miles through the network, to the alates'
chamber. There they stopped, confused. "Gone," the large
one said.

The chamber was empty. Afriel had never seen it empty
before, and it was very unusual for the Swarm to waste so
much space. He felt dread. "Follow the food-giver," he said.
"Follow smell."

The springtails snuffled without much enthusiasm along
one wall; they knew he had no food and were reluctant to do
anything without an immediate reward. At last one of them
picked up the scent, or pretended to, and followed it up
across the ceiling and into the mouth of a tunnel.

It was hard for Afriel to see much in the abandoned chamber; there was not enough infrared heat. He leapt upward after the springtail.

He heard the roar of a warrior and the springtail's
choked-off screech. It came flying from the tunnel's mouth, a
spray of clotted fluid bursting from its ruptured head. It
tumbled end over end until it hit the far wall with a flaccid
crunch. It was already dead.

The second springtail fled at once, screeching with grief
and terror. Afriel landed on the lip of the tunnel, sinking into
a crouch as his legs soaked up momentum. He could smell
the acrid stench of the warrior's anger, a pheromone so thick
that even a human could scent it. Dozens of other warriors
would group here within minutes, or seconds. Behind the enraged warrior he could hear workers and tunnelers shifting
and cementing rock.

He might be able to control one enraged warrior, but never
two, or twenty. He launched himself from the chamber wall
and out an exit.

He searched for the other springtail—he felt sure he could
recognize it, it was so much bigger than the others—but he
could not find it. With its keen sense of smell, it could easily
hide from him if it wanted to.

Mirny did not return. Uncountable hours passed. He slept
again. He returned to the alates' chambers; there were warriors on guard there, warriors that were not interested in food

and opened their immense serrated fangs when he approached. They looked ready to rip him apart; the faint reek of aggressive pheromones hung about the place like a fog. He did not see any symbiotes of any kind on the warriors' bodies. There was one species, a thing like a huge tick, that clung only to warriors, but even the ticks were gone.

He returned to his chambers to wait and think. Mirny's body was not in the garbage pits. Of course, it was possible that something else might have eaten her. Should be extract the remaining pheromone from the spaces in his vein and try to break into the alates' chamber? He suspected that Mirny, or whatever was left of her, was somewhere in the tunnel where the springtail had been killed. He had never explored that tunnel himself. There were thousands of tunnels he had never explored.

He felt paralyzed by indecision and fear. If he were quiet, if he did nothing, the Investors might arrive at any moment. He could tell the Ring Council anything he wanted about Mirny's death; if he had the genetics with him, no one would quibble. He did not love her; he respected her, but not enough to give up his life, or his faction's investment. He had not thought of the Ring Council in a long time, and the thought sobered him. He would have to explain his decision. . . .

He was still in a brown study when he heard a whoosh of air as his living airlock deflated itself. Three warriors had come for him. There was no reek of anger about them. They moved slowly and carefully. He knew better than to try to resist. One of them seized him gently in its massive jaws and carried him off.

It took him to the alates' chamber and into the guarded tunnel. A new, large chamber had been excavated at the end of the tunnel. It was filled almost to bursting by a black-splattered white mass of flesh. In the center of the soft speckled mass were a mouth and two damp, shining eyes, on stalks. Long tendrils like conduits dangled, writhing, from a clumped ridge above the eyes. The tendrils ended in pink, fleshy plug-like clumps.

One of the tendrils had been thrust through Mirny's skull. Her body hung in midair, limp as wax. Her eyes were open, but blind.

Another tendril was plugged into the braincase of a mu-

tated worker. The worker still had the pallid tinge of a larva;
it was shrunken and deformed, and its mouth had the
wrinkled look of a human mouth. There was a blob like a
tongue in the mouth, and white ridges like human teeth. It
had no eyes.

It spoke with Mirny's voice. "Captain-doctor Afriel. . . ."

"Galina. . . ."

"I have no such name. You may address me as Swarm."

Afriel vomited. The central mass was an immense head. Its
brain almost filled the room.

It waited politely until Afriel had finished.

"I find myself awakened again," Swarm said dreamily. "I
am pleased to see that it is no major emeregncy that concerns
me. Instead it is a threat that has become almost routine." It
hesitated declicately. Mirny's body moved slightly in midair;
her breathing was inhumanly regular. The eyes opened and
closed. "Another young race."

"What are you?"

"I am the Swarm. That is, I am one of its castes. I am a
tool, an adaptation; my speciality is intelligence. I am not often needed. It is good to be needed again."

"Have you been here all along? Why didn't you greet us?
We'd have dealt with you. We meant no harm."

The wet mouth on the end of the plug made laughing
sounds. "Like yourself, I enjoy irony," it said. "It is a pretty
trap you have found yourself in, captain-doctor. You meant
to make the Swarm work for you and your race. You meant
to breed us and study us and use us. It is an excellent plan,
but one we hit upon long before your race evolved."

Stung by panic, Afriel's mind raced frantically. "You're an
intelligent being," he said. "There's no reason to do us any
harm. Let us talk together. We can help you."

"Yes," Swarm agreed. "You will be helpful. Your companion's memories tell me that this is one of those uncomfortable
periods when galactic intelligence is rife. Intelligence is a
great bother. It makes all kinds of trouble for us."

"What do you mean?"

"You are a young race and lay great stock by your own
cleverness," Swarm said. "As usual, you fail to see that intelligence is not a survival trait."

Afriel wiped sweat from his face. "We've done well," he

said. "We came to you, and peacefully. You didn't come to us."

"I refer to exactly that," Swarm said urbanely. "This urge to expand, to explore, to develop, is just what will make you extinct. You naively suppose that you can continue to feed your curiosity indefinitely. It is an old story, pursued by countless races before you. Within a thousand years—perhaps a little longer—your species will vanish."

"You intend to destroy us, then? I warn you it will not be an easy task—"

"Again you miss the point. Knowledge is power! Do you suppose that fragile little form of yours—your primitive legs, your ludicrous arms and hands, your tiny, scarcely wrinkled brain—can *contain* all that power? Certainly not! Already your race is flying to pieces under the impact of your own expertise. The original human form is becoming obsolete. Your own genes have been altered, and you, captain-doctor, are a crude experiment. In a hundred years you will be a Neanderthal. In a thousand years you will not even be a memory. Your race will go the same way as a thousand others."

"And what way is that?"

"I do not know." The thing on the end of the Swarm's arm made a chuckling sound. "They have passed beyond my ken. They have all discovered something, learned something, that has caused them to transcend my understanding. It may be that they even transcend *being*. At any rate, I cannot sense their presence anywhere. They seem to do nothing, they seem to interfere in nothing; for all intents and purposes, they seem to be dead. Vanished. They may have become gods, or ghosts. In either case, I have no wish to join them."

"So then—so then you have—"

"Intelligence is very much a two-edged sword, captain-doctor. It is useful only up to a point. It interferes with the business of living. Life, and intelligence, do not mix very well. They are not at all closely related, as you childishly assume."

"But you, then—you are a rational being—"

"I am a tool, as I said." The mutated device on the end of its arm made a sighing noise. "When you began your pheromonal experiments, the chemical imbalance became apparent to the Queen. It triggered certain genetic patterns within her body, and I was reborn. Chemical sabotage is a problem that can best be dealt with by intelligence. I am a brain replete, you see, specially designed to be far more intelligent than any young race. Within three days I was fully self-conscious. Within five days I had deciphered these markings on my body. They are the genetically encoded history of my race . . . within five days and two hours I recognized the problem at hand and knew what to do. I am now doing it. I am six days old."

"What is it you intend to do?"

"Your race is a very vigorous one. I expect it to be here, competing with us, within five hundred years. Perhaps much sooner. It will be necessary to make a thorough study of such a rival. I invite you to join our community on a permanent basis."

"What do you mean?"

"I invite you to become a symbiote. I have here a male and a female, whose genes are altered and therefore without defects. You make a perfect breeding pair. It will save me a great deal of trouble with cloning."

"You think I'll betray my race and deliver a slave species into your hands?"

"Your choice is simple, captain-doctor. Remain an intelligent, living being, or become a mindless puppet, like your partner. I have taken over all the functions of her nervous system; I can do the same to you."

"I can kill myself."

"That might be troublesome, because it would make me resort to developing a cloning technology. Technology, though I am capable of it, is painful to me. I am a genetic artifact; there are fail-safes within me that prevent me from taking over the Nest for my own uses. That would mean falling into the same trap of progress as other intelligent races. For similar reasons, my lifespan is limited. I will live for only a thousand years, until your race's brief flurry of energy is over and peace resumes once more."

"Only a thousand years?" Afriel laughed bitterly. "What then? You kill off my descendants, I assume, having no further use for them."

"No. We have not killed any of the fifteen other races we have taken for defensive study. It has not been necessary. Consider that small scavenger floating by your head, captain-doctor, that is feeding on your vomit. Five hundred million years ago its ancestors made the galaxy tremble. When they attacked us, we unleashed their own kind upon them. Of course, we altered our side, so that they were smarter, tougher, and of course, totally loyal to us. Our Nests were the only world they knew, and they fought with a valor and inventiveness we never could have matched. . . . Should your race arrive to exploit us, we will naturally do the same."

"We humans are different."

"Of course."

"A thousand years here won't change us. You will die and our descendants will take over this Nest. We'll be running things, despite you, in a few generations. The darkness won't make any difference."

"Of course not. You don't need eyes here. You don't need anything."

"You'll allow me to stay alive? To teach them anything I want?"

"Certainly, captain-doctor. We are doing you a favor, in all truth. In a thousand years your descendants here will be the only remnants of the human race. We are generous with our immortality; we will take it upon ourselves to preserve you."

"You're wrong, Swarm. You're wrong about intelligence, and you're wrong about everything else. Maybe other races would crumble into parasitism, but we humans are different."

"Certainly. You'll do it, then?"

"Yes. I accept your challenge. And I will defeat you."

"Splendid. When the Investors return here, the springtails will say that they have killed you, and will tell them to never return. They will not return. The humans should be the next to arrive."

"If I don't defeat you, they will."

"Perhaps." Again it sighed. "I'm glad I don't have to absorb you. I would have missed your conversation."

PEG-MAN

by Rudy Rucker

An obsession with computer games and video contests is the current madness of the young. Fighting off invaders from space, battling against weird foe in fantastic combat, or just eating up the enemy while evading hot pursuit . . . these are the pastimes of millions. Naturally there is a story in all this and the author, a professor of mathematics, has produced it.

It was hot. Polly was driving Rhett home from work. Pretty Polly, fresh out of college, driving her husband home from his job at the arcade. Rhett had been fresh out of college three or four years earlier, but it hadn't took.

"Eat her, Polly, eat her fast," cried Rhett. A fifty-year-old woman in a pink alligator shirt and lime-green Bermudas was in the crosswalk.

"Peg-Man, Rhett?"

Rhett made change and serviced the machines at Crasher's, a pinball and video arcade in the new Killeville shopping

246

mall. He left about a third of his pay in the machines, especially Peg-Man and Star Castle. Sometimes, when Rhett had been playing a lot, he'd come home still *in the machine's space,* the Peg-Man space today, a cookie-filled maze with floorping monsters that try to eat you while you try to eat all the cookies, and there's stop-signs to eat too: they make the monsters turn blue and then you can eat them back till they start flashing, which is almost right away on the third and fifth boards. . . .

"Yeah. I broke a hundred thousand today."

"My, that's a lot." The uneaten fifty-year-old preppie was out of the road now. Polly eased the car forward.

"Sixteen boards," added Rhett.

In Peg-Man each time you eat all the cookies and stop-signs, the screen blinks and then goes back to starting position. Almost all the video games include some similar principle. Killing off all the monsters in Space Invaders, blowing up the central ship in Star Castle, making it through the maze in Berzerk: in each case one gets a reset, a new board. The rules of the game usually change somewhat with each new board, so that as one moves to higher levels, one is exploring new space, probing unknown areas of the machine's program.

"There was an incredible show after the fifteenth board," Rhett continued. "All the monsters came out and took their robes off. Underneath they were like pink slugs. And then they acted out their roles. Like the red one is always first?"

Polly smiled over at Rhett. He was long and skinny, with a pencil-thin mustache. He knew that he was wasting his life on the video machines, and she knew, but it hadn't seemed to matter yet. They had time to burn. They were married, and they both had college degrees: till now that had been enough.

"I went for the interview, Rhett."

"Yeah? At the bank?"

"I think I can get it, but it looks kind of dinky. I'd just be a programmer."

"You don't know computers."

"I do too. I took a whole year of programming, I'll have you know."

"A useful trade," mused Rhett. "Killeville College prepares its students for a successful career in modern society. The New South. Why did I have to major in English?"

"You could get a better job if you wanted to, Rhett."

Rhett's fingers danced across phantom controls.

"Tfoo, tfoo, tfoom!"

The next day, Polly decided to take the bank job. It was dinky, but they paid five dollars an hour; and Mr. Hunt, the personnel officer, promised that there were opportunities for rapid advancement. After signing up and agreeing to be there Monday, Polly drove over to the mall to tell Rhett.

The mall was a single huge building jig-sawed into a lake of asphalt. Crasher's was in the middle, right by Spencer Gifts. It was dark and air-conditioned with a gold carpet on the floor. A row of machines was lined up along each wall, pinball on the right, video on the left. Polly liked the pinballs better; at least there you were manipulating something real.

The pinballs glowed and the videos twinkled. A few youths were playing, and the machines filled the room with sound.

Intruder alert, Intruder alert.

mmmwwhhhaaaaAAAAAAAAAA-KOW-KOW-KOW!

Welcome to Xenon.

Doodley-doodle-doodley-doo.

Budda-budda-zen-zen-BLOOOO!

Try me again.

There at the back was Rhett, grinning and twitching at the controls of Star Castle. He wore a news-vendor's change apron.

"I took the job," said Polly, coming up behind him.

"Just a minute," said Rhett, not looking up. "I'll give you change in a minute." He took her for a customer, or pretended to.

A fat spaceship rotated slowly at the center of the Star Castle screen. Surrounding it were concentric rings of light: force-fields. Rhett's ship darted around the perimeter of the rings like a horsefly, twisting and stinging, trying to blast its way to the machine's central ship. Eerily singing bombs pursued Rhett; and when he finally breached the innermost wall, the machine began firing huge, crackling space-mines. Rhett dodged the mines, firing and thrusting the while. One of his bullets caught the central ship, and the whole screen blacked out in a deafening explosion.

"That's five," said Rhett, glancing back. "Hi, Polly."

"I went to see Mr. Hunt like we decided, Rhett. They're really giving me the job."

"Far out. Maybe I'll quit working here. The machines are starting to get to me. This morning I saw a face on the Peg-Man screen."

"Whose face, Rhett?"

The new board was on the screen and Rhett turned back to the controls. **Wi-wi-wi-wi-wi-wi** went his bullets against the **ee-EEeeEEeeEEeeEEee** of the smart bombs and the **mmmm-MMMMMwaaaaaa** of the force-fields.

"The president," said Rhett, sliding his ship off one corner of the screen and back on the other. "The president of the United States, man. He thanked me for developing the software for some new missile system. He said that all the Peg-Man machines are keyed into the Pentagon, and that the monsters stand for Russian anti-missiles. I ran twenty boards. Nobody's ever done that before."

There was a big hole in the force-fields now. The fat, evil ship at the center spat a vicious buzz-bomb. Rhett zapped it **wi-wi-wi** from the other side of the board. Then the ship. **BLOOOOOOOO!!**

"Six," said Rhett, glancing up again. "I'm really hot today. I figure if the Pentagon put out Peg-Man, maybe someone else did Star Castle."

Polly wondered if Rhett were joking. In a way it made sense. Use the machines to tap American youth's idle energy and quirky reflexes. A computer can follow a given program as fast as you want, but a human operator's creative randomization is impossible to simulate. Why *not* have our missiles trace out Peg-Man monster-evasion paths? Why **not** tape every run that gets past twenty boards?

"Did the president say you'd get any money?" asked Polly. "Did he offer you a job?"

"No job." **Wi-wi-wi-wi-wi-wi.** "But he's sending a secret agent to give me a thousand dollars. If I tell anyone it's treason Aaaaaauuuugh!" **Crackle-ackle-ackle-FTOOOM.** Rhett's ship exploded into twirling fragments.

"Change please?"

Rhett changed a five for one of the customers, then turned his full attention on Polly.

"So you're taking the job at the bank? They're really hiring you?"

"Starting Monday. Did you *really* see the president?"

"I think I did."

"Why don't you phone him up?"

"It was probably just a tape. He wouldn't know me from Adam." Rhett fed another quarter into the Star Castle machine. "I'm gonna work on this some more. See who's behind it. Will you hand out change for me?"

"O.K."

Polly tied on Rhett's change apron, and leaned against the rear wall. Now and then someone would ask her for more quarters, always boys. White males between 14 and 34 years of age. Interacting with machines. Maybe, for men, women themselves are just very complicated video machines. . . . Polly pushed the unpleasant thought away. There was something more serious to think about: Rhett's obsession. The whole time she made change, he kept plugging away at Star Castle. Ten boards, fifteen, and finally twenty.

But no leader's face appeared, just the same dull target with its whining force-fields. A flurry of bombs raced out like a flight of swallows. Rhett let them take him, then sagged against the machine in exhaustion.

"Polly! Are you working here?" A big sloppy man shambled up. It was Dr. Horvath, Polly's old calculus professor. She'd been his favorite student. "Is this the best job a Killeville College math major can aspire to?"

"No, no." Polly was embarrassed. "I'm just helping Rhett. Rhett?" Wearily her husband straightened up from the Star Castle machine, "Rhett, you remember Dr. Horvath, don't you? From the graduation?"

"Hi." Rhett gave his winning smile and shook hands. "These machines have been freaking me out."

"Can I tell him, Rhett?"

"Go ahead."

"Dr. Horvath, this morning Rhett saw the president's face on the Peg-Man screen. Rhett says the Pentagon is using the twenty-board runs to design the new anti-anti-missile system."

Horvath cocked his big head and smiled. "Sounds like paranoid schizophrenia to me, Polly. Or drug psychosis."

"Hey!" said Rhett. "I'm clean!"

"So show me *der Führer's* face. I've got time to kill or I wouldn't be here."

"Right now I'm too wrecked," confessed Rhett. "I just blew the whole afternoon trying to break through on Star Castle. But there's nothing there."

Horvath gave Polly a questioning look. He thought Rhett was crazy. She couldn't leave it at that.

"Come in tomorrow, Dr. Horvath, come in before ten. Rhett's fasest in the morning. He'll show you . . . and me, too."

"At this point Rhett's the only one who's been vouchsafed the mystical vision of our fearless leader?" Horvath's pasty, green-tinged features twisted sarcastically.

"Put up or shut up," said Rhett. "Be here at nine."

That night, Rhett and Polly had their first really big argument in ten months of marriage. Ostensibly, it was about whether Polly should be allowed to read in bed when Rhett was trying to sleep. Obviously, it was also about her reluctance to make love. But deep down, the argument was triggered by the slippage of their relative positions: Poly was moving into a good, middle-class job; but Rhett seemed to be moving down into madness.

There was a lot of tension the next morning. Crasher's didn't open to the public till ten, so Rhett and Polly had it to themselves. Rhett fed a quarter to the Peg-Man machine and got to work.

"What a way to spend Saturday," complained Polly. "That machine doesn't connect to anything, Rhett. You might as well be shouting into a hollow tree. The president isn't in there."

Rhett didn't look up. . . didn't dare to. Three boards, six.

Horvath arrived, rapping at the metal grill that covered the entrance. As usual, he was wearing shapeless baggy pants and an oversize white nylon shirt. His glasses glinted blankly in the fluorescent light. Polly let him in.

"How's he doing?" whispered Horvath eagerly.

"Ten boards," shouted Rhett. "I'm in the groove today. Ten boards and I haven't lost a man yet!"

Horvath and Polly exchanged a glance. After all the nasty, wild things Rhett had said last night, there was no question in her mind that Rhett had imagined his vision of the president. Surely Dr. Horvath knew this, too. But he looked so expectant! Why would an important professor take the trouble to come watch her crazy husband play Peg-Man at nine in the morning?

Horvath walked over to stand behind Rhett, and Polly trailed after. There is a single control on a Peg-Man machine, a sort of joystick. It controls the movements of a yellow disk on the screen: the disk moves in the direction in which you push the joystick. It's not quite a disk, really; it's a circle with one sector missing. The sector acts as a munching mouth, a hungry Chinese, a greedy Happy-Face, a peg-man. As you move it around, the peg-man eats the cookies and stop-signs in the maze. **Muncha-uncha-uncha-uncha.** Later there are also cherries, strawberries, grapes, birds, and bags of gold. **Gloooop!**

Rhett was on his fifteenth board now, and the four monsters that chased his yellow disk moved with a frightening degree of cooperation. But, **uncha-uncha-uncha,** the little peg-man slipped out of every trap, lured the monsters away from every prize. **Uncha-uncha-uncha-uncha-gloop!** Rhett ate a bag of gold worth five thousand points. That made a hundred-and-three-thousand. Horvath was transfixed, and even Polly was a little impressed. She'd never seen Rhett play so well.

The next few boards took longer. The monsters had stopped speeding up with each board. Instead they were acting smarter. Rhett had to expend more and more time on evasive action. The happy little peg-man moved about in paths so complex as to seem utterly random to anyone but Rhett. Seventeen boards. Nineteen.

On the twentieth board the monsters speeded back up. Rhett nearly lost a man. But then he knuckled down and ate the whole board in one intricately filigreed sweep.

The screen grew gray and staticky. And then there he was: Mr. President himself.

"The supreme commander," said Horvath nastily. "I don't believe it."

"See?" snarled Rhett. "Now who's crazy?"

". . . thank you for helping our country," the video screen was saying. The president looked friendly with his neat pompadour and his cocky, lopsided smile. Friendly, but serious. "Your photograph and fingerprints have been forwarded to the CIA for information retrieval. An agent will contact you to make payment in the sum of one thousand doallars. This offer cannot be repeated, and must be kept secret. Let me thank you again for making this a safer world."

"That's it," said Rhett; straightening up and kicking the kinks out of his long, skinny legs.

"Are you sure?" demanded Horvath, strangely tense. "Couldn't there be a higher level?"

"The screen's blank," shrugged Rhett. "The game's over."

"Push the Start button," suggested Horvath.

"Peg-Man doesn't give free games," replied Rhett. "And I've got to open up in a few minutes."

"Just try," insisted Horvath. "Push the button."

Rhett pressed the Start button with his skinny forefinger. The familiar maze appeared on the screen. The monsters moved out of their cave and the little peg-man started eating. **Uncha-uncha-uncha-unch.** Mesmerized by the sound, Rhett grabbed the joystick, meaning to dodge a hungry red monster.

But when Rhett touched the control, something about the image changed. It thickened and grew out of the screen. This was no longer a two-dimensional video image, but a three-dimensional hologram. The peg-man was a smiling little sphere sliding around a transparent three-dimensional maze. Rhett found that he could control his man's movement in the new dimension by pushing or pulling the joystick. With rapid, automatic motions he dodged the monsters and set his man to eating cookies.

Polly was not so accepting of this change. "How did you know that would happen?" she demanded of Horvath. "What are you up to, anyway?"

"Just don't disturb Rhett," said Horvath, pushing Polly away from the machine. "This is more important than you can realize." His hands felt strange and clammy.

Just then someone started shaking the steel grate at the entrance.

"Let them in," called Rhett. "It's almost time. I don't *believe* this machine!" His face was set in a tight, happy smile. He'd eaten every cookie in his cubical maze now, and with a flourish of music it reset itself. Twenty-second board.

"Hey!" shouted the man at the grate. "Let me in there!"

He already had his wallet out. *Can't wait to spend his money,* thought Polly, but she was wrong. The man had a badge to show her.

"CIA, Miss. I'm looking for Rhett Lyndon."

"That's my husband. He's playing Peg-Man. Do you have the two thousand dollars?"

"He can only collect one. But he shouldn't have told you!"

The secret agent was a fit, avid-faced man in his thirties. He reminded Polly of a whippet. She rolled back the grate; and he surged in, looking the whole room over at once.

"Who's the other guy?"

"Beat it, pig!" shouted Horvath.

Polly had always known Dr. Horvath was a radical, but this outburst really shocked her. "You can leave, Dr. Horvath. We have some private business to discuss.

Rhett glanced over with a brief, ambiguous smile. But then he had to give his full attention back to the game. The maze he was working seemed to have grown. It stuck more than a meter out of the machine now.

"I can do better than the Pentagon's lousy thousand," hissed Horvath. "I can give you anything you want, if only Rhett can help us defeat the Rull."

"Freeez," screamed the secret agent. He'd drawn a heavy pistol out of his shoulder-holster.

But rather than freezing, Horvath *flowed*. His whole body seemed to melt away, and thick gouts of green slime came surging out the bottoms of his pant-legs. The agent fired three wild shots anyway, but they only rippled the slime. And then a pseudopod of the stuff lashed out and struck the CIA man down. There was a moment's soft burbling while the alien flowed over and absorbed its prey.

And then, as suddenly as it had started, the ugly incident was over. The slime flowed back from the agent, revealing only a clean spot on the carpet, and Dr. Horvath's clothes filled back up. The head reappeared last of all, growing out of the nylon shirt's collar like a talking puffball.

"I'll admit it, Polly," it was saying. "I'm an extraterrestrial. But a *good* one. The Rull are the bad ones. They don't even eat what they kill. We are, of course, fantastically advanced compared to you primitive bipeds. But we need your animal shiftiness, your low cunning!"

"Rhett," screamed Polly. "Help! Horvath is an alien!" She darted past the slimy deceiver to stand near her husband, as near as she could get.

Rhett's upper body and head were inside the maze now; it had grown that much. A glowing two-meter cube of passages surrounded him. The peg-man and the monsters raced this way and that. Bobbing and weaving, Rhett watched and controlled the chase. The planes of the hologram bathed his features in a golden, beatific light. The peg-man completed its circuit of a randomized space-filling curve . . . and the cube flickered to reset.

"Thirty," said Rhett.

"Go!" shouted Horvath. "Go Rhett! Finish this board and we'll be able to eat all the Rull worlds without losing a single ship!"

With each **uncha** Polly imagined a planet disappearing into some huge group-Horvath. Rull-monsters darted this way and that, trying to foil the peg-man, but crazy Rhett was too fast and random for *any*one. She wondered what to ask Horvath for. Riches, telepathy, the power of flight?

Suddenly the board was empty. Rhett had done it again! The huge maze drew back into the Peg-Man machine's screen. The image of a jubilant extraterrestrial appeared, burbling thanks. And then the screen blanked out.

"That was our leader," said Horvath. "We can't thank you enough. Anything you want is yours. Make a wish."

"Peg," said Rhett distantly. "P,E,G. P is Pentagon, E is Extraterrestial . . . I wish I could find out what G is."

"You got it," said Horvath. "Just push the Start button. And . . . thanks again." With a slow zeenting nosie the extraterrestrial disappeared, feet first.

"Was he for real?" said Rhett.

"I can't believe it," wailed Polly. "You just blew our big wish. Who cares what G stands for!"

Rhett shrugged and pushed the Start button. There was a sizzling sound, and slowly the machine, and then the room, dissolved into clear white light.

"Greetings," boomed a voice. "This is the Galaxy speaking. I wonder if you could help me out?"